Things
I Know
Are True

Original title: *Las cosas que sé que son verdad*

Copyright © Pilar López Cárdenas 2022
All Rights Reserved

Registered in The National Library of Australia
NLApp98300

ISBN: 978-0-6451896-0-5

Cover and interior illustrations:
Katherine Giannina Moreno Rosso

English version translator:
Jacqueline Maurelos

Follow the author on Facebook @Pilar López Cardenas
E- farfalle7@icloud.com

ISBN 978-0-6451896-0-5

9 780645 189605 >

Things
I Know
Are True

PILAR LÓPEZ CÁRDENAS

These pages are dedicated to the strong women in my family.
To my daughter Adriana, my mother Emilia, and my sister Isa.
All of them peaceful warriors full of light, who face life
with the infinite courage to be themselves.

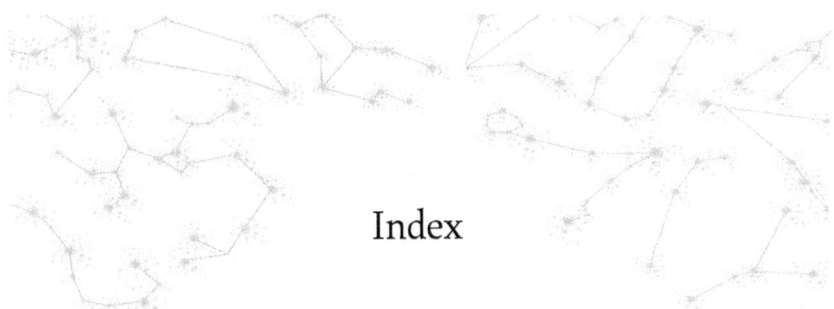

Index

Acknowledgements   9

Chapter 1. The Final Fight   11
Chapter 2. The Awakening.   27
Chapter 3. Elsu   41
Chapter 4. Closed for Repairs   53
Chapter 5. Dream's Caress   65
Chapter 6. There Was a Time.   83
Chapter 7. Letters   99
Chapter 8. Crazy Things   115
Chapter 9. Love Without Fear   131
Chapter 10. Tooth and Nail   147
Chapter 11. Your Grandfather Esteban   159
Chapter 12. We are the Cosmos   169
Chapter 13. The Message from Venus   181
Chapter 14. The Deflowering Ceremony   193
Chapter 15. Lessons from the Sea   207
Chapter 16. Taking Flight.   219
Chapter 17. A New Beginning   233
Chapter 18. Winter Soldiers   245
Chapter 19. The Shoebox   257
Chapter 20. Someone Like Me   269
Chapter 21. The Frog's Leap   283
Chapter 22. The Afar Brotherhood   295
Chapter 23. Uniting Promises   309
Chapter 24. Tango Steps.   321
Chapter 25. The Pendulum   335
Chapter 26. Journey to My Destiny.   347

Book soundtrack   365
About the author.   367

Acknowledgements

This is always the toughest part of the book. Not because I find it hard to thank people, but because I'm aware of the divinity and grandeur of the most powerful, healing and magical word I know. I want gratitude to be my mantra – gratitude for each and every person who helped me in one way or another, holding my hand along the journey to where I am today.

Thank you baby, honey, my love, for giving me my space and for spending so many hours on the couch watching TV or reading alone, waiting for me. For dreaming this dream with me, for giving me the power to fly each and every day, and for showing me that, together, we can fly even higher.

Thank you to Cowland Management, my sponsor for this book, for believing in the person first, and then the project. Thank you for the vision that made it all possible.

Thank you Carmenchu, my dear friend, for accompanying me in every chapter, for lending me your ears and your heart, and for showing up unfailingly every day to our date with destiny, despite being eighteen thousand kilometres away. Thanks for being my number one fan.

A million thanks to the readers of my first book *How To Create An Amazing Life,* for sharing your success stories with me and for following me every step of the way. Thank you for choosing me once again, and for choosing yourselves.

Thank you to all the master architects who helped to design, build and decorate this special project that has seen the light of day thanks to the efforts of some very special people.

And, as always, thank you to my children Adriana and Darío, for being my inspiration.

To everyone…. Thank you so much

Chapter 1

The Final Fight

One year later, without even being recognised by her neighbours, Rafaela López Aguilar returned to the place she had called home for most of her life. The story could have been different, but this is what happened and how she, herself, told it to me. Some stories begin very far away and end very near. This is one such story. Endings are always surprising, even if they have already been written ahead of time.

———∞———

I could feel the warm blood gushing from my wounded nose, gliding over my split lips with a slightly salty taste. This feeling, once again, awakened my survival instinct. As I lay on the floor of the boxing ring, my unconscious mind could still hear the anonymous voices yelling my name.

'C'mon Iris, keep fighting. Don't give up.'

I had promised myself that this would be my final fight, my last combat for a good cause.

I knew all the secrets of the psychology of boxing very well. In fact, I applied them outside the ring, with my patients, every day. Conan, my trainer, had prepared me to compete, for victory and for defeat, and had shown me how to stay motivated.

I always thought I had started boxing as a consequence of my work as a psychologist. I knew how important it was to win the psychological battle before even stepping inside the ring. According to Conan, the trick was to come out of the changing room leaving behind any trace of anxiety and replacing it with a large dose of self-esteem. In just a few metres, I would go from fearing failure to feeling completely invincible.

I used to perform a mental trick that consisted in maintaining unwavering eye contact with my opponent until they looked away. At that moment, I knew I had struck first, that I'd hit them psychologically, and that this would, in turn, increase my chances of winning the fight.

I first met Conan when he answered one of my ads as I was looking for someone to rent the ground floor of my house – an indigo blue Andalusian house whose walls were covered in hanging pots filled with red and white geraniums. As soon as I set eyes on him, I was impressed by his confident demeanour, and I was drawn to his American accent. He told me he had left the marines when he fell in love with Granada, the beautiful southern Spanish city that is bathed by the Mediterranean Sea and scented by its green fields, during one of his missions. He was fresh and spontaneous, and I knew right away he was the one.

I remember our long conversations beneath the coloured lanterns that adorned the orange tree courtyard of Cantina El Romero, a tavern round the corner from the gym where we trained every afternoon. I would talk to him about my frustration and about how unfair life was to some of my patients, who included young drug addicts unaware how great the gift of life was, women beaten over and over again by those who ought to love and protect them, successful executives living in the poverty that is having nothing but money, desperate people with terminal illnesses, and children trapped in the welfare system in an uncertain world.

As Conan, whose Irish name means 'little warrior', used to tell me boxing and life itself have important similarities: both knock you down constantly.

'Tell me, Rafaela, why did you decide to become a psychologist?' he asked me curiously while firmly gripping his mug full of frothy beer.

I hesitated for a few moments, looking for an answer that would make me feel like a superhero. After all, I *was* saving lives, wasn't I?

'There's a turning point in every superhero's life when they go from being just a normal person to discovering their purpose,' I answered, while plaiting my long jet-black hair.

'I understand; and what happened that made you dare to take such a big step?'

—⦂∞⦂—

Suddenly, I was back in the fight, slowly coming back to reality. The referee was about to finish counting and declare my opponent the winner by knockout, that fateful moment when you take so many punches that you get weaker and weaker until you receive the final blow that makes you unable to continue fighting. My body wanted to give up and end the agony, but my mind refused to throw in the towel. I didn't want to be part of the great majority that gives up just short of the finish-line.

At that moment, I reconnected with my earliest childhood memory. We had a very unique orange cat that loved to get wet when it rained. Ágata had given birth and I wanted to give one of the kittens to my friend Sebastián, who lived nearby with his alcoholic father. His mother had died on the day Sebastián was born. In his father's eyes, her death was all his fault. He never fully recovered and this made him turn to drink.

Sebastián was a fearful child with large grey eyes and an emaciated body. He cried as he picked up the tiny animal in his arms.

'Why are you crying, Sebastián? Don't you want the kitten?'

'Yes, it's very soft,' he answered while he caressed his fragile little back. 'But dad won't let me have him. He always says I can't do anything, not even take care of myself. Yesterday, he punished me without dinner when I spilled some milk on the living room carpet, and then he slapped me when I said I was still hungry.'

'Don't worry, Sebastián. I'll adopt you and we'll be brother and sister. That way, we can take care of the kitten together and we'll come up with the magic words that will make your dad disappear.'

Even today, if I close my eyes, I can still see him hugging me tightly and following me everywhere. We would play make-believe, imagining that we were travelling on a spaceship to a planet called Iris, where each colour gave us a superpower. I was eight years old, I think Sebastián was a little older when he succumbed to a final beating after one of his father's drinking sprees. That image gave me enough courage to get back on my feet and return to my corner, where Conan and my team revived me in a matter of seconds.

'Rafaela, I don't know what's going through your head right now,' he whispered with determination while dropping a towel onto my shoulders. 'Remember, a champion is someone who gets up when they can't go on.' His voice had a magical power over me and reminded me that, although I was fighting alone, I did so with the strength of many. With Sebastián's strength, and that of each and every one of my patients.

I had learnt that the superhero and the coward both feel the same way, but the former uses that fear and projects it onto their opponent, while the latter runs away. I had nowhere to run, even if I wanted to. For the past few months, I'd been facing an existential void, or what I referred to as 'the something more syndrome'. I was supposed to be a superhero and protect all those who were lost and defenceless in a hostile world, but who would save me from the edge of the abyss on which I now found myself?

I adjusted my mouthguard, while I felt the weight of my sweaty gloves pulling me towards the centre of the ring. I normally wore one orange glove and one green one as a good luck charm in honour of Sebastián, which is why I was known as the 'Andalusian Iris'; although, to be honest, I could barely distinguish any colours after that last hook I'd taken from my rival.

The second round was about to commence and the sound of the bell brought me back to attention. At some point in our lives, we all hear that sound telling us we must go on, no matter how much we want to stop, and reinvent ourselves professionally, free ourselves from a toxic relationship, break away from everything and go somewhere new, or simply chase that crazy dream that no one else believes in except us. We are experts dancing on that ring to the rhythm of the bell and, just like in boxing, we often feel caught between the ropes, unable to escape.

I had lost my passion for my work, much like when you still love your partner, but you just don't want to be intimate with them any more. My special touch had vanished, or maybe I never had one in the first place.

Conan, my great friend and trainer, was the only one who could occasionally snap me out of that state. He suffered from a strange condition that made him incapable of not telling jokes. Often, he would wake up in the middle of the night and, if he saw light through my window, he would come over to tell me about his latest idea. I suppose I couldn't really blame him for having picked up the peculiar Andalusian sense of humour which, combined with his American accent and melodious laugh, made him a truly irresistible being.

'*Chiquilla*, are you awake?' asked the American as he tapped on my bedroom window, as if wanting to confirm his suspicions.

Wide awake and bored, I gestured for him to come in.

'I'm going to tell you a joke that's perfect for your unmotivated patients,' he said as he took a seat on the wicker rocking chair next to my tiny balcony , which was bathed in the light of a large silver moon.

'The boss asks one his workers, "Martínez, why aren't you working?"

He hasn't seen the boss arrive.

"You have to come motivated, Martínez."

"I know, boss, I *was* really motivated when I came, but then something happened and my motivation disappeared."'

Conan began to laugh so vigorously that I couldn't help but laugh along with him, and we laughed and laughed while looking at each other in amusement. Then we stopped, remaining completely still, looking up at the stars in the dark night sky.

'If you had the choice, who would you be?' I asked, suddenly breaking the silence.

I suppose the question caught him off guard because it took him a few seconds to react.

'I'd be a very astute reporter,' he said finally, with utter conviction. 'Specifically, a correspondent in a large, chaotic city. Somewhere that never slept and with thousands of interesting events to tell the rest of the world about. I'd like to be brilliant at my job, not just a familiar face in the crowd but someone with intelligence and daring, and with real talent.'

I immediately recognised the twinkle in his eyes, the musical tone of his voice, and the passion that surrounded each and every word as he imagined being the hero of his own life that nobody elso could replace.

'And what about you, *chiquilla*? Who would you be?'

In a sudden burst of honesty, I answered, 'I feel lost, Conan. I feel like my life has no meaning. I don't like anything that's happening around me. Every morning, I look in the mirror and see an equation with a constant value – inertia – and a whole bunch of variables I just can't make any sense of. Apathy's got a tight hold on me. What am I doing with my life?'

It was clear. I'd knocked my friend out with my answer. He scratched out the tobacco from the pipe he usually smoked when he was nervous, as if searching for the perfect words to make me feel better. He then began to fill the pipe from a carved wooden case, flattened the tobacco and lit it, inhaling repeatedly until it began to burn steadily. He was large and muscular, with a tattoo of an archer on his right arm. He was also one of the best boxers and friends I'd ever known, but he was ill-equipped to emotionally handle a highly complex organism such as myself at that precise moment.

'Rafaela, life is like boxing; the loser isn't the one who falls down, but the one who doesn't get back up. C'mon, it can't be that bad. You have an amazing house, a job where you're respected, you're the most beautiful girl in all of Granada and, more importantly, you have me,' he argued, while making one of his funny faces. 'You're not going to become a depressed psychologist, are you? That'd make one hell of a title for a bestseller,' he went on, trying to make me smile.

'I guess I've lost my motivation, like your friend Martínez, the one from the joke.'

'We're not always motivated, *chiquilla*. You have to learn to be disciplined. If you persist, and stand strong, you can do anything you want.'

I knew this speech well. I even used it on patients myself as I tried to make them focus on the positives, on everything they had versus what they were missing. It's the theory of plenty versus the scarcity mentality. How easy it is to advise others from the other side, don't you think?

I was suddenly brought back to reality when my opponent threw a right hook that I barely had time to dodge. I was fighting in support of my local children's residence, managed by the foundation House to Grow. The truth is that, when I began to box, I became their sponsor and had already spent several years taking part in competitions so that orphan children could go to school and have better lives. At least, that's what I told myself to make me feel better every time I hit my opponent. I was doing it for a good cause.

We often look for an excuse to soothe our souls, and so we allow our egos, our fury a our frustrations to take control. Something wasn't right inside me; the effect of this deceit was fading, as if a spell had been lifted.

Weak and on autopilot, I was trying to win two ongoing battles at the same time; my ego didn't want to lose the title, the hero wanted to win for the cause. I weathered the storm, hiding behind my bruised arms. The public continued to cheer.

'Don't give up, Iris! We're all with you!'

'Hit hard, champion! Show them what you're made of!'

My bloodied gaze met Conan's, who gave me instructions using our coded signals. I felt like a gladiator about to be devoured by lions.

It was a titanic effort but, with my failing reflexes, I became an easy target. The only glory I wished for was to be out of that battlefield. The last thing I remember is an intense headache followed by a dark cloak covering my eyes. I broke.

As a psychologist, I had always been interested in the science behind the visions people swear they have when faced with death, those that both literature and cinema have used to entertain us. In 'Hamlet', Shakespeare describes it as *the undiscovered country from whose bourn no traveller returns'*. But what happens if they do return?

I grew up with my grandmother, Isabel, a woman of short stature, with a slim waist that contrasted with her wide, exuberant hips and opulent rear. Her quiet, drowsy gaze curiously collected each tiny detail around her. It was impossible to escape her radar. She would always catch me in one of my mischievous endeavours before I could even carry it out.

She was a true Andalusian beauty, with round cheeks and lips the colour of red wine. Everyone said I looked exactly like her, and they were right. My Arab features were, without a doubt, part of her legacy.

Belly, as I called her, was ahead of her time in a patriarchal society where women were only expected to take care of the home and raise children. But that didn't stop her from becoming a designer of haute couture hats and gloves for the most glamorous European fashion houses. She was a true pioneer and a trailblazer. That was my grandmother!

As a child, I enjoyed smelling her sandalwood-scented hands that had been dyed black by the sun. When everyone went to mass on Sundays, while everybody else when to mass, we would model her latest creations, sashaying across the courtyard to the rhythm of our own off-key melodies. I was absolutely spellbound by the museum she had made for herself in her attic, housing all kinds of hats: woollen hats, Gavroche caps, large hats with lace for weddings and funerals, wide-brimmed straw hats, travelling hats, even hats inspired by the canotiers worn by Venetian gondoliers.

The kids at school would laugh at me when I showed up wearing exuberant brightly-coloured hats with impossible bows. But I couldn't have cared less. Belly had taught me that I could be whoever I wanted to be, and that's just what I did. Over time, I learnt that true love is nothing more than wanting to help someone else be exactly who they are. No one can know anything for you. No one can grow for you. No one can do your soul-searching for you. No one can do for you what you're meant to do yourself. You can't live by proxy.

I know for a fact that I also inherited her love of collecting. One of my hobbies consisted in compiling motivational phrases for my patients; I had hundreds of them printed on magnets all over my fridge. I also collected small vintage wooden frames that I would buy on my travels, colourful postcards for every occasion, playing cards featuring Japanese phrases, and even a book that I wrote with my favourite phrases, titled *If You Can't Do It, I'll Help You*. But my favourite has always been *'no matter what happens, you'll always have a story to tell'*. I often wondered what mine would be, what story could I tell and how. I never imagined that, one day, I could be the star of an incredible, passionate tale.

A professional boxer is only as good, or as bad, as their cornermen. It doesn't matter how fast or talented a boxer they are, they will be at a great disadvantage if there aren't any people to refresh and revive them.

The bell rings. The public is silent, the lights go out and a spotlight shines on the warriors as they cross each other in the ring. At no other time will an athlete feel lonelier than this. Your corner is there, but at least for two minutes your only weapons will be your hands and everything you've learnt during your training. When you hear the bell again, it's the moment you've been waiting for, the moment to feel safe and supported. Your corner is there. Seventy per cent of the merit goes to the boxer, but the other thirty per cent is due to various other factors controlled by your corner.

Outside of the boxing ring, my corner had dissipated like the steam from my kettle shortly after falling silent. My person, that person we all need when we fall apart in floods of tears and curse the world. The one who spontaneously becomes the architect of your crushed soul, very carefully putting the pieces back together without you even noticing. My person, who never tired of hugging me, regardless of how hot it was. My number one fan and the only presence who could understand the things I left unsaid. My person. The one who knew how to cultivate dreams instead of doubts and who disarmed my pain with silly laughter and poetry. We were the ultimate accomplices in an imperfect yet eternal story that no longer existed. The love we had was good for breaking fear, not hearts. Wait... did I just say good for not breaking hearts? Well... you can tell me what you think later.

I tried to get back to that corner over and over again, unable to accept that he was no longer there to comfort me and whisper 'It's going to be OK, babe. We're an invincible team.'

I still remember the day we met, when I first looked up and saw him. He greeted me with that white smile of his, waving his hand excitedly. He introduced himself as Jared. We met at university in Jerusalem, while I was completing my doctorate in psychology and he was working at the library canteen to pay for his philosophy degree. His bright, sparkly eyes looked over a pair of black-rimmed glasses that rested on an aquiline nose, giving him a modern, intellectual look that was both cocky and a little flirty, just like him. I soon found myself drawn to his passionate and somewhat nutty character. We'd get lost in endless existential conversations, never agreeing on anything.

'Rafaela, philosophy comes from the Greek word *philosophi*, which means a love of knowledge. You study the human mind and its behaviour. I'm one of those people who try to understand the meaning of our existence. You ask about the mind, while I listen to the soul,' he used to tell me, ending his discourse with a playful wink.

It was a red July sunset, barely three weeks after our very first meeting, when Jared handed me my breakfast receipt along with a crumpled paper napkin, stained with coffee and sugar, on which a note had been written:

All spiritual gurus
Apprentices of genius
Psychologists who speak of not tying themselves to anyone
Mystics who promote the path of self-healing
Those who help us with our personal growth
Happiness experts
Those who recommend being strong
and depending only on oneself.
They're right,
But I'm happier when you look at me.

Conan knew how to revive me in less than the minute rest given to us between rounds. Sixty seconds can mean the difference between victory and defeat, between life and death, and between happiness and a life without meaning. It isn't long, but it's long enough if you make the right decisions. We all have one thousand four hundred and forty minutes each day and the final human gift: free will. This legitimate privilege to choose gives us freedom. The philosopher Sartre defines it very clearly in his famous phrase *'man is condemned to be free'.* Simply saying nothing in itself implies a choice. What decisions of mine could have brought me to this state of nothingness? Where exactly did I go wrong?

'Quick, adrenaline! C'mon, c'mon!' yelled Conan to his assistant, without taking his eyes off my disfigured face, covered in raw cuts, while stretching out his rough forceful hand, as if searching for the planet's last elixir.

Adrenaline is the only chemical substance allowed in the corner because it constricts blood vessels an stops bleeding.

'Put more Vaseline on her face, she's a mess,' said the technician, who knew well just how important this petroleum-based lubricant was in keeping the skin elastic, thus minimising the risk of cuts.

The bucket of iced water on my head not only lowered my body temperature but also abruptly brought me back to life.

At that precise moment, my mind broke away from 'reality', taking me back to the memory of my first training session with Conan.

'You've got to be quicker, Rafaela. The quicker one always punches twice.'

'But I need to think about the strategy,' I said, trying to play it cool, but in truth I couldn't stop thinking about his gorgeous naked torso and how sexy he looked in those patterned Thai shorts that hinted at the firmness of his well-shaped backside.

'Boxing is like life, *chiquilla,* it flies by at breakneck speed. There's no time to think or reflect. Each time we make a decision, we're giving up the chance to make others. Our decisions are like the two sides of a coin: on one side is what we want, on the other is the price we must pay for it.'

'But that means it's a path strewn with pitfalls, one of which is our propensity to act.'

'That's it, *chiquilla,*' he said, sure of his argument. 'It's a quick, violent and impulsive process. That's how we humans act most of the time.'

I came back to the ring.

'Iris, we're almost there. You've got them cornered. Don't let up. Hit and don't get hit, that's the aim of this noble art,' voiced Conan.

Dazed by the flurry of punches, I could barely hear my trainer's voice, though I could see in his gestures the fury I no longer had within me.

'Breathe deeply. Finish the job and let's go home.'

'Job?' said my faltering voice, 'Boxing is the only job where they keep on punching you while you work. What kind of job is that?'

Every fight was a story, a non-verbal drama that was helping me discover who the woman behind the colourful gloves was. Life had dealt me some low blows, but it had also been the best sparring session. People only move on for one of two reasons: they've either learnt enough or they've suffered enough. I was in the latter category. Wounded and broken, I still had one of my best allies on my side: that rebellious, idealistic woman who still lived inside of me, who was determined to knock out adversity at any cost.

The first days of summer began to unfold. Belly had left the large arched window in my bedroom half open, with the hope that my laziness wouldn't make me miss the first day of holidays. The warm rays of sunshine eagerly shone through, landing on the paprika-coloured terracotta floor and reflecting off some ancient furniture pieces she had brought over herself from Morocco, Italy and the north of Belgium. Decorating the alcove were some restored sixteenth century pieces, family mementos and travel souvenirs, all bathed by the soft, fresh colours of the walls, giving the room an authentic, personal touch.

I was upset and disheartened because, yet again, my mother wouldn't be spending the holidays with us. Every year, I would eagerly await the moment she appeared behind the courtyard gates, with her worn brown leather suitcase and her hair in a French twist. That's when summer would truly begin for me. Nothing made me happier than walking hand-in-hand along the shore of the 'together forever' cove, as we had named it one warm July sunrise. I'd heard several of the townspeople say that she'd lost her mind, that she was crazy and delirious. But I only knew a being of perpetual light who made my world stop when she curled me up between her knees and told me stories in which I was turned into a giant, a hero, a magician or a nymph. I was seven years old when I saw her for the last time. Her absence still seemed like an illusion, an unbearably loud silence I was unable to quieten with words.

They called her crazy because she exuded rebellion and spoke when she should have been quiet. They said she didn't fit in, because she refused to accept the world as it was. They spoke about her as though she were a random verse with no poem attached to it, and yet she was one of the most lucid people I ever knew, despite the fact she would put lipstick on just before going to bed. 'I want to be beautiful in my dreams,' she'd tell me. I liked telling her all about my day, what had happened at school, what I'd learnt as night fell before going to sleep, when I would whisper to her:

'I don't want you to sleep, *mamá*, so you can spend more time with me.'

'Don't worry, my love. I've learnt to look at you always, even when my eyes are shut.'

Then she would hug me, and there was nowhere else in the world I felt safer. Those were the few memories I had of my mother, although I probably invented many of them because, after all, we all need a mother.

She taught me to love books. She would take me to the 'enchanted bazaar' that, as I later discovered, was just an old bookshop that she had made absolutely magical for me. My bedroom was full of invisible friends and dust-covered pages, whose smell I still treasure. What story had my mother told me then? Yes, I'm sure she would have told me the story of the prodigious washerwoman. That was one of my favourites.

There was once an old washerwoman named Niku who lived in the Himalayas. She had built a small and modest wooden house on a mountain near a great flowing with cool, clear water that gave life to a beautiful valley. The old woman supported herself with the silver coins that the locals paid her for her hard work. Each sunrise, Niku would make her way along the rocky paths leading to the village, accompanied only by Canela, her mare, loaded with wicker baskets full of clothes. The ritual would then take place in the main square. Her clients would wait anxiously to collect their clean, folded clothes and hand over their dirty ones.

The old woman's fame had travelled far and wide, even drawing in clients from neighbouring villages, to the point where she had to turn some jobs down.

'My sheets smell like mint and rosemary, the scent relaxes my children so much they fall asleep as soon as the sun goes down, and they never have nightmares,' said the baker to one of her neighbours.

The neighbour nodded, adding, 'My husband stopped complaining about his stiff trousers since I started giving our clothes to the washerwoman. He says he can feel the softness of the material and that the hours he spends working in the fields are much more pleasant.'

A young woman with long golden plaits rode by distractedly on her bicycle. She couldn't help but overhear what the women were saying and how highly they spoke of the washerwoman's work, so she joined in.

'I think the secret is in the water of the river where she does the washing,' she said with conviction. 'There must be something very special there. Ever since she's been washing my dresses, more and more suitors come to call. They say I have a special glow about me, which no doubt has to do with the vibrancy of the colours and how bright they become with every wash.'

The old woman was also widely revered for her wisdom, and many went to her to seek advice whenever they had a problem. Niku had a compassionate, generous heart and was always willing to help people in need. However, time and exhaustion had been tough on her health and, although she loved her work, she finally decided to retire to her mountain to meditate and to sunbathe on the banks of the mighty river.

Despite her decision, groups of selfish people would still go to her house in search for answers to their problems, believing that only she could calm human hearts.

'If you can't wash our clothes anymore, at least help us to be happy with your advice,' demanded a sulking postman.

'My situation is just awful,' continued a man with a brown hat at the back of the crowd that had now gathered in front of Niku's home.

'That's nothing compared to what I'm going through,' said a flustered woman wearing yellow boots and a checked apron, defiantly placing her hands on her hips.

'How can you possibly think you're the worst off?', said the mayor haughtily. 'You have no idea what kind of problems go hand-in-hand with a job like mine.'

Soon, the situation turned into absolute chaos: a multitude of voices all yelling at once, people crying, men and women desperately trying to elbow their way through the crowd in order to be heard, each and every one of them sure that the washerwoman knew how to solve all of life's troubles.

Niku said nothing. Instead, she simply asked them all to take a seat and take some time to meditate. People continued to arrive for the next three days. When there was no more space, she addressed the awaiting crowd that had formed at her door.

'I will give you all the answer you seek. But you must promise me that, once your problems are resolved, you will tell everyone that I have left this place, so that I can live my life in the solitude I crave and enjoy my final days in peace.'

The men and women present swore a sacred oath: if the wise washerwoman kept her promise, they would build an enclosure along the river so that no one could climb her mountain or bother her every again.

'Tell me your problems,' said the old woman. Someone began to speak but was immediately interrupted by others who knew that this would be the very last audience they would ever have with the wise old woman and, as such, were worried that she wouldn't have time to listen to everyone.

The wise old woman, who was patient but had a strong character, finally yelled, 'Silence!'

The crowd went quiet instantly.

'Go home and take the whitest item of clothing you own, write your problem on it and hang it up in the main square tomorrow at dawn.'

The answer perplexed those in attendance, as they couldn't understand how this would put an end to their problems. Pensive, and placing their trust in somebody who had never failed them, they each returned to their homes and prepared what Niku had asked of them.

The next morning, the square was overflowing with clothes featuring everybody's problems. The expectant villagers had gathered at the meeting point, waiting for wise Niku to ease their suffering. Suddenly, the old woman appeared from behind one of the large hanging sheets that rustled gently in the cool morning air, and said, 'Very well, here are all your problems. Take a walk around the square and choose an item of clothing with a problem you consider to be smaller and more insignificant than yours. Then, you can exchange your problem for the one you have chosen, or you can take your own original problem back with you.'

The people gathered there all walked through the square excitedly, thinking that their lives would finally be free of problems. However, the more they read what their neighbours had written on their clothes, the more horrified they were. Eventually, they concluded that what they had originally written, no matter how bad, was nowhere near as serious as what the others were going through. Relieved to know that their issues were not as serious as they'd originally imagined, they took their own clothes back and returned home convinced that they were happier than the rest.

Grateful for the lesson they had been taught, the villagers fulfilled their promise and never allowed anyone to disturb Niku or her peace from that moment on. She was never heard from again. In her honour, and so that future generations wouldn't forget this lesson, the mayor ordered the construction of large stone plaque with bronze letters in the centre of the square, with the endorsement of the entire village. It read, *'Bring your problems here and return home full of cheer.'*

I could feel my grandmother's suffering hiding behind her sad smile, haunting her like a shadow. Despite her sudden bursts of joy and her efforts to go on as normal, she wasn't able to fill the infinite void left by my mother either. Her light and her warmth lived on in every part of that house.

'Belly, why don't I have a mother like the other kids?'

'Your mother's very special, Rafaela. She's an angel,' she answered, wiping away my tears with her long fingers.

'But sometimes I can't remember her face. Could we visit her where the angels live?'

'Very soon, Rafaela, very soon.'

With the faith of a small child, I waited for that magical event to take place, but it never did. Since that day, her black and white portrait sat on the chest of drawers, presiding over our living room. Her image brought me moments of pain, while it also forged a strong desire within me. I longed to learn enough so that I could penetrate her mind and get to know her inner world. Understanding the human psyche became my personal crusade.

We all have an 'if only' in our lives. Someone who could have been something special but never got any further than the door. A spark that never quite became a flame. Someone who hangs around your thoughts and who occasionally makes you wonder 'what if'. Amelia López Aguilar would always be mine.

Each round in boxing is like a book published as part of a series: four, eight, ten or twelve rounds. That fateful afternoon, the last of my chapters was being written, the one Conan named 'the sweet science of the beating'. For the first time – after one hundred and ninety-seven fights under my belt, two Amateur Champion titles, twenty victories by knockout – I didn't want to be yet another disciple of a science whose participants proudly show off their flattened noses, greet each other with hooks that send you to the ropes and whose ripped bodies reminded me of Florentine sculptures.

It's amazing just how quickly you think when so much is at stake. Boxers possess extraordinary awareness; they respond to their opponent's change in strategy and are even able to sway the public's emotions, just like writers do. My thoughts, bathed in sweat and blood, wandered off on an unknown path following my opponent's overwhelmingly final blow.

Conan knew me well; he knew I wasn't one to throw in the towel, which is why he had no choice but to ask for the fight to finish, putting an end to my agony.

'It's over, Iris. We're going,' he said hurriedly, knowing there would be no argument from me.

'Can you hear me? Rafaela, look at me. Stay with me,' he insisted, sounding a little desperate as he watched me slipping away.

'Call and ambulance, now! I can't feel a pulse,' said the doctor in his effort to keep me alive as he removed all the trappings of the fallen hero and leaving me again a mere mortal.

Conan had always been sensitive to my feelings, even though they were lost on him most of the time. He was an enthusiastic mentor who genuinely enjoyed witnessing my physical and emotional growth.

'There will never come a day where I put your health or your safety at risk in exchange for victory, Rafaela. I'll measure my success only by how much you respect me. My job isn't to push you to achieve things that are beyond your reach but to teach you to fight for your dreams, regardless of the end result. Never forget that my interest in you as a person far outweighs my interest in you as an athlete.'

His words resonated loudly somewhere inside my dishevelled head that now lay on a narrow white stretcher, shooting through the crowd that wasn't quite ready to leave. Then the lights went out. My life was lit only by the vermilion of the wailing sirens that desperately cleared a path that night, on the way to my inevitable destiny.

Chapter 2

The Awakening

I woke up with an intense headache. I tried, unsuccessfully, to budge on that soft place that appeared to be a mattress but a stabbing pain in my temples, as though I was being pierced by sharp knives, and an immense pain in my shoulder made me abandon all efforts to move. I opened my eyes and noticed that I was immobilised, my arms hooked up to IV drips that fed a yellowish fluid into my body. The room's silence was interrupted by mournful voices and the clicking of high heels. I looked around me, taking in every detail, trying to remember why I'd ended up in what seemed to be a hospital. However, my memories appeared to have vanished into obscurity.

My radar detected another bed a few metres away where a woman of about fifty, with a rather aged appearance, tried to conceal her suffering beneath a flannel nightgown printed with tiny daisies. She was passing by the time counting colourful pills, which she then put into a small transparent box.

'Nurse, the girl's awake,' she said, struggling to speak, while she pressed the red button hanging to her right.

Barely seconds later, a nurse approached me in her blue uniform and white clogs. She took my pulse and looked at my pupils.

'What happened to me?' I asked in a broken voice, not wanting to interrupt what she was doing.

'You arrived two months ago with a serious concussion that result-ed in a stroke. You've got two broken ribs and liver trauma.'

'Two months?'

'Yes, you've been in a coma this entire time. You've been very lucky. The medical team never lost hope. You have many followers that believe in you, Iris.'

'Iris? Is that my name?' I asked, completely disoriented.

'Your real name is Rafaela López Aguilar. Iris is what they call you in the boxing world.'

Seeing the look of confusion on my face, the nurse explained, 'I'm not a big fan of that sport, but everyone here has been talking about you and your boxing triumphs. Looks like you're quite the star in Granada. Over the past few weeks, the press has really taken an interest in your case and there've been lots of articles written about you.'

'Really? Is that what I am? A boxer?'

'Actually, you were a renowned psychologist.'

'I *was*? Does that mean I'm not any more?' I asked again, trying to find some clues as to my own identity.

That question seemed to make her uncomfortable, so I changed the topic.

'I can't remember anything. Just vague images and a few blurry faces. I remember the face of large man with dark skin surrounded by some mystical music, but I don't know who that is.'

The woman smiled. 'Don't worry, that's due to your head injury. All that information will come back eventually, and things will fall into place. The neurologist is coming to see you shortly. Take it easy. This type of amnesia isn't permanent.'

Then she hurriedly picked up all the medical material and disappeared, leaving behind a halo of mystery and a simple 'now rest'.

My roommate eyed me curiously, not quite knowing how to start a conversation with someone like me, who had no answers.

'Don't push it, sweetie, your family and friends will help you put all the pieces back together again. Especially the lady who comes to see you every day; she seems to know you very well.'

I couldn't tell whether her words were comforting or disturbing, but I wanted to know more.

'Do you know who she is? What does she look like? Have you spoken to her?' I asked, interrogating her like a secret agent working for Interpol.

'She usually comes in the evening, outside visiting hours. She never speaks to anyone, but smiles at everyone. She sits at the foot of your bed and reads you books in a language I don't understand. Do you have any foreign relatives?' she asked, as if trying to make sense of it all for me.

I searched through my memories but couldn't come across anything that would provide a clue.

'I don't remember,' I answered, looking at her indifferently.

Without fully understanding what was happening, I was sure I'd experienced this feeling before – the feeling of being lost and not knowing who I was.

'Can there be anything worse that being lost?' I whispered rhetorically, while I challenged my body to sit up slowly. I didn't expect an answer.

'You're not lost, sweetie, you just have to remember who you are,' said my roommate without hesitation.

Those words resonated within me like a hurricane. For a second, I felt as though I'd uttered them myself, as if they were my words coming out of a stranger's mouth.

Looking through the half-open window, past the faded and languishing curtains, I figured it must be autumn because of the smell of wet earth and the ochre, red and orange colours of the landscape outside. I associated that season with melancholy, maturity, stillness and reflection. Autumn represents change, when trees rid themselves of all that is superfluous in order to rest throughout the winter and then be reborn, beginning a new cycle. I enjoyed watching the effects of autumn, where each fallen leaf gave way to a new flower. I identified with that part of the yearly cycle that corresponds to early sunsets and a culmination of life's maturity. It was a time of culmination and decline. Spring light is young and unruly, while autumn light is wise and mature.

This feeling awakened some memories in me. I could see myself taking notes in almost illegible handwriting, with a silver pen, while actively listening to the account being given a familiar-looking woman who seemed to be calmly reclining on a white leather couch. A minimalist desk of light wood, its contents perfectly arranged and surrounded by shelves full of books and certificates, were also a part of that vision. I concluded that it must be my consulting room, and that I was providing therapy to one of my patients.

'Every time autumn comes, I get depressed, I feel sorry for myself, I latch on to solitude and don't let anyone in,' said the patient with her eyes closed, resting her arms loosely on her ample bosom.

'Lucia, the melancholy that seems to invade you during this season, and that disturbs your moods and your emotions, is often due to the changing pattern of light and darkness. This reduces our levels of serotonin – a central nervous neurotransmitter – and this can directly affect our moods. Emotions sync up with nature.'

'That's interesting. I've never noticed that connection.'

'Tell me, how do you feel?' I asked, genuinely interested.

'Really tired. I can barely sleep. I can't concentrate on anything I do, and the worst part is that it's affecting my productivity at work. Can you help me?' she asked from her horizontal position.

'In Chinese philosophy, autumn is the season of *yin* and has a tendency towards receiving, opening up to intuition and internalisation. It's when the sap in trees flows from the leaves and branches back to the roots. Animals reduce their activity. The sun sets earlier each day and, little by little, the cold returns. It's a time of death and rebirth. According to Buddha, *'this existence of ours is as transient as autumn clouds.'* Practising the art of detachment and freeing ourselves of all but the essentials, syncs us up with this season. This autumn metamorphosis also requires us to change. We must retreat from the physical and psychological world and look inwards,' I explained, as she listened intently.

I realised from my answer that I was not a conventional psychologist, and I tried to prolong that memory.

'I think what you're saying makes a lot of sense. I've just realised that I've been hanging onto a toxic relationship, and it's taking over my entire life. It's time to let it go. This feeling returns every autumn, reminding me how unhappy I am and triggering my feelings of melancholy.'

I let her lie silently with that thought before continuing.

'There are times in life when we have to let go of that we no longer need, tear ourselves away from certain behaviours that are no longer of any use to us, and find a bit of internal peace that takes us away from the obsolete. And we have to prepare ourselves to embark on the path of transformation, clearing the way for new spaces and possibilities,' I pointed out as I set my eyes on a tiny hourglass that discreetly measured the time that was slipping away.

The screeching sound of a trolley approaching suddenly interrupted my memory, bringing me back to the reality of my hospital room.

'Are you hungry?' asked a nurse, excitedly.

She headed to the foot of the bed and looked at my chart. 'This'll be your first dinner in some time. It'll be bland food for a while, until your body adjusts,' she said as she uncovered a steaming ceramic bowl accompanied by a soft bread roll and a tiny portion of butter that had already begun to melt.

The truth is I was hungry, even though I found the meal rather disappointing. I must be a very polite person, or an extremely sensible one, because I didn't want to hurt her feelings with my reply.

'Yes, thank you,' I said, hiding my frustration.

I continued to watch her as she served my roommate something that appeared to be vegetables and a piece of seasoned fish. I couldn't help but envy her, and I began to drool unconsciously. That particular signal told me that it was exactly the type of diet I had lived on until now. My intuition told me I was vegetarian. I took a couple of sips from my bland broth and turned to the nurse.

'Excuse me, did I have any personal belongings when I came here?'

'Yes, they're in the small white cupboard in the bathroom. Do you want me to bring them to you?'

'Yes please,' I said gratefully.

The helpful nurse seemed to show even more curiosity than I did to discover the secrets hiding there. She hurried off and returned with a Wayuu, a Colombian backpack in a bright emerald green and brown pattern. Upon first glance, it looked quite heavy. She very carefully left it on my bedside table, making sure I could easily reach it, and then waited for me to do something. The woman in the next bed also directed her nosy gaze towards it. I felt my privacy being invaded so I held back until both women had gone back to their own routines.

When no one was looking, I tried to guess what kind of objects I'd find inside, putting my hand in first and then attempting to guess what it was before taking it out of the bag. The first thing I found was a very soft toiletry bag with a zip. I figured it contained makeup and maybe a small mirror. I was not mistaken. Just as I expected, there was a bubble-gum pink lipstick, black mascara, an old makeup brush and a pearly eyeshadow, along with a small round mirror with a cracked lid.

Unable to contain myself and somewhat suspicious, I brought the mirror to my face. I wanted to see what this woman, trapped in her own labyrinth, looked like. Despite my dull complexion, a skinny face that had survived on a liquid diet for eight weeks, and a bandage covering half my head, exposing a clear forehead with some tangled pieces of hair, I liked what I saw. I was horrified at the sorry state of my unkempt eyebrows, but was relieved to recognise myself in the depth of my own gaze, which I held for a few seconds.

I quickly recovered from that initial impact and moved on to the next object. I could tell it was some kind of lingerie from the feel of lace and silk, maybe a camisole. But, why would that be in my backpack? I took it out and saw that it still had the tag of a luxury department store attached to it. It had never been worn; was I expecting a night of romance with someone special? It cheered me up to think that maybe I had someone, a person that aroused my basic instincts.

The third item was some paper, a sheet that had been folded into an envelope. It wasn't hard to deduce what it was. The note was as small as the white envelope it came in. There was no sender, just a faded stamp and my name in big letters, written with what seemed to be a fountain pen. When I read what it said, I was in absolute shock.

My son, your father, has just died. This is the first time I have written your name, though I have said it out loud many times. He would have liked nothing more than to have had you visit the land he so adored, beneath the sun that tanned his golden skin. The land to which you also belong. In accordance with our traditions, we will travel there next Tuesday at sunrise, and the dust he has now become will return to heaven.

Song for returning spirits:

May the sky's warm winds blow softly in your home.
May the higher spirit bless all those who pass through it.
May your shoes leave many happy footprints in the snow.
And may the rainbow always shine down on you.

Signed:
Wakanda,
he of internal magical powers

Taken aback, I rubbed the sleep from my eyes and reread the note three times. I could not believe those few, but troubling, lines.

'My father, my father, my father has died,' I repeated over and over to myself, like a broken record.

The letter was dated the twelfth of August of that same year.

'What's the date today?' I asked out loud, not realising I'd woken up my roommate.

'It's the thirty-first of October,' she groaned in pain.

Suddenly, I burst out crying, not quite knowing why. I was a mess. I didn't remember my father, but still I felt an immense sadness. That being who had given me life was gone, and I had not been there to say goodbye. My torment was so overwhelming that all physical pain disappeared from my body, fading into inexistence. I didn't even have his memory to hold onto.

After a few minutes of crying, I dried my tears with the same sheet that covered my half-naked, shivering body.

'Bad news?' asked my roommate softly, witnessing the scene.

I shook my head. I didn't feel like talking to a stranger about my findings. What could I tell her? There were no words to describe it. I needed answers and all I had was a flurry of questions.

Why was that letter in my bag? Who was my father? And, more importantly, who was I?

I opened the backpack once again and continued my investigation. I found a state-of-the-art mobile phone covered in a cheerful phone case with butterflies on it. The battery was obviously dead. I felt around and found a charger in one of the small pockets inside the backpack. That insignificant discovery gave me a flash of hope. Surely that small device had a lot to say. There would be messages, contacts, emails... an entire arsenal of information, which was exactly what I needed in order to shed some light on so much darkness.

My memory fluttered incessantly, throwing random images at me, as it pleased.

I was sitting in a circle with a group of people. My outfit was casual, but I'd but a lot of effort into it. I was wearing brown knee-high suede boots; a sheer immaculately white shirt hanging loosely over tight, torn jeans; and a simple hippy-style belt. Over the top was a beautiful blue jacket with a bright red lining. There was not a scrap of jewellery on me.

I immediately ruled out the possibility of meeting up or partying with friends, as everyone there, including myself, looked serious and pensive. I counted fourteen people in total, a mix of men and women.

'What the hell am I doing here? I should be spending what little time I have left doing something much more useful than listening to other poor dying people like myself,' said an emaciated and bald man, shooting me a defiant look.

'I don't feel like a poor dying person,' said a young woman wearing an amazing, beautifully styled, blonde bob wig. 'We're not dead yet.'

A young man with Asian features, sitting to my right, also wished to speak.

'It's not fair. I'm turning twenty-three in twenty days' time. I've just met a beautiful girl at university whose name's Amanda. The music in my heart is much louder than the noise in my head, which is yelling at me that the metastasis will not only kill my body but also my story.'

A short but liberating silence signalled the group's agreement. It was then interrupted by a woman who stammered as she prayed, holding a slippery set of rosary beads in her trembling hands. She stood up, clumsily, and continued to pray out loud.

> Lord, I come to you today with all my hope and trust,
> I need your help, oh Lord.
> God, Almighty Father,
> I thank you for being by my side,
> For making me feel protected when I'm alone and have no way out,
> I thank you for being present always,
> During the difficult times, when I can find no solution.

The young lover stopped her, spouting fury.

'Enough. Where is your God? Do you really think your cancer is going to disappear just by repeating those stupid prayers all day long?' The devout woman burst into tears as the others looked empathically.

I then remembered the group therapy sessions I held on Thursdays with terminal patients in the city centre. Experiencing death while still alive felt very familiar to me. The programme was called 'On Death and Dying' in honour of a book by Doctor Elisabeth Kubler-Ross, possibly the world's greatest expert on death, dying people and palliative care.

I helped people cross over into another form of existence, yet I could not do the same with my own father. How ironic.

I wonder what had happened to him. What were his beliefs on this topic? I felt as though I was getting to know a man by the end of his story, not the beginning.

I was a child of Jupiter and this fact undoubtedly marked my positive outlook and extensive views with regards to the 'great beyond'. Like Elisabeth, the Swiss doctor and psychiatrist, I believed that dying meant moving to a nicer house. I read that, on one particular occasion, she had visited one of Hitler's laboratories in Poland where prisoners had engraved butterflies on the walls. Years later, she found an explanation for this. We abandon our body, which holds our soul prisoner, just as the cocoon encases the pupating butterfly. Once we are free, like the beautiful butterfly, we are able to return home. The process is almost identical to that of birth as it involves the beginning of another form of existence, passing from one state of consciousness to another and growing spiritually. We feel overwhelmed with unimaginably indescribable and unconditional love. I've never been a religious person, but I am deeply spiritual.

We all have a purpose, a mission that we have been sent to fulfil in this crazy world. My maxim has always been not to leave this world, with a headstone that reads *'Here lies someone who was born, lived and died, but who never really knew why she existed in the first place.'* The one and only indisputable truth is the importance of life.

When we take our journey's final turns, edging closer to the other side, we face the one question we must answer. If you have lived according to the plan that brought you here in the first place, then there is no reason to fear death. The pieces of existence don't always fit together perfectly, but experience has taught me that coincidences do not exist. If we pay attention, we see that everything that happens to us leads us on the right path to discover our life's purpose.

Is this really how I want to live my life? We have all asked ourselves this question at some point. The problem is not that life is short, but that sometimes it takes us too long to understand what truly matters.

I wondered what all these developments could mean. All my ideas were back to front. If, as I believed, there was life after death, then perhaps I could meet my father again someday and solve the enigmas that had affected so deeply my emotions.

That night, I slept very deeply. My last image was that of a seagull spreading its newly fledged grey wings on the windowsill, watching me with its beady eyes. The cool breeze helped calm my thoughts and carried me off to the land of dreams.

—✕—

'Good morning, Rafaela, how are you feeling today?'

Still drowsy, I opened my eyes. The man was holding a bunch of unwrapped blue daisies in one hand, the other reaching out to hold mine. His warmth ran through me like an electrical current, cutting me in half.

'You look incredible. Even at your worst, you're still the sexiest girl I've ever met. The doctor told me you'll be discharged in a couple of days,' said the mysterious visitor.

I felt as though I'd been dragging boxes all night, maybe due to bad posture.

'I feel much better,' I said, still unsure of whom I was speaking to.

The fresh scent of his cologne invaded the room and my senses. There was no doubt about it; this was clearly someone important in my life.

'You have no idea how relieved I am. I've been so worried about you and it's made me realise just how much you mean to me,' he continued, flashing a broad, heartfelt smile.

He carefully arranged the flowers in a slim, hand-painted glass vase. His behaviour made me fear we might have been romantically involved, but I could no longer remember. The sparkle in his eyes felt familiar and made my stomach flutter.

'The neurologist thinks I'll get my memory back soon,' I said, not daring to ask anything too personal until I knew what I was dealing with.

'Everything is going to be OK. Do you know who I am?'

He leaned in towards me, caressing my face with the palm of his hand. That moment opened the gates.

'Are we in a relationship? What's your name?'

'Jared. My name is Jared.'

'Jared?'

'Yes, we were married some time ago, but you moved back to Granada after the divorce. The project I'm working on in Israel brought me back here a few weeks ago. Our team is carrying out some research in your city. By coincidence, I came across a newspaper with an article about your accident. I was shaken to the core. These past few weeks have been very tough.'

His Spanish was pretty good, and the sweet way he pronounced his words gave him an air of sophistication. The rolled-up sleeves of his black linen shirt showed off the toned muscles in his arms. A pair of Ray-Bans hung from a pocket on his mustard-coloured chinos. His rugged facial features and light stubble revealed him to be exactly the type of manly man I was attracted to. I guess it was my professional bias that led me to determine his personality profile immediately. I couldn't help it; even outside my job as a psychologist, I analysed every living being. I'm not sure to what exact extent was conditioned by it but I was almost never wrong.

I categorised him as a confident and intelligent man with a strong personality. Most likely independent and successful.

'Why did we break up?' I asked him, incredulous but curious.

'It's complicated. Sometimes things don't turn out the way you planned. You write the story and then life changes the plot.'

I detected a hint of bitterness in his voice, but it sounded like the typical excuse of a man who'd had an affair and didn't know how to get out of the mess.

He buried his fingers in his raven hair, combing it back firmly as his coal black eyes pierced mine.

Our conversation was interrupted by the same nurse, who looked like a travelling pharmacy.

'It's time for your medicine.'

Jared moved aside to make room for the nurse, who was dragging her tired feet as though she'd been on night duty for a month.

'It's great to have you back, Rafaela. I have to get back to work now. I'll leave you my card with my phone number on your bedside table. Call me any time.'

With that invitation, he retraced his steps out of the room, leaving me to my ruminations once again. In my ignorant solitude I asked myself how it was possible to have been married to a man and to have lived in a foreign country, and yet have no trace of those memories within me. But there was no answer. Only my intuition shone a glimmer of light inside my brain.

'My life is an absolute mess. In just a few short hours I've discovered that my father is dead and that my marriage failed,' I thought to myself, sadly. I felt as though I was living someone else's life and was mentally unable to travel back in time. I had no autobiographical memory.

I'd waited anxiously for my phone to come back to life and could finally turn it on. Suddenly, my heart was beating faster. It asked me for my PIN and my fingers quickly typed in the magical number as if guided purely by instinct. Eureka! I was in. I was impressed by the level of activity reflected in that tiny device. A whole living, parallel world that had gone on without me, barely noticing my absence all that time.

I felt sick. I had that dizzy feeling you get when you're going up and up on a roller coaster, and you fear you might die, but you want to do it anyway. The brightly-lit screen showed ninety-three messages, three hundred and two emails and a mass of voice messages on WhatsApp. I started with these first. I noticed that there were a lot of them from the twelfth of August, most of which came with heart, smile and kiss emojis.

> Hey champion. Be bad and have a good day! I hope all your dreams come true in this new stage of your life.

> Good morning, Rafaela. They say that honesty is the most important part of any friendship. Don't be upset, but... you're getting old. Happy birthday, grandma!

> 'Hey, its Raquel again. Where are you? We're all waiting for you at Cantina El Trébol to celebrate your birthday. C'mon, don't freak out, Turning thirty-seven is still worth celebrating!'

'Stop the world, I want to get off!!' I yelled.

That thirty-seven burned itself into my mind like a tattoo. It was obvious that I had missed my own birthday, though that disappointment faded when I realised that it was the same day that my father had died. Coincidence? Then I remembered that Jared had also used that word to explain our re-encounter.

Our rational mind calls synchronicity 'coincidence'. One of my greatest teachers, the psychoanalyst Carl Jung, uses this term to refer to apparently unrelated but meaningful events that are simultaneously linked by chance. The universe has its own order, one that is unknown but fascinating.

This phenomenon occurs when certain events sync up with our internal state. We all have a hidden inner universe and go through life projecting and attracting through our feelings. This is how we use our human ability to open new fields.

I liked having everything under control; it gave me security. However, that had all come crashing down like a house of cards. Were those unexpected coincidences confirmation that I was merely a puppet in a predetermined plan? I'd become obsessed with understanding the human mind since a very young age. I knew that, as humans, we had a tendency to find meaning in everything, shunning the unpredictable, and seeking an explanation behind every disturbing truth. What looks like a simple accident unequivocally becomes our destiny.

'Rafaela, don't fool yourself. Calm down. You're seeing things where there's absolutely nothing to see. Use your analytical skills and everything you've learnt over the years.' That was my rational mind speaking. But what I felt transcended all reason. It had nothing to do with magic or coincidence. What we call internal wisdom, conscience, intuition, or 'x' was flying ahead, leaving all traces of unpredictability behind. My spiritual side was yelling that my 'master plan' had been activated. Albert Einstein himself had said that *'the intellect has little to do on the road to discovery. There comes a leap in consciousness, call it intuition or what you will, and the solution comes to you and you don't know why or how.'*

No matter how hard scientists try to control every factor and answer every question, there will always be unknown variables out of our control. We use reason to reduce those variables but sometimes improbability can play an important role. Was there a combinatorial analysis, or mathematical explanation, to explain that series of coincidences?

I wasn't sure if this sudden burst of clarity was clearing a path like a bolt of lightning cutting through a storm, or if it was simply my need for comfort that clutched me tightly, like a frightened koala, approving of my own self-deceit.

I had met hundreds of patients that were far removed from their own internal coherence.

'Rafaela, you're not walking along the same tightrope now, are you?' I asked myself, trying to maintain my mental balance.

I'd heard that these synchronicities occurred more often during times of transition, self-doubt or crisis, particularly following a death or events that shake us to our very core and send us on a journey of self-discovery. It is then that the world becomes a place full or opportunities and openings, where strings wait for us to pull from them, tying them together in what will ultimately become the tapestry of our purpose, visible only to those who are ready to see it.

There's a cosmic order no one tells us about, whereby we can trace a dialogue if we pay attention to the signs and symbols or gut feelings that have no connection to anyone else but us. I myself was determined to read those signs. I had to follow this path wholeheartedly and listen to my destiny.

Following this moment of introspection, I moved on to the photos. There was an infinite number of them, proving that I had a rather active social life. I also found photos of me in boxing poses, photos of me surrounded by children, beautiful natural landscapes immortalised together with different people, and lots of selfies. I was startled when my iPhone began to vibrate without permission between my frozen hands. A nervous melody played along with a message that read 'Conan incoming video call', which I read as I tried to stop it from shaking. The clock read eight minutes past twelve. 'What a coincidence,' I thought, looking at the combination of numbers.

Chapter 3

Elsu

Even when your name means 'falcon among the clouds', it does not make the experience of flying in a gigantic metal bird any easier. Although I had prepared for this momentous adventure my entire life, the small spaces, the cabin pressure and dry air were all beginning to take their toll on a free spirit like myself.

'The falcon always takes flight against the wind, never with it,' my father would tell me with his deep voice whenever one of the wild horses would throw my small elastic body to the ground. Sulking, I would run to lie down on top of the bison skins that were kept over the long winters piled high in our tepee. My father would then come and deliver a life lesson right into my soul, that I would never have learnt otherwise without that 'defeat', allowing me to take flight again, this time higher, stronger and wiser.

'Elsu, life is an invitation to succeed, conquer and be happy. It calls us to be fighters or victims. There is no other category. Life is a cry that calls for pacific warriors to fulfil the most glorious of all conquests. Our own.'

From my earliest childhood, I learnt that the situations we experience, which appear in our lives in a multitude of ways, occur simply to give us an opportunity to learn from them. They are not hurdles, but a step forwards on the path of self-awareness, allowing us to discover the different layers that live within us that we often do not believe are there, or which we feel are dormant, waiting to be awakened. Learning is the start of wealth and spirituality.

I travelled alone, but was accompanied by the strength of many who eagerly awaited my return. Despite the circumstances, I was happy to travel abroad for the first time, and to experience the feeling of floating in space. It was the perfect occasion to honour my name. The plane was full of passengers and I guess I seemed as unique to them as they did to me, because I could feel their stares penetrating my skin like arrows. I avoided their eyes, feigning indifference, and stretched my neck to see how the violet sky appeared to swallow us through the tiny round windows.

A freckly kid with blond hair and honey-coloured eyes playfully watched me from his seat to my left. He tried to imitate the Indian yell, placing the palm of his hand in front of his mouth, moving it quickly and intermittently. The woman sitting next to him, whose hair was the same colour as her son's and tied in a long golden po-nytail that fell in a cascade of curls over her shoulders, sheepishly stopped him.

'Leave the gentleman alone, Ryan. Let's put a Disney movie on for you,' she said, trying to distract him from his innocent behaviour.

'I want to watch a movie about Indians just like him,' said the child, while she lovingly smiled at him and adjusted his seatbelt, paying no attention to his request.

In our ancient culture, children are the music that make our spirits dance. We love them deeply, lavishing care and affection on them. When a baby is born, we keep the umbilical cord. Once it's dry, we roll it up and coat it in the parents' saliva and some herbs, and keep it in a small suede pouch adorned with beads. We place this next to the crib as an amulet, and it will then form part of every important ceremony in that child's life. Twenty-six years later, my mother still keeps mine like one of her greatest treasures.

As is our tradition, my grandparents gifted me my name shortly after being born – a name I abandoned for the one with which I am known today, 'Elsu'. As they get older, children in our tribe change their name for another one that has greater meaning for them, according to their personality and achievements. It is also normal for both men and women to change their names as they transcend into new levels of spiritual intelligence.

It had been over five hours since we had left Montana, with its vast horizons and never-ending skies. No wonder they called it Big Sky Country. I had always heard that our tribe had secretly remained hidden in the Rocky Mountains for thousands of years, protected by snow-covered peaks that touch the sky. For generations, we had shared that land with herds of wapiti that grazed among the abundant tall grass, a place with three times more animals than people.

I was seated in an aisle seat on one of the front rows, in economy class, naturally. The hours dragged by, until it was dinner time. The lights came on and an immaculately uniformed flight attendant wearing a red hat, a fitted blouse and pleated knee-length skirt approached me to ask whether I wanted beef or fish. I curiously observed the meal composition, presented in tiny boxes, which was all completely new to me.

'No, thank you. Just a little water for me, please.' I said, using a hand motion for emphasis.

'Of course,' said the accommodating young woman.

I knew that I was going to remain immobile in that small space for almost fifteen hours until I reached my destination, taking into account the connections I would be making, so I began to pass the time by examining the other passengers. I found this quite entertaining. Suddenly, a well-dressed man in his sixties with impeccable white hair, sitting to my right near the window, interrupted my thoughts.

'Can you believe it?' he said to me with a snide laugh.

'Excuse me?' I answered, not quite understanding the question.

'It's amazing. I can't travel with my dog Lua in the cabin with me, but those Arabs wearing their white tunics can keep their falcons on their arms like it's no big deal,' he continued indignantly, pointing at three passengers a few rows back.

I turned my head towards where he was pointing and finally understood what he meant. I had not noticed up until then but, personally, it seemed entirely normal to me. I even felt a little more at home surrounded by those animals that meant so much to me.

'They are harmless; they will not hurt you,' I replied, trying to reassure him.

'So is my Lua. This is unheard of!' he protested, raising his voice.

A flight attendant came over immediately upon hearing the man yelling hysterically, waving his arms and shaking his head.

'Sir, you're travelling on an Arab airline. We allow passengers to travel with their falcons here as we consider them sacred animals,' she explained very politely, trying to calm him down.

'And what about other animals? My dog is sacred to me.'

'I'm sorry, sir, but dogs are not allowed,' she declared respectfully.

'That's outrageous, what discrimination! This is the last time I travel with this airline. It's surreal,' he concluded.

I was captivated by the young woman whose features resembled those of the men in white. Her words had touched me and I wanted to know more.

'Miss, could you please tell me more about your falcons and the place they hold within your tribe?'

'Tribe?' she repeated with her red lipstick smile. 'In the Middle East, falcons are the highest status symbol. Hunting with falcons goes back thousands of years and has become a very important part of our culture. Traditionally, these birds were used to obtain food, but nowadays they are kept as pets and are used in sports. In order to travel, they must have their own passports issued by the Ministry of the Environment and Water Resources, to prevent smuggling. Some families even have hundreds of them. For us, they represent bravery, perseverance, determination and freedom,' she concluded, looking over also at the annoyed man while he listened on, feigning disinterest, furrowing his brow and stroking his long white beard.

The lights in the plane were dimmed beneath the stars and the soft vortex of night. I decided to rest so I would be fresh the following day, when my life's most important mission would commence. I removed my moccasin boots and took one of the magazines that peeked out from the seat pocket in front of me. While I eyed it curiously, I recognised the image of the Alhambra, the fortress and palace in Granada, a masterpiece of Islamic art in Europe that my grandfather and then my father had told me so much about. I imagined myself wandering the streets of that city. I admit I was eager to experience everything that lay ahead of me; I could not believe the moment had finally arrived.

A few hours later, a voice came over the loudspeakers confirming that we had arrived at our destination. Without a second thought, I got out of my seat and took my carry-on luggage from the overhead compartment – my brown leather backpack that accompanied me on all my expeditions – which contained only the bare necessities. I said goodbye to some of the passengers and smiled at the flight attendants who wished me a pleasant stay.

Before I knew what was happening, I found myself surrounded by a mass of people, running in every direction like an antelope stampede. There was a mixture of stress and adrenaline in the air, and the energy and speed of the atmosphere overwhelmed me. Where I come from, peace and balance are what keep us alive. The training I received from my teachers gave me the power to survive in a chaotic world such as this, where the noise of the human mind far exceeded the acoustic noise produced by that civilisation – a civilisation that called itself 'developed', despite not having crossed the first Arch of Light, one of the seven Arches of the Temple of Light that the guardians of the Elove Galaxy had protected for millions of years.

It was written that a child whose name would be attributed to the Falcon Totem would guide humanity through the seven Arches of Light, thus fulfilling the prophecy that would complete the universe's sacred cycle. The guardians of the Elove Galaxy, which included my own father, would be my greatest allies.

I first saw her bending over, clumsily tying the laces of her red suede stiletto boots. A messy auburn mane with the occasional red streaks covered half of her face. I looked at her from the corner of my eye without imagining for a second that this slender young woman, dressed in all the colours of the rainbow, was in fact the guide I had hired. She suddenly looked up, revealing her grey feline eyes, clutching a printed sign up to her chest featuring my name, preceded by 'Mr'. This was amusing to me because, for the first time since mixing with that civilisation, I did not feel like the only odd one out. I stopped in front of her, noticing she was in her twenties. The look in our eyes as we met said it all – she was just as surprised to see me as I was. Maintaining a professional demeanour, she approached me with determination, adjusting her crossover bag that was covered in yellow stars.

'Are you Mr Elsu?' she asked confidently.

'Yes, I am. Thank you for coming.'

'Welcome to Granada. My name is Amelia and I'll be your guide during your stay in this beautiful city. I'm sure it will not disappoint. I've prepared a list of places of interest, monuments and activities for the next few days. Do you speak Spanish? Where would you like to start? Would you like to go to the hotel first to rest and freshen up? It's almost lunch time, I know one of the best tapas restaurants in the city.'

'I am sorry, but I am not here for leisure. I need your help to fulfil a very specific mission. And yes, I speak your language.'

'Mission? I don't understand...' she asked. Her face was expressionless for while, before a look of disappointment set in.

I showed her the palm of my hand, on which I had etched a map showing a tiny star near the word 'Purple Lagoon'.

'Do you know this place?'

Surprised, she read it out, repeating it as a question.

'The Purple Lagoon? I was born here, I grew up here and I've been working as a tourist guide for over four years. I've never heard of any place with that name or anything like it around here.'

'Maybe it has another name nowadays. It is a very old map. Do you at least know that area?'

Amelia thought for a moment, fixing her eyes on what appeared to be a hieroglyph with no meaning, as she held her chin with her fingers.

'According to your map, that spot would be to the north of the city, about a hundred kilometres from here. If you like, I can do some investigating tonight. I'll ask one of the city's most senior historians and then pick you up at the hotel tomorrow morning so we can inspect the area. Are you looking for anything in particular?'

'Yes, an extraordinary place,' I said, without going into any detail.

I noticed that Amelia was becoming more and more curious, though she was still notably unsure and suspicious. I decided not to give her any more information for the time being. I knew that this civilisation had a tendency to fear the unknown, and even reject it altogether. Familiarity made them calm, while the exotic or difficult to understand frightened them. What fed the fear of those weak minds was their inability to understand, which ultimately annulled their own autonomy and made them prisoners of their own emotions.

In Elove, we learnt that fear feeds off ignorance, while knowledge frees us, making us wiser and more capable.

'C'mon, I have the *mirabragas* right in front of the airport,' she said as she began walking, inviting me to follow her by tilting her head.

She soon realised that my literal translation of *mirabragas*, 'look at panties', made no sense at all. She smiled cheekily and explained.

'*Mirabragas* is what we call cars with rear-hinged doors. Sometimes, I also call mine *rust-bucket* because it's pretty old but, don't worry, it still works.'

I followed her to her car, a small beat-up bright green car full of maps and books that would take us to the hotel. I struggled to get my almost six-foot frame into the tiny space, but finally managed to wedge myself in like a contortionist. It was winter and it was drizzling. A gust of wind lifted up her pleated skirt before she could take her seat, exposing one of her toned buttocks.

'Shit! Damn wind!' she cried, composing herself after the incident.

'Well, I guess now the car's lived up to its name. We can probably drop the formality,' she said jokingly as she laughed, again in her unique style, which was beginning to grow on me.

'Of course,' I answered, sharing her laughter.

'The wind that your civilisation normally hates so much is an essential part of nature's balance. As a child, I loved watching the vegetation dance from one side to the other around our tepee, beneath a cloud of straw, dust and thousands of other minute particles that would come together and fly over the mountains. We recognise and feel our brother, the wind, who spreads seeds and pollen to make the plants grow. Wind carries life from one place to another and allows birds to glide and move freely.'

Amelia's face changed. Her metallic eyes welled up as she continued driving.

'Years ago, we had a vegetable garden where my father would grow seasonal fruit and different vegetables. My mother would complain because he would come inside dragging dirt in with his shoes and leaving footprints everywhere. Whenever I asked, "Where's *papá*?" she'd say, "The mole is around there somewhere, digging." They were always complete opposites. He was the passionate lover who became a husband, a man of the earth who enjoyed living a slow-paced life, peeling beans and watching chickens scratch the dirt. She was a refined woman who didn't have much of an education, but had cultured spirit and a passion for beauty and fashion. They were two souls living in incompatible worlds. I think that, to him, she was always a kind of ethereal presence that he never fully possessed, but was happy to share a home with.

'I was only around six years old when my father took me to the side of the house and told me, "You're not going to be my helper anymore, from now on you'll have your own vegetable garden." I'd plant things and water them, just like in my dad's giant garden. I remember getting angry at the snails when they would eat the seedlings and I'd always try to get out of pulling weeds.

'When he died of a sudden heart attack, he left a tray of tomato saplings ready to be repotted, and my mother with a broken heart, her happiness stolen from her. Since then, I haven't exactly got along well with Mother Nature.

'The truth is I have no idea why I'm telling all this to a perfect stranger. I don't usually share my feelings with anyone, but something made me do it. I'm sorry,' she said, holding back tears.

We, the children of Elove, can feel the emotions of unevolved beings and experience them, simultaneously. I felt Amelia's wounded, burning heart, galloping like a young foal with no direction, rules or control. I then understood the first teachings of the secret doctrines, the ones that the guardians of our galaxy transmit to the initiated. One of the true mysteries that can only be understood by those who have crossed the seven Arches of Light, thus opening the innermost doors that lead to the Temple of Light.

The civilisation to which Amelia belonged suffered when faced with death because the darkness blinded them. They faced it with immense fear, rejection, sometimes even preferring to ignore it as they had declared it the enemy of life. Some sought refuge in their beliefs in order to alleviate the pain, orphans of knowledge, holding onto their fragile egos, fears and reasoning, all of which made them incapable of accepting it, and therefore unable to open themselves up to the mystery and wonder of the infinite journey.

The vehicle stopped in front of a white Art Nouveau building adorned with red and purple flags. In the centre, a revolving door followed the guests as they entered, like a sunflower following the sun.

'Well, this is the hotel. I'll pick you up tomorrow at nine. I'll do some investigating about that mysterious place of yours before then.'

Amelia then said goodbye as if in slow motion, as though she really had no interest in letting me go.

'OK. I'll see you tomorrow,' I agreed, truly astonished at how hectic life was in this place that was so different to anything I had ever known.

I awoke at dawn as the first rays of sunshine pierced the slats in the blinds. I was used to a night so deep that I could not help but miss the stars. I did not need to check the clock hanging on the turquoise wall to know that it was exactly twenty minutes until our meeting. I had showered the night before and eaten some food at the hearty hotel buffet, as an experiment. I put on some cotton trousers and a matching camel-coloured suede shirt adorned with porcupine bristles and fringes, and I used my fingers to comb my long dark hair, which hung around my shoulders like a weeping willow, before adjusting the red headband that ran from my forehead to my nape. It was the first time I had seen my tanned complexion and golden eyes reflected in a mirror. In Elove, we learn to recognise ourselves through the eyes of our brothers. They tell us who we are and we thank them by returning the favour so they, too, can discover themselves. We have no need for glass contraptions that show only what is superficial, without delving into the true essence of the bare soul, our favourite place.

Amelia was leaning against the bonnet of her car, arms crossed, waiting for me when I arrived. I was surprised to see a silver-grey dog with thick fur and pointy ears leaning its head out one of the back windows. I immediately recognised its brave, inquisitive and active temperament. It was a tall and strong Czechoslovakian Wolfdog.

'I hope you don't mind,' she said trustingly as she caressed the animal's muscular, symmetrical head. 'I always bring him with me when I know I'm spending the day outside. You won't even notice he's here,' she insisted, trying to downplay his presence.

'I love animals,' I said, approving of her initiative. 'I have always spoken the language of nature, animals and trees.'

'Really? That's great! Maybe you can convince Vodka to stop eating my breakfast in the morning,' she answered jokingly, giving no credibility whatsoever to my statement.

'C'mon, get in. I'll tell you what I've found out on the way. We have a few hours of driving ahead of us.'

I had to move aside some travel brochures that had piled up on the passenger seat before I could sit down. I felt my adrenaline rush, my breathing speed up and my pupils dilate. It was then that I understood the excitement that Amelia was feeling.

'You seem to enjoy your work a lot. Where do your travels take you?' I asked, curious.

'Where do they take me? Anywhere. I feel the need to move, to know what there is beyond just this. I think I have fernweh, "farsickness".

I feel immense longing for places I've never been. *"When the snow melts, the stork arrives and the first steamships race off, then I feel this painful travel unrest,"* as Hans Christian Andersen would say. I pack my beat-up suitcases that sit by the door impatiently and I give in to my need to take off. I can't help it,' she replied, as we left the city behind.

'Travelling is both fleeing and seeking, in equal parts. An interior, existential experience that seeks to fulfil our longing for what is missing in our lives. But life is the real journey. One never completes the way back,' I said, pausing for reflection.

'You're probably right. Like Buddha says, *"You cannot travel on the path until you become the path itself."* Every time I leave for a long period of time, I come back a different person. What impacts and moves me the most is seeing the same people go on with their ordinary lives, doing their jobs like robots. They live on autopilot, paying their bills, buying their food, having the same conversations over and over again and worrying about the same trivial matters. I'm really into just sitting somewhere unknown and remembering things I haven't thought about in years that maybe, had it not been for the strong smell of violets or picturesque streets, I may have forgotten altogether. Dreaming in different beds, feeling like you're discovering new worlds without borders, makes me feel like I'm experiencing everything for the first time, but in an eternal kind of way. My mother's convinced that my trips are just a disappearing act I've been using since my father died. Don't take this the wrong way, but I prefer to travel alone. I only do this type of thing to make a living.'

Her words were sincere but, at the same time, I felt a connection beyond just a professional one, drawing her to me like a moth to a flame. She enjoyed my presence in restless peace. At that precise moment, I wanted to give her what she needed, to give meaning to her solitary, travelling spirit.

'I really appreciate your honesty. I am not offended at all, on the contrary, I completely understand. Every journey finds its maximum expression when experienced alone. There is no way to see what cannot be seen when in the company of others. The important part of the journey is not the destination but the person you become along the way. This introspection can become confused or distorted by the impressions of others. Herein lies the paradox. Good company will obstruct the view and bad company will fill the silence with trivial matters. The clarity we find when alone is essential if we are to capture our true essence. This is the also why humans travel alone when they leave their physical bodies behind in order to cross over.'

Vodka was lying down on the backseat, his head between his front legs, following every movement both inside and outside the car. He also sniffed me constantly, as if trying to remember who this person sitting next to the object of his affections was. Suddenly, an unexpected bark interrupted our conversation, and we fell silent for a few seconds. Amelia took this opportunity to change the topic.

'I've been consulting the oldest maps I could find and asking anyone I thought could help us in your search. An elderly archaeologist and astrologist told me about a forgotten legend, where beings who came from the stars founded a civilisation in a purple city thousands of years ago. Apparently, it consisted of an enormous network of communities arranged like the constellations. You could only get there by following a star map, which became visible once every millennium. The gates to that metropolis is believed to be around six hours south of our current position. It's so crazy, don't you think? Old folks love talking about legends like that. Only fools believe them, though.'

I had expected Amelia's disbelief and hermetic reaction from the moment I met her. I had embarked on this mission forewarned and aware that it would not be easy to explain to this fiery, dreamy creature that the richness of our reality is actually not in what we see, but in what we do not see. When you come across the unknown, your superficial self is surprised, but the mystery of truth is far deeper within us than we could ever imagine. We must have an open outlook, not cover our view with cement and block out the light.

'And what if it's true?' I asked, prompting her to let out a resounding, spontaneous laugh.

'C'mon, Elsu, you're not one of those naive people who believe in these tales of prophecies and intergalactic beings, are you?

'Actually, I am,' I declared.

Amelia shot me a quick glance, peering over her oversized retro cat-eye sunglasses.

'Of course you would. And what exactly do you expect to find in that mysterious purple city?' she added with a condescending tone.

'I am looking for the writings about the mysterious truths that created the human race, before it was corrupted.'

'C'mon, tell me the truth. You're a science fiction writer, consumed by monotony and boredom and in search of inspiration. Even your strange dress sense and your behaviour… you're a character from one of your novels, aren't you?'

'Is that what you think?'

'Naturally, writers have the job of turning truth into fiction and fiction into truth. They have to make the former sound like an interesting story, and the latter seem believable enough for the readers to enjoy it.'

We both laughed, infected by each other's laughter.

We were gliding over the asphalt of a winding road that followed a wide river, swollen by the season's rain. On one side was a stretch of land populated with stunted trees and shrubs. On the other, was a dense forest with the occasional meadow. It was the ideal stage from which to observe the native wildlife. The hills that rose at the four cardinal points opened up to reveal a landscape of scattered clouds coming in from the west, while the setting sun bathed them in pink light. I could sense that our canine companion was becoming increasingly tense, and he began to turn around anxiously, growling and fixing his gaze on the windscreen. I knew immediately that something was wrong.

'Vodka, relax. We're almost there, buddy. Sit down,' said Amelia sternly, but the animal ignored her order. Instead, he began to jump uncontrollably, wagging his tail and changing his expression. 'One day, I'm really going to have to do something about training you' she continued, then adding, apologetically, 'I don't know what's wrong, he's usually not like this when we travel.'

I turned towards him, extended my open hand and howled, much to the surprise of Amelia, who incredulously observed the scene through her tiny rear-view mirror. Vodka responded, relaxing his body and offering me the information I needed, in a fluent and innate language we both shared.

'Stop the car, please. Someone needs our help.'

'Where? Here? Now?' She asked, flustered, swerving off the road and breaking suddenly, with an almost kamikaze-like blind faith in my words.

Chapter 4

Closed for Repairs

This experience is probably the sort of thing that happens to other people, but never to us. There are also memories which, despite our best efforts to bury them and hide them beneath better ones, manage to remain fresh, hostile and defiant, popping up in our minds over and over again, like a jack-in-the-box. We believe in music, cinema, sex and, of course, lifelong love because deep down we're romantic souls who need to dream.

The scene could not be more depressing. The microwave pinged for the millionth time that morning. The tea, or whatever I had put in the mug, was ready. I placed it on the marble kitchen worktop, along with the other nine cups of cold herbal teas that remained untouched. I wiped down the formica tabletop yet again, and tucked the chair back in its place. It was a time for boleros, rancheras and sad ballads. *'Esta Tarde Vi Llover' ('Yesterday I Heard the Rain')* by Armando Manzanero was playing. I abruptly wiped my tears away, letting out a sigh from the very depths of my tortured soul. On the fridge was a bright blue sticky note with an obsolete message *'We're so close to having it all'*, with Jared's Hebrew signature. Even more ammunition for my pity party.

I then remembered the story of Gana the gorilla, an inhabitant of Germany's Münster Zoo that was featured on the news a while back. Gana refused to let go of the body of Claudio, her three-month-old son who had died from unknown causes. Experts were unable to perform an autopsy as the mother refused to abandon her baby, trying constantly to revive him with gentle taps and caresses. Gana was mourning the loss of her son, and carrying his dead body on her back for several days was part of these primates' funerary ritual – the way they grieve when clan members die. We humans also carry the bodies of our dead relationships, refusing to let them go. We insist on maintaining that connection, even if the memories are particularly painful for us.

Esther is my soul sister. Although we share no DNA, I adopted her when I discovered that she was one of those rare creatures who become true friends for life when you show them love. She is always there to bring positivity and encouragement, and is, without a doubt, one of my absolute favourite people. She is also a nut for Feng Shui – the Chinese discipline based on the belief that, just as fresh air and clean water feed our bodies, so does the Qi, or life energy. The Chinese recognise that the human organism is highly influenced by landscape and surroundings. Both are part of the same energy system that gives rise to life, which is supplied by the Qi that connects the spirit to matter.

'Look, Rafaela, really, what you have to do is follow this Feng Shui tip that says, and I quote "order and cleanliness are essential, as they allow Qi to flow freely. Organise your storage areas and avoid accumulating useless items that take up the space destined for new and useful ones." There's nothing better for getting over a break-up than cleaning out the cupboards and letting go of all the old junk that gathers dust and that you no longer use, especially everything to do with him. It'll make everything flow better,' said Esther, pulling my arm towards the bedroom.

'I really don't feel like it. I just want to feel sorry for myself, eat ice cream and watch films that make me cry. Some days, like today, everything's a mess, my hair, the bed, my heart, my life… and that's OK.'

'Remember when you first told me about Jared? You said you'd met the perfect man to play sponge with. I went blank, I asked you what you meant and you almost passed out laughing. Eventually you told me it was the game where *"he kissed you and you scrubbed him from the waist down"*. Don't ever let anyone tighten that loose screw of yours, Rafaela,' she said putting her arm around me, inspiring feelings of home, a fireplace and honey.

Though exhausted, I forced a smile to reward my friend's efforts.

We live in a society of happiness, where we aren't allowed to be sad. Sadness is overrated and has no appeal whatsoever. We run away from people we can smell it on, or who are afflicted by the mourning virus, just in case they ruin our chakras or mess up our vibes.

Marcela, one of my patients, told me that one of the things she hated the most when her partner of over fifteen years left her for a girl on the basketball team he coached was the constant bombardment of 'well-intentioned' messages.

'C'mon, it's not the end of the world.'
'You're young, you'll meet someone soon.'
'Chin up, life goes on.'
'Don't cry, it's not worth it.'

We deny our mourning, and we think that, if we ignore it, it will disappear like a rabbit in a magician's top hat. But, unfortunately, grief is stubborn and awaits patiently just around the corner to fulfil its mission before we can even think of moving on and starting again. There are certain people and situations that deserve our tears. Pain that must be shouted. Our tiredness disappears when we sleep, our hunger is soothed by eating, and pain is healed by crying. Every emotion is valid within measure.

Belly had never been in favour of our whirlwind relationship, much less our wedding. Before we met, she always said 'Rafaela, if you fall in love with a cat, the cat will come home with you.' I guess she forgot to tell me that the cat's name couldn't be Jared. She thought I was far too young to settle down. She would often murmur, 'That man has *trouble* written all over him.' The fact that her only granddaughter was throwing herself into a man's arms, a Jewish man at that, was not the kind of promising future she had envisioned for me. As a liberal woman, she prided herself in being an atheist with no affinity for any religion in particular. However, her true colours would show when things got ugly and she secretly prayed to Jesus. When she carried on about it, I'd hug her around her waist really tight, like a bear, and she'd laugh and say that if I didn't let go, she'd make a hairy rug for the living room out of that clingy bear. Despite having shrunk with age, she still filled that house with her enormous presence.

Twenty-four months, three weeks and two days. That could be the title of a Hollywood blockbuster in which I play the lead: a romantic drama where, following an intensely passionate love story,

I find that he isn't the exotic leading man he appeared to be during the auditions.

I was determined to be the director of that film. As Virginia Woolf said, and I couldn't agree more, *'There is no gate, no lock, no bolt that you can set upon the freedom of my mind.'* I would change the soundtrack, the script and even the setting. My diet would consist only of what made me feel good, gave me strength, brought me joy and filled me with optimism once again.

The aim would be to cover the entire story, passing through the required grieving period, until I could find my feet once again. This 'bad love' would become nothing more than a memory that I could file away in my heart as something positive and painless.

My adventure in Jerusalem began when I was granted a scholar-ship to complete my psychology doctorate at the holy city's Hebrew University. All I knew how to say in Hebrew was *'ani lo medaberet ivrit'*, basically 'I don't speak Hebrew'. But what I lacked in vocabulary I made up for in enthusiasm and a desire to discover the world. Belly would always tell me I had my mother's travelling spirit.

Those memories would forever be burned into my retinas: the walks hand-in-hand with Jared through the bustling Arab bazaar in the Old City with its organised chaos. It was filled with shops selling wood and textile handicrafts, hookah cafés, stalls piled high with spices and fruits and vegetables, and metal workshops with their irresistible colourful pieces. In the afternoons, we'd sit at a café that offered tiny pastries and sweets on copper plates such as *knafeh,* and of course pita bread with hummus, falafels and freshly-squeezed carrot juice, with promises of love and dreams of forever finding their way onto the menu. Such a vivid postcard. Jared was convinced that the change humanity so desperately needed would come from Jerusalem.

I had lost all notion of time, which is what happens when habits and routines fall by the wayside. The sight of the calendar with its bloodstained poppies brought me crashing back to reality. It had been a week since Esther had been sleeping in Jared's side of the bed. She had set up camp in my house like the perfect friend, playing a part that I'm sure was extremely difficult. After the death of a sentimental relationship, the division of friends isn't usually set out in the will. On the other hand, what happens if a friend closes ranks around one of the parties, saying all kinds of things about the other one, and then an unexpected reconciliation happens?

Esther was always more than just an unconditional friend. She also filled the holes left by my absent mother, and by the father I'd never met. She was my safety net, the soft cushion ready to catch me whenever I fell.

'Frankly, Rafaela, I don't know what to say to you. When someone dies, you offer your condolences. When there's a wedding, a birth or an important achievement, you congratulate the person. But when a love story ends, you don't know whether to feel sad because the person is still in love, or be happy because they've been set free,' confessed Esther, pulling my hair back into a low pony-tail as I had breakfast and blankly stared at the brown corduroy jacket I'd given Jared during *Rosh Hashanah,* Jewish new year, which he'd left behind on the couch.

I felt my tears burning my throat, but I was brave and refused to give in. I found no solace in being strong, but I put myself to the test, sure that in some hidden part of me was a free Rafaela who was able to spit out all the fury she had been swallowing. 'Girl, I think it's time for our dance, take out the first-aid kit and hit play.'

'Woohoo, I was dying to hear that!' cheered Esther, knowing exactly what that meant: chocolate, scented candles, face masks and singing karaoke to *'I Will Survive'* by Gloria Gaynor, our song, which always aroused the amazons within us. Suddenly, we were Greek warriors descended from Ares himself. We were the two-girl band Hippolyta and Penthesilea.

Whenever someone arrived at my consulting room fatally wounded by love or loss, I would make them all the same promise before commencing therapy. It was a promise I almost never broke.

'I promise you that there will be days when fury, doubt or sadness take over, so much so that living will become unbearable. People will speak of a light at the end of the tunnel, but don't hold onto that, it always comes far too late to save you from the depths of darkness. I promise you that there will be days where reality will have absolutely nothing to offer you, and still you'll let it in because you won't be strong enough to fight it. I promise you that despair will be a constant in your life for some time, and that there are no magic tricks or miraculous methods to silence the soundtrack of sorrow. I promise you that there are no shortcuts or anaesthetic to free you from the pain of grieving, and that you'll experience violent battles between your crushed heart and your rational mind, where neither will win. I also promise you that your memories will stick to you like leeches, depriving you of your sleep and your present for a while. I promise you that you'll have nowhere to hide from the barrage of bleeding questions and excuses that you'll inflict on yourself. But I also promise you that, one day, everything will begin for the first time. You'll make peace with your smile in a refurbished life where you will no longer have to sit at a table where love is not on the menu. I promise you that you'll find another way to coexist with those you have loved and who are no longer here. I promise you that the clock will start ticking again and, more importantly, that you'll come back wiser, stronger and braver, ready to walk down the red carpet of life. I'll be by your side to shine a light when your own goes out, to remind you who you are when you can't remember, to open the window when you need air; but you'll have to use your own hands to turn that page and to write the next chapter.'

We were going to be married in the month of March, in a wedding for three hundred people at the Sheraton Hotel. Live music, kosher catering, partying beneath the stars until morning. By the way, for those of you who are unfamiliar with the term *kosher*, as I was at the beginning, it refers to food that is prepared in accordance with Jewish dietary regulations.

As the son of a traditional family of Orthodox Jews, keeping kosher was expected of Jared. And his future wife was also expected to be Jewish, or at least willing to go through the long conversion process.

Completely immersed in that temporary insanity caused by love, I thought it was utterly romantic the way my 'nutty philosopher', as I called him when I was feeling affectionate, felt about the ceremony.

'Tell me about your customs. What's a Jewish wedding like?'

'For us, the ceremony is the coming together of two twin souls who were separated at birth,' answered Jared, tracing small circles with his thumbs on my naked shoulder. 'The *kallah*, bride, wears a white dress and the *chatan*, groom, smashes a glass beneath the *chuppah*, the canopy, while the family yells "*Mazel Tov!*" which is a Hebrew expression that literally means "Good luck!"'

'That sounds fun! You smash glasses and the Greek smash plates. I remember when Adonis invited me to his wedding with Adrienne, both Greek, and all the guests started smashing plates to the rhythm of Zorba as a way of wishing the couple good luck.'

'I guess you have to release the day's adrenaline in some way or another. It's always better to smash the plates first and not throw them at each other after the wedding, don't you think?' he joked. 'The more devout or radical Jews have different customs and rituals.'

'Really? I thought all Jews were Jewish?'

Jared laughed, showing off his pearly whites.

'We have a saying, *"Two Jews, three opinions"*. Bear in mind that our people have been around over three thousand years; that's long enough for different groups to form. Some don't read general newspapers or watch TV, and they want nothing to do with the Internet. They have large families with as many children as God decides to send them, they congregate and pray three times a day and, in some places, live cramped together in neighbourhoods that follow the laws of the Torah and the preaching of the Rabbi.'

'The Torah? You mean the equivalent of the Bible for Christians?'

'Yes, something like that. The Torah contains all the laws and teachings of Judaism.'

'And what does it say about marrying a free, rebellious spirit like myself?'

'I'm sure you believe in something too.'

'Of course, I believe in spirituality.'

'Isn't that the same?'

'Of course not. I'll give you some examples: religion isn't just one, there are hundreds, whereas there's only one spirituality. Religion is for those who want to follow the rituals and formality of the masses, while spirituality is for people who want to achieve spiritual transcendence without dogmas. Religion is for the dormant; spirituality is for the awake. Religion is for people who need to be told what to do, who need guidance. Spirituality is for those who listen to the voice within. Religion threatens and intimidates; spirituality gives you freedom and inner peace. Religion speaks of sin and guilt; spirituality tells you not to sweat it, get up, learn from it and move on. Religion is forced on you as a child, like the soup you don't want to eat; spirituality is the nourishment you seek for yourself that fills you and satisfies your senses. Religion doesn't investigate or ask questions; spirituality is an eternal question. Religion follows the precepts of a sacred book; spirituality seeks the sacred in every book. Religion dreams of glory and heaven; spirituality invites you experience it here and now. Religion causes division and wars; spirituality is based on unity.'

'We'd better drop the subject. You can't possibly understand what it means to be Jewish.'

'Of course I do. Jewish means someone who is born from a Jewish mother, or who has converted to Judaism.'

'That's it. And you're neither one nor the other.'

At that moment, at just twenty-three years of age, little did I know what I was getting myself into. Cupid, the son of Mars and Venus, of love and war – the cheeky child that shoots arrows in every direction with his eyes closed – is a terrible shot with terrible judgement in most cases. I was hit suddenly and squarely. Euphoric, full of energy, and overrun by the chemical cocktail of dopamine and serotonin, which is what a brain in love releases when you're in the state of 'transient stupidity', I had become completely addicted to the 'Universe of Jared', undoubtedly the worst state of mind in which to make intelligent decisions without collateral damage. You feel like not even a tsunami can take you down when, in fact, you're so vulnerable that the gentlest breeze could knock you over in an instant.

'No man is more blind than he who refuses to see'; 'unrequited love equals wasted time'; 'a passionate heart does not listen to advice'. These are popular Spanish sayings we often hear and which Belly would have recited to me, particularly the last, had I spoken to her about my situation – something totally unheard of when you're living on a cloud, without direction and with a feeling of omnipotence. What advice or opinion would I have accepted if it didn't agree with my own fairy tale? My ears only paid attention to the comments that reaffirmed my reality.

'You guys are the perfect couple.'
'You're so lucky to have found Jared.'
'I can tell you're made for each other just by looking at you.'

It's only later on, too late, that you find your bearings again and try to figure out how you ended up so far from home in the first place.

Now that it's over, I see my story reflected in one of my patients. Julio, aged fifty-seven, was a successful surgeon who came to me for help because of Sabrina. Their relationship looked more like an obstacle course than a happy shared life. Julio had a lot of admirers, but he'd fallen under the spell of Sabrina, a young twenty-five-year-old with modelling aspirations who looked like she'd stepped right out of a catalogue and was friends with his daughter. Apparently, she liked the fast life, she enjoyed toying with substances that took her to places that sex with Julio could not. She also loved going out at night and everything we normally associate with a young woman that age. Julio provided her with finances, security and a pedestal he had built just for her. His blindness seemed inexplicable from the outside. Julio was capable of doing the impossible just to please his goddess, the being whose likeness he had himself forged. His friends, his family and even his own daughter could see what all other mere mortals could see. They were two human beings who were destined to never understand each other. Love would never be enough to bring their incompatible worlds together, but Julio insisted on believing a completely different story. 'Envy is a national sport'; 'they're just too prejudiced'; 'love has no age'; 'I'll change her'; 'I'll bring out the wonderful woman inside her' were arguments he used to convince himself until, three years later, reality came crashing down on him like a ton of bricks. His unhappiness finally took its toll, affecting his work, his mental health and his closest friends and family. It's clear that sometimes things are just clearly impossible. They're not meant to be. However, unless you're completely immune to passion or you've renounced your human condition, it's easy to fall for that improbable promise and believe that, despite all evidence to the contrary, only you can see the real truth and only you can perform a miracle.

Immersed in my own romance and adventure novel, I resisted the onslaught of cultural and religious shocks, particularly with my future mother-in-law. I met Jared's mother, an authentic *idishe mame*, one Sabbath, the seventh day of the Jewish week that is considered sacred. The celebration of the Sabbath begins on Friday afternoon and ends on Saturday evening, symbolising a day of rest. Particularly interesting to me was the fact that not even animals could perform any tasks to serve humans – as an animal-lover, I appreciated this fact.

I admit that, even though I considered myself more Spanish than a Spanish omelette, I was soon taken with those exquisite dishes and the magical ritual of those Friday nights, which I still miss today. The image of a woman lighting two candles as she recites the Sabbath blessing has always fascinated me.

Jared had taught me *'Shalom Aleichem'*, the song with which the dinner traditionally begins. We had been practising for three weeks non-stop. He had invested all his effort and interest into it so that my official introduction to his family would be a resounding success.

'C'mon, Rafaela, one more time. You have to make an effort to learn it. Everyone will be watching you.'

'I'm exhausted; we've been practising for hours. You know how hard Hebrew is for me. It won't matter if I'm the only one not singing. Look, I'll just mouth the words, I'm sure no one will notice my terrible accent.'

'You're not showing any respect for me or for my family with that attitude. How do you want them to accept you if you don't even try?' he said authoritatively, but clearly hurt.

'I'm hungry. Let's eat something and we can continue later. A break will do us good.'

'No way, there'll be no food until we finish.'

It was two in the morning when I was finally allowed to go to bed, exhausted and starving. Another popular saying would have been appropriate here, *'for better or for worse'*. My stomach grumbled desperately at the lack of food. But my love for Jared was all the food I needed. How could I have been so selfish? I'd been so ungrateful that I hadn't valued everything Jared was doing for our happiness. With that thought, covered in guilt, I went to sleep.

A young woman of my age, with a well-coiffed brown wig, a neat and demure outfit but with no flair whatsoever, stared at me as if hypnotised. Her eyes were two drops of blue silver shining like precious diamonds. Sitting across from me, one of the thirteen other women and nine men surrounding that impeccably-set table, she followed my movements with discreet curiosity. Clearly, the low cleavage of my orange angora jumper and my tight jeans were scandalous to most of those present, although I suspected her look was more one of secret admiration for someone who didn't hide her body or her thoughts beneath the decent image that a dignified woman ought to present, both to her husband and to the rest of the Jewish community. That was the very first time I met Esther. A complete stranger who would become an essential part of my story.

Esther was the wife of Jared's older brother. Despite her youth, she already had three children and a round belly that announced the imminent arrival of number four.

The meal consisted of *challah,* a plaited bread covered in seeds; oriental salmon and cauliflower salad; and *gefilte* fish, accompanied by roast potatoes and green beans. Their vivid colours contrasted with the white tablecloth, over which were set porcelain dishes, wine glasses and the shiny silverware.

We hadn't yet made it to the traditional honey *leicaj* dessert when Jared's mother broke through the whispering diners with a question that was both unexpected and unfortunate in equal parts, considering it was our first meeting.

'Jared, have you begun the preparations for Rafaela's conversion yet?'

'Mum, Rafaela will convert if she wants to,' answered her son, dryly and without emotion.

Later that night, in the privacy of our tiny apartment, he said, 'It's important to me that you convert. I'd like you to. But I don't want you to do it if it's a problem for you.'

'I don't want to. I don't understand why I should give up my beliefs and my way of life just because I love someone. Besides, I'd basically have to be reborn, and I refuse to go through that entire traumatic process all over again. I'll just go on being the *goy,* as you call foreigners.'

'Let's marry in secret, then. Once I finish my philosophy studies, we can move to Granada. What do you think? Give me one year.'

We sealed the deal with an endless hug, as my nutty philosopher whispered in my ear, with his deep, warm voice, 'Rafaela, did you know that a hug is two hearts kissing in secret?'

'Why should it be a secret?' I asked, like a child interested in everything around it, posing a series of endless questions and challenging any explanation that doesn't satisfy its curiosity. 'I was taught not to express my feelings, to suppress my emotions. When I was eight, I made up a new language to communicate with the people I loved.'

That fleeting victory that made me feel in control was tinged with sadness following Jared's story. At the time, I was unaware that I'd taken over the role of mother to a child who was both defenceless and tyrannical. This is often the case with many men and women: they continue to revolve around that infant, and despite having a moustache or wearing a bra, seek partners who are willing to die in order to fulfil their needs. This role was made for me, like the glass slipper for Cinderella. I had put a cape around my neck and identified as Super Rafaela. After all, had I not chosen saviour as my profession?

The story of Amanda and Ricardo is the clearest example I can think of to explain this insane relationship model. In my first therapy session with Amanda, alarm bells went off in my head when she said, 'I can't leave Ricardo, he needs me. What will happen to him if I'm not with him?' I wanted to know more about Ricardo so I could understand just how defenceless he supposedly was. Ricardo was forty-six and drove around in the latest model car on the market. The son of a wealthy family, he practically lived off the rent he got from apartments in an exclusive part of the city. He met Amanda while she was working nights at one of his family's café's to pay for her nursing course. He would call her at all hours of the day, saying he hadn't eaten and that he only liked omelettes when she made them. He would pick monumental fights when Amanda was talking to her friends and didn't laugh at his childish jokes. Ricardo never wanted children as he claimed it would take time away from their relationship, despite the fact that Amanda's biological clock had started ticking very loudly three years earlier. She'd taken over his appointments and would literally take him to the dentist when he was due for a check-up, comfort him like a helpless puppy every time he had an unwarranted outburst, and feed him on demand, worrying only about his sexual satisfaction. Ricardo would then roll over and sleep like a baby, cared for by a proud and selfless mother. She always had a disconcerting explanation for it, 'No one knows him like I do. If I leave him, he'll die.' Amanda had lost herself to motherhood, despite never having given birth. Our therapy together was an adventure that lasted almost ten months.

Last Christmas, I ran into Amanda at a department store. She was pushing a pram with a beautiful green-eyed girl; she was married to a divorced engineer and appeared to be very happy. She told me that Ricardo was still living with his Peter Pan Syndrome – a syndrome first described by Dr Dan Kiley in his book 'The Peter Pan Syndrome. Men Who Have Never Grown Up' – unable to assume his circumstances, still anchored in the past, refusing to take any responsibility for his actions or his life.

Chapter 5

Dream's Caress

'I think they put these bum-exposing gowns on us so we don't escape from hospital.' That was how I answered Conan's call, to which he replied, 'Sleeping beauty is finally awake! When are you getting out of that place? I miss you.'

I recognised my friend and trainer's voice immediately, and with it all the memories about out relationship, or so I thought, came flooding back.

'I'll be discharged tomorrow if my CT scan results are positive. I can't wait to go home.'

'Great! I'll pick you up then! You have a lot to tell me about your trip to the other side,' he said with his typical wit, ending the conversation with a burst of laughter than rang in my ears like an echo for a few seconds.

As I write about this experience, which has forced me to dig through my memories, conversations, details, and so many experiences, I realise that, thanks to Conan, a sense of humour has been a faithful friend to me along my journey. As strange as it sounds, laughing at oneself, at just how absurd and complex some situations are, is one of the healthiest and most effective healing exercises Conan ever taught me. It's a necessary exercise and a true emotional catalyst when faced with uncertainty and catastrophising thoughts as it creates a strong mind capable of withstanding anything.

Over four thousand years ago, in the ancient Chinese empire, there were temples where people would gather to laugh in order to improve their health. In India, there are sacred temples where people also practise laughter. Other ancient cultures had the figure of the 'sacred clown' or 'clown doctor', a wizard who wore a costume and makeup to invoke the therapeutic power of laughter in order to cure sick warriors. In the Bible, the Old Testament says *A cheerful heart is good medicine, but a crushed spirit dries up the bones.* Freud also believed that laughter had the power to free the organism of negative energy.

One of the doctors in charge of performing all the tests came bursting in to the room where my body was lying inside the CT scanner, a type of tunnel or tube with a bed in the middle used to obtain very detailed images of the body and its different organs. I felt his breath on my shoulders; he was clearly coming towards me. His lemon-scented aftershave, mixed with his own masculine smell and that of bandages and alcohol, activated my olfactory perception as if waiting for something unexpected to happen. His slight build moved with surprising coordination. His hair had a tendency to flop over his forehead and a few grey streaks were beginning to show. My attention was drawn to his small, brown eyes, and to his face, which conveyed serenity and intelligence. He exuded professionalism in everything he did. I trusted him from the moment I met him.

'Now you must stay completely still, Rafaela, just like a statue. Don't be afraid; it's completely painless.'

I'm convinced I was already claustrophobic inside my mother's belly, which is why I was born early. Small and cramped spaces terrified me and led me to feel an intense irrational fear of being trapped somewhere closed or restricted. Whenever I entered an enclosed area, I'd always check where all the exits were and stand near them, and I'd also avoid driving during rush hour so I wouldn't get stuck in a traffic jam.

I was experiencing all the familiar symptoms. I became tense and alert and I began to hyperventilate. My heart was beating faster by the second. Thoughts of imminent death bombarded my brain. Even my extremities began to shake uncontrollably.

'I know, I know. You want to see the innermost secrets of my body because there's nothing good on TV tonight, right?' I said to the medical staff, clinging onto my sense of humour as if it were a life raft.

Before getting into the scanner, I moved to undo the bow on the back of my gown that had been incorrectly tied, when a seemingly shocked male nurse shouted out, 'Don't take it off, it's not necessary!' I finished that sentence for him in my head, 'Please lady, nobody wants to see that!' I thought to myself just how unappetising my soft white body must be after my long hibernation.

Dr Alex did his best to calm me down, 'It'll be over in an hour.'

'Oh, OK. Just sixty minutes of getting to know the monster and having to deal with my friend, the neurotic claustrophobe, who's driving me over the edge?' I added, ironically, faking a smile. Alex gave me a thumbs up and laughed with his team. The white coat he wore, for me, was a symbol of life.

If I've learnt anything throughout my life, it's the true power of laughter and its impact on our mind when we start catastrophising. While as many realities exist as can be invented, it's safe to assume that he same also applies to fears. During what seemed an eternity, I recalled Miguel's case.

Miguel came to seem me one May afternoon at the recommendation of another patient. He was dour faced, dishevelled and dragging his feet as though carrying a ton of bricks. He gave the impression that he'd never smiled in his life and that he was feeling cold despite the warm spring weather. He was so sparse with his words and had such an overriding air of melancholy that he couldn't help but inspire sympathy. The company he worked for had closed two years ago and, unable to keep up with the mortgage payments, the house he shared with his wife Ana and his two children, aged four and seven, had been foreclosed. They had moved in with his in-laws, who helped them financially while he looked for work. What little money there was came from the few hours Ana spent working as a cleaner in a paper factory and from her father's modest pension.

Miguel told me he'd always been a positive man, someone happy and energetic, the life of every party and the friend everyone went to when they needed cheering up. Even his old boss used to bring him along to all the tense meetings so that he could break the ice with one of his jokes but, since that fateful event, he no longer had the will to live and had even considered taking his own life. Each time he tried to tell a joke at home, his father-in-law would say, 'How can you laugh at a time like this? I don't think misfortune is funny, do you? Cut it out with the jokes; no one's in the mood.' On her part, Ana seemed to have inherited her father's pessimism. If Miguel suggested an outdoor activity with the kids or maybe spending time alone with Ana, she would refuse, saying, 'How can you think about that at a time like this? It's like you're living in a parallel universe. I don't know how you can possibly enjoy yourself in this situation...' Every joke was offensive and any sign of happiness was quashed. Miguel had given in to misery and had renounced the joy he no longer felt he deserved. He needed seven months of intense therapy to realise that the most important natural resource he needed in order to recover was, precisely, his sense of humour and positive attitude. He had to shut down the emotional masochism he'd become so accustomed to.

Happiness can be painful to people who don't experience it. However, it's important to understand that humour doesn't trivialise a tragic situation, nor does it deny reality; it simply allows us to accept it. Comedy isn't a cure, it's merely provides temporary relief. Although it doesn't resolve a bad situation, it motivates us to handle it better. Every joke has an element of truth to it, which is why it makes us laugh. It ridicules a well-known truth and makes us feel strong when faced with our fears. A sense of humour empowers us momentarily and, in general, that helps us to be the best version of ourselves.

Back in my room, awaiting the results that would give me my freedom to go on with my life, I stopped in front of the only window that broke up the long third-floor corridor where I was an unwilling guest in that hotel for the somnolent. Outside, a refuse truck roared. It was filled with the remnants of things that had once been new, useful and wanted, much like everybody staying in this place. A van featuring the words 'fresh news' was parked alongside the kerb, waiting to be given the green light to supply a daily dose of necessary data and information, adding to our mental pollution. People resembling colourful ants crossed each other without looking, lest they discover another presence in their tiny private world. The only exception to this were workers at a construction site staring lasciviously at some attractive girls as they passed.

The flatscreen TV in a corner of the room revealed the day's news, gushing out of the reporter's bright pink lips. She was made up like a Barbie doll that had just been taken out of its box and was standing in front of the camera wearing a light blue Kate Spade knit dress and low-heeled grey shoes. In one hand she held a giant microphone that in no way detracted attention from her long French-manicured nails, and in the other was a silver clipboard.

I observed as my roommate made her way back after buying a cappuccino from the vending machine located near one of the visitor areas. She seemed happy to see me on my feet and said hello as she approached.

'Have you got your results back yet?' she asked, in a somewhat overly loud tone of voice.

'No, not yet.'

'No news is good news,' she replied, one foot already in the room.

I've never understood why we just assume that the absence of news is a good thing. Maybe the news is still making its way to us, fighting to reach its destination. Maybe the news hasn't been made public yet, or we're simply in the wrong place. Belly would say that bad news flies while good news crawls. The truth is that the speed of the news has nothing to do with how good or bad it is, just as it is wrong to assume that knowledge doesn't take up any space. In fact, knowledge takes up the most space. If knowledge didn't occupy space, why do we forget so many of the concepts, dates, doctrines and battles that we've learnt off by heart during so many hours of study?'

As discouraging as it sounds, our brain only has a limited amount of storage. We forget around ninety per cent of what we learn and only retain the truly essential knowledge required for the purpose of staying alive, or information that has a strong emotional impact. We can act intelligently and create a strategy so that all the knowledge and information that goes into our brain is useful and beneficial to our lives. Or we can become 'information gluttons' – the kind of people who consider themselves to be more cultured, better informed and better conversationalists than the rest of us, who are constantly encouraged to continue with their consumerist culture, not realising that much of the information they receive is bad quality, biased, incomplete or politicised.

Another memory returned. It was a couple of years ago, when I first went to Japan for a month to represent the charity I work with in Granada and for which I've been boxing. I almost turned down the invitation as I was stressed preparing for my final exam that would allow me to head the department where I practised psychology. I felt I couldn't refuse, seeing as I was one of its main ambassadors. I was also eager to meet the wise man I'd heard so much about, and see first-hand if his fame was merited.

Despite working hard for several weeks, I was terrified at the thought of going blank or getting stuck, as if frozen, unable to answer any of the questions I had no trouble with the night before. I was suffering from the effects of the 'eternal student syndrome'. No matter how much I knew, it was never enough; there was always another course I needed to take in order to be ready, another book to complete my knowledge, another seminar to keep me up-to-date with the latest statistics and findings. In other words, I was an information glutton starved of wisdom. It's scary to think that we generate approximately the same amount of information each year as was produced by the entire human species since the beginning of time until now. That's some infoxication!

I ended up living with that Buddhist monk in the Kumano Mountains for a couple of weeks. Thanks to that experience, I had the pleasure of meeting incredible people and visiting places I would never have discovered otherwise, had I travelled as a simple tourist.

With the help of a European volunteer that had been living in that uniquely beautiful and charming place for almost a decade, and who knew it like the back of her hand, I was able to visit the most secluded and picturesque parts of the historic Kumano region, where we walked along the famous sacred Kumano Kodo pilgrimage route.

The famous monk wore a rustic saffron-coloured *kasaya* that left his right shoulder exposed, an ochre belt and sandals that didn't cover his toes. He practised Shugendo; a Buddhist discipline that seeks direct contact with nature, overcoming physical limits through a tough daily training schedule in order to achieve peace and mental well-being. My host was waiting for me at the end of the road, where the volunteer and I parted ways. The young monk placed his hands on his heart to welcome me, lowering his head as a form of greeting. I responded by copying his movements.

'Welcome, Rafaela. You can call me Jien. Please respect the silence and follow me,' he said in a serene voice, setting my feet in motion.

He uttered no more words as we walked immersed in nature. We crossed trails and wooded mountains until the sun decided to call it a day, probably as tired as I was. Despite the long journey, I didn't dare say a word, not even to ask him to stop so I could soothe my dry throat at one of the wild streams or waterfalls that surprised us along the way.

Along the way, we came across dozens of *ojis*, small shrines to guide the pilgrims. Finally, we arrived at the temple that would be my only shelter for the next few days and that, as I later learnt, was over two thousand years old. A majestic arch indicated the gateway to a sacred place. There were figures of dragons everywhere. At the entrance, another ten people, almost all Korean and wearing similar white linen tunics, celebrated a type of ritual. Some played instruments that I didn't recognise and others lit hundreds of candles, which they later placed everywhere. It was a surreal atmosphere like something straight out of a David Lynch movie.

'Rest, Rafaela. I shall see you tomorrow at meditation, after breakfast.'

Jien had taken his leave that night with such an expression of humility and kindness that he made me feel at home.

For the next few hours, I couldn't sleep. I woke up early and left my room – an austere and minimalist, but very cosy square room measuring three metres by three metres and with an open shower. Excited at the thought of being able to chat to the monks and drink from their wisdom, I was surprised not to see anyone in the dining hall and convinced myself that I'd woken up too early. After about twenty minutes spent wandering around looking at the installations, a monk approached me with an unnerving calm.

'Did you enjoy your breakfast?'

'Actually, I was waiting for the others to wake up,' I answered, proud to have been the first to arrive.

The fragile monk reminded me of Gandhi himself. His smooth skin was that of a young person, but his white beard and curved back were those of an elderly man. He smiled shyly, lowering his gaze. He put his hands together delicately to greet me.

'We finished breakfast over two hours ago, right after the first prayer of the day. They are all meditating now.'

'But it's seven in the morning!' I exclaimed in shock.

'Indeed, it is. You must be new as you do not yet know our customs. I shall serve you breakfast.'

'Thank you so much,' I replied, grateful for his hospitality.

He soon returned with a wicker tray carrying five small colourful bowls and placed it on a small table along with a cushion – pretty uncomfortable, as a matter of fact – for those of us not used to sitting on the floor. Gandhi's dead ringer pointed out each of the dishes to me as he explained that, according to Buddhist teachings, *shojin ryori* must be completely vegetarian and is based on the five tastes, five cooking methods and five colours. Every meal must include a barbecued dish, a fried dish, a pickled dish, a tofu dish and a soup.

Accustomed to my cereal with coconut milk and blueberries in the morning, it felt very strange to start the day with that particular menu, consisting of pickled seaweed, white rice, miso soup, omelette and tea.

The same monk later accompanied me to the meditation area. It was a cemetery decorated with hundreds of tombs and commemorative monuments where the moss and shadows blended into the texture of the rocks, and where the gigantic cedars and other more ancient trees were the guardians of silence. I was beginning to fall in love with those wild colours and scents.

I struggled to recognise Jien among the sea of monks wearing identical clothes, with shiny shaved heads, all sitting in the lotus position. He did the work for me by inviting me to enter that spiritual territory with an almost imperceptible gesture. All I can say is that I did my best to blend in, like a chameleon fading into the colours around it until you can no longer see it.

I closed my eyes and tried to disconnect, but it didn't work. A tiny voice inside my head kept telling me, 'you're wasting your time; you should be studying for your exam; you won't learn anything here; if I leave my mind blank I'll forget everything; if only there was a newspaper or a TV so I could watch the news…' Slowly, a feeling of emptiness came over me. The deafening silence was overwhelming, suffocating even. I decided to take a deep breath and take as much clean air as I could into my lungs, as if I were a camel that didn't know where the next drink of water would come from.

After more than two hours resisting the silence, Jien spoke to me, giving me a small rock he had picked up from the ground. I accepted it without question.

'Rafaela, let us walk. I would like to show you a place that is very special to us.'

'Of course,' I said, happy we could finally talk.

'I feel your anxiety flittering around about your head like a little lost bird. I sense you are carrying some baggage with you.'

Although I didn't have a close relationship with this 'enlightened being', I felt inspired, at ease and safe around him. I opened up, sharing my worries and my thoughts.

'I understand. Humanity has allowed itself to be carried away by continuous chatter. It is the noise that masks everything, allowing the powerful army of words to intimidate the inner universe, thus keeping it prisoner and not giving wisdom the space to breathe. People are not only trapped, but are also completely unaware of it.'

'Is that why you practise silence and meditation?'

'Yes, Rafaela. Silence and meditation are our weapons against the 'high command' that directs the turbulent universe of empty words.

'But don't you consider information and reading necessary for humanity to evolve?'

'We understand that knowledge is the bridge that leads us to wisdom. However, humanity that is ignorant and lost among all the questions and answers is one that indiscriminately consumes much more than what the soul actually needs. If the soul is to understand and remember, it must first be connected to the speaker in silence, just as the shape that is modelled in clay must first be connected to the potter's mind.'

'But how do we silence that noise?'

'The great noise is barely audible, Rafaela. That is why it is so important to allow silence to exist. It crises unexpectedly when all voices go quiet, and it contains all whispers and roars alike. To us, silence is a light that shines high up on a mountain top, illuminating the darkness around it.'

'I think I understand. You mean to say that silence is illuminating and provides clarity, right? And that it helps us find what we can't be read in books or in newspapers?'

'That's right. Silence is the raw understanding of words and thoughts. In order to flourish, we must keep our mind in a natural state, without imagination, thought, analysis or reflection.'

'Why are we so scared to empty our minds?'

'Many people are scared to empty their minds for fear of falling into the abyss. They fail to understand that, in fact, their mind is the abyss. Silence teaches us to learn to be present in life, instead of running away from it. We practise silencing our bodies, voices and thoughts.'

'Silencing our body? How does that work?'

'In general, people are scared to sit still because they feel they are missing out on the feeling of existing, that they always have to be doing something, instead of just being still.'

I was so wrapped up in the conversation, I almost was almost unaware that we had arrived at a small curved wooden bridge decorated with red handrails. Barely two hundred metres away was a tiny house surrounded by a colourful Japanese garden. Jien explained that it was a tea house, and that all the foreigners were surprised at its small size. My walking companion argued that a tea house only required two square metres, had to be located in a secluded garden and should have a very small door so that everyone who entered, no matter how powerful, was forced to bend down just like the others. Jien invited me to enter with a solemn gesture. I experienced my first tea ceremony that day. The ritual takes over four hours and is intended to provoke feelings of tranquillity, purity and respect, as a result of sharing such a confined space with others, far from the world's troubles. As Jien filled my tea bowl, I wanted him to know more about me, so I began to tell him proudly about my recent titles and personal achievements. He continued pouring until it spilled over onto the table.

'Thank you, it's full enough,' I said, not wanting to embarrass him for his clumsiness.

'Just like your mind, Rafaela. You are so full of you that there is nothing I can teach you. In order to fill your bowl, you must first empty it, and this can only be done through silence,' he said, exuding peace and serenity.

I was silenced by Jien's 'checkmate' and hung my head, embarrassed. I still hadn't quite recovered when he asked me, 'Rafaela, why do you still keep the rock I gave you in the cemetery?'

I'd completely forgotten about the smooth blue rock I had been carrying since that moment.

'Well, you gave it to me,' I answered, awaiting another of his lessons.

'And do you accept everything you are given, without asking yourself what use it may have or what intention lies behind it? Words are full of information and knowledge; half belongs to the one who utters them and half to the one who receives them.'

With that experience held firmly in my heart, I returned to 'civilisation' once again, grateful and fascinated by that kind man's devotion to understanding the depth of truth that lies beyond our lives. He gave me a simple tea bowl as a farewell gift, with a Japanese inscription that read *'When you wish to speak, stay silent. Let silence be your shield and your sword'*.

If you're an obese person carrying around a hundred kilos, other people see it as a problem. However, if you spend all day consuming all kinds of information non-stop, no one gives it a second thought, no one tells you that you have a problem.

That trip was much more than just a physical journey; it also became a spiritual one. Today I am satisfied with my hypo-informative diet, having distanced myself from newspapers, television news and over-exposure on social media, consequently freeing myself from an incessant battle against being consumed by nothingness.

At the calmest hour of the night, as I drowsily stirred in my bed, I saw a slim shadow stealthily approaching me. Its tall, thin silhouette was neatly projected onto the wall. It stopped in front of me for a few moments, finally sitting with a swift, elegant movement in the chair located next to my slow-moving body. Previous days had been dreamless. I struggled so much to disconnect, my head spiralling out of control. I slept on and off, and this lack of rest was affecting my body, the bags under my eyes announcing this fact to the world. Stopping the conscious mind was a priority for me, but it was a challenge. I was the embodiment of contradiction – on the one hand, silence and meditation; on the other, the battle between reason and giving meaning to all my life's events. I was sure that the tempting red pills the nurse left on my bedside table every night would knock me out, but I didn't want to depend on them and insisted on visiting the house of blessed relaxation, the ultimate lover for our nervous system, which involved letting go, releasing, alleviating, softening... leaving behind all physical and mental tension.

The dark entity watched me as I, far from being fearful of that shapeless presence, made the effort to remain lost in what I believed to be one of those dreams that I no longer remembered.

It was one of the coldest nights I had spent in that hotel for the somnolent, I was frozen to the core. I instinctively curled up beneath the blanket, turning my head towards the shadow that continued to radiate a soft, penetrating warmth. A noise came from that flexible column of dark smoke that seemed destined only for my ears. Another element seemed to become part of the figure, I deduced by its shape that it was a book. Its voice was a beautiful melody, a sweet sound that produced both a horrifying yet soothing effect on me. Those words I couldn't understand were full of meaning. The sounds of drums became louder and louder, carrying me away. For the first time in a long time, I felt in sync. I just wanted to soak in all those words that came flooding like a river, evoking memories of true happiness and peace.

I've always taken notice of my dreams, never ignoring them. I receive them like intuitive information filled with signals. Dreams are wide-open doors that send us messages and invite us to interpret their meanings. Could this be a lucid dream? Was I experiencing that weird phenomenon of being aware that we are dreaming despite being asleep? In that case, I could guide and control its content and its outcome to my convenience. I had read that fifty per cent of people have experienced a lucid dream at least once in their lives. Some even have the ability to control their dreams at will. Dreams have always been a source of mystery for scientists and psychologists, alike. In my case, I can say that I've always had a great deal of respect for the subconscious. I'm acutely aware of it and pay close attention to what it says.

The voice was undoubtedly that of a middle-aged woman. It seemed so familiar, yet the language she spoke threw me off completely. She seemed to be reading a story. Suddenly, she began to whisper a song that unlocked a hidden folder in my brain, urging me to sing along to the chorus, hypnotising me with that enchanted melody like a rat spellbound by the pied piper of Hamelin. Clearly, it was not the first time those sounds had emerged from my throat but, for some reason, they'd remained silent until the arrival of the mysterious visitor. It was evidently not the kind of song I would download from iTunes, despite my broad musical tastes. It sounded like a children's song, and I associated it with something very deep and special, something rooted in me and wrapped around my entire being like ivy. Where could it have come from? It wasn't just the chorus, it was the entire song! Where had I heard it before? And why was it permanently burned into my mind? Was this a sign?

There I was, absolutely intrigued and concentrating on my internal noise, immersed in that dream that felt so real, when the voice went silent and the black silhouette began to grow as it came closer, slowly but without stopping. She took my hand and smiled. That's when I knew. It's going to hurt so much when she lets go again. Not even my amnesia could tear that memory away from me. The memory of my mother's silky hands that looked like birds in flight when they plaited my hair, when she caressed me with her magical touch, when I didn't want to go to school for fear of missing out on spending time with her, and she'd hold my face and say, 'Rafaela, you have to learn that a pencil weighs far less than a shovel.' My mother's hands were full of love and smelled like fresh lilies.

I wanted to evoke each and every one of those few and fleeting moments that filled my soul with hidden doubts. I wasn't ready to let anyone save me from this delicious torture, so I decided to take over the reins of this story, even if it was only an ephemeral dream of a shadow somewhere in my unconscious. I addressed the only thing I had left of my mother – her shadow. Without letting go of her hand, I told her everything I always wished I could tell her. Somehow, in this particular timeless space, we had found each other again.

'*Mamá*, I want you to know that I think about you all the time. I ask myself every day what would have happened if you hadn't left. I often smile because it's easier than explaining why I feel so desperately sad. I've found my passion: helping people. If you were here with me, I'm sure you'd be so proud of me. We'd go to photography exhibitions, museums, concerts, book presentations, and we'd travel the world together. It would be amazing. *Abuela* filled my world with love, but she wasn't strong enough to give me the answers I needed. Your absence still hurts. My job has helped me to discover many things, to observe people and to better know myself, but I never got to know the most important person in my life – YOU. I sometimes let my imagination take flight as I try to guess what you'd be like today. I also dream that we're walking down the street together, arm-in-arm, my head resting on your shoulder. Maybe, in another lifetime, we'll get another chance. In the meantime, please, don't forget me, no matter how much destiny stands in our way. This is going to sound very strange, but I miss who I could've been with you, even though you weren't there. I still remember the last day we spent together. I would have liked to have known then that I'd never see you again so I could hold you tighter and tell you that I always would wait for you.'

The shadow hugged me tight, crushing all my bones. It was the strength of love. The tears from her eyes wet my skin like much-needed rain wets the earth, and a few halting words planted the seed of hope in my heart.

'My little Rafaela, you're all grown up. I love you so much. Help me find my story.'

The day opened its doors to the public once again. Still a bit dazed, I put my feet on the floor with the aim of heading to the bathroom to have a shower. Despite having slept for nine hours, I was truly exhausted, like a cocktail shaker might feel after a night of constant use. Once inside the shower, I adjusted the temperature of the water and let it wash over all my senses.

My mind suddenly went on high alert when, from behind the half-opened door, I heard my roommate humming the song I had been dreaming about the night before. I immediately got out of the shower, half naked and incredulous, wondering if I was still dreaming or if it was all part of some cruel joke.

'Why are you singing that song?' I asked, firmly and straight to the point.

'I couldn't help it after hearing you both sing it all night. The chorus is very catchy, what is it called?'

'You heard *us*? Who exactly?'

'You and your mother, obviously. Who else would it be?'

'Wait… what are you talking about?'

'Rafaela, maybe you're still experiencing some kind of memory loss. Look, bout midnight last night, the lady I told you about a few days ago, the one who visits you often, came back. She read to you, as she always does. This time, you even sang that beautiful song together and I couldn't help but listen. I ended up falling asleep, like a baby listening to a lullaby.'

'What did she look like? Did you hear anything else?'

'Rafaela, you ask the strangest questions. Don't you know what your own mother looks like? I don't think you'll be leaving the hospital for a while…'

'Please, this is very important!' I begged, as though my life depended on it.

'Well, it was pretty dark, but she's an extraordinary beauty. She must be in her late fifties, with a good figure and dressed very young for her age. You can tell she loves you very much by the way she treats you.'

My feelings were all over the place. I felt like I was standing in the crater of a dormant volcano of my own making, one that had just begun to erupt, shooting up a cloud of volcanic ash that blinded me, made me lucid and shocked me, all at the same time.

Over the past few hours, the mysterious letter notifying me of the death of the father I had never met and now my mother's return as a nocturnal ghost had become intermittent explosions of fire and lava in my head.

Active volcanoes are fascinating; they remind us of the power of nature that we humans simply cannot control. At that moment, I could feel the spirit of contradiction rearing its head. My neuron connections shot into action, creating a retaining wall. Their mission? To insulate me from the extremely high temperatures and protect me from the toxic gas, unless I wanted the molten rocks to bury me alive under the lava. My heart, however, told me to have some faith, to go with it and give into intuition, that long-forgotten friend. I was tired of the chains that tied me to reason and the nonsensical need to make sense of everything, to have a perfectly-defined structure and all the answers. A superior force was shouting, 'Free yourself, Rafaela!' I let my eyes close and envisaged myself swimming naked in the ocean, allowing the waves to rock me, covering me in soft white foam. That was, without a doubt, the closest thing to freedom I remembered. My weightless body floating in the water. Just a second. Stop, stop… I ordered my mind, while also asking, 'Why was I swimming naked with Conan? Why had my thoughts taken me to that man at that precise moment of pleasure and freedom? And why had my body shivered at that image?' I breathed in deeply and told myself, 'Rafaela, relax. You're experiencing "a tunnel moment".' Yes, one of those moments in your life when you pass from one reality to another. That moment of darkness that comes with many emotional rollercoasters and important decisions. A familiar darkness that invades the carriages of a train as they enter a tunnel, eventually finding the light again.

The arrival of Dr Alex in the room saved me from my own thoughts. I saw happiness in this face, or at least I thought so. That hero, with his inseparable stethoscope around his neck and using science as his shield, brought out enormous feeling of gratitude in me. I felt I owed him much more than just my life, I owed him my chance to be reborn.

'Doctor, I have a date with a very handsome man, so I hope you have some good news for me because I can't stay in this hotel any longer, no matter how much I enjoy the buffet and nightly parties,' I joked, my irony, protecting me from any possible bad news.

'I see you haven't lost your sense of humour, Rafaela. That's very important. We're going to miss you around here.'

'Does that mean that your little machine has given us the green light?'

'The CT scan results are clean. You may still have some ongoing form of memory loss, but it will all come back to you eventually, once you return to your normal routine.'

'That's exactly what I wanted to hear, doctor.'

'There's something else you ought to know, Rafaela. You'll never be able to box again. You won't survive another blow to the head. Getting back in that ring will mean risking your life. I'm sorry.'

I felt like he'd just poured a bucket of cold water over me. Another blow. I was mute for a moment, not quite knowing how to take it all in. I remember having thought about quitting many times, but now that it was no longer by choice, it was far more painful. I began to spiral at breakneck speed. What would happen to my kids at the foundation? What about those training sessions with Conan that I enjoyed so much? I could imagine the disappointed looks on my followers' faces when they found out. A part of me had died. Iris was much more than just a character. She was a link to my dear childhood friend, Sebastián, the hero who saved the needy with her victories, the strong woman who punched back at life when her patients could not, the sexy girl who appeared in the calendar every year, but also the fragile woman who hid behind her colourful boxing gloves. Iris would forever remain in that hotel.

'You're going to need some time to assimilate all these changes, Rafaela. It's very normal for you to experience a type of catharsis. Life has given you a new opportunity and there's a whole world waiting for you out there,' said Alex, encouragingly, more like a friend than a doctor this time.

A whole world waiting for me? That's precisely what was so terrifying, facing that topsy-turvy world, with a feeling of emptiness and ruin.

'I've signed your discharge papers; you can leave the hospital at five. I'll see you in six months if everything goes well for your routine check-up. Good luck on your date with the handsome man!'

I said goodbye with a simple 'thank you so much for everything'. I never saw Dr Alex again, and I never went to my check-up.

I took my phone out of my backpack and messaged Conan: *free at five*. It seemed a bit flat, so a few seconds later I added one of those little winking faces. I changed into the only spare clothes I could find. They were so big I actually doubted for a moment they were mine. The bra had nothing to support as my breasts had been reabsorbed into my body. My jeans danced the lambada around my waist and the zebra-print shirt looked like something I might inherit from a big sister. Only the black boots fit my feet perfectly.

I looked back bittersweetly at the place that had been my home for the past few months. I gave a goodbye hug to my roommate – a first-hand witness to key events in the story of the new Rafaela.

Chapter 6

There Was a Time...

Three children were relaxing on the rocks by the water. The girl who was lying on the warm rock let her dark hair fall freely, sweeping the golden leaves from the ground that brimming with life. The two boys were somewhat older. The girl observed how the water made tiny waves when she caressed the shiny surface of the Purple Lagoon with her fingers. Behind them a breeze blew through the forest full of rock trees that resembled columns growing straight up towards the sky. This had always been a favourite place for the kids to lose themselves playing their games.

'Don't get too close, Narin,' said one of them. 'You might fall.'

But ignoring the warning, the girl extended her arm towards the mysterious depths.

'She's going to fall, isn't she?' said the second boy, agreeing with the first.

Narin disappeared below the deep purple waters, as the boys desperately shouted her name. Vodka was the first to arrive on the scene. Restless, he began to circle the lagoon as he barked, making sure Amelia and I were still following him.

On the dimly-lit water, two swans glided perfectly in sync like a pair of professional ice skaters, unaware of the boys who were frantically trying to save the ill-fated girl.

Amelia observed the area perplexed and incredulous. I could feel her emotions acutely. We had entered the Purple Lagoon abruptly and completely by surprise, where another space-time continuum existed, without having warned her or prepared her mind and soul for the adventure – an adventure that was light years away from anything else she had ever experienced on her travels.

One of the boys, with a moon face and an angelic look, addressed us immediately in a millenary tongue, while the other seemed to give Vodka directions so he could trace the missing girl.

'My sister fell in the lagoon. Please help us,' he begged sobbing, barely getting the words out.

I removed my moccasins and dropped my fringe jacket on a bed of small pink cuckooflowers that shared their kingdom with other light green star-shaped wild flowers and leaves resembling grey feathers. I jumped into the water without thinking. I used the ability we Elove beings have to perceive and connect with people's emotions and dived deep, following the fear that floated in the water, heading to the bottom of that magical underwater forest inhabited by old sea wolves and striped dancing octopuses. The lack of oxygen was not a problem for me. Our lungs are able to go without the precious air that humans need to survive. However, I knew the intrepid girl would not last much longer without it. I slid quickly through the currents and the festoons of seaweed that insisted on holding me within its soft, tireless grip. I found the tiny sleeping body of Narin trapped in some branches, so I picked her up as carefully and as quickly as I could and carried her up to the surface. There, the boys and Amelia waited anxiously, full of hope. Even Vodka remained still, his ears up and his gaze fixed on the same spot where I myself had disappeared moments earlier. They all seemed to expect the miracle that, finally, was not to be. I placed Narin's lifeless body on my jacket. The boys approached and began yelling her name, crying, shaking her body in an attempt to bring her back to life. Vodka licked her wet face, making a sound somewhere between a bark and a howl, clearly expressing his sadness. Amelia had been engulfed by silence. The situation had completely overcome her, and she stood there observing the scene like a marble statue. I hugged her. I knew it was what she needed the most. She hugged me back, shaking, burying her head in my chest. I always believed that this tragic moment joined our hearts and our destinies together forever. There were no introductions, no farewells. The nameless boys disappeared with Narin, blending in with the forest beneath the dark starry night. Amelia, utterly heartbroken, wanted to follow them, comfort them, accompany them in this terrible loss, explain to their parents how sorry we were and how we did everything we could to save her. I persuaded her not to. She obviously thought like an adult from Planet Earth, but things worked differently at the Purple Lagoon. Other laws applied, which were difficult to understand if you were not from here.

'What does all of this mean, Elsu? Is this place real?' asked Amelia, sitting in front of the purple water, and leaning against a large tree as she took her shoes off. She was sure I would enlighten her. She always said I had all the answers in a world full of questions. I always told her she was the only question I had no answer to. That made her feel like the most exceptional woman in the universe. It did not matter how many times I told her, she always responded with a genuine smile, as though she were hearing it for the very first time.

'We seem to have passed through the gate leading into the Purple Lagoon, the place we were looking for. I thought we would only find a few ruins, but I never expected there to still be life here, or that its beauty would remain intact thousands of years later. The guardians of the Elove Galaxy lost their connection to the beings that lived here a long time ago.'

'Wait, are you saying that the Purple Lagoon is not on our planet? That it's not on our maps or even in our consciousness?' asked Amelia, holding her head in her hands, as if her fragile brain were being weighed down by the very idea.

'As you have said, the borders of the Purple Lagoon are not shown on any map. It exists on a parallel dimension.'

'You mean, the people we call insane for believing in aliens and UFO's are actually right? And that all the scientists are wrong?'

'Amelia, what you call science is nothing more than a tiny island in a vast ocean of ignorance. Your species on Earth tries to broaden its understanding, yet remains ignorant regarding most matters of importance. Your arrogance is due to the fact you have not found any other form of life such as your own. Even today, you continue to look for it, while remaining lost to yourselves. The life form you seek remains hidden from your eyes and from your hearts. It is much more advanced than you. You humans may not be as intelligent as you think. If you find it one day, I am sure you will learn a lot from them but, more importantly, you will have the opportunity to develop a more mature sense of your place in the universe. You will not think that you are so unique and special, and your absurd and egocentric belief that you are the centre of the cosmos will come to an end.'

'What do you mean by we're not so intelligent?' asked Amelia, somewhat hurt and offended.

'You are not particularly intelligent as a species; just look at how you behave. You fight amongst yourselves and you do not take care of the environment as you should. You continue to provoke global disasters, sometimes by accident or through lack of awareness, and other times intentionally. Pollution, desertification, seas full of plastic, mountains ravaged by fire, oil spills in the ocean, melting polar ice caps, defiled rivers, these are just a few examples... does that sound like a symptom of intelligence to you?'

Amelia thought for a moment, searching for something within her to fight back and defend her human pride.

'And what about our capacity to feel solidarity, affection, kindness and compassion for others? Humans are also all of those things, and we're constantly evolving.'

I looked at her and smiled, thinking how fond I was becoming of this creature. I did not want to hurt her with my words, but it was important for her to understand.

'You proclaim to be human beings, but you still have a long way to go to become proficient in humanity. You are just people, individuals who cause suffering, waving the flag of selfishness in the name of survival, encouraging violence due to a lack of empathy and excess of ignorance, faithful followers of the laws written by the worst part of the human condition, endorsed by your own egos. You have become half-baked soldiers, fighting visible and invisible wars without a cause, loaded with ammunition that ends up exploding in your own souls. The humanity project is in serious jeopardy, as is your place as the planet's caretakers. You have to wake up.'

'Of course we've evolved,' she replied, continuing her argument. 'A clear example is the technological era we're currently living in.'

'Amelia, you have to recognise that even after several centuries of history, you are still stuck on your own involution. The fact you have been touched by technology is not a sign of human evolution, but a result of the development of knowledge. While polar bears have developed a thick skin with many layers in order to resist the Arctic cold, you humans continue to skin them and wear their fur just to parade around in.'

I realised then that this had been a checkmate for someone who loved animals as much as Amelia did. She lowered her head and caressed her faithful friend Vodka in a special way, conveying deep and profound feelings. The animal received the gesture with gratitude and gave her a wet kiss near her lips in return. For a moment, I envied him and experienced a new emotion not yet registered on my emotional ladder. I did not wish to name it.

'Perhaps you're right,' she replied disappointed, facing the facts. 'I can't help thinking of the martyrs in the Roman circus and the intermittent persecution suffered by Christians for over two centuries. It wasn't only the gladiators who killed each other in the Colosseum to entertain the Roman people, Christians who were being persecuted by the empire were also thrown in so they'd be devoured by the beasts. Even families with children were thrown in there. They were exposed publicly so they'd fight the lions with no weapons, but what they really wanted was to see how they were eaten. The little ones were even dressed up as sheep so that the lions would attack them. These became popular entertainment shows, giving rise to the famous Latin expression *panem et circenses*, literally 'bread and circuses' for the people, a saying still used by modern politicians today. Nowadays, this seems barbaric.

'However, how's that different to boxing matches, where many athletes die from fatal blows? Where's this human evolution present in animal fighting, such as cockfighting, dog fighting and others, including bullfighting, where even today people still pay to watch the pain, suffering and even death of these living beings? Legal and illegal forms of entertainment which we embellish with the wonderful words "sports", "tradition" or "culture" so we can sleep guilt-free at night.'

I let her speak. She was awakening, and that was precisely the state I needed her in.

'I remember how much of an impact it had on me to watch my first football match with my father, who was a huge fan of the sport. I didn't want to go, but he could be very convincing when he wanted to be. He promised me that he'd quit smoking if I went. He was a chain smoker. *Mamá* always got upset with him and warned him that he'd have a heart attack one day if he didn't quit. I thought it was a fair deal, and for a good cause. It's such a shame he died just one week after we made that pact, just as my mother had predicted. *Papá* always played at an advantage, I'm sure he knew his death was around the corner.

'I was shocked to see how some fans constantly insulted the players, the referee and even fans of the other team. Children, in the company of their parents, repeated the same insults and violent gestures, encouraged by their parents. I couldn't understand the extreme violence displayed by some of the fans, who were emotionally unable to manage the frustration, anger and aggression they'd probably built up in their daily lives and then released at the match, as it wouldn't be allowed in any other public situation. This sowed the seed of hatred and aggression whose purpose was only to defend a set of colours, a club, or simply as an excuse to hurl insults. I saw a clear reflection of a part of society that hurt me deeply, even more so than the bottle of water thrown by two brawling fans at the back that came flying like an out-of-control spaceship and hit me in the eye, causing it to bleed.'

Amelia was still sitting, meditating deeply in touch with the silent voices floating around her. They were spirits of remembering and truth, flapping around her like a boiling hot tornado.

'Lately, especially when I stop to think about the state of the world, I feel like I'm experiencing a déjà vu. It's like the story just keeps repeating again and again, confirming that human beings are the only animal that stumble twice, three times and even four times against the same stone. The hard stone of involution. They say that history repeats itself, but its lessons are not learnt. Learning is the first sign of evolution, and despite knowing the history of our people, we're destined to make the same mistakes. Even though we know just how damaging a war can be, the world's peoples have been in constant battle since the dawn of time with no obvious ability to come to terms. What is it about the human psyche that leads us to ignore the lessons we've learnt and to repeat the same mistakes despite knowing how bad the ending will be?

'Maybe history's greatest lesson is that no one learns theirs. That is why you survive amidst the same human dilemmas, between the best and worst of human behaviour.'

'Elsu, is there hope for our species?' she asked, anxiously.

'The course of your future evolution will be decided by yourselves. It will depend on your species' ability to change the world. I'm here to help you. It's not too late. You must know that there was a time when things were not like this. The guardians of the Elove Galaxy created this place, the Purple Lagoon, where human beings planted their seeds for the first time under the rule of the secret doctrines found in the seven Arcane Truths. It was a civilisation where pain died of pleasure, love was the hardest drug there was, and everything worked in perfect symphony. They were later assigned Planet Earth.'

I guess that answer calmed her momentarily, though I could sense her curiosity in the form of dozens of questions fluttering around in her restless mind, like newborn butterflies in an eternal spring.

'We have to find the thousand-step staircase that leads to the Temple of Light. We do not have much time,' I said, leading the way.

My only guides were the constellations, those brilliant specks of light in the night sky, opening a path through the darkness. I was specifically looking for the constellation of Cancer, the crab, one of the twelve signs of the zodiac, as it would lead us to the centre of the Purple Lagoon, to the mother, the origin of life, the fertile and fruitful land. That is where we would find the closest thing to a home. The area ruled by Cancer would undoubtedly contain drinking water and food, as well as a safe place to rest where we would be protected and illuminated by the giant lunar lamp. My father had taught me that Cancer was the gateway into the world of feelings, and that people born under its influence possessed great emotional sensibility and a deep faith. If we could find those beings, I was sure they would show us their hospitality.

We walked in single file along a trail surrounded by some kind of blue mushrooms. The sound of our feet stepping on fragile sycamore leaves frightened some animals that resembled grey rabbits, who ran away without sound, while Vodka chased them to no avail. A bird with three wings laboriously took flight and headed downstream. For a brief moment, everything was still. After walking for several hours, Amelia began dragging her feet a short distance from me, disoriented and weary, showing the exhaustion from travelling to a place that was light years away from everything she had ever known. Her inquisitive eyes scanned every tiny detail like a radar. We emerged from the trail into an open space on the other side of the lagoon. I raised my eyes and confirmed that we were, in fact, in the land of the crab people.

We heard the sound of singing voices and followed them until we reached a series of caves and cliffs by the water, surrounded by wild vegetation. A round woman with a high brow and slightly curved legs played with four children of similar ages that looked alike. The children's reddish skin was much more intense than that of the woman who appeared to be their mother. They moved strangely through small marine galleries, using lateral movements and some spins, splashing and laughing as their protector, with her sweet and mysterious features, showered them with constant love and affection.

Our hairy companion's barks startled the youngest in the family, who ran to hide beneath his mother's strong arms. Their red faces and shiny black eyes turned towards us. As we neared them, I noticed that the woman was carrying a baby on her back.

'He's harmless, he just wants to play with you. Don't be scared,' said Amelia immediately as she caressed Vodka, trying to inspire confidence in those peculiar beings that observed us with hesitation and fascination in equal measure.

Two of the children approached shyly to caress the animal's back, having received their mother's permission.

'Which constellation are you from?' asked the woman.

'Our home is not of this world. We are only passing through in search of the thousand-step staircase. Have you heard of it?' I enquired, hoping to obtain some clue that would help us advance.

'I cannot help you with that, but you look like you could use some food and a place to rest before continuing on your journey. It is almost dawn and it is time for us to go home. Please, come with me and enjoy our hospitality.'

We happily accepted the invitation. Their house was just a few short metres away – a natural cavern in the midst of a hotbed of crabs. The woman introduced herself as Ninan and explained that they went to bed at dawn, only to resume their frenetic activity at dusk. The community was characterised by its slow, consistent work. They did not believe in quick and easy results. Their strength lay in their unlimited intelligence and prodigious imagination. Inside the cave, Ninan's partner anxiously awaited his family, tirelessly mixing the fertile earth that housed flowering plants in a multicoloured garden. The culinary skills of our hostess, along with the cosiness of her home were, without a doubt, a treat during our quest. Peace and harmony permeated every corner of that cave. The kitchen was a volcano of flavours and aromas that drew you in. The light of the full moon illuminated everything.

'Elsu, have you ever been in love?' asked Amelia, wistfully.

I remained silent. That unexpected question unsettled me. 'I do not know,' I answered. 'I can feel love and connect with your feelings.'

'I'm not talking about sentiment, I mean crying because you love someone too much. Planning uncertain futures that you long to share with that person. Putting aside your fears and becoming the bravest person you can be so you can continue to risk it all, even when the game's already over.'

'Maybe not in that way,' I replied, unsure of my answer.

'If you're not sure about whether you've ever been in love, then you haven't been. It's something you just know without having to think about it. You know right away, from the moment it happens, because you look at that person differently and want to devour them with kisses.'

'I gather you have been in love, right?'

'Yes. And I know that we don't share our clothes or our dreams with just anybody. Many bodies can pass through your bed, but very few souls reach orgasm together. You don't seek their kisses just to pass the time, you want those same kisses forever. In return, you offer glances that don't need to be filled with words.'

'It seems as though the other side of that kind of love is suffering.'

'Sometimes, it reopens old wounds without meaning to. With new blows, you bleed from the same place that once hurt, and you realise that you're not as strong as you thought you were. One day, you find yourself in front of someone who makes you vulnerable again. Suffering is always a price you're willing to pay in return for running the risk of truly living, feeling that to love again is always worth it.'

Her sad, mascara-stained eyes resembled the most beautiful Montana winter I could remember. They were undeniably the perfect labyrinth through which to lose oneself in the depths of her soul.

We were in Cancerian territory. I knew the emotional implications of this fact. I myself had to make an effort to resist my impulses and not allow myself to be carried away by affection and be turned into one of those cyclothymic beings. Amelia sailed on the ocean of her emotions, showing me a world of infinite depth that was completely new to me. I knew she was not being entirely truthful when she declared herself an expert in love, and that she was actually feeling that emotion for the first time, but I did not want to reveal this knowledge.

Following a few hours of deep restorative sleep, we awoke just as darkness was falling. The sunset had revitalised the Cancerians once again. Ninan was nursing her offspring as the rest of the family devoured a type of nocturnal breakfast, rich in plant shoots and a varied mix of colourful fruits and flowers. Vodka sniffed around every inch of the kitchen, as if searching for a menu that was more suited to his canine tastes, eventually accepting the fresh fruits Amelia had prepared for him in a small coconut shell bowl.

I peeked through one of the kitchen's small rocky holes to see how the Cancerians automatically gathered in a circle around someone who addressed them in an impassioned and endless stream of verbosity.

'What is happening out there? It looks as though an important meeting is taking place,' I asked, taking my place at the table and taking what appeared to be white grapes.

'It most certainly is,' said the mother crab without taking her eyes of her baby, whom she cared for as though he was the centre of her universe. 'One of our neighbours from the constellation of Gemini brings us the news of the world.'

'Of what world?' asked Amelia, playing with a piece of hot seaweed bread in her hands.

'He travels through all twelve constellations over three hundred and sixty-five days and then shares the most important events with us at the Purple Lagoon. He is our greatest connection with everything that happens in our world. My husband woke up early so as not to miss anything. You should go and meet him. I'm sure he could give you information about the thousand-step staircase you are looking for. He knows everything about everything,' she suggested with prophetic intuition and a noble nature.

Like a perfectly synchronised team, my companion and I looked at each other, got up from the table and headed off together. A few minutes later, we made our way through the red crowd and stood in front of that hypnotic being. His eyes were light like glass, sparkling constantly and moving from side to side. He seemed incapable of resting his captivating gaze on a particular spot for more than a second. His body was thin and his extremities seemed too long for this trunk. He was amazingly flexible, adopting impossible postures and moving in such dramatic ways that it seemed as though there were two people inhabiting the same body, each moving in opposite directions. It seemed incredible that so many words could come out of such a tiny mouth in such little time. His clothes were very ambiguous, best defined as 'pauper and prince' style. Covering his head was an elegant green suede top hat with a black band around it and a golden buckle at its base. A scarf surrounded his slim neck, with dozens of fine pastel-coloured strips covering his buttoned-up grey corduroy jacket featuring shoulder pads and large pockets. Completing his look were slim black trousers adorned with patches covered in phrases, and a pair of hot pink worn-out trainers with clear plastic laces. The character read with impressive speed while, maintaining eye contact with his audience, as if the words were just sliding off his tongue.

'And this terrible event occurred just recently. A young crab girl lost her life while playing near the forest with her brothers, near the Gemini border. The eight-year-old drowned in the lagoon, and no one was able to save her,' he said with a sad expression.

He soon became aware of our presence. He stopped his newsreel and made his way over, swaying cheerfully. He left his old newspapers and magnifying glass on a big trunk covered in rings that reflected its longevity, which he often used as a lectern, and asked us in a friendly voice, 'Who are you? Where are you from? What are you doing here? How did you get here?'

Before we could say anything, Ninan's partner took a few steps to the right to get closer to the insatiably curious being and said, 'They are my guests. These visitors come in peace in order to carry out a mission,' in a serene and protective tone.

'What mission? Why do I not know about this? Please tell me, I have to know,' he asked anxiously, moving his hands like an out-of-control fan.

'I am Elsu, a descendant of the guardians of the Elove Galaxy. My people have lived since time immemorial in the mountains of Montana in a different space-time continuum to yours and to the rest of the planets in the cosmos. We founded the place that you know as the Purple Lagoon with the purpose of creating a civilisation that would be pure of heart and soul, advanced and intelligent, and follow the seven Arcane Truths that rule our Galaxy. The Elove guardians established twelve zones of equal dimensions, influenced by the twelve areas of the celestial sphere that you refer to as constellations. The idea was for the inhabitants of each area to learn from the others, thereby evolving together from their own essence and eventually improving the species through subsequent generations.'

The crowd listened to my every word in silent attention. The restless being from Gemini interrupted me.

'Of course, that is why each of the life forms that live at the Purple Lagoon are so different, yet so complementary. That is something I have learnt after more than twelve decades of travelling, delivering news all over the constellations. However, I wonder why it is that we continue to live apart from one another, without mixing, after so many years of coexistence?' reflected the ingenious, enigmatic being who appeared at first glance to know everything.

Amelia whispered in my ear, 'Isn't it amazing that this eloquent creature with a childish face is over twelve decades old? Time has barely aged him at all.'

'Amelia, you have to stop comparing everything to what you know, because you will only make yourself smaller in your own world. The comparisons that are so common among humans erode and empty your minds, distorting your perspective on everything and clouding your view of what is possible.'

She nodded and cracked a faint smile. She had understood my message.

'The woman and that strange animal do not appear to come from the same place as you. How is that? Is there another constellation I am yet to know about?' he continued, pointing to Amelia and Vodka with his long fingers.

Without waiting for an answer, he took a small brown leather-bound book with folded-down corners from one of his enormous jacket pockets.

'Let me take some notes. I don't want to forget anything so I can report on it as accurately as possible,' he said as he watched us, writing as he moved around us.

'You're right. I'm Amelia and he is my dog. We both come from a planet called Earth,' said Amelia.

'Earth... Elove Galaxy... Mission... Dog. OK, OK, I understand. This is the most interesting and exciting piece of news I have ever heard! But, what are you doing here?' he insisted, stepping all over Amelia's introduction.

As they obtained more and more information, the Cancerians' mood began to change. The feeling of insecurity and lack of control made them very nervous and irritable.

'What will happen now, then?' asked one of them, shyly.

'The truth is that the guardians of the Elove Galaxy were convinced that your civilisation had disappeared thousands of years ago, when they lost all contact for some reason. The only hope left for Earth and for the survival of humankind, to which Amelia belongs, is to find the thousand-step staircase illuminated by the seven Arches of Light. Each arch houses one of the seven Arcane Truths that must be understood and assimilated by humans. Only then may they access the Temple of Light.'

'Elsu, why is it so important to access that temple? And what makes you think that you will find that staircase at the Purple Lagoon?' asked the Geminian as he stroked his goatee. 'Well, perhaps it is here...' he said contradicting himself. 'I remember one piece of news... but I need more details. I need to put my ideas in order.'

'When the guardians of the Elove Galaxy founded the Purple Lagoon, they chose this place to protect the Temple of Light because the Galaxy was under threat from dark forces conspiring to destroy it. The constellation map that leads here could only be interpreted by one of our own, so it was the safest place to protect it. We only have one chance to access this place whenever the alignment of the planets allows it, and that moment is now. That is why we are here.'

The two-minded being revealed his analytical nature in an effort to recall all of his memories, connecting ideas at the speed of light. Like a child, thrilled to have completed a difficult puzzle, he finally spoke.

'I remember hearing a story about an infinite staircase an eternity ago,' he declared, staring vacantly as he concentrated. No matter how much time has passed since then, meeting that beautiful woman is still fresh in my mind. She sang a beautiful song as she turned the pages of a very old music manuscript, covered in dust and chewed by mice. What did she call it? Oh yes, the stairway to the sky, that was the name of the song.

'Consistent with my curiosity and dazzled by the light of her deep gaze, I approached the young woman and asked her where she came from.

'"I am made of music, that place where we all coincide at some time or another. The destination that never disappoints. No one *knows where I am from, because I was born deep within a heartbeat, and yet I keep her secrets because Music herself told them to me. I unleash new horizons and strip sunsets,'"* he said without taking his eyes off his notes, covered in lines, semi-circles, triangles, among other things, speaking his language. 'Naturally, her enigmatic reply inspired me to continue digging. The song seemed to be a coded message that penetrated you and made you fly without wings.

'"Did you write that song? What inspired you?" I asked.

'"I dreamt of writing a ballad on the moon. One night, while bathing in moonlight, I discovered a stairway to the sky and that was the closest I ever came to fulfilling my dream. The stars of the twelve zodiac constellations all leaned over open doors facing the Purple Lagoon. I felt like I was suspended over the musical notes of the stellar concert. From there, I could hear all the music of the world."

'At that moment, I didn't think the story of the infinite staircase was significant. I was drawn by the passionate chemistry and irresistible mystery of that woman, who disappeared on her bare feet, moving her hips seductively to the rhythm of her own melody, dropping verses as she went. It was clear that she wanted to protect her privacy and left without saying goodbye, completely sure of herself.'

One of the crab people asked, 'What was the song about? Judging by your description, could she have been a daughter of the constellation of Scorpio? What do you think?'

The Geminian thought for a moment before answering.

'I seem to recall that the lyrics went something like this:

Music is like thousands of stars lighting your way.
Beneath a blanket of jacarandas in bloom, hugged by arches of light,
The Rainbow Eucalyptus by the stream bows down at the foot of the
steps that take you to the sky...

'It was such a long time ago but I still think about it. I could not tell you exactly in which constellation it took place, though I am fairly sure she was a Scorpio. She was beautiful, not just by the shape of her body but by the very architecture of her soul.'

'Could you identify any setting such as the one you describe in the song? You know the land better than anyone. It might be the key to finding the place,' asked Amelia, who already felt completely involved.

'I have no idea, I have never seen a place like that on any of my travels around the Purple Lagoon. It may have simply been a fantasy for that woman, a song that was the fruit of her imagination and her desires. I do not believe it actually exists. Anyway, I think it is time for me to continue on my way. Good luck on your mission,' he said, folding up his old newspapers and pushing them hastily into his giant pockets in a sudden and unexpected turn of events.

The multifaceted Gemini being was lying. I could feel the lies hiding within him. My instinct as a hunter of emotions had been triggered by this deceit; my internal sensors detected an enormous absence of truth. He began to swallow more often, his breathing became more agitated and sweat was beginning to form on the palms of his hands. Nervousness had been tattooed all over every cell of his being like stripes on a zebra. He became opaque, silent and somewhat pessimistic. I could not read his thoughts, I simply tuned in to his brainwaves, understanding his contradicting emotions much more than even he could. Why the sudden change in attitude? What was he hiding?

Chapter 7

Letters

'Where to, young lady? I took the day off just for you. Shall we have drinks by the sea? A romantic candle-lit dinner holding hands? Or shall we just head home and make love until we're completely worn out?'

I didn't react. There was silence. I rolled down my window. I'm not sure if it was to breathe the air that had been sucked out of me, or to keep me busy, pretending that those words weren't meant for me. As we drove along the same road I'd taken hundreds of time to go home, I wanted to vanish in the traffic noise and amidst the hustle and bustle of the crowds of people making their way through the city. I looked at myself from time to time in the passenger-side wing mirror, and then at him out of the corner of my eye. It was like comparing a lush apple with a withered flower. I looked awful and felt even worse. My head slumped, possibly beneath the weight of my crushingly low self-esteem. Luckily, my female pride came to the rescue when I remembered one of the many legendary phrases Belly would use at times like this.

'Rafaela, you must only ever look down to admire your beautiful shoes. A woman's value isn't in her appearance, but in her essence. It has nothing to do with clothes and everything to do with class. It's not in her beauty but in her manners.'

This all happened in a matter of seconds but, to me, it felt like an eternity. I held up my weak body, with the intention of possessing the space and conveying confidence with the response I had prepared. Luckily, Conan helped me out with one of his classic outs.

'Did I hear a hot herbal tea and a conversation in good company? I may be willing to accept that too,' he said, letting out a warm laugh.

'Yep, that's exactly what I said,' I answered, playing along.

'I took care of your plants in your absence, and I picked up your mail. I also cleaned the house and filled your fridge with all your favourite foods. That way you can just rest for the first few days.'

'Thank you so much, Conan. You don't know how grateful I am.'

'I didn't do anything you wouldn't do for me. That's what people who love each other do, right?'

'Of course,' I agreed, forcing a smile, not wanting to delve any further into that.

I was dying to get home and get back in touch with my surroundings, resume my life or, rather, the pieces that were left of it. I needed to think, to piece all the morning's disconnected events together. I felt like the entire universe was playing a bad joke on me; nothing at all made sense and, although I didn't find it funny at all, someone was surely having a great laugh at my expense. Going home meant much more than just returning, it was an awakening, taking a deep breath and reconnecting with everything that had been my entire world before I'd been ripped out of it. That house was where I grew up, the refuge where all my memories lived, where the smell of Belly and my mother still lingered. It was what kept me grounded, and at the same time, it was the launchpad that lifted me into the air like a paper lantern. Despite my grown-up appearance, the little girl inside me was more alive than ever.

Conan parked in front of the wrought-iron gates leading to the front porch. I got out of the car and approached the house slowly, taking in each and every detail, as if I were discovering them all for the first time. The garden was very well-maintained; Conan had obviously done an extraordinary job. The Mediterranean blue wooden shutters were open, as I usually left them.

I stepped over the threshold and headed straight for the staircase leading up to the second floor. I walked past the door to the room that had been Belly's for many years until she died. When I saw the multi-coloured butterfly with her initial hanging from the wooden doorknob, I couldn't help but run my fingers over it, caressing the giant B formed by its wings. I remembered the day I made it myself and gave it to her, around Christmas time. I felt the need to go in. As soon as I opened the door, I was overcome with a feeling of melancholy. I could smell the scent of my childhood mixed with hers, as if someone had preserved it hermetically in a small glass bottle, just waiting for me to come and open it and get drunk on its aroma. I had read that our sense of smell is the most sensitive of all our senses and the most closelyconnected to our memory. We are able to recognise over ten thousand different smells, yet one was unique. Belly's floppy straw hat, one of her favourites, waited faithfully on her vanity chair, unaffected by the passage of time. I took off my shoes and climbed into her slippers as I used to do when I was little. They were as soft as her hugs. Belly used to tell me that they were like floating clouds because she would constantly trip over when wearing them. I remembered how angry she would get when I'd go in her room and move her things around. She'd always had the character of a fighting bull. Whenever that happened, I would, burst into tears like the extremely sensitive being I've always been, and she never failed to perform the same ritual.

'Rafaela, have you run out of smiles? I have one in my hand. If you want it, I'll give it to you. Do you want it? I'll open my hand and you catch it before it flies away.'

I would smile shyly at first, and then nod my head, still crying. Belly would open her hand and I would smile fleetingly, until my salty tears reached my mouth and I'd be upset all over again. She didn't give up.

'I have another hand and another smile, this one's from ear to ear. Do you want it?'

It was her infallible trick. For a second, I could still hear the echo of her voice. She never ran out of smiles. She was the most vibrant and joyful person I've ever known. With her, every day was a celebration.

I sat on the bed, beside the embroidered satin pillows on which her kind body and brave heart had rested so many nights. I breathed deeply, taking in some of that immensely personal, magical air, as I observed the tiny sepia-coloured photo of Belly and her husband on their wedding day. It felt odd to refer to my grandfather as *abuelo*, maybe because I had never met him, or perhaps because Belly had misplaced all of his memories and therefore never mentioned him. There were so many secrets in my family that I may not live long enough to be able to uncover them all. I came from such a short lineage that not even family gossip could shed any light.

I felt a bittersweet sensation upon remembering the date when Belly died. It happened on a Tuesday, the seventh of November, with the same simplicity and elegance with which she lived her life. Nobody noticed that she had prepared for her trip until the last minute, when it was already too late to intervene, aware of the courage required to leave this life all alone. What would an old person's heart sound like when it shattered? It probably didn't even make a noise, or at the most it made a tiny, imperceptible, sound. I wondered if an X-ray could show the pain of an old speedboat, accustomed to sailing the seven seas of life and whose hull had undergone many repairs, as it bid a final farewell to the shore.

The neighbours told me it had been the coldest day of the year, in spite of which, they'd found her lying on the bed uncovered, with a lock of my mother's hair tied to a white piece of string resting on her sunken chest. My own theory is that, on that epic day, Belly took away with her the warmth that illuminated everything and everyone. I could never forgive myself for not being there on the day she set off on that journey. Just as Dr Alex had said, remembering that detail meant my memories would return as soon I went back to my usual surroundings. But remembering this particular fact crushed my soul all over again. Belly was generous right up to the end. She got sick the same year I went to Jerusalem. She never held me back; on the contrary, she encouraged me to experiment, to live. Today, I know that she began to die the same day I started packing. She seemed to be a big fan of secrets. She never told me of her illness, despite our daily phone calls. I didn't really tell her everything that was going on with Jared at the time, either. I just noticed a long silence on the other end of the line whenever I told her I missed her. I couldn't imagine that she needed me even more than I needed her. Nor that she who had armed me with the munitions to face the battle of life would be shipwrecked on the rocks of existence, far away from me.

A very large and very old oak trunk, stained blue and embellished with metal corner guards and decorative silverwork with metallic corners and silver fittings, stood guard at the foot of the bed. This trunk had accompanied Belly on all her travels. She said it was her life. She was always reluctant to open that piece of furniture that decorated her room. I tried to open it once, but it was locked. What secrets could my grandmother have been harbouring inside this stylish trunk that had accompanied her everywhere for over half a century? I rummaged through the drawers of her bedside table and inside the wardrobe. I also went through the little box decorated with sailing motifs where she kept a few items of jewellery of little value, but found nothing. I then remembered one of her famous phrases, 'Sometimes, the most obvious things are the hardest to see.' I tried to put myself in Sherlock Holmes' shoes and decipher that enigma. I pondered briefly before catching a glimpse of a tiny gold key hidden inside the one corner guard of the trunk that seemed to remain intact. My triumph, however, was short-lived: when I put the key in the lock and turned it, the metal twisted and then snapped, leaving the bottom half inside the lock.

'Shit, shit, shit!' I yelled in frustration.

A few seconds later, Conan appeared at the door. He had charged up the stairs like a racehorse when he heard me scream.

'What's wrong? Are you OK?'

'Yes. Well, actually I'm not sure,' I answered, showing him the broken piece of metal in my hand. 'I was trying to open the trunk and the key broke off in my hand.'

'You just got here and you're getting into trouble already? I can't leave you alone for a second, *chiquilla*. Shouldn't you be resting instead of hunting for long-lost treasure like a pirate?' he said gently, taking my hand by the wrist and coming so close to me he was skimming my breasts.

To be completely honest, I was dying to be held by that large happy, passionate and fearless man, in those arms that could crush a person, though he never used them for that. I wanted to hear the words devoid of all embarrassment that he would whisper to me whenever we had sex anywhere, and I would have given anything to fall asleep with him again, my head resting on his tattooed arm. I was having flashbacks, and for a moment I found myself back in that different world we call the past. It was clear that my need for intimacy was mutual. The temptation to let myself go was invading my entire body. My legs could barely hold me up. Undoubtedly, the best part of leaving was always coming back and trying everything out as though it were the first time.

'Do you want to wear the camisole I gave you for your birthday?' he whispered seductively, very slowly placing his fingers on my bony shoulder.

I had no idea how I was meant to behave, or what I was like with Conan before the accident. Maybe I should just go with the flow and let my basic instincts take over, pounce on him like a lioness and devour his muscly body but, what if he expected a more erotic, sensual me? Or perhaps a very shy and submissive lover? Who was I? How had I lived my sexuality up until now? I didn't want to disappoint him. I felt insecure, ridiculous even, like a silly girl meeting a boy for the first time and not knowing how on earth to seduce him.

At least one piece of the puzzle made sense now. The black lacy lingerie I'd found in my backpack was from Conan, so there was clearly something between us. Or was I just filling in the gaps with juicy details?

'I won't pressure you. We have all the time in the world,' he said, noticing my fragile emotional state. I longed for him to take another step closer, but he didn't.

'I think I can help you with the trunk. Back in the navy, I used to always have to repair the locks on the cabin doors because they got stuck from the humidity and the rust. I became quite the locksmith. Let me see.'

He knelt down in front of the mysterious piece of furniture and fiddled around with the lock for a few minutes using a couple of paper clips that he, apparently, always carried in his pocket for an emergency. Or at least that's what he told me when he saw the look of surprise on my face. Four rusty staples on the sides made it harder to open, but he finally succeeded and the heavy domed lid was flipped open. Nostalgia gave way to to curiosity. Conan moved aside, letting me have the honour of being the first to discover what was inside. The scent of sandalwood with traces of pine and wet earth, like that of a waking forest, was freed from its enclosure and enveloped us. Inside, all the objects were perfectly arranged to make the best use of every inch of space. I immediately recognised her wedding dress, the same one she wore in the photo on her bedside table – a beautiful boatneck dress with puffed sleeves, a voluminous pin-tucked skirt and a matching veil whose colour had gone from white to vanilla and now smelled musty. A dusty photo album wuth the words 'Discover me' in shiny letters. Some old fashion books and records by singers I'd never heard of. My heart skipped a beat when I found Lesly, my favourite doll, my playmate and adventure companion, given to me by my mother on my sixth birthday. I threw her away when our cat, Ágata, destroyed her. Apparently, Belly had rescued her, sewn her up and kept her all this time. A melon-coloured silk blouse with buttoned cuffs was wrapped around a small box at the bottom of the trunk. I took it out and opened it. Inside was a bundle of old yellowing letters that had been arranged very carefully to keep them from wrinkling them and were tied together with a scarlet ribbon. To my surprise, the first one I saw was addressed to me.

Conan watched me, quietly. But when he saw the petrified expression on my face after making that unexpected discovery, like that of Tutankhamun's mummy, he broke the silence by shooting me the obvious question.

'So, aren't you going to read them?' he said, pointing to the letters with his head.

'Why would Belly never tell me about these letters? If she wanted to keep them a secret, who am I not to respect her wishes? I suppose she had her reasons,' I pondered, somewhere between nervous and excited.

'Rafaela, we all have secrets locked away in the attic of our soul, chapters of our life we don't read out loud. Sometimes those words mature in silence.'

'I guess so. But we had each other. She knew she could trust me. I always wanted to know and she always avoided my questions.'

'Maybe now you have the opportunity to discover all the things you ever wanted to know about your family. It's been a very intense day for you. You don't have to decide right now. I'll make you a hot chocolate. Get some rest now, and, you'll see how everything makes much more sense tomorrow.'

From the window, I could see the church clock marking ten to eleven at night. I looked up at the stars dancing in the black velvet sky one last time and followed Conan's advice.

I woke up ravenous, but happy to see I was back in my bedroom and surrounded by my things, all of which seemed familiar and very personal. I lay on the bed for a while just letting my senses kick in. The sound of a plane in the air, the tiny bark of Troy, the neighbour's poodle, even a pair of birds singing hopefully from a tree, as if the sun's weak rays had tricked them into thinking spring had already arrived. I fixed my eyes on a pair of boxing gloves hanging on the white brick wall. That made me upset, so I immediately turned my gaze towards Belly's letters. I never imagined that remnants of the past of one of the most important women in my life would wash up like a shipwreck in that house.

Whenever you have to make an important decision that will change your life, take several slow deep breaths, enjoying the air that will transform your existence as you know it, and let your heart take the reins. That was the advice I used to give my patients, just before they made a choice between one option or another. That's just what I did. I filled my lungs, taking in my surroundings, allowing my heart – that wise muscle that is the source of every one of our passions – unravel the coded message and show me the right path. Aristotle had already said that two thousand five hundred years ago, before today's science would eventually back up his theory. He believed that we all think with our hearts, and that the brain simply cools down the warm blood sent by the heart after having thought. Numerous scientific studies prove the connection between the brain and the heart, and how both function as instruments within the same orchestra.

An internal force pushed me inevitably to read those letters and to discover what had remained hidden for far too long. The decision had been made; there was no doubt now. Before beginning to read, I needed a good breakfast. I went down to the kitchen and immediately noticed one of the bananas in the fruit basket on the table. Written on it, in capital letters and a few spelling mistakes here and there was, *'Good morning, chiquilla. You're the universe's way of telling me how beautiful life is. I'll be in the gym until seven. Conan.'*

The spelling mistakes didn't surprise me, he still had trouble writing some Spanish words, especially those containing an 'r'. His wit and sense of humour were his signs of identity, but this romantic note didn't sit well with me. Conan wasn't that type of man, suave and overlysweet; I remembered that perfectly. He showed his affection through actions. He made sure you could see how much you meant to him in everything he did. He gave himself unconditionally to those he cared about, always attentive and ready to make their lives easier. For example, I remember one birthday when he gave me a bottle of oil for my car, saying that I would kill myself if I continued to drive with no oil as it was essential for safe driving. The truth is, he wasn't wrong, I had always been very bad at maintaining my car, but at that moment I understood the gesture and his special way of looking after me.

After one of the best breakfasts in my life, or at least that's what it felt like on that clear morning, I sat on the balcony and untied the ribbon holding all the mysterious letters together. I opened the first one slowly and extremely carefully, as if the words could come unstuck from that old paper and fall off.

Dearest Rafaela, my sweet girl,

If you're reading this, it is probably because I'm dead. I don't know when you'll read it, but I hope it helps you. I was originally going to tell you about the trunk, but then I thought it would be better for you to discover it yourself. These letters will tell you everything you've always wanted to know. I hope they're not too late, and I trust that you'll know what to do with it all. You've always been a wise, determined woman, like all the women in our family. Please forgive my bad handwriting. With half my body paralysed from the stroke, my hands are shaky and it's hard for me to write, but what's truly important is the message.

When I was young, things were much worse for women. We lived with the ceiling right above our heads. We couldn't study what we wanted. I, for example, barely learnt to read and write thanks to my love of fashion and all the magazines I would hide away when I decided I wanted to be an independent woman and initiate my own personal revolution. I'd always dreamt of travelling around the world, learning different languages and falling in love hundreds of times like Hollywood actresses did, but at the time society wasn't made for me. A man appeared, I got married and I had your mother. I'll tell you more about them later on.

Now that I face my own mortality, I don't regret making the decisions I did, but I would've liked to have done so much more than I did. So many frustrations were hidden in the depths of this trunk, now a an old and rusty ship, like sad relics I couldn't bear to look at. I discovered my illness the same day that you told me that you'd won a scholarship to study in Jerusalem. I recognised the excited sparkle in your eyes, you were so happy that a torrent of contagious energy flowed through your veins. You had opened the door to that beautiful creature who, like a hungry wolf, emerges free and in search of its own territory. I didn't have the strength or the right to forbid you from living and discovering new horizons. My illness couldn't be the thing that held you back. I never would have forgiven myself! Rafaela, life's a gift with an expiry date, often too short for us to stop and think what actually makes us happy, or is good or correct. We all arrive in this world completely free. However, we are moulded a little at a time by the many hands of our families and the society that surrounds us. Waking up from this sad dream requires bravery. I brought you up to become your own artisan, and that's why I didn't want you to live anchored to a dying woman, having to give up your dreams. Keep on walking along the path of life with an open heart and make sure each and every moment counts.

I love you,
Belly

I read those lines over and over again, stopping on every word, imagining her aged hands gliding on that notebook paper. It made me feel so much closer to her. I pressed that paper against my chest while unexpected tears fell. 'Belly, you'll always be the most beautiful mark that my emotions have imprinted on my soul; each one of your caresses and all your advice remains tattooed on my skin,' I told her, sure that she could hear me. They say we don't stay with our bodies but where we are missed the most, and all my memories were keeping her here. Our connection went far beyond blood and love. I tried to comfort myself by holding onto one of her phrases, *'No one leaves a minute before or a minute after they're supposed to.'*

Now that time has passed, I know I was escaping the fact that Belly was no longer around. I never thought that when I said goodbye to her with that Eskimo kiss, rubbing my nose against hers, that it would be the last. And although there were no certainties, I was overcome by inconsolable fear once I realised that her hidden behind her encouraging words were tear-filled eyes. That day I felt as though she already knew it would be our last one together. One of my favourite songs says *'There were things I'd never do again that I thought were right at the time.'* I think this phrase perfectly expresses what I feel today. When you're young, your energy gives you wings and you get lost in the abyss of dreams, tangled up in your own feelings. It's only later, sometimes too late, when your feet land firmly on the ground, that you delve into the deep, dark caverns of your conscience and realise how short life truly is.

I had barely finished the first letter when I could clearly see that this trip through time was going to shake everything up within me. The smokescreen that had covered our entire family was beginning to dissipate. For the first time, the elephant in the room that nobody seemed to notice was right in front of me. I felt strong enough to face its gaze and to rid myself of the chains that had kept me away from the truth. I needed to know about my origins and why Belly had remained silent for so very long.

As a therapist, I often witnessed the complexity of those grey areas in the lives of families. I encountered some patients who were forbidden from even discussing certain family issues and had no idea why. Others were like sentinels, guarding within them events that inspired shame, pain or guilt that they had not been able to process psychologically. Family secrets and trauma often go hand-in-hand. Whenever you hit a raw nerve with families, it's likely to be rooted in a closely guarded secret. But, what could possibly be Belly's motive? Perhaps her silence was the shield with which she protected herself from her own suffering, avoiding certain information in order to protect me and the pain it would cause. I considered the tremendous emotional exhaustion involved in carrying such a burden, and how negatively this can impact the mental and emotional well-being of, both the people who know the truth and the ones who are oblivious to it. I wasn't the only victim. It's incredible how human beings can live seemingly normal lives inside a pressure cooker, when they actually conceal layers upon layers of suppressed suffering beneath their skin. It was only now that one of Belly's legendary phrases began to make sense. *'Rafaela, life must come first, above everything else.'*

We pretend to go on with our lives, as if sweeping it under the carpet and not talking about it could make it simply go away. But the truth is that the more you run from it, the faster it will catch up with you. Revealing a secret is, itself, healing and has the ability to rewrite history. I decided that I wouldn't read anymore that day. I needed to digest and take stock of everything, drink it in one small sip at a time, and let my mind get some air. I put the letter back in its envelope and placed it beneath the others. I put on a plain white linen dress and a sky-blue panama hat from Belly's collection, in her honour. I went downstairs, ready to make the most of my time, which had taken on a special meaning since coming back to life. I was feeling romantic and mysterious. The sky was blue and clear. The sunlight left a pleasant warm feeling on my skin. I walked carefully, measuring each and every step, my eyes wide open, appreciating how wonderful, simple and miraculous it is to walk, ready to dissolve into my own perception of reality, leaving the hurry and my obligations behind, feeling infinitely fulfilled and grateful to be alive. I walked along the wide avenue where I was able to greet some of my neighbours, who were happy to see me again and took an interest in my health. A few teenagers even asked me for my autograph and had photos taken with me. I felt uncomfortable and surprised at the fact they'd recognised me looking like that outside the ring. I almost signed my real name, but one of the boys called me Iris and that sudden reality check reminded me that it was not actually Rafaela the boys were interested in. I ended my stroll along the lake whose waters cooled a spacious park. It was an indescribable pleasure to be able to observe the living images, natural beauty and charm that I had completely forgotten. It's interesting how things change when you change the way you look at them, or simply when you've gone without them for a while. Those little things that were once insignificant and often went unnoticed become the most important. The feeling of the breeze on my face, a spontaneous smile, some sincere words that bring a tear to your eye, a flower in your hair, the look of those few magical people that walk the earth pretending to be normal but capture you forever once they touch your life. Little things that trigger giant emotions. Why are we here if not to experience these small victories? Like the satisfaction that is felt by the nerve endings of a bear when it manages to grab a salmon out of the water. Powerful, and profoundly healing. Life is full of simple moments that we assume will be there forever, either because they're everyday events, or simply because we have them, and we completely ignore their true value. We mustn't forget that life is fragile and vulnerable; it can take a sudden turn at any time, without warning, taking it all away from us. According to Stephen Covey, *'the main thing is to keep the main thing the main thing'*. I would never box again, but was that the main thing?

Bryan Dyson's inspirational words when leaving his position as the president of Coca Cola were incredibly eye-opening and an invitation to reflect on our own lives. *'Imagine life as a game in which you are juggling some five balls in the air. You name them – work, family, health, friends and spirit – and you're keeping all of these in the air. You will soon understand that work is a rubber ball. If you drop it, it will bounce back. But the other four balls – family, health, friends and spirit – are made of glass. If you drop one of these, they will be irrevocably scuffed, marked, nicked, damaged or even shattered. They will never be the same. You must understand that and strive for balance in your life.'*

I sat on one of the newly painted benches, under the shade of a large old oak tree, and observed a group of four old men playing one of those endless card games. They were occasionally interrupted by coughing, probably from smoking too much, a bad habit they had been unable to quit. Other strollers barely took any notice of them, perhaps thinking that they were the typical old folks who want nothing more from life, living a boring routine existence to which they were resigned. The image of those venerable old men, filled with memories and unforgettable days, somehow validated the urgency to squeeze as much out of life as we can before the game is over.

Yes, life is a fascinating, unique and exciting game. When we're born, the cards are shuffled and dealt randomly depending on your place of birth, your cultural surroundings, your genetics, your personality, your skin colour, your family, your star sign, your ascendant and the moon's position at the exact moment you were born. Life deals us an equal hand in each game. We can't choose the cards we're born with, but we can decide what we do with them. Good players are not always the ones who are dealt the best cards, but ones who play the best possible game with the cards life has given them. The only thing we know for sure is that our moment of glory will come as long as we pay careful attention to our strategy. As the game advances, we receive new cards that can improve or reduce our chances of winning. Only losers and amateurs complain about their cards.

At that point, I felt overwhelmed by the hand that I was holding, particularly because I couldn't understand the new dynamic the game of life was offering me. There are always options, we just have to be creative and daring. We mustn't be afraid to face new challenges because we learn to be brave by taking risks. It's not over until we stop trying. Anyway, we don't really have to take part in the game; we can always just sit back and watch how others enjoy themselves or we can choose to participate. Life is like poker: you never know if you have the winning hand until the last player reveals theirs. I wasn't ready to let the final bell ring without having first played all my remaining cards. I would play until the end in order to resolve the puzzle of my existence.

Conan's words the night before lingered in my memory like fresh morning dew. He said, 'I was wondering the whole time what you'd be like when you woke up. Whether you'd be the same woman or if we'd have to get to know each other all over again, like strangers. You might come back with no memory and I would have to patiently tell you everything we'd been through and that we'd shared together. I went to the hospital every day just to hold your hand and give you hope. I needed the same hope if I was going to survive without you. The doctors told me that being in a coma was like a dreamless sleep, a mysterious state, and that you felt nothing. I would walk around the second-floor hallways looking for specialists to give me more information. The fact that your life was in someone else's hands, beyond my protection, terrified me. I never learnt to pray, but I'd repeat to myself, over and over again, "Chiquilla, if you can hold on, so can I." I was delirious at the thought that we would have months, maybe even years to put all the pieces of your past back together again, or better still, invent new memories to match your fantasies so that our love story could be the way you always wanted it to be.'

I wondered what kind of player Conan would be in a relationship. What would be his strategy when the cards dealt out are all of the same suit, all hearts, the cards of love?

I don't know why, but my brain just couldn't retrieve the memory of my relationships, but for some reason it could access the stories of some of my patients. Thanks to all the excellent teachers I'd had, I learnt how to recognise the profiles of all the different players.

There are some who place their bets blindly, ready to lose it all for love; then there are the cheats, the toxic people who play with marked cards, profiles that resorted to deceit and trickery, and using the good faith and unconditional love of the other players to their advantage. There are players who insist on using flawed strategies over and over again, clinging to losing cards, fascinated by their shine or texture. And we can't overlook the ones who turn the other way if they know another player is cheating, unable to take back the control of their own lives; the emotionally self-destructive ones who bet it all on one hand; the ones who stubbornly remain in the game knowing that they have no hope of winning; the cold calculating players who plan their strategy well before sitting at the table; the ones who learn from defeat; and the ones who complain about their bad luck and blame the dealer when things go wrong. Would Conan be one of those players whose game is above board? Was he keeping a card up his sleeve or was he showing me all of them?

Chapter 8

Crazy Things

I still haven't heard any specialist call what's happening to me by its real name, as if not mentioning it kept them safe. I've read some reports diagnosing it as a depressive and depersonalisation disorder. It's as though you are an external observer of your own life, completely disconnected from your surroundings. Of course, none of those academics or experts had ever studied anything about 'attacks of reality'. My mother never uttered the word 'asylum' in my presence, as if that somehow made it a more inhabitable place. But let's start this story at the beginning. Something happened on my last trip that shook my life, transforming everything I had ever known up until that moment. At first, I couldn't explain it. Who would believe such a story? I ended up creating a protective shell around me in order to survive; I began to suffer from anxiety, particularly in social situations. I found it hard to relate to strangers, and being in the presence of more than three people at once was far too exhausting.

I remember the day it all started. At precisely the magical moment of daybreak, I began to hear an ominous sound, much like a hysterical whale crying. I looked out from the balcony and saw a woodcutter from the city council dressed in a green uniform and wearing a helmet and protective goggles. He was up on a boom lift, and was pruning all the trees along the avenue with a chainsaw, leaving them completely bare. I hadn't been the same since getting back from my trip. I'd started speaking to the trees and establishing a special connection with them, particularly with the giant elm tree with exposed roots that was planted in our garden, to whom I told everything that happened to me. I was no longer indifferent to the troubled existence of the sparrows and lizards that sometimes came into the house. I felt deep inside me as though nature was yelling, as I watched the chainsaw decimate the harmless elm. I wanted to run, scream, protect it. I ran out of the house in my nightgown, desperate, and began hugging all the trees, one by one, as I spoke to them. I felt such freedom, as though I was entering a deeply profound spiritual relationship. The woodcutters called the police when I refused to heed their warnings to leave the area. From then on, I couldn't escape the inquisitive looks and derogatory comments, such as 'what a fruit loop!'; she must have escaped from the loony bin'; and 'she's completely lost her marbles'. I was even nicknamed the 'crazy koala'.

At the beginning, my mother did support me. 'Amelia, of course what they're doing isn't right!' she'd say. 'But what are you going to do? Stop being yourself?'

'No, of course not. I want to be me!' I'd reply, crying uncontrollably.

But, for some reason, being myself had suddenly become something bad. The stigma had won.

Nowadays, we know that hugging a tree is an officially recognised form of natural therapy, part of what is known as balneotherapy, which heals and prevents certain illnesses through the use of natural elements such as water or mud and has been used for centuries. However, in the context of a city and particularly in my nightgown, it was considered a mental illness. My mother encouraged me to see a doctor. But, understandably, nobody believed my story about the Purple Lagoon and everything I'd experienced there. After being hospitalised for three days at the National Institute of Neurology and Neurosurgery, it was determined that I'd suffered a psychotic episode and the recommendation was that my mother should have me committed to a specialist facility until I was stable. That's when I heard the famous trick question, 'How would you like to spend three days at a facility?' You don't go somewhere like that unless the situation is really dire and unless you fulfil one of the following three criteria: you have lost all concept of reality, you pose a risk to others, or you pose a risk to yourself. I knew that I had never been saner in my entire life. They sold it to me like a holiday at one of the best resorts, with an all-inclusive bracelet, where I ended up being put away for more than three decades. Suddenly, I found myself walking down winding hallways and travelling in service lifts. The screams and the sounds of keys locking and unlocking doors was terrifying. 'Please, give us your bag, take off your earrings, your belt, all your accessories… you're far too stylish for this place,' said the nurse who welcomed me. She looked more like one of those evil English governesses who lacked all empathy and were ready to become your tormentor. If you hadn't already lost your mind when you arrived, you were sure to do so here. On the way to the 'torture chamber', I came across two patients wearing matching pyjamas a couple of sizes too big who asked me, 'Are you new?' I said that I was and they replied, 'We're going to Japan to eat sunflower seeds in a Buddhist temple. Want to come?'

The white surroundings were asphyxiating – the perfectly white walls, the dining room tables, the rooms, the psychologist and psychiatrist coats, even the straightjackets I'd occasionally see on one of the 'crazies', the people with whom I shared the enormous, cold building that they referred to as a mental health centre. The users of this service were called many things: ill, unstable, incapable, demented, intellectually disabled and a variety of other more sophisticated terms. In the end, it didn't really matter which category you fell into, we were all treated like dangerous people who had lost their sanity, and locking us up was the logical solution for people who, like me, were devoid of logic. A broad range of mental and emotional worlds coexisted beneath the same roof and, according to society, they represented a danger to ourselves or to others.

It was the second time that week that Daniela had taken all her clothes off in the communal area during our post-dinner TV time, in front of a drug-dazed audience staring at a rose-coloured screen. Despite the strip show, they were like statues, completely unaffected without taking their eyes off the idiot box. At eighteen, she was the youngest of the bunch and belonged to the 'Hearing Voices' group, people who heard voices and manifested auditory hallucinations.

'Amelia, after constantly being attacked by my own voices, and living in fear of being controlled, I decided to accept and even ridicule them. And now, after a lot of hard work, I've finally managed to interrupt that negative thought pattern.' That's what she herself had told me the day before, as we strolled through the neglected garden surrounding the building. However, it seemed that the call to expose herself in a free and natural way had once again prevailed.

If people were to see a naked woman in the street, they might think she was mad, but perhaps their opinion would be different if they knew that she was actually participating in one of the mass nude photos by renowned American photographer Spencer Tunick. Daniela had been labelled a 'schizophrenic', though, in my opinion, this supposed condition was a myth. It was an attempt at explaining and controlling strange or abnormal behaviour, like that of a sheep that was walking in the opposite direction to the rest of the flock. Madness is such a relative term that it is often misused or abused for the benefit of certain entities, such as pharmaceutical companies, and social and religious contexts, all of which open the door to social exclusion, incomprehension, injustice and a lot of suffering. If I talk to God, I'm religious. If he talks back, I'm schizophrenic. And yes, I know how insolent that sounds, but I've met and lived with more 'crazies' than those who consider themselves to be sane. I like to call them 'enlightened geniuses'; some of those extraordinary beings were truly ingenious! There's actually a very thin line between insanity and brilliance. Personally, I never had the pleasure of meeting any of those people who forever changed history, but I wonder how much insanity was behind their brilliant work.

Let's take John Forbes Nash, the American mathematician who received the Nobel Prize for Economics in 1994 and inspired the movie *A Beautiful Mind*. At the age of twenty-nine, he was diagnosed with paranoid schizophrenia. This basically excluded him from society and made him unfit for scientific work for two decades. He began to suffer delusions of grandeur and claimed that the most important figures in the world had reached out to him. After thirty years battling the disorder and 'wasting time' in and out of hospitals, he experienced a significant recovery in the 1980s.

And what about Vicent Willem van Gogh, the Dutch painter and distinguished Post-Impressionist? Despite his tortuous life, he painted nine hundred paintings and drew one thousand six hundred drawings. It is widely known that he cut part of his ear off and even, supposedly, tried to eat paint. He eventually committed suicide. Some authors of Van Gogh biographies, as well as psychiatry experts, claim he suffered from bipolar disorder. Others say it was schizophrenia.

Another of the greats was Ludwig van Beethoven, the German pianist and composer. His contribution to music was monumental, and yet the famous musician had a very tough life as the son of an abusive alcoholic father. One of the most tragic aspects of his life was his deafness. Incredibly, he was able to compose some of his most valued and acclaimed pieces after losing his hearing. His internal struggle is documented in letters to his siblings where he toys with the idea of suicide. Several authors have written that Beethoven most likely also suffered from bipolar disorder.

Another magnificent example was Isaac Newton, a British scientist, physicist, philosopher, inventor, alchemist and mathematician. The man who discovered the law of universal gravitation. Among his other scientific discoveries are his works regarding the nature of light and optics. He was truly a brilliant thinker, even more influential than Einstein himself. Despite his many achievements, Newton suffered from psychotic tendencies and mood swings, and is also believed to have had bipolar disorder. His delirious writings also give credibility to the theory that he was schizophrenic.

And, lastly, Edgar Allan Poe, the American writer, poet, critic and journalist, renowned as one of the universal masters of the short story and considered the inventor of modern detective novels. His letters revealed his battle against suicidal thoughts. Edgar Allan Poe himself may have observed a correlation between creativity and mental illness in himself. He once wrote:

> Men have called me mad; but the question is not settled whether madness is or is not the loftiest intelligence – whether much that is glorious – whether all that is profound – does not spring from disease of thought – from moods of mind exalted at the expense of the general intellect. They who dream by day are cognizant of many things which escape those who only dream by night.

I had just turned twenty and had a life growing inside of me. I immediately connected with Daniela and we became good friends. We shared everything you can share in a mental asylum. I fondly remember all those times we spent together. I would give her really extravagant hairdos, she would sneak over to my room to borrow my clothes and I would make her up like a true catwalk model. She always said I shook things up at the asylum, that I made everything more colourful and whimsical with my originality, and that she admired my strength and my positive attitude to life, even when surrounded by so much negativity as we were in that place. But there were few moments of joy to be had in that place. I never witnessed the use of water jets to calm the patients, insulin shock therapies or terrifying lobotomies, but there was an enormous amount of anguish, fear and suffering in that prison. If hell exists, I'm sure that place was in it. After over thirty years locked up in that institution, between individual and group therapy sessions, seeing specialists who would constantly change my medication and indiscriminately adjust the doses, I was considered one of the privileged few. I was allowed to take part in recreational activities, and even go out for walks for a few hours in the open and green space surrounding the asylum grounds, conveying the illusion of freedom. The truth is that I was just as scared to go out as I was when I went in. I understood far too late for my future life that I would never be allowed to rise from the ashes, and that they would not rest until I told them what they wanted to hear.

I would get up at eight o'clock. My diet consisted mainly of colourful pills, which we all took with no complaints. I resisted them, at first. I still remember the taste of the nurse's latex glove as she put her finger in my mouth to make sure I had swallowed them and how nauseous that made me feel. I later developed some rather sophisticated techniques that I learnt from some of the veterans to avoid taking them. I had seen how psychoactive drugs paralysed other patients' nerve functions to the point they could no longer fend for themselves. We drew mandalas and played dominoes. It was utterly boring. I suggested we create a rap group so we could express ourselves and have fun in that concentration camp, where people were being annihilated in the most legal way possible. It was a physical and emotional abattoir, a reflection of the violence of our time. Daniela thought to call it 'Crazy Pride' and each of us contributed our ideas. The rap was titled 'Careful with Outsiders' and began with 'they call me mad, crazy, demented, loopy, loony, lunatic, nuts, disturbed, perturbed, just because I live on the other side...'

'Amelia, the first thing you have to do is accept that you have a mental illness,' said the latest psychiatrist that had been assigned to me. I looked at him defiantly. He was nothing more than another white coat with hands and feet. I wasn't ready to let another 'nobody' walk all over my mind with his dirty feet.

'How do you feel today?' he continued.

'I feel invisible; I live concealed, in hiding, silenced, denied, kept away, locked up, covered. I don't exist because I'm invisible.'

'Why do you think you're here?'

'Haven't you read my medical history?

'No, I haven't. I don't really trust what other people think, I prefer to hear the original version.'

For the first time, I thought I saw genuine interest in his answer, which caught my attention. He had ventured away from protocol and caught my attention. The Thursday therapy sessions would typically result in a series of silences and blank faces. I expected another stranger to look at me over his glasses, which would slide towards the tip of his nose, and systematically take notes while attempting to delve into my childhood traumas.

'Oops! How clumsy of me,' he said, accidentally dropping a pile of messy reports and a golden fountain pen on the floor. I wondered if that was one of those infallible techniques to appear approachable and make the patients relax, putting aside their fears and anxieties so that they open up and talk about their problems. Appearing vulnerable always brings people closer and helps to establish trust.

'I know you're not here to be my friend, so don't bother trying to act normal.'

He laughed and said, 'Normal? Normal is so boring. Wouldn't you like to get out of here?'

Again, it sounded like a trick question, but I was willing to play along.

'Yes, of course. Could you sign my discharge papers today?' I replied, ironically.

'First I need you to tell me your story. I'd hate to miss out on something so exciting.'

'Do you really want to hear something exciting? Very well. When is your birthday?'

'Excuse me?' he asked, taken aback.

'What's your date of your birth?'

'The nineteenth of March.'

'So, you probably belong to the constellation of Pisces. Do you believe in astrology and in how things like planetary alignments can affect our personalities?'

'Actually, I'm more scientific. I believe in things that have been empirically proven.'

'Naturally,' I said without letting him finish. 'Science is dominated by reason. But who says that something has to be scientific in order to be true? Could astrology be an occult science only for the eyes and knowledge of those who don't wish to know? Have you ever heard of hermetic wisdom?'

'What is it about?' He asked, intrigued, sitting back in his black leather chair.

'Both the universe and human beings are governed by the seven hermetic laws. These principles remain secret for the great majority, and only few individuals are prepared for the truth or to recognise it when it is presented to them. For many, something that is hidden is considered negative, but that's not true. It's only one perspective. One of the laws, the law of correspondence, says that what is below is like what is above, and what is above is like what is below, thus consuming the miracle of Unity. In other words, the entire macrocosm is repeated in the microcosm. If you're religious, this may ring a bell in the Lord's Prayer that says "On Earth as it is in Heaven". The law of correspondence acts like a mirror in the universe; it's the foundation of astrology as it explains why the alignment of planets at the moment of our birth symbolically represents our vital energy. As it is above, so it is below. Likewise, planetary transits at a particular time and their relationship to our birth chart symbolise the internal changes we experiment at a particular moment in time.'

The 'white coat' tapped his pen on the notepad a couple of times and, without taking his eyes off mine, asked, 'So, according to your theory, we all come to this world predestined, right?'

'The truth is that there's a synchronicity or coincidence between the planets and ourselves, and there's also a sacred, esoteric and enormously complex yet fundamentally simple language, known as Astrology, that acts as a translator between what exists and what we're able to understand.'

'As far as I know, we've never locked up astrologists or their followers for their ideologies. We wouldn't have enough space!' he continued in good humour, with a friendly smile.

'You scientists are intellectuals, but you're not truly intelligent because you live in a constant state of rigid scepticism. You've lost your creative aspect and you defend an atheism that completely annuls the spiritual mind. You think the universe exists purely by accident. You are submissive, naive and blind, and you can't see beyond what you can prove with your own limited tools. Isn't the fact that that the lunar phases affect crop quality and production, and can stimulate or delay germination scientific? It's scientifically proven that the different lunar phases affect plant sap and bird migration, and even heal some illnesses afflicting humans. The power of attraction the moon exerts over water and the tides make it easy to understand how it can also have similar effects on human beings, bearing in mind that our bodies are seventy per cent water.

'In your position, you should know about the great many accounts regarding the increase of violent crimes, suicides, hospital emergency admissions and cases of anxiety and depression during a full moon. That doesn't even include the studies on how the moon affected people suffering from psychiatric disorders before electricity was invented.'

'Tell me, Amelia, what does astrology have to you with your presence in this psychiatric facility for more than three decades?'

'Creation is governed by an infinite plan and nothing happens by accident. Humans also fall into that plan. The stars are a fundamental part of that project initiated thousands of years ago by the guardians of light, masters who protect the supreme wisdom of the cosmos.'

'Please, continue, I want to understand you.'

'Really? And what if you can't understand me?'

I realised at this stage that I was becoming far too familiar with him. This 'white coat' had managed to bring us closer. After all, given his age, he could easily be my son.

'Give me a chance. And yourself.' He challenged me, looking at me with his dark green eyes and long, giraffe-like eyelashes.

'OK, but in your attempt to understand what I'm going to tell you, you must make a conscious effort to open your mind. It's important for us all to have a healthy dose of scepticism, but at the same time, we must be willing to retain an idea in our mind, without immediately accepting or rejecting it. I'm not looking for you to have blind faith in what I tell you, but I'd like you to keep a balance between both states, otherwise you'll be very disappointed by what you hear. I've learnt that the heads of most people are awareness-control mechanisms. I was actually one of those people for a long time.'

'Very well, Amelia. Go ahead.'

His unusual pronunciation, which was only occasionally perceptible, added to the pleasure he clearly got from sipping his *maté* tea, led me to believe he was Argentinian. The aromatic infusion of bitter green herbs filled a mango-coloured cup shaped like a pumpkin that appeared to be glued to his hand. I then recalled our neighbour Marcelo, with whom my father would have endless conversations that inevitably ended in ridiculous arguments. He was an Argentinian widower who, according to my father, worked as a snake oil salesman and was the kind of person who knows nothing yet understands everything.

'Amelia, never trust an Argentinian. No matter how entertaining they can be, they're the biggest liars, cheats and scoundrels you'll ever come across,' my father would warn me after every encounter with Marcelo, who always had the last word. My father told him he spoke too much and always pretended to know everything. He always had to have an answer, even when he didn't understand the question. My father would often stop talking altogether, and he would just go on, speaking alone like a preacher in the desert, even though no one was listening to him. However, this 'white coat' didn't give the impression of being an enemy of silence, or of being one of those lying charlatans who had an opinion about everyone and everything. In fact, he appeared to feel quite at ease in the art of reflection.

He reclined his seat, as if preparing himself to hear one of those ghost stories that grandparents tell their grandchildren before bedtime.

I stood up and walked towards the large window facing the garden. Contemplating Mother Nature's varying tones relaxed me. I sat on the windowsill, looking outwards, and embarked on a voyage to my past once again. A blind journey guided by instinct.

'I've always been fascinated by travelling. When I was a little girl, I already knew all the flags of the world and I loved playing with atlases and reading about different countries. I guess the love of adventure flowed through my veins. My mother travelled a lot for work, and I always had a thousand questions for her when she returned. I loved hearing her accounts and seeing all the photos of her trips. I felt a curiosity to come into contact with different cultures and different people. But who would've thought that one day I'd travel to a place that's not on any map, and that I'd meet creatures I could never have imagined?'

'Where exactly are you referring to, Amelia?' he interrupted discretely. The psychiatrist's name, Dr Fred Martínez, was impeccably embroidered onto his top left pocket, but to me he was always 'white coat'.

'Its name is Purple Lagoon – a place so far from anything we know, and at the same time so near, that once you've been there you can never look at life the same again. First, it leaves you speechless, but then it turns you in a teller of incredible stories.'

'Wow! It sounds amazing. Do you mean the stories that brought you to this facility, and that have kept you here for so long?'

'It appears so,' I said firmly, abandoning the image of the garden and holding his gaze.

'The root of my problem has always been the same: people's inability to accept what seems natural to others, and our irresistible tendency to express opinions that no one wants to hear, all of which has culminated in recent times. Indiscreet questions and the revelation of truth have both always been tremendously unpopular, and a dangerous and destabilising weapon for a society as ignorant as ours. We are educated, but receive no wisdom.'

'I understand. And how did you get there?'

'It just happened. The last thing I remember was clambering over a fallen tree. Suddenly, I felt like I was being sucked in through a tunnel at lightning speed. In a matter of seconds, at least that was my impression, I felt like I'd travelled billions of kilometres at the speed of light. I found myself in one of those scenes that you only associate with fantasy films, like *Avatar*. The first thing we saw was an endless lagoon surrounded by lush nature. The light, the smells, the colours… There are no words to describe any of it. I could feel it all so intensely as though it was a part of me. I was so overwhelmed by everything I was experiencing that I didn't stop to think.'

'Wait a second, did you say "the first thing we saw"? Was someone else with you?' enquired the 'white coat' with an enlightened face, as if he'd made a huge discovery.

'Oh yes, of course, my dog Vodka was with me.'

I couldn't avoid tearing up at the recollection of my faithful friend, whom that was not allowed to come to this place with me. I requested he be allowed to live with me as a therapy animal, but the director cruelly denied it, horrified at the thought of his hospital smelling like dog. He died ten months after I arrived. The Argentinian empathised with my pain, offering me the box of tissues that was ever-present in this office for those waterworks moments.

'This might sound strange but, ever since we returned from that place, I noticed a change in him. His look became so sweet, clean and piercing that he transmitted an indescribable feeling of peace. I felt as if Vodka conveyed love with his eyes. I'm sure his soul was also changed by the experience. I'd like to think that he's with Elsu right now, and that their spirits soar the skies together like falcons.'

Who's Elsu? A family member you've also lost recently?'

'No,' I smiled fondly. 'Elsu will never die. He's my love, my daughter's father, a being of light and a guardian of the Elove Galaxy.'

Although he tried to hide it, he raised his well-shaped eyebrows into a confused expression that completely transformed his face. I guess the story had already completely surpassed him and his logical, sensible mind was now taking control.

Despite this fact, he asked a new series of questions, which I figured was to determine just how crazy I was. I wasn't sure whether to be happy or concerned.

'What would you think if someone told you what you've just told me?'

'I'd believe them, obviously, because I've also been there.' I joked emphatically.

'You say you have a daughter. How come she doesn't visit you? Is she aware of your situation?'

'How do you know she doesn't visit me?'

'I took the liberty of looking at the visit register and, since you've been here, only your mother's name appears. There are also a couple of names written in that book. Two people have come regularly to check on you.'

'Two names, you say? I don't remember anyone else besides my mother setting foot in this hellhole to check on me. I assure you, I'd remember.'

'Well, the notes clearly reflect the visits made to room twelve, on the eighth floor. I personally checked and you've never changed rooms, so there's no mistake.'

'I guarantee you, it's a huge mistake.'

Not even my emphatic response made him doubt in the slightest. It was the testimony of a brainless woman against the diligence and professionalism of an expert administration team, so that battle was lost before it even began. I won't deny that it was an expected surprise.

Between those damp, peeling walls, the constant barrage of the same questions over and over again pierced through the building's paper-thin walls. It didn't matter what answer you gave, it had already been marked down as crazy before you even uttered it.

The director, who had run the asylum for the past thirty-five years and was better known among the residents and even by the employees as the 'Unholy Father' for his utter lack of mercy, boasted he had been chosen by God, whom he always had on the tip of his tongue like a stamp. Dressed in a white clerical collar and black robes, which he paraded around taking tiny symmetrical steps like a sparrow, he made sure absolutely nothing moved in the San Patricio Mental Health Centre without his permission. Much like Pontius Pilate, however, he often washed his hands of the place. Everybody feared him, and he had no trouble kicking anyone who contradicted him out of his kingdom of terror. If any of his flock dared to complain about how they were being treated and asked for mercy, his reply was always the same, 'My child, going mad isn't a luxury many people can afford, so enjoy this privilege.' Yes, he also handed out slaps regularly, the kind that leave a bitter taste in your mouth and the outline of his fingers on your face. In truth, the hood does not make the monk, and not everyone is worthy of the position, but it gives him the power to play with the lives of others and condemning their souls to the deepest darkness without punishment. At first, I tried to pick up 'God's red telephone', but God never picked up.

San Patricio was run by a Catholic religious congregation that was known for secretly coming to the aid of the needy. It was the best my mother could afford at a time when she was going through economic hardships. As a widow with a granddaughter to raise, she had to stop travelling to promote her hat and accessory collections, which led her to experience some tough times. However, she always held her head high despite all the gossip and the snubs of others who had previously been considered friends and neighbours, and defended me with lion-like fervour. She didn't like anyone knowing her business. As she used to say, *'Amelia, even if the house is on fire, one must never see the smoke from the outside.'* She confessed on more than one occasion that she would have liked me to be closer to God, but I was never able to overcome the infinite distance between us. To be honest, it wasn't that God, from whom I'd always been orphaned, that had kept me going all that time. Instead, it was the love that had grown inside my heart during my adventure to the Purple Lagoon, and my dream of getting my daughter back.

I felt like the survivor of a collective shipwreck who was awake and grateful to be alive. Maybe it was maturity, all the years that had passed years, or maybe even resignation, but one day I simply discovered that some conversations were just no longer worth having. Instead, I opted for silence and a smile which, though quiet, in no way admitted defeat. I finally understood that there's no point providing any explanations to someone who can't read the look in your eye.

The door to trust that had slammed shut suddenly opened again with the Argentinian's unexpected question, which brought me back to the game at hand.

'And what's your destiny, Amelia?'

It could have either taken an entire lifetime to answer that question, or simply use the words of Jorge Luis Borges, *'Any life, however long and complicated it may be, actually consists of a single moment, the moment when a man knows forever more who he is'.*

'Do you know who you are?' I asked, playing another card.

'Well, I could tell you that I am a psychiatrist working at San Patricio, a single father to an autistic son, a fan of crime novels and a cricket buff. Yes, that would describe me pretty accurately,' he answered, nodding his head like those car toys with the springy necks.

I knew that the code of practice didn't allow psychiatrists to reveal information and feelings to patients. That figure must be a blank canvas, a neutral person onto whom patients can project their unconscious conflicts, free of any countertransference. But, from the beginning of our conversation, the 'white coat' had made it clear he wasn't like other psychiatrists. We were so starved of human and approachable figures in that place that to smell the empathy he projected was similar to the pleasure you got from an orgasm, or from an endless standing ovation.

I imagine he saw the disappointment reflected in my eyes when he asked, 'Were you expecting a different answer?'

'I expected something along the lines of, "Who am I? That's the only question that can heal the human being. In our search to find ourselves, we often incorrectly recalibrate our compass. Most people identify with their jobs, with their role within their families, their hobbies, distancing themselves from the true essence of their being. To know oneself is not only the most difficult thing to do, it is also the most uncomfortable. This challenge can last an entire lifetime, which is why many choose to float on the water's surface instead of diving in the immensity of the ocean and into the true essence of themselves."'

'What you say is very coherent, Amelia. I'm sorry if my simplicity disappointed you. How did you reach that level of consciousness? Did you study philosophy or were those thoughts instilled in your as a child?'

'Nothing like that. I, like you, also lived a numb life, hooked onto the giant pendulum of the superfluous for a very long time, until the extraordinary creatures of the Purple Lagoon removed my blindfold.'

He observed me, perplexed and curious, pointing his chin at me.

'And what did those creatures teach you?'

'Each and every one of them knows their place in the cosmos. They don't ask themselves who they are because, since birth, they've made it their business to understand their inner map, so there's no possibility of getting lost or hesitating. Just as a tiger knows it's a tiger, and a horse knows it's a horse, and they act accordingly. The tiger doesn't ask itself if it's a rat, and the rat doesn't wonder if it's, in fact, a bat. The creatures that live there spend time with themselves, proud of who they are and honoured to fulfil their mission.'

Suddenly, the air was sucked out of the room and I held my breath as the Unholy Father appeared with no warning. I felt the beat of his hardened heart and the putrid stench of his tyranny filling the space. The years had only nourished the seed of evil that lived within his soul. He slid his bony white fingers with unkempt nails from this forehead to his chest, and then from shoulder to shoulder, making the sign of the cross before the wooden crucified Christ that hung on the room's main wall.

'Dr Fred, I think there's been a misunderstanding. The case of Amelia López Aguilar will not be one of your responsibilities here, at San Patricio.'

'I'm sorry, I don't understand. Amelia's on the list of patients for the psychiatrist I'm replacing,' said the 'white coat', confused.

'I repeat, Dr Fred, that this case has been assigned to another psychiatrist. I'm sorry about the confusion and that you've wasted your time listening to Amelia's delusions. Please, give me her reports and continue with the other patients,' he demanded, holding out his hand as he waited for his order to be executed.

'Father, if you don't mind, I'd like to continue working with Amelia,' he insisted, not giving up, unaware of the other speaker's dark personality.

The priest clenched his fists unconsciously, trying to control his outrage at the doctor's lack of submission.

'Dr Fred, I repeat: Amelia is already in good hands. Thank you very much for your interest. Amelia, you can go back to your routine,' he ordered me authoritatively, as he pointed towards the door with a burning look that could have melted the entire North Pole.

Those words were a direct missile aimed at the newcomer, which forever opened Pandora's box.

Chapter 9

Love Without Fear

S ometime we live 'onion stories' – ones that make you cry the more
layers you peel away.

I awoke that morning with the intense, very real, feeling that I'd
met my knight in shining armour, my soul mate, my other half. I was
covered in a heavy, thick and gloopy layer of happiness, like the cough
syrup I was given as a child. And there was no doubt whatsoever that
I was the most loved woman on Earth. This wonderful man couldn't
stop telling me how much he loved me, and even that he was willing to
leave his country and his family to spend the rest of his life with me.
Jared ticked all the boxes on my 'Perfect Man' list. I mean, he fitted
me better than my favourite t-shirt.

I was experiencing that feeling of longing to form a large family,
convinced that it would fulfil me. A false assumption, as it turns out,
but one that the mirage of my dream partner wouldn't let me see.

I remember writing that list with Helena, my best friend from high
school, when I was barely fifteen years old. My sidekick had the most
beautiful eyes I'd ever seen. I knew they were light, but they looked
like two drops of silvered glass. I don't even know whether they had a
colour or were simply a reflection. Her honey blonde hair was always
held up messily above her head, like a bird's nest.

'What will he be like?' she would ask, as we swung on the swings
at the top of the vineyard, where we'd go after class. That doorway to

the sky hung down from ropes fastened to the branches of a centenary holm oak. We pointed towards the endless horizon with our knee-high socks printed with innocent pictures. I licked a strawberry and pistachio ice-cream, letting not only my changing adolescent body fly on that hanging wooden board but also my candid imagination.

'He has to be very special, a spiritual man who, although he lives on Earth, is not from this world,' I answered confidently, closing my eyes with every swing, my warm tongue licking the melting ice-cream that slid down my virgin lips that had never been kissed.

'And how will you recognise him, Rafaela?' asked my confidant, raising her voice as she pushed herself, higher as if wanting to touch the sunset with her fingertips.

'He'll be more wise than intellectual. Sensitive and romantic. With a great sense of humour, and he'll laugh like a child at my terrible jokes and my clumsiness. He'll know how to listen in silence and admire the divinity of nature. A man that, rather than go to all the museums, is amazed looking up at the stars, and who stops to watch a sunset as though it were the first. He won't need a crowd, because his body and mine will make up the entire universe.'

'You'll have to go to Tibet or Mars to find him! You'll never find all those qualities in one man!' she exclaimed, teasingly.

'As Belly always says, "*What is truly yours can be for nobody else.*" I'm convinced he'll be looking for me too.'

'Well, I want the love of my life to be exactly like my dad,' said Helena proudly.

'Tell me, what's your father like, Helena? Is he very handsome?'

'He sure is,' she said. 'I hope my children have his genes one day. My father has always been the Adonis in my family. You know, the Greek god who was so attractive even the goddess Aphrodite couldn't resist him.'

'Wow, in that case I'm not surprised. And what's he like with your mother?'

That question carried special meaning for me as I lacked that particular reference. I'd never heard the story of my parents and never even saw them together. I wanted to know what it was like to experience the love and support of your parents in the same house. I never even witnessed my grandparents' love story. I sometimes imagined them to be idyllic relationships. Companions and travel mates. Though I'm aware that a perfect relationship isn't when two perfect people meet each other but when two imperfect people learn to love each other's differences.

Helena continued to sweeten her story, drizzling her descriptions like honey.

'My mum says he kisses better than anyone. When she's feeling stressed or is about to go off the rails, he can stop her mind from spiralling. He knows exactly what her tastes are and what her favourite food is. Sometimes, he surprises her with her favourite dish when she gets home tired from work, unable to lift a finger. If they have anything in common, it's that they would both kill for a sweet. My mum always takes one of his liquor chocolates, the ones he keeps in one of the glass jars in his office, guarding them like jewels. Even so, he continues to leave them in the same place so she can take them, and he pretends not to notice. He looks at her lovingly when he sees her coming out of his office with chocolate on her lips, while she only manages to mumble the occasional compliment about his ties.'

Finding our 'perfect man' was part of our bucket list, which we eventually put together, swing after swing, one ice-cream at a time, over the space of two years, until one day Helena moved away to Mexico with her family and we lost contact. I wonder how many things she's ticked off her list by now, and if she walks hand-in-hand with little Adonises who speak with Mexican accents.

At the time, we felt no giddiness or fear in our recklessly high flights. Those swings were symbols of freedom and happiness. We called it the 'love is in the air' moment because our flights became mixed with two fifteen-year-olds' dreams of love.

I didn't feel giddy either at that particular moment, when everything was about extraordinary views and fun. Jared became the water that quenched my thirst for adventure in Jerusalem, an exotic place in my eyes. It was a supernatural love that went beyond the physical or the spiritual. I would have loved to tell Helena that I'd found that wonderful being that I had so often described. However, Belly taught me that we must never lose significant people with insignificant lies.

But let's not get side-tracked. At the beginning, I was in a permanent state of excitement that was being constructed naturally by my mind like a feat of psychological engineering and had taken over my heart – that poor, neglected being that constantly whispers the truth, despite the fact we ignore it most of the time. If only listening to our hearts became a compulsory subject at school, perhaps there wouldn't be so many unhappy people in the world.

Jared had taken it upon himself to build a love bubble, a 'Wonderland', which ended up popping in my face when it turned out to be a real house of horror. We lived like a normal couple of university students in love for the first few months. I would work on my thesis until two in the afternoon, then I'd go back to our tiny apartment and eat something light, do a bit of tidying, run errands, or simply keep myself busy with one activity or another until Jared finished his classes and work at the university cafeteria. Afterwards, we still had a couple of hours to go out, make love, or do whatever we wanted.

It was almost twenty to seven in the afternoon when Jared called me and invited me to dinner at a brand-new restaurant in the city centre that had apparently become a big hit and the new place to be. It was popular among tourists and locals alike. It offered fusion cooking and good cocktails, music and a lively atmosphere at night. The project was linked to several international celebrities and was so Instagrammable that no one could resist a good photo op. I'd even seen a few posts on my own Instagram advertising the Polisón, as the hugely famous place was called. It was described as one of those places you absolutely must go to if you want to have a truly unforgettable night. And, unforgettable it was!

The truth is I wasn't planning on going out that night. I had my period and, like many women all over the planet, I was at the mercy of my hormones every twenty-eight days – those same hormones that take over, control you, and push you to your physical and emotional limits. I felt terrible, low in mood and energy, completely overcome by apathy and exhaustion. I would have given anything to be one of the lucky ones who go through it and barely even notice, but in my case, it was a painful experience. As if that wasn't enough, add my deformed body to the mix. The hormones had already begun to do their thing and my bloated abdomen looked like that of a toad, my breasts looked like melons and my eyes were more sunken than the Titanic. It's at those moments when you wonder, 'Why didn't he ask me out last week, when I felt fabulous and sexy, and ready to take on the world?' No, of course it had to be today, when the world was ready to eat me alive. I looked in the antique mirror with its carved and gilded frame that hung in the entry, and I was presented with a horrific image of an ugly, dishevelled woman, utterly incapable of setting foot outside.

'C'mon Rafaela, we'll have a great time!' said Jared's enthusiastic voice over the phone, warning me that the Polisón was usually booked solid and that I shouldn't be late.

I bit the bullet and put into action my plan for success, which was useful for those times when your body isn't cooperating and you need your mental strength to take control of the situation and employ any tool necessary to make you feel better, cheer you up and motivate your senses. Better than anyone, I understood how important the psychological aspect was, and how necessary it was to rid the mind of pessimistic thoughts, so I cast my mind back to days when I felt at my best, like a queen, letting those feelings wash over me. Why couldn't I hold my head high when, after all, being beautiful was simply a matter of attitude? That was already a good start.

I've never been able to stand those tedious nosy questions, like 'You don't look too good; what's wrong? Are you sick? Did you have a bad night? Have you been crying?'

A quick, traditional shower wouldn't do on this occasion. I had to pamper my skin, so I began my ritual with a hot scented bubble bath, followed by a massage using a herbal oil that brought me back to life. I bid farewell to my deathly face and applied night-appropriate makeup using intense colours, drawing attention to my plump, sensual lips. I then headed for the wardrobe. After creating a massive pile with clothes I didn't even know I owned on my bed, I decided to go with my tried and true winning look: a short asymmetrical electric blue satin dress with an oriental vibe, spaghetti straps and an open back. It looked like it had been designed especially for me and never failed to have the 'wow factor'. At times like this, improvising is never a good idea.

As I underwent this transformation, I turned up the volume on one of my favourite songs, 'Cry to Me', by Solomon Burke, which my body could never resist. Broom in hand, I writhed around like a lizard in the sexiest, most outrageous poses we strike when nobody is looking, in front of the mirror that had once again become my friend. I stood tall in my black ankle boots, which enhanced my long legs – one of my best features – and had an immediate effect on my self-esteem. I concluded this ceremony with an irreverent perfume that combined all the deliciousness of peach, sandalwood, orange blossom, coffee, cashmere and a hint of liquorice. This exquisite perfume was one I only used for special occasions as it elevated the attitude of anyone under its influence, capturing the senses even in the most crowded settings. I bought it at a large and exclusive department store, when the advertising caught my attention: 'For enigmatic and determined women, who refuse to follow the rules.' I immediately identified with that. Since then, it has continued to leave an intoxicating trail in my wake, announcing my arrival and extending my departure, giving me a lingering presence wherever I go. The final touch was a white jacket with feather detailing that added style and night-time glamour to my daring outfit. I was ready to rule the dancefloor!

It wasn't hard to find the restaurant, I just followed the multitude of young people who came together from all the tiny winding streets to join the same procession, exuding excitement. Eventually, we all ended up in front of a lively garden that welcomed guests by gently caressing them with a sea of veils and crystals hanging all around. The place was completely packed and a resounding success. I felt my phone vibrate inside my minuscule handbag, 'We're inside, sitting just behind the bar, in front of the dancefloor,' said the message below the name 'nutty philosopher', which is how I had registered Jared's number on my contact list. Fantastic! We had managed to avoid that infinite queue, now I just had to work my way through the crowd and enjoy the evening. At the time, I didn't notice the plurality of that message, 'we're inside'. It was only when my radar zeroed in on Jared's unmistakable outline that I noticed three other people sitting at the table. I thought it was going to be a romantic evening, just the two of us. My heart fell. I walked ahead confidently, feeling sure of myself, showered by compliments from some European-looking guys. I felt utterly glamorous as I neared my love. Jared was so engrossed in conversation with his three companions that he barely noticed my arrival. I identified his brother, Esther's husband, but I'd never seen the other two men, undoubtedly also Jewish, one of whom was very dark-skinned and had an afro.

'I'm here! I thought I wasn't going to make it!' I announced, smiling broadly, as I casually removed my jacket and my bag, placing them on the backrest of the only empty chair. I felt like the entire scene had frozen when I leaned over affectionately to kiss Jared. He pulled away, nervously, offering me his cheek instead, eyeing me as if I were a ghost. He cleared his throat and introduced his entourage.

'Rafaela, I'd like to introduce you to David and Leiz, they're friends of my brother's who are on holiday in Jerusalem for a couple of days. I thought it would be a nice idea to ask them to have dinner with us.'

'Yes, of course,' I said as I looked at them, trying to hide my discomfort.

His brother was glaring at me, daggers in his eyes.

'How are Esther and the kids?' I asked, trying to soften the situation, which was feeling increasingly tense. His only reply was, 'At home, where they should be.' Although his words were clearly aimed at me, I decided not to take them personally in order to prevent the situation from boiling over. It was already hot enough with all the lights, candles and steaming plates balancing on stressed waiters' arms, feeding dozens of hungry diners like chickens in a farm. Jared didn't say a single nice thing, nor did he make any affectionate gestures towards me all night. I'm not the type of woman who needs my partner's constant attention to feel validated, but his radical change in attitude made me feel completely out of place. He felt like a total stranger. I tried to participate in their boring, mundane conversation about the power of banking and its political implications, but they wouldn't let me in. Leiz was the only one who occasionally let me in, like maybe he empathised with me a little and even thought I was quite pleasant. I'd go as far as to say that he was as bored as I was, which is why he asked me to dance when the first song played.

There are certain people that have the gift of lifting your spirits anywhere, anytime – people who exude energy and good vibes and, as a result, always become the life of the party. Any reason is good enough to celebrate, have a dance and start a conga line, without giving it a second thought. Their personality and sense of fun is as contagious, if not more so, than their magnificent laugh. Well, it turns out that Leiz was one of those people, so I immediately accepted his invitation, much to the surprise of my rather flat significant other.

The young Jew, son of a Cuban father, was a very pleasant and fun guy who happened to also be exceptional on the dancefloor. I imagine that the fact he had grown up and studied as a professional dancer in Paris had given him a broader and more relaxed view of the world and the opposite sex. As we danced, he admitted that there were people in certain religious groups, even within his own community, who attacked this type of art and who didn't allow him to dance in public, unless it was a traditional Jewish dance. Despite this, he never gave in to the pressures to quit dancing because all he really wanted was to fly on the wings of music and live life to the fullest. He was eager to break the stereotype that ballet dancers had to be blonde and white. Now, he travelled the world as a principal dancer in the Houston Ballet, playing the role of Romeo in *Romeo and Juliet*, a role that had only ever been reserved for white dancers. His story moved me and I was thrilled to be able to share that moment with such a special person, someone brave enough to break moulds. Jared appeared suddenly, grabbed me forcefully by the arm, and took me aside.

He said, 'Rafaela, you're shaking the hornets' nest and this won't end well.'

'What are you saying? You've ignored me since I got here, and now you drag me away from the dancefloor to tell me I'm shaking the hornets' nest?'

'You're acting like a floozy, with that slutty dress, carrying on and provoking my friends. How do you think that makes me look? Do you want me to be a laughing stock? Have you no shame?'

He shouted at me as though he were completely possessed. His irrational act made me run out of the hornets' nest altogether. A bee that's busy collecting nectar rarely stings, except when it's frightened or stepped on. I was humiliated and stepped on by the person who supposedly loved me the most, and I rebelled. When a bee feels threatened or is warned by the scent of attack pheromones, it reacts aggressively and stings.

'Maybe your inferiority complex doesn't let you see the woman standing right in front of you, so you have to follow your backward flock, surrounded by nunnish women, in order to feel more like a man.'

Then, full of rage, he pushed me hard and I slipped and fell near the bathroom door, hitting my forehead on one of the marble columns that decorated the restaurant, to the shock of people wrapped in laughter and alcohol who witnessed the incident. Jared freaked out and tried to help me up. I didn't let him. I headed straight for the table, picked up my things and went back to the apartment without a word, completely petrified and in disbelief at what had happened, my emotions spiralling out of control.

The worker bee's sting is covered in bristles and, when it buries itself in its victim's skin, it breaks away from their abdomen, causing their death a few moments later. However, the queen bee's sting has no bristles. She can sting over and over again without dying. My days as a crownless monarch had begun.

Jared arrived thirty minutes later. I guess it was enough time for him to explain what happened to his guests and prepare his speech. I was in the bathroom, trying to wipe away the black, wet tracks my mascara had left on my face, courtesy of my tears. He approached me from behind, wrapping his arms around my waist and resting his head on my shoulder. He kissed me tenderly on the bump that had appeared on my forehead, and gently mumbled into my ear.

'I behaved like an idiot. I'm so sorry. Forgive me, my love.'

My cold body was still shaking from within the emotional bunker I had built for myself as protection. His eyes and his burning body crushed me like a steamroller. I went silent, unable to react. Jared was reassured by my silence.

'I know what happened today was horrible, but it's only because I love you so much, I want to protect you so nothing happens to you. You put me in a very delicate situation, I didn't know how to react.'

He slid his tongue along my nape, working his way down my back, as I tried desperately not to lose control of myself. I wanted to believe his words and forget that painful episode so badly.

His hands climbed up to the tip of my breasts, as I tried to defend myself with feigned indifference.

'I'll take care of you, Rafaela. I know you only have me.'

Those words made me feel fragile and vulnerable, like a newborn. Up until that moment, I had never felt so alone. Was it really true that he was all I had? The air was filled with his intentions and the other half of me, the one that refused to reason with him. All of a sudden, a summer storm broke and unruly breeze blew through the window – a promise of rain to come. I felt as if the first lightning strike had torn right through me, my body now in flames, waiting to be put out by Jared. Trying hard to push away those erotic thoughts, I concentrated on what I was doing, clutching the cotton pad to my face.

'You're the most special person I've ever met. The things I like most about me, are the ones I've learnt from you,' he whispered, and I came undone.

I replied 'I love you' without sound. I felt myself tense up, excitement pulsing through our bodies, like crackling metal that has been heated up too quickly.

'Please, don't ever do anything like that to me again,' he repeated, placing the blame on me, making me doubt what had really happed, so much so that I eventually apologised.

I loved him with all my being. I became a white flag, fluttering as I fell into his deadly trap. He was dynamite, ready to explode, and I was gunpowder, ready to shoot. As though the storm had broken through the walls, I was wet, and my fantasy became sublime and explosive all at once. My suppressed desires came undone to the sound of his fast breathing. I felt an electrical spark within me that sent me to the point of ecstasy. Makeup sex was a classic that always worked for us, maybe because we were both passionate lovers who didn't hold back; there were no boundaries, fear or shame between those lustworn sheets. Over time, I came to learn that love is soul first, flesh second.

People think that emotional abuse is not as serious as physical abuse, but let me tell you: it leaves scars just the same. Little did I know that, years later, I would end up helping other women like myself.

Sandra was born in Switzerland and moved to Spain when she was very young. She came to my consulting room in the throes of a panic attack on Halloween morning. I remember it clearly because I was wearing the Wonder Woman costume I had hired for a work party as a therapy tool that day. Sure, my psychology methods didn't always follow protocol, and I'd had a few problems as a result, but they allowed me to continue doing it because I was the psychologist with the most success stories in Spain. In fact, I'd been asked to write a manual based on my techniques, but I never did. Back to Sandra. She was thirty-two years old at the time. She told me she'd been having problems with her partner for two years, and that anxiety had made her gain twenty kilos. She never used the term 'abuse'. Actually, victims are mostly unaware that they are being abused at all.

'I can't take it any more,' she said, completely broken, sobbing and ashamed. 'Everything turns into a huge fight. Even the most insignificant details not worth talking about, like my mood or my feelings. He says I'm paranoid, I exaggerate everything and that it's all in my head.

I end up believing him. I feel like I'm not good enough so I keep quiet to avoid disappointing him. At first, I'd try to get my point across, but I never got anywhere, which made me feel worthless. I don't remember that last time I answered back or expressed my opinion.'

Sandra had been completely negated as a person; he had absolute control over her. She was exhausted and had no strength or energy left. She was constantly worried about upsetting or disappointing him. She walked on eggshells to avoid disturbing him on the days he worked from home.

'If I contradict him, he insults and rejects me. I can't live like this. This isn't normal,' she repeated, over and over again, staring at the floor.

A winner of the Women Economic Forum's Woman of the Decade Award, Sandra was the founder and director of one of the most powerful technology companies in the world. She was the first European woman to lead a unicorn company, a start-up valued at over one billion dollars. She was widely-recognised as a self-made champion, and yet, she went to bed with her worst enemy every night. Cut open to her very core, she relived each and every one of the situations that kept her oppressed.

'He uses my nationality to bring me down with comments like, "what you're saying makes no sense, you don't know what you're talking about, you're foreign, you have no idea, you should be grateful." Lately, he's become more violent in the way he treats me. He makes me call him "sir" and has forbidden me to drive.'

This was a clear case of gaslighting. This type of psychological violence involves a man subtly manipulating his partner, convincing her that she's imagining things, that she's remembering the fights incorrectly, ultimately making her doubt her own sanity. The abuser alters the victim's perception of reality, making them unaware that they are victims of abuse. Gaslighting is a very perverse form of violence because it's ongoing, and is achieved by subjecting the victim to constant subtle harassment that is indirect, repetitive, and serves to create doubt and confusion in their mind, making them feel guilty and deserving of the abuser's violent conduct, doubting everything that happens around them.

She couldn't stop crying and, when she finally caught her breath, she was incredulous.

'Me? Abused?' she said, as I explained my theory.

Her partner manipulated her constantly. Whenever she reminded him of something along the lines of, 'You promised me this,' he would respond, 'I didn't promise you anything. Why are you making things up? Are you crazy?' She also gave me examples where he invalidated her point of view when she expressed her feelings or complained about something. 'I didn't see that you're obviously exaggerating. What on earth are you talking about? How can you say that?'

Her partner was a master of the intermittent reinforcement technique. Occasionally, he would show love, affection, remorse, respect, and make promises of future happiness to make her feel as though, if she could change for him, then he would too, and that she would only ever be truly happy by his side.

My technique to overcome Sandra's fears required her to feel empowered. Firstly, she had to choose a superhero capable of solving all her problems. She said she loved Wonder Woman as she represented a fight for justice, love, peace and equality, so my costume was ideal. Then, she had to get in character and identify with her powers, see the world through her eyes. In essence, she had to 'pretend' that the character was within her, and that it would help her end her suffering. A good old case of 'fake it till you make it', basically. She closed her eyes to invoke that half-Amazon, half-goddess and absorb her strength and superpowers into every cell of her being. Sandra was visualising herself in the moment of transformation, becoming strong, with endless agility and the power to teleport anytime she needed to get out of danger quickly. She became a warrior with superhuman resistance and durability to combat the threats and humiliations she suffered at the hands of her partner. She imagined herself transforming into Wonder Woman, now completely in control of herself, battling any type of black magic that posed a threat to her fantastic world. She used the power of supreme knowledge, given to her by Athena, the goddess of wisdom, to become aware of her situation and plan her exit strategy. Finally, the power of super healing completed the package. Having this healing power made her a true hero in a patriarchal world and invincible to her enemy. She got so into character that I watched her as she stroked her long, black hair, even though her natural mane was a fresh, modern, platinum blonde pixie cut.

It wasn't a walk in the park. In fact, it was more like a trek in a long desert, full of challenges. But I still remember what she told me in her last email, convinced that when determination surpasses fear, we can make history.

Thanks to the powers obtained for me by the gods of my ancestors, and to hard work, I have once again become who I always was. You'll be happy to know that I still hold on to my special superhero weapons that give me courage every day. I feel the tiara on my head offering me protection, and I've learnt that the stones that don't kill me make me stronger. It was worth it, Rafaela.

Sandra,
the Swiss Wonder Woman.

It was only later that I discovered, purely by coincidence, that the character had been created 1941 by a psychologist by the name of William Moulton Marston – an American who also invented the polygraph lie detector test, and was no doubt inspired by it when creating the magic lasso of truth that hangs from the hips of the Amazon warrior princess. This invincible golden weapon is her most important one because, both in fiction as in real life, nothing is more powerful than the truth.

———⦅∞⦆———

After the scene at the Polisón, Jared returned to being the extraordinary man I'd fallen in love with, spoiling me rotten. He would fill our bedroom with blue daisies, my favourites, and would surprise me with gifts I never asked for, though I was always grateful. We were in our honeymoon period all over again.

As if by some miracle, an ad appeared on the university forum a few weeks later looking for psychology students who were also native Spanish speakers. Anybody interested had to go to a majestic human resources office in Tel Aviv at nine o'clock the following morning, CV in hand. I didn't have to think twice. It would be an amazing opportunity for me to kickstart my career, and some additional income to add to our emaciated bank account, kept alive only by my scholarship and by Jared's part time job.

Belly taught me something very important. She said I could be anything I wanted to be, but that if I wanted to be a princess, I had to build my own castles. I was taking a leap into my first serious job. I closed my eyes, overcame my fear and jumped, feeling like my body and heart were floating off the ground. I took the fast train that links

Jerusalem with Tel Aviv and arrived ten minutes early, thinking I'd be the only candidate, but that wasn't the case. Another seven people had the same thought as me, incidentally all of them men. I was the last to go in. Much like your first kiss, you never forget your first job interview, especially if it was anything like mine. When it was my turn, I entered a well-lit office, decorated in the industrial style with futuristic details. A coordinated series of greys and reds reflected from the wooden floor, giving it a cosy feel to my liking. I was met by a tall, gangly character, wearing a grey striped blazer with a matching bow tie. He must have been around fifty but appeared older. He had a prominent nose, deep wrinkles marking his skin and sparse hair on his head. He reminded me of a vulture. He asked me my star sign and smiled when I answered. He too was an Aquarian and, according to him, we were the best-suited for that position. I felt like I was off to a good start. He then began to ask me the typical questions to break the ice. How are your studies going? Why do you want to be a psychologist? The most interesting part for me was when he asked me what my favourite district of Jerusalem was. I began to speak of one in particular, the Christian Quarter, but added that I no longer liked it as it become rather run down. The man began to make strange faces, and I gathered that he lived there, so I changed arguments, got carried away and spent five minutes talking about how wonderful it was, unlike the Jewish Quarter.

'I live in the Jewish Quarter,' he said, to my shock and horror.

I didn't know where to hide, but I stoically stood my ground and waited for the next question.

'How's your Hebrew?'

'I manage OK,' I answered, though it was a lie. I couldn't put two words together. Then the interviewer changed into an unknown language. Maybe it was Hebrew to him, and he talked for a while. Up until then I had communicated in something vaguely resembling English. I looked at him, dumbfounded. I was going to answer, but then I pretended someone was calling me. Except, I was so nervous, my phone fell on the table just in front of him. He could see that it wasn't ringing and, even so, continued.

'How would you define yourself?'

'I don't know. Stupid, I guess,' I replied, like a ventriloquist doll being controlled by dark forces. I was sorry as soon as I said it.

He was silent and unsure of what to say next. I was sure it was all over. It was the typical moment when the world comes crashing down on you, and he wasn't letting up, constantly putting salt on my wounds.

'What do you mean?'

I tried to explain it, saying that I was stupid for having done a stupid thing, not because I wasn't smart. To top things off, I had a particularly bad cold that day and, before I could stop it or cover my mouth, I let out one of those uncontrollable sneezes, shooting a cloud of thousands of minute germ-laden droplets directly onto his face. I apologised and offered him a tissue stained with chocolate. I think he felt sorry for me in the end; he told me not to worry, that if I'd gone to the interview in that state I must really want to work. To top it all off, he asked me what my relationship with spirits was like.

'Pardon?' I asked, as if I hadn't understood the question.

He looked frightened. I thought he was exhausted by the whole interview process. Finally, he told me that the building was located just behind the main funeral parlour in Tel Aviv, and that he'd just seen two spirits in the foyer where I had been waiting earlier. He accompanied me to the door, a halo of mystery around him, and said goodbye by taking my hand in his, that felt like a dead wet fish. I left feeling like that had gone terribly. In fact, the experience had been worthy of a comedy script. I wasn't proud of myself at all, so I decided to keep it a secret and not tell Jared about my interview. The next morning, I had set about cooking some pasta and was at that precise moment when the water was starting to boil and you had to add the salt or it would be too late. My ringtone sounded cheerfully from the table. It was the vulture. He told me I'd been selected to support a team of consumer psychologists from a multinational advertising agency. I would have to identify and analyse public consumer trends and design promotion and commercialisation strategies. One of my dreams. The news was too good to be true! He admitted that my authenticity and determination had convinced him; he typically found interviews boring, although he'd quite enjoyed mine.

Such wonderful news should have been celebrated with fireworks, but it instead became a Greek tragedy.

Chapter 10

Tooth and Nail

M any people in the outside world will judge me, perhaps people who are as insensitive as they are mad, for believing that any of this could exist. But this inner world is where all living beings transit through as we head to the other side like arrows, bereft of memory, convinced that it's the only real world. There's a living, transparent circle surrounding us, connecting to our source and to our final destination. We know nothing of what exists from the edge of that world towards infinity. It's the final frontier for all living beings. We can't even possibly imagine it.

A strange feeling in the middle of my stomach began to spread over my entire body. Maybe I was about to discover the final purpose of this adventure. Drops of sweat were racing down my temples and I began to fan myself with a very large and shiny leaf, whose bright blue colour and purple veining would have made it a real treasure for any collector or botanist. Incredibly, another leaf quickly grew from a bud on the plant that was identical in size and beauty to the one I had pulled off. In that world, everything regenerated with amazing speed. Elsu encouraged me to eat the leaves, due to their high protein and nutrient content. He assured me that doing so would allow me to sustain my energy and would act as medicine, as it was the best natural antibiotic for human beings such as myself. I did as he said, though I felt like a slug chewing that bitter and somewhat pungent plant tissue.

'Elsu, did you see that?' I asked, pointing at the horizon, like a child catching sight of their favourite Disney character walking around at Disneyland.

'Yes, it is truly unique. It must be very impressive for you.'

'It's much more than that,' I mumbled, unable to look away from that phenomenon.

Eight suns shining brightly painted the sky an intense orange. One by one, in a single file, they each crossed the moon, appearing to be swallowed up in a ball of fire and then leaving it behind to join the sun circle once more as they revolved, suspended like an enormous ring of light.

'What you are seeing is the hunting ritual of the eight brothers that will take place over the next three hours. We must be close to the constellation of Leo. Let us find a shady spot to protect ourselves until it finishes. You and Vodka will not survive the high temperatures. This marvel can become the doorway to hell for those who are not children of this constellation.'

As we ran with no clear direction, the landscape became an arid desert. I was desperately trying to breathe, like a fish out of water, and Vodka's sandy tongue dragged on the floor. Elsu was the only one still standing strong, like an Egyptian pyramid. Meanwhile, my thin papery skin began to suffer the burns of that torrid, infernal heat. His skin, on the other hand, became colder as the temperature rose. All over his skin, a series of tiny trumpet-shaped thermoreceptors appeared, turning it into a perfect slippery, viscous layer that was thick enough to protect him from the intense solar radiation. His ability to adapt to the changing climate was astounding.

I felt like we were advancing like a limping turtle, uphill and without crutches. We were in the middle of nowhere, surrounded by burnt rocks and vast expanses of spectral solitude that made up that gruelling desert.

Elsu took Vodka in his arms when he saw him collapse along the rocky path. He spoke to him in a language that seemed to inject new life into him and, like a father protecting his child, he covered him with his jacket while we continued to walk up a rugged slope that led to the top of a hill.

'We will wait here,' he said, guiding us through a humid opening on the other side of the hill that seemed to be an animal's burrow.

We crawled through its narrow tunnel until we fell into a pool of purple water that became our oasis for a few hours. Millions of phosphorescent insects illuminated the dark space. At first, I thought they were butterflies, but I soon realised they lacked bodies. They were simply transparent wings that fluttered around a few short centimetres from the rocky walls and released drops of almost frozen dew that saved us from deadly drought.

'Do you think there can be life in this place?' I asked with what little breath I had left.

'There is, Amelia, and I believe it will not be long before we are found.'

'What do you mean?'

'The hunting ritual of the eight brothers is about to end.'

'How can you be so sure?'

I felt like burnt toast, but he looked at me with the kind of tenderness that could be wrapped up and sold as a Christmas present.

'Sun number seven is entering the moon. That means that day and night, much like the constantly-moving hands on the universal clock, will soon give way to sunset. The children of the sun, the lion people, will come out to hunt.'

Elsu was not mistaken, the light was beginning to fade, inviting dusk to the spectacle. The fan of blinding rays was closing through infinite space. We left our refuge following our respite from that horrific heat wave and ventured out into a landscape dominated by a haze that floated up from the ground, making everything look blurry and confusing, presenting an image of dull colours. We were stopped in our tracks by a distant chorus of long, deep roars that became shorter and more explosive as they neared. Vodka raised his ears as he tried to identity where that sound, which seemed to be surrounding us, was coming from. He lunged his head and bared his teeth aggressively as if preparing for an imminent attack, barking compulsively. Our relief from the heat had given way to the stress of uncertainty.

Like an apparition, a dozen creatures closed ranks around us. I expected to find aggressive beings, expert hunters with predatory instincts for whom we'd be easy prey. One of them, probably the leader, approached us while projecting two lasers from its round coffee-coloured eyes, scanning the floor at a rate of millions of pulses per second, using echoes to map our outlines, creating an attractive three-dimensional map.

I could practically feel the rhythmic movement of the creature's shoulder blades and its stealthy steps, as if it were creeping up on an unsuspecting impala. I counted up to five male and seven female felines.

I wouldn't know whether to call them a tribe, a pride or a pack of fantastic creatures because they were a mix of everything all at once. I felt like I was living in a dream, something that wasn't real, but that didn't make it any less frightening.

Elsu must have guessed what I was thinking because he whispered to me, 'They are beings from the constellation of Leo. Do not be afraid.'

I was worried that something would happen to me and no one would ever know the truth. I thought about my mother and how much she would suffer with the disappearance of her only daughter. The idea that all of this could be true, or a lie, or both, was disturbing. Regardless, I was living a most wonderful adventure. I promised myself that, if I survived, I would make sure to publish this story. Half the readers would probably not believe a word and the other half would simply call me crazy.

While they scanned us, Vodka and I remained perfectly still. We instinctively became reflections of Elsu, copying his behaviour and every one of his movements, which were practically inexistent. If anyone knew what to do, it was him; of that we were sure.

Why wasn't Elsu reacting? Was he planning out the next step? That thought gave me a strange sense of security.

Their majestic figures were of a much greater size to ours. Their muscly bodies supported a head that was slightly larger than the rest of them. In the centre of their flat foreheads was a tattooed sun, which was a little smaller on the females. A short wide snout showed two upper canines, shining like gold, some of which were still dripping with fresh blood. The matriarch, with her dominant attitude, shook a thick, messy greying mane that covered her shoulders, while she cradled her tail, also crowned with a white streak. There was no doubt whatsoever that this robust and impressive figure was a lioness. Her physique made no secret of it either. The males had shorter manes.

I tried to hear even the tiniest sound, but could only make out the beating of my own heart, growing exponentially louder. The more I tried to reason and overcome my fears, the less calm I was. My human mind immediately came up with a prognosis. I told myself, 'Amelia, you're safe. If they've already had their fill, they'll no longer be hungry and that's a good sign.' But there were also other possibilities, much more agonising and uncertain, that I couldn't specify or reason, which is probably what made them all the more terrifying. Every second felt like a century.

In my mind, I saw images of the Metro-Goldwyn-Mayer lion, the lion prince from *Beauty and the Beast*, the cowardly lion from *The Wizard of Oz*, and many others that have roared and conquered Hollywood over time, starring in an endless array of movies. However, I met the most important lion of my life when I was only eight.

As a child, I suffered from nyctophobia, an extreme irrational fear of the dark. Every object and every shadow looked like the most terrifying monsters, and I couldn't figure out why. They made fun of me at school, and that bothered me a lot. I would avoid going to the bathroom because they'd turn off the light when I was inside, just to see me run out half naked and terrified, fleeing from that dark place. Every day, my father would patiently explain to me that they weren't monsters, but I couldn't avoid feeling intense fear every time the light was gone. I couldn't be in the dark even for a second because I'd be completely overcome by panic, imagining the dangers hiding there. One night, before going to bed, he sat me on his lap and drew a lion's face on my own. Painting had always been one of his hobbies so this wasn't difficult for him. He drew two ears on my forehead, applying orange-reddish tones on my cheeks and giving them the appearance of movement. Small touches of brown on my tiny face gave the illusion of fur. He completed his work of art by drawing long black whiskers and applying a layer of Vaseline on my nose to stick golden glitter to it.

'Amelia,' he said, taking me by the hand and placing me in front of a large mirror. 'Do you see that? That's you. Now you're the king of the jungle and therefore a symbol of courage and strength. He lives within you. We all have a lion inside us. You're much braver than you believe you are, much stronger than you look and much more intelligent than you think. Never forget who you really are.'

'Does that mean I can fight them all and beat them now?' I asked innocently, having fallen for that feline.

'Amelia, being a lion means that you have to stand your ground with your head held high and face whatever conflicts and situations arise in your life. However, bravery is not synonymous with fighting every battle, but with having the wisdom to choose the ones worth fighting.'

My father had never set foot in a school. Life was his teacher and he was an excellent student. While he spent hours sitting on his tractor ploughing; he didn't just dig furrows in the soil but he also opened up his soul to life's truths. What I thought was a fun game at the time, became the repellent for my night terrors. I felt so sure of myself that I could scare even Phobos – the embodiment of terror and horror in Greek mythology. I learnt that by waking our inner lion, we could change our perception of things. As Steven Covey says, 'We see the world, not as it is, but as we are.' That paint covering my innocent face, far from scaring me, reconnected me with my inner strength and power, ending my nightmares forever.

I then thought: if we all have an inner lion within us, why should I fear them? What could I hold against a being that, far from doing anything wrong, is actually just living according to its DNA, fulfilling its purpose? They were simply living up to their name. Nevertheless, the closest I'd ever been to a real lion had been at the Granada Zoo, and those certainly did not resemble these albino creatures one bit.

I abandoned my self-absorption for a moment as I watched one of the youngest lions cough up a hairball, bones, horns and teeth, possibly the remains of his last feast, followed by a fierce roar that cut through the air. I couldn't hide a look of disgust. This seemed to offend him, and he got ready to attack. I observed as the tattooed sun on his forehead lit up with his reaction. Later, I learnt that his happened anytime anger and rage manifested in their bodies. The leader stopped him, giving him a stern look, not to intimidate him but to reclaim her authority.

'I am Kalu. What can we do for you, travellers from other worlds?' she asked with determination, her voice deep and hoarse.

A leader is a leader because they think first about what they can give others before thinking about what they can take. Her question confirmed her natural temperament for leadership.

There were as many tongues as there were constellations at the Purple Lagoon. And yet, even with this dialectic diversity, everyone was able to communicate with each other fluently. It was amazing how Elsu could speak each and every one of them, performing some kind of instant telepathic translation so that I could also understand them.

The leader's scan had already given her most of the information she needed. We weren't enemies looking to conquer her territory, nor were we interfering with their hunting. We were no threat to them at all. She knew exactly why we were there. A lion's gaze always sees what lies beneath the surface.

'How far is the next constellation? Do you think we could reach it before sunrise? You already know what we are looking for...' said Elsu in a friendly manner.

'You could reach Virgo in four moons. Travelling during the day would end the woman and the dog's lives, whereas if you move at night, you'll become the perfect target for other nocturnal creatures.'

Some of the tribe members were beginning to eye Vodka like a child eyes a cream puff with a cherry on top. In an irrational, instinctive act of survival, Vodka began to run, three of them chasing after him. I never would have thought to do the same. I'm not sure anyone can outrun a lion.

They executed a perfectly-synchronised team strategy, immediately surrounding him from different angles. One of them paralysed him, grabbing him by the neck with his big, strong hands, covering half of his body.

I yelled, 'No, Vodka! Let him go!' as I ran towards my faithful friend, who was trying to resist death, whimpering softly.

Kalu arrived long before I did. The sun on her forehead was emitting a powerful light that made the wild creatures stop. Vodka, now free, ran and hid behind some shrubs in the empty terrain. Elsu addressed Kalu once again.

'I understand the essential, beautiful and complex cycle of life. The ecosystem sustains itself thanks to that cycle and nobody should underestimate any of its pieces, however I ask that you please respect our existence as our elements do not form part of the life cycle in your world.'

She looked at him as only a leader looks at another leader. Following a large yawn, she agreed in a generous and noble tone.

'That is correct, Elsu. It is an infinite cycle of beginnings and endings, which is why we lions are not afraid of living short lives because they cannot be compared to a long existence. We all have something to contribute that puts us all on the same level. No one must feel better than anyone else.'

Our journey through the constellation of Leo taught me very important life lessons, thanks to Kalu. Firstly, about biology – how the ecosystem works and the role of all the food webs, that is, the cycle of life. The lion hunts the suka, something like an antelope on

Earth, the suka eats the grass, and when the lion dies, it goes on to form part of the grass again. Therefore, the carbon, nitrogen, phosphorous and other organic components all form part of the biological cycle. Each one of us fulfils a purpose, and although reality is not quite so simple, in my world we were still arguing over whether some species were ecologically more important than others. The balance of our ecosystem comes from the part played by each and every species. Predators, prey, plants, fungi, insects and worms were all necessary. It's like a puzzle: if you take one piece away, it doesn't work anymore. Likewise, you are part of the world and no one can take your place, but remember to respect others and understand that no one is better or worse in this cycle. The politician caught up in the fight for power is no better than the person who cleans our streets. The surgeon, despite high social status, is not superior to the person who serves them food after work. The director of a successful company is no better than the stay-at-home mother who cares for her children. Money, culture, beauty and intelligence – none of these things distinguish us from the each other. Only if you learn this lesson, will you be worthy of your own existence, as it is through others that we become ourselves.

We stayed with Kalu and the others that night. After weighing up the options, they offered to guide and protect us the next day at sunset, so we could cross the border into the constellation of Virgo. She even took us to see the place where the cubs were raised, admitting that the youngest ones could sometimes be relentless, particularly the males, but that the fundamental values of loyalty, love and family ties were always above everything else.

During the day, we rested and sought refuge from the extreme, suffocating heat, while moving again at night in the company of the most loyal protectors we could possibly have. We covered great distances and had many hours of observation and conversation, through which I was able to understand the world and personality of those beings with human forms.

'Elsu, did you notice how fascinating these beings are? And how brightly they glow?'

'Of course. It is no coincidence that they are the children of the sun. Part of the star's characteristics live within them. Like the sun, they make themselves noticed. The sun is the central power that sustains all of the planets because of its large size and because of its magnetism, which keeps them spinning around it. That is why these creatures become the centre, exercising a power of attraction on the others. Think about it, Amelia. The sun does not rule by force. It does not have all the planets tied up with string to prevent them from flying around space, it simply attracts them, and that is enough to keep them there. Just as a true leader does not exercise their power over their followers. True lions are strong, energetic and motivated enough to make others want to stay around them.'

It was hard for me to associate the amount of time they spent inactive, resting and taking long naps in the sun, with leaders as I understood them. Elsu gave me the key.

'Amelia, make no mistake; leadership does not mean taking on a large number of tasks. A good leader does not waste time on details or wanting to be everywhere at once. They know what is truly important and which button to press to make things happen. They only spring into action to manage what is essential. They concentrate on doing only what is crucial for the success of those to whom they have made a commitment.'

I immensely enjoyed those days spent in darkness in the wilderness, as the shadows became longer and took on a life of their own, the clouds took on all kinds of shapes and every corner seemed to hide something new and magical. I remember those moments when my imagination was filled with ideas and my conscience filled with light. My eyes, like precision cameras, captured moments as scenes brimming with mystery and excitement.

Kalu was an extraordinary conversationalist, and Elsu could listen to and understand others like nobody else. Kalu knew everything about everybody. You could tell she was truly interested in others, and perhaps this is why she had been chosen. I never saw her impose her ideas on anyone; instead, she would collect them, put them together to make them her own and present them afterwards. One of her phrases stayed forever in my novice ears, 'A leader takes others where they never would have gone alone.'

I could barely sleep long enough to dream. I seemed to be getting used to our new destination, but the nostalgia for my home and for everything I had left behind surrounded me incessantly like the promise of a kiss.

Elsu would spend hours gazing up at the stars. He said he was interpreting the star map, but I was sure he was also weighed down by the absence of his loved ones, and by responsibility. I guessed we were very close to the next constellation. The sun, suspended high up in the sky like a golden coin that someone had dropped, was gradually losing intensity during the day, and the landscape began to offer more signs of life. On the last day, we rested next to a pool whose floor consisted of tiny blue and green rocks, which ended in a waterfall that was white with foam.

'Elsu, how about a swim,' I suggested.

We were so dirty! Our clothes smelled terrible. I didn't wait for his approval. I dived into the refreshing water that felt like Mother Earth herself was caressing me. Our purple oasis was a collection of waterfalls and cascades, grottoes and small natural pools filled with crystal-clear waters. He eventually joined me when he saw me splashing around having fun like a frog in a pond, or maybe it was my insistence as I challenged him to catch me while I submerged my playful body.

'C'mon! Don't falcons like the water? Or are they too slow to catch earthling away the infinite horizon?'

'You should know that falcons are the fastest animals in your world, Amelia. They can reach up to three hundred sixty kilometres per hour,' he said in response to my provocation as he swam towards me.

I threw myself at his neck, forgetting we were strangers, drowning all embarrassment and prejudices into the bottom of that place that had brought us together. We were two paths running in the same direction. I'd swapped the dirt and dust I had accumulated for the courage those lion inhabitants had inspired in me. He took me by the waist and threw me into the air, filling my ears with laughter, 'Now you will fly too!'

I felt like I was being dragged away by his current, drowning in his eyes. I feared his ability to make me feel completely naked without taking off my clothes, exposing my heart. I didn't expect him to understand what had awakened in me when I didn't even understand it myself. Even so and without wanting to, I couldn't help loving him sometimes.

For a moment, time stood still and became a convenient accomplice. I was fifteen all over again. I didn't know what fifteen would look like for someone such as Elsu or in a world like his, but I knew he was feeling the same way. We hugged in silence for a while, knowing that words could never mean more than that particular moment in time.

Kalu and her tribe rested like guardian sphinxes around us, uncon-cerned with our games. To Egyptians, sphinxes were probably a way to blend beauty with the ferocity of a lion and the wisdom of a king.

'Elsu, I'm worried about time. What will happen to me? What will happen to my world and everything I've ever known if we don't find the thousand-step staircase soon?' I asked in a sudden burst of awareness.

'Amelia, you are time, eternal, infinite, immortal and beyond measure. The soul of man is immortal and enduring. Time does not end, it is simply spent. Imagine there is a bank, and each morning it deposits eighty-six thousand four hundred euros into your account. However, this strange bank does not carry over your balance from one day to the next. Instead, every night it wipes out whatever you have not spent that day. What would you do?'

'Well...' I lowered my gaze and thought about it. 'Then I'd withdraw the full amount each day and spend it, I guess.'

'You are a customer of a bank called life, and your account is called time. Every morning, the bank deposits eighty-six thousand four hun-dred seconds into your account for you to spend only during that day, and, whatever you have not invested towards something beneficial is considered a loss and wiped every night. You cannot carry over your balance from one day to the next. Every morning, your account is reset and every night you lose what has not been spent; there is no way back. You must live in the moment, using today's balance. Do not use your wealth thinking that you have no time left because that makes you poorer. Treasure every moment you are alive, which becomes much more valuable if you share it with someone special – someone special enough with whom to spend your time. The important thing is not time but how you spend it, it is how you spend it.'

The memory of the smell of my mother's delicious jam, which she made using the fruit from our garden, took me back to the kitchen where she prepared breakfast every Sunday. She hated cooking and, more often than not, a layer of burnt milk would form on the bottom of the pot before my distracted mother could do anything to stop it when it came to the boil. Even so, she would wake up early just to spend time with me.

'Amelia, don't eat your toast standing up in the bathroom while you do your makeup,' she would complain while she patiently waited in front of my empty seat. 'This isn't the place to eat. Sit with me, let's chat.'

'I'm late, *mamá*! I don't have time! Time's flying! I'm almost out of time!'

'For God's sake! It's like we're living in the city of "maximum speed". Time is a cannibal that eats you up and spits you out. Don't you see? Come and sit down and tell me all about that book you're reading and about that new friend of yours.'

I saw myself running all over the house, going up and down the stairs like a madwoman, checking all the clocks, as if I was part of a competition and my life depended on it, ignoring the voice that was calling me. With some people, we feel like we're wasting our time. With other very special ones, we lose track of time, and very few have the ability to give us back that lost time.

What I wouldn't give to sit in that chair now and talk to my mother about all my little things, the ones that were always the greatest reward for her early mornings. If only we could preserve those flavours, those aromas, all those moments. How wonderful it would be if we could vacuum-seal them, preserving their freshness, so that we could open them anytime we wanted and relive them, adding whatever was missing the first time in order to make them perfect. In my case, I'd add large doses of quality time spent with my favourite people. The truth is that we never think about how long we have left; we feel like we'll always have another chance to do the things we love and to share those moments with those we care about. And you? If you knew exactly how long you had left to enjoy those people, what would you do?

Like a movie that ends with the words 'to be continued' and, whose sequel we await excitedly, I bid farewell to the creatures with fiery hearts, having learnt so much, and yet suspecting that there was still much more learning to do. Life was turning out much more mysterious than I'd imagined, and a new chapter with other living beings lay in store. Surely, they'd be the ones to help us figure out this thing called life, because all journeys have secret destinations that travellers know nothing about.

Chapter 11

Your Grandfather Esteban

There are people who see what happens in life, others who foresee it, and others who make things happen. Then, there is a fourth group of people who wonder what happened and why. I belong to that last group. I was a tormented mess that needed to find my place in the world.

With these words began Belly's second handwritten letter. Her words broke up the blank spaces of the trembling page with the same force of a wild, ocean's waves crashing on the rocks, overwhelming me that afternoon where the wind was quiet and a small bonfire was burning, soothing my still open wounds. I had chosen that secluded, secret cove, my favourite place, where a few fleeting memories with my mother remained buried in the sand like treasures. It was a sacred place to me, where soft seaweed wrapped around our feet, only to disappear into the depths of the ocean later on and a large net protected us from jellyfish, allowing us to swim naked, free from the gaze of curious tourists. Even the fish seemed to be in love with the place. The warm breeze caressed my hands as they held a future rooted in the past. It felt like the freest place in the world. My memories and my childhood felt so far away. Here, my only concern was to be happy surrounded by all the blue. Despite how much time had passed, I was still tied to this place where I had been a swallow, where my innocence had sparked the glow of truth. It was a starting point, where three generations of women were coming together, joined by one voice.

Dearest Rafaela, my sweet girl,

I'm sorry I never spoke to you about your grandfather Esteban, and for having deprived you of the memories that every little girl should have of her forebears. Although it pains me, I think it's time for you to know about the man I loved the most and with whom I suffered the most. I was the seventh of eight children and worked as a waitress at one of the finest restaurants in Granada. I was about sixteen years old then. My parents were farmers and couldn't afford to send us all to school. Not a month went by when they managed to fill our bellies without eating through their savings because they could barely afford to feed us all gruel. I never liked farm work. I found it so tiring, especially when it was windy and when it rained. It made my head and my feet hurt. The sight of ploughed fields tormented me even in my sleep. No, I really didn't like farm life. Just the idea of seeing a poor farmer covered in mud, all ragged, looking more miserable than his skinny horse wading through black, muddy soil, seemed to me to be the embodiment of brutal primitive force, and I was born to be surrounded by beauty and elegance. Little did I know I'd end up marrying a man who loved the earth more than life itself? Just like Jean de La Fontaine said, 'a person often meets his destiny on the road he took to avoid it.'

In order to escape my inevitable destiny of picking melons like the rest of my siblings, I worked in that restaurant serving the city's rich and famous. That's where I discovered my love of fashion, watching in awe as those elegant women paraded through the dining area. I was in charge of keeping their coats, bags and hats in the cloakroom and of taking their orders. I was fascinated by the way they spoke and how the pronounced the French names of some of the dishes. Every single day I left that place I promised myself that, someday, those glowing, soft and sophisticated ladies would wear my own designs all around the city.

In my day, if you didn't have a boyfriend by the age of eighteen but hoped to get married, you were already on the way to becoming a 'spinster'. What a word... so awful and cruel. Sure, it was innocent, but it had unhappy, condescending, disrespectful connotations. Basically, what everyone saw as a bitter old woman who's over the hill. It's funny how by just changing that terrible word to 'single' it can suddenly make you a woman who's independent, young and desired nowadays. In my day, we weren't so lucky! Nowadays, being single is fashionable. When someone tells you about their single neighbour, we immediately think of a young woman, a hard worker who lives alone, does yoga, eats macrobiotic food and walks around her minimally decorated loft apartment in lingerie. However, fifty years ago, that same woman was seen very differently. They were considered nosy spinsters who spied on their neighbours, lived with five cats and a parrot for company, played solitaire on a table with a crochet doily and watched endless hours of television on the days they had no one to gossip about.

I'm sorry, but maybe single people are too independent and that bothered society back then as it was obsessed with relationships, and there was a point in life when you absolutely needed to have a steady partner and children. My head was too far up in the clouds to think of marriage. I didn't feel mature enough to become anyone's wife and to attach my destiny to someone else's for all eternity, no matter what anyone said, or how much my mother would pray to Saint Anthony of Padua every thirteenth of June as, according to tradition, he would help women of marrying age find a boyfriend or husband so they wouldn't be left on the shelf. Even female solidarity was non-existent. Half a century ago, we were subjected to high expectations and were forced to live in the hope of one day achieving the patriarchal ideal of becoming the 'perfect woman', a beautiful submissive woman devoted to her home and to raising her children. No way, that wasn't for me! It broke my heart to watch as my mother spent years preparing my trousseau, filling it with bed sheets, exquisitely embroidered towels and tablecloths, considered real treasures, particularly for a modest family such as ours.

Despite my youth, I had sworn to myself that I'd never depend on anyone economically or, in truth, in any other way. Contrary to my mother, I wouldn't fall in love and get married hoping that someone would fill the void in my life, turning me into a baby factory, robbing me of my dreams and my energy. I triumphantly declared that I didn't need a husband by my side in order to be happy.

Rafaela, you don't know how happy I am that you haven't had to carry the burden of a conservative, chauvinistic society's stereotypes, and that you can decide freely whether or not you want to be involved with another person, without the stigma of being 'incomplete'.

I can still see that young guy that looked like James Dean coming into the restaurant with his enormous trolley of fruits and vegetables through the kitchen door. His sweet face and rebellious personality made all the women melt and even, dare I say some of the men. His scent of wet earth was lost behind his innocent appearance and his body, worthy of being declared a World Heritage Site. Tall and agile, he looked healthy and athletic. Just as James did, he always held a cigarette between his lips and wore a white t-shirt, stained green by the radish leaves that rubbed against him when he loaded and unloaded the produce.

Up until that March morning, we hadn't exchanged a single word. I ignored him because I didn't want him to think that I was another one of his fans, fainting at his feet. I've always been very proud.

'The cook will be in later today. He asked me to pay you,' I said, addressing him indifferently.

'It's a miracle!' he said without even looking at me, concentrating on unloading the boxes of pumpkins and tomatoes he had brought.

'Miracle? What do you mean?' I asked seriously, but without getting upset.

'I thought you were a mute. You haven't said a word to me in the two years I've been coming here,' he answered, puffing on the almost finished cigarette.

'What a miracle! Is that honestly the greatest miracle you've ever witnessed?'

'No, I see thousands of them every day. Everything's a miracle! Isn't it a miracle that the Earth is just a ball floating around in this infinite universe? And what about the fact that your heart beats one hundred thousand times per day, thirty-five million times per year, and two and a half billion times over an entire lifetime, without stopping? Tell me, would you allow me to listen to yours every night until mine stops beating?'

That night, my eyelids closed and opened again, in an endless fight between sleep and energy, provoked by that rude young man's question. After that fight to the death, my eyes gave in to the magical sands of feelings. I learnt that your grandfather was a very wise and simple man. His mouth was pure sin. His lips had been carved by expert hands, they were the perfect size – not too thick or too thin – and were shamefully sensual. They were framed by a strong chin, a sharp jaw and tanned skin. He was impressive to any woman. However, what intrigued me about him lay beyond the physical. He had a confident walk. He knew what he wanted and lacked the necessary patience to pretend otherwise. He knew the secrets of life and of the country like the back of his hand. For weeks after we had broken the ice, your grandfather Esteban would seek me out with his desperate wide-eyed look, leaving a bunch of fresh wildflowers on the cloakroom counter for me. My mind was at war between my independence and the idea of us two, together.

Inside every human being is the profound desire, and maybe even need, to know that their life means something, that it has a value. I was hanging on tooth and nail to my dreams of independence. I wanted to travel the world and became a famous designer of haute couture, but one that was accessible to everyone, even to modest girls such as myself. Creating my own brand and style at economic prices was all I wanted. I'd be the first female designer to break the barrier of class, using the power of the fabrics and their colours. I couldn't allow anyone to cut my wings off on my flight to freedom – those same wings that spread out as I soared through the sky, seemingly touching the stars, so bright and yet so far away.

One afternoon, as I was leaving the restaurant, I saw him in front of the door on his battered and rusty lime green bicycle surrounded by a cloud of cigarette smoke.

'They've opened a boutique in one of the towns on the coast near the best icecream parlour in the world. The grand opening is in a couple of hours and they're having a fashion show with Italian brands. Do you fancy an icecream?'

For the sake of adding a little excitement to my boring life, I nodded and accepted that surprising and original invitation. So we headed to the coast. He stood up to pedal, leaving the seat for me, and we rode against the strongest wind I'd seen in a long time. In those situations, physical resilience was just as important as mental stamina. After all, his legs had to fulfil a tough but simple task. However, Esteban's head may have been dealing with such ridiculous thoughts as I was and, if he didn't keep his cool about it, he could easily lose his balance.

As we pedalled along, little by little, I found myself feeling more comfortable hugging him around the waist, pressing his body against mine. A lock of my hair was tickling my lips, but I didn't want to take my hands off his body. He remained silent, I imagine he didn't want to use up what little breath he had left. His eyes were darting from the challenging road to the fogged up bike mirror projecting my image. After several kilometres swallowing dust, we could hear a distant murmur coming from our destination. Esteban put one foot on the floor, slowly and gently bringing that screeching vehicle to a stop.

'What do you think about all day on that bicycle?' I asked, as I smoothed down my wind-blown hair.

'About where the journey is heading,' he replied, resting it against the street lamp that shone on the boutique's large sign.

I assumed he meant the journey he completed on his old bike every day, delivering goods to all his clients, dragging a heavy trolley full of freshlypicked fruits and vegetables.

Obviously, I hadn't delved deeply enough into his answer.

'I think about the meaning of the journey, about the meaning of life and of humanity. I assure you very few people are able to spend as much time alone as I do, and to think while the body goes into automatic mode, like when you're pedalling a bike for twenty-five kilometres in a straight line,' he added, smiling.

I looked up at the sky. A very thin letter C floated placidly over the rooftops. Even the moon was different that evening.

'The moon is as sincere as I am,' he said, following my gaze. 'When it forms a C shape, it's growing, the way I grow whenever I see you dreaming. You know you're unique, don't you? I've been watching you. You're creative, imaginative, and you have a different way of seeing things.'

'Yes, I'm unique. But, even so, I'm only one person. I can't change the world,' I said, observing the event's glamorous atmosphere that raised my spirits to the sky and let them fall, in a constant battle of 'yes, but...'

I almost didn't survive the shock at the prices of the garments behind the shop window. For a few moments, I felt small and insignificant.

Esteban smoothed my hair and said, 'Maybe you can't change the world, but don't ever let the world change you.'

I'm convinced my answer was contaminated by one of my most recent memories, when my father had asked me on the porch as I looked at the melon patch, 'Amelia, if you didn't have to pick melons or work in the restaurant, what would you like to do?' I didn't have to think twice. I replied, immediately, 'I'm going to be someone important. I'll be an haute couture designer, and even mamá will be able to wear my collections on Sundays to go to the market.' My father held my gaze for a few seconds, and then let out a thunderous laugh. My siblings and my mother saw him and followed suit.

Esteban insisted, 'Sure, but you can do something. And just because you can't do everything, that doesn't mean you should give up on doing *what you can do. You may just be one person, but you have it in you to do great things in the world. It's the power of one. Your life can make a difference,' he replied, firmly.*

'I'll tell you another thing; when I ride my bike, I don't just improve my mind. Pedalling also requires me to make some sacrifices – not just physical effort, but accepting that there are some places I'll get to go with it, landscapes I'll never get to see on my brown leather bike seat, and yet that thought will never take me off the road. I've learnt that there are always new paths opening up, and that there are countless new routes waiting to be discovered. The reward is always there, waiting for those who never stop pedalling, as long as you don't betray your journey's principles and you recognise the power of one. Life will accept some stops along the way to carry out your bike maintenance, and to invoke some personal mantras to help you stay motivated with every pedal, helping you resist the temptation to go backwards or to give up altogether. You can't travel with your head down because you'll miss the beautiful views that remind you to keep on pedalling.'

That guy with his infinite vitality was not after a body he could transform into a wife, he was after the greatest conquest of all: my soul.

With him, I learnt that the longest journey begins with just one step. The greatest achievements begin with a dream. The greatest fortunes were built with the first euro, and the best books are written just one word at a time. When we believe we can't change things, we let ourselves go and let others decide for us. Giving up on ourselves and not pedalling any more is just one possible alternative, but it's not the only one, nor is it the most dignified. This, Rafaela, is the greatest legacy your grandfather left me, which I have also tried to pass on to you.

I love you,
Belly

I searched anxiously for more words after Belly signed off that letter. How ridiculous could I be? When someone says goodbye, it's goodbye, that's it. If only there was a PS... Actually, it would never have been enough. Every time she signed off in her letters, it was like losing her all over again, leading me to desperately search for her in the next one. I knew that not even a million words could bring her back, but I couldn't help waiting for the hello after every goodbye. Belly had opened up her heart to me, and for the first time, I could hear it beating to a different rhythm.

I thought that my grandfather Esteban must have been an amazing man. I'd liked him from the beginning and was learning to love him through Belly's story. How I would've loved to have engaged in philosophical conversations with him! I felt like he was one of those special people who, in this dark grey world, manage to be a beacon of colour that attract you, cheer you up and bring you back to life. And although part of my buried roots began to come alive again, there were still many puzzle pieces missing, and so many questions remained unanswered. Why did Belly never tell me about him? Why didn't we visit his grave, or remember his birthday? This man I was beginning to discover, who formed a family with love and who was so deeply adored, was beginning to lose his invisibility and his absence was being filled with memories.

Belly's love story aroused a morbid curiosity in me. In particular, the message 'You are capable of more, connect with the *power of one*' made my head spin for a long time.

Again, the stories that truly inspire me don't spring from fiction but from reality: nothing moves me more than ordinary people, or those close to me, who dedicate their lives to improving the status quo of their surroundings.

I remembered Hernán, a yoga instructor who dreamt of changing the world. The first time I saw him in my consulting room, I was impressed by his passion, his big heart, and the idealism with which he tried to convince me about the need to bring his dream to life. He wanted to completely revolutionise the world of education and introduce yoga techniques into schools. He said it would help to create better people and, in turn, a more just and engaged society. So what was the problem? Why was he explaining all this to a psychologist such as myself?

He didn't think he was capable of achieving such a feat. The fire burning in his heart was all-consuming. 'It's just me on my own' he would say. 'A modest yoga instructor. How can I possibly lead such a movement?' Psychologists have an endless list of words for that: lack of self-esteem, limiting beliefs, learned helplessness, etc. How easy it would have been to call it by its name, a disconnect with the *power of one*. Each and every one of us should learn that small things can often outdo large ones. That people considered by society, and often ourselves, to be insignificant can perform feats that are well above their strength or resources.

That young man who broke through my door with the strength of a buffalo, but with the fear of failure on his shoulders, had been to Thailand to meditate and practice his discipline for a few years, only to return to Granada and completely revolutionise a school. He invited a team of international instructors that he put in charge of an innovative environmental programme. Hernán connected with the *power of one*, seeing further than his own eyes could see and allowing success to flourish. More than thirty schools are applying his practices today.

Abraham Lincoln and Mahatma Gandhi are classic examples of social-political feats achieved primarily by just one person. The fantastic *power of one* encourages us not to underestimate ourselves but to do things to the best of our ability, regularly stretching the limits just as a woman in labour widens her cervix in a loving act of giving life. Every change begins with a single person. When that person decides to unleash their power, extraordinary things happen. One is more than just a simple number; it's the number that can make all the difference. One tree can be the start of a forest, one bird can announce spring, one vote can change a nation, one ray of sunshine can light up a room, one star can guide a boat at sea, one handshake can raise a spirit, one step can begin a journey, one word can save a life, and one life can bring about a revolution.

At just seventeen years of age, Jadav Molai Payeng began a personal crusade that would occupy much of his life: he planted one tree a day for over forty years. Since the 1970s, Jadav Payeng, has been planting trees in order to save his island of Majuli, India. To date, he has single-handedly planted his own forest, transforming what was once a desert into an exuberant oasis of vegetation and life. Known as the 'Forest Man', he's a humble person who is truly passionate and philosophical about this work. It all started in 1979 when the young Indian found dozens of dead reptiles in the city of Jorhat, on the banks of the Brahmaputra River, the result of a lack of shade. After alerting local authorities, he was given twenty bamboo seeds to plant. Anybody else would have thrown them away, mumbling about how badly the system works and how little public institutions actually do to help, but Jadav wasn't just anybody. He decided to do something about it and get involved. He took those seeds and did what he had to do – he planted them.

Later on, forestry authorities from the Golaghat district started a project to plant two hundred hectares of trees in a nearby area. Jadav was one of the people who worked on it for its entire duration of five years. Not satisfied with this, he continued to plant trees at his own initiative. The final result is a forest almost twice as big as New York's famous Central Park. In this way, the *power of one*, in this case Jadav, has helped create a new ecosystem that has changed the local landscape and is now home to tigers, rhinoceroses, elephants and many bird species, making it a true natural reserve for these animals. Yes, just one person can change the world and their own lives. If you ever wonder 'What can I do to change my life? it's just me on my own!' You'll find the answer in the *power of one*.

The power to transform what happens is within each and every one of us. The key to change is believing that we have the power in every situation, because if we can imagine it then, without a doubt, we can achieve it. Maybe the changes we observe are only small, but we must never forget that endless beaches are made up of minuscule grains of sand. Perhaps the round shape of our heads was designed that way so that our thoughts can change direction, so we realise that nothing is static and that change depends on us.

Chapter 12

We are the Cosmos

According to an ancient Serbian proverb, '*Be humble for you are made of earth. Be noble for you are made of stars.*'

We mothers have a very sharp sixth sense, particularly for anything that has to do with our children. It's a unique and special gift that allows us to perceive something that is outside the reach of our more developed senses. An inner compass is activated in mothers that allows us to intercept dangers, even from a distance. It doesn't matter how far they are, we can hear and feel the state of our children's souls, and mine was very tightly linked with Rafaela's. It always had been.

That night, I couldn't sleep. I had a strange feeling running through every cell in my being, a constant bombardment of relentless, negative thoughts that disturbed me and robbed me of my sleep. I dozed off for a little, but in the middle of the night, I woke up suddenly from a deep sleep, shaking and completely drenched in sweat. The image of Rafaela shot through my mind like a lightning bolt. I felt a violent shock as though I had taken a classic leap into the void, like when Indiana Jones was searching for the Holy Grail. Stunned and frightened, I began to shout her name louder and louder. Something wasn't right. My heart was in my throat and I couldn't control my hyperventilating body, contracting and dilating like a giant accordion.

It didn't take long for a pair of male nurses to come, armed to the teeth and ready to silence me in any way necessary. They told me to go to the infirmary, but I couldn't walk. My legs were shaking. They then dragged me from the bed and put me in a chair, my hands and feet in restraints, and poured a jug of cold water all over me, saying as they laughed that if I didn't shut up they'd make sure I didn't wake up for a week.

I was lucky that 'white coat' was on duty that night and decided to intervene. Normally, the offences carried out by some of the nurses and guards at San Patricio were part of their entertainment activities and included in their salaries.

'What are you doing? It's nothing more than a night terror; it'll only last a couple of minutes. There's no need to sedate her,' he said defiantly.

One of them, the leader who would instigate the others to participate in his morbid torture games, pursed his lips in displeasure, while I pulled on the arm of the 'white coat', desperate for some compassion.

'My daughter's in danger. I have to go to her. Please, help me!' I begged.

'We've already told you a million times, you don't have a daughter. Stop carrying on about that,' said the leader.

'Why do you talk to her like that? What kind of cruelty is this?' asked Dr Fred, outraged, addressing the daring nurse.

'The director warned us that she's deranged, and that she made up the story about having a daughter. She's been repeating the same thing over and over for years.'

He looked at me, surprised, and caressed my back as a small token of mercy, offering me a tiny seed of compassion amidst all that pain.

'Relax, Amelia,' he said. 'We'll sort this out, but you have to promise me that you'll try to sleep. I'll come to see you tomorrow and we'll talk all about it.'

His response didn't help me relax. I was exhausted. I couldn't even feel my own heart. I was furious, but I also felt a profound sadness, like an anchor dragging me every which way. However, deep down, I knew that it was my best option at that time. I realised that if I didn't fight, I wouldn't survive my own downfall. I told myself that if I had even the slightest molecule of energy left in me, I had to find it and multiply it. I had to survive and leave that place, not just for myself, but also for my daughter, for humanity and for the entire cosmos , from which we come, and to which I owed so much.

One of the male nurses took me back to my room that was as white as my future, scrutinising me with an arched eyebrow and a malicious smile. With my body as stiff as a mannequin, I allowed myself to let go on the bed. I heard the symphony of my bones resting on the bed. The fluorescent light was flickering like a firefly. I blinked several times and closed my eyes, trying to forget that I was in that prison for forgotten patients, trapped by desperation. Then I heard a silent voice, a gentle sensation like a memory from long ago, whispering into my ear like a singing robin.

'Look at that dot, Amelia. That is here. It is our home. It is us. To-day, I will take you to the best place to get lost in. I will bring you up to the sky and to its fascinating arch. You will fly with me up to those sparkly points in the dark night sky that are full of light and truth. Together, we will discover the secrets of the invisible universe. Come with me, we will look at our cosmic home, we will venerate the celestial bodies hanging from transparent strings beneath the majestic dome that creates and launches our magic. We will let our silhouettes dance like trapeze artists over the imaginary lines of the constellations. If you dare to follow me, you will be welcomed by Polaris, the North Star, the brightest star in Ursa Minor. We shall close our eyes, I shall hold you tight and we shall make a wish every time a shooting star surprises us. Do not be afraid, the moon will be our protector as soon as it falls in love with your stunning eyes. This voyage will push you towards the absolute, it will fulfil your desire for infinity, you will experience the start of transcendence and you will go beyond the limits of your being. For a while, I shall become the magician who will open the trunk of secrets, as long as you never forget that you are a daughter of the stars.'

Elsu visited me often. I could feel his presence in my dreams, in the light fresh breeze that caressed my face, every time a butterfly placed its delicate wings on me, spreading rainbow dust, or whenever a flower mysteriously fell from a tree and adorned my hair. That was our code. He promised me that his music would accompany me always, and somehow it always did. What felt like a second seemed to last an eternity. The doorway to the stars suddenly slammed shut when I felt the voice of the 'white coat' in my ears. I hated him for waking me up from my wonderful dream and ruining one of the few happy moments I'd had in that place. Half asleep, I fumbled around for my purple slippers under the bed and I sat up, covering myself with one of my greatest treasures – my mother's brown woollen jacket, covered with little fluffy balls and and missing a few buttons, which she'd wear on cold winter days and whose sleeves stretched with wear seemed to hug me tightly when I wrapped my own arms around me.

'Amelia, how are you feeling?' he asked with interest as he put his hands in the pockets of his ink-stained coat that smelled strongly of eucalyptus lozenges.

My rusty tongue was fighting to rid itself of the courage of impossibility. I had become accustomed to the perfection of silence. I walked in circles along the grey floor tiles, tracing their outlines with the tips of my worn-out slippers. Finally, my obstinate mind gave the order. I accepted to talk in my dimly-lit cell, looking towards the door through which the morning was trying to enter, stopped only by the pale walls.

'They don't want to listen to me. No one ever wants to listen to me. When they look at me, all they see is a crazy person.'

'I shouldn't be here. You know I'm no longer your psychiatrist, but after what happened last night I wanted to make sure you were OK. I'm really sorry you had to go through that. You should know I informed the director so he can take the appropriate measures.'

'You mean the Unholy Father? It's a waste of time. That won't help you or me. Do you seriously think that they do anything here without his blessing? I'm a veteran, you know. I know who I'm dealing with. Every day, I see how they reduce the doses, how they open and pour pills into metal cups as comfortably as a Vegas drug dealer. I've witnessed such frightful scenes that they could be put together to make one of the best horror films of all time.'

'You have such imagination, Amelia!

'I like that you call it imagination and not insanity. When we switch on our imagination, we are transported to worlds that never were, and yet without it we wouldn't go anywhere. With it, we conquer the impossible. I live with eternal hope. I believe that, somewhere, something incredible is always waiting to be discovered. The soul thirsts for knowledge. It's one of the most powerful impulses in existence; it can't be stopped because it's like a giant magnet that is drawn by the call of the greatest of mysteries.'

'If only everyone thought like you.'

'It doesn't matter if someone doesn't agree with me. They should still be allowed to exist. You probably won't find anyone like them in one hundred billion galaxies.'

'Do you really think there can be extraterrestrial life out there?'

'It would be a huge waste of space if we were all alone in the universe, don't you think? The absence of evidence isn't evidence of absence.'

'Well, even if that were the case, I don't think we should so much as consider running other planets, considering what a terrible job we're doing with our own. There are those who say that the universe is nothing more than a god's dream.'

'I actually think that rather than humans being dreamt up by gods, it is the gods that have been dreamt up by humans. The immensity of the cosmos is truly unfathomable and should make us humble.'

'But that's very hard to understand.'

'In fact, it's purely a question of logic. If the human race is the product of natural processes, and with the universe being as large as it is, by pure mathematical logic other advanced civilisations must also exist on planets with equally favourable conditions such as ours for complex life forms to develop. It makes no sense to think that we're the only intelligent species in our own galaxy, and much less in the universe. Tell me, have you never doubted this, even for a moment?'

'My ex-wife used to tell me that doubt was my greatest virtue, and that it's the reason I became a scientist.'

'Well, then let me tell you that scientists such as yourself have managed to study the distribution of elements throughout the galaxy for the first time and have concluded that ninety-seven per cent of the human body is made up from materials that have come from the stars. Throughout history, many have tried to tell us this. We are stardust. Maybe science is a source of spirituality, don't you think?'

'The possibility of being literally made up of stardust is one of the most scientifically poetic ideas I've ever heard.'

'That's right. The truth is that we're made up of the same substance as the stars and the cosmos is also within us. I had the enormous fortune of discovering this a long time ago on my voyage. Elsu taught me.'

'I see,' he said, wide-eyed.

'Yes, he taught me that to touch someone is to caress the cosmos, and that when we see our own reflection, we're facing the cosmos itself. We are stars enjoying our own presence. To contemplate the cosmos is in fact an exercise in introspection.'

'Don't you find that a very risky mind game?'

'Think about it for a moment. If the planets orbit the stars, receiving their light and warmth, then our lives are inevitably suspended by their influence. Maybe it's because of that connection with our destinies and the map of the planetary positions at the moment of our birth that we're so familiar with such expressions as 'to be born under a lucky star'. Not even you can know that the light is inside you. Not even you realise that you are the Universe.'

'But how do you reach this consciousness?'

'It is written. Get to know yourself and you'll discover the greatness of one who has everything and knows everything.'

He went quiet for a few seconds, like a bird when night falls, while I continued with my explanation.

'Stars are a universal symbol, one of the first symbols used by man, and they carry enormous significance and represent knowledge, wisdom, light and happiness. Since ancient times, humans have looked at the sky in search for answers. The stars have guided many civilisations and cultures, and explanations have been sought in their contemplation and study. The Celts, the Greeks, the Egyptians, the Mayans, the Incas, all indigenous peoples were observers of the celestial celestial orb and even made predictions using their calendars. They were convinced that man's destiny was written in the stars. Some animals also use star patterns, and sailors follow night sky charts. Our DNA contains the same fibres used to embroider the stars and nebulae that inspire us from the infinite every night. Therefore, as children of the stars, we too are made to stand out, to shine, and to touch the sky. Every cell in our heart and every calcium particle in our bones has a cosmic story written in it.'

'You make it out to be something magical.'

'Does it seem magical to you? There's no doubt. We're meant to shimmer, reflecting one another's light like diamond dust. We're part of a unique and wonderful symphony. We are magic in motion. We've been made to believe that magic is something that occurs outside us, that it's something that only very few of us can do. Magic is embodying our true essence, our spiritual truth within our human experience. Magic is bringing heaven to Earth. It's assuming your role and your purpose in the mandala of life from your truth, from your heart. Magic is serving life and not letting the apparent reality rob you of your unique and authentic expression. Magic is honouring and embracing your journey, your steps – every one of them, as they have brought you this far and will lead you to become the person you are meant to be. Magic is knowing that everything changes in love's light, that everything is awakened, flourishes and finds its pulse, its rhythm, its frequency, its future, its true manifestation. Magic is beauty and integrity. Magic is respecting all other life forms and all other beings, and their choices, their paths, their stages of evolution and their free will. It's understanding the unique and perfect rhythm of every being and their cyclicity, their value, their perfection. That the divine order carries out its mission so that true nature can flourish and manifest itself is perfection. That's magic. That's what you are, what we are, what they are.'

'I'm not sure I agree with you, Amelia, but I don't think you belong at San Patricio.'

'Unfortunately, not everybody who should be here is here, and not everybody that is here should be here. It's time for me to no longer be here.'

I wanted to stop feeling like a burnt-out boat in a country from which the sea had withdrawn, where its waters only come to visit every once in a while.

My soul needed to connect with people who were also awake. To connect with someone who spoke the same language, who vibrated on the same note.. I didn't want to talk about everyday trivia, I wanted to talk about the soul, energies, the moon, lives and the evolution of beings. I dreamt of San Patricio's open door, with its metal doorframe, full of promises. Beyond those steel doors that sealed off the psychiatric wing lay my freedom, Rafaela, and a truth to deliver.

Here, freedom was achieved in exchange for rules laced with submission. That was the key. You had to appear to be a nice girl, not cheat, finish your plate and go along with everything – something I had refused to do for decades. Fail, misbehave and the key to your room will turn once again, with the subsequent descent into hell.

'The darker the night, the more the stars shine,' whispered Elsu when fear would take me by surprise. 'Go to the large window and admire infinity. A simple connection is sometimes all you need to get your breath or your inspiration back because it reminds you who you are. Do not feel like the stars are something distant or superior to you; allow yourself to understand and accept that we are a whole, that the astral material is found in every fragment of your being, therefore giving you a magical power and capacity – that of shining on any stage, in any situation or adverse moment, not worrying about the darkness around you. In life, there is no point fearing, only understanding. It is here that fear sees the strength in your face and dissolves in your light.'

It's not easy to shine, we know this. We tend to make our way over oceans of darkness, through marshlands of perpetual unhappiness, and across arid lands where the seed of self-esteem can no longer grow. The dark human underside tests us on many occasions, forcing us to participate in a perverse and macabre game that makes us forget our own cosmic destiny.

If we ever forget that we're made out of stardust, there will always be another star by our side, giving us part of its magical matter in order to relight the fire of our hope and our happiness. There's nothing like caressing the soul of another star to perceive the immensity of the cosmos. In challenging situations, I like to remember Oscar Wilde's words *'We are all in the gutter, but some of us are looking at the stars.'*

'Don't you find it amazing to imagine the possibility of becoming close, in the deepest sense of the word, with beings that we generally perceive to be as distant and impersonal as the stars? When your conscience connects and discovers your presence within the universe, the cultural precept that "everything is out there" comes crashing down, and you embark on the indescribable journey to self-awareness. Part of our being knows that's where we come from. Each individual is connected to the cosmos. Their behaviour depends completely on their star sign. We're eager to return, and we will, because we're made of stellar matter that will, irrevocably, return to its origin.'

'So, basically, the future of man depends on what the skies decide. We're under the constant influence of the cosmos. Conscious or not, we're at their mercy. What's the purpose of our existence, then, if we're nothing more than puppets?'

'That's not exactly right, although our activities are guided by the same universal rules. Consciousness gives us the opportunity to establish contact with the great power of the cosmos, to restructure our life maps and make the necessary connections in order to avoid secondary influences that wreak havoc on our civilisation and bring chaos and disorder to our lives. Despite the inviolability of our destiny's basic design, we have an almost unlimited degree of freedom. We can determine how the process will come to pass in our present lives. Life is a game, and we have to know the rules.

'We each have a metaphysical DNA that corresponds to the alignment of astral bodies at the moment of our birth. We'll follow a route in accordance with the positions of the stars that will lead us in the right direction, but there's an element of free will so we can make corrections.'

He looked at me as though I'd just come out of a flying saucer and said, 'Let me see if I understand this, Amelia. Are you suggesting that the exact time, day and place of our birth reveal the main pattern of our lives, as well as our potential power, our preferences and our problems?'

'Bingo! You've got it. Our birth chart reveals the limitations and restrictions that prevent us from feeling free. It shows us our strengths as well as the methodology with which to improve our weaknesses. There are also dangerous areas and favourable skies to take into account.'

'But if that were true, such knowledge would be absolutely essential for our lives and for the destiny of all mankind. Why don't we apply it?'

'Short-sightedness, intolerance and non-spiritual attitudes usually prevent us from using the tools available to us, through which we can transcend to another level of consciousness and change our destiny. I'll tell you something else. The cosmos is geared towards sharing its benevolence with us, even more so than we are to receiving it. There's actually no need to become an Indian yogi, a Mexican shaman or a Tibetan lama in order to recognise our grandeur and experience an awakening.'

'It seems as though the universe and all our lives are programmed into computerised cosmic maps.'

'Maybe that way of describing it can help you understand it better. The cosmic group of celestial actors is predetermined, but each of us is influenced by our astral intelligence in different ways. That explains such different lives, with such unique and particular characteristics. In the metaphysical universe, stars don't shine or transfer energy constantly, they radiate only at established intervals. Each unit of consciousness or intelligence returns to its original position once it has fulfilled its purpose. Therefore, our mundane universe and our own physical bodies reflect a constant back and forth between the terrestrial reality and that of the celestial systems.'

'And where would the soul fit into all of this?'

'That's a very good question for a scientist. Our soul's consciousness possesses an energy-intelligence that has the desire to receive and a purpose, which is to share. The soul is a metaphysical force that creates life within us. When the soul leaves the body it creates death, given that the body itself doesn't contain life. Physical existence no longer has a purpose. It's only when the soul's consciousness dominates the body's consciousness that this is completely integrated into the whole.'

'Does that mean that our tendency to divide the physical and metaphysical worlds in to separate concepts is nothing more than an illusion?'

'Just take the sun and the moon, for example, and look at their strong and profound influence on our lives. The moon makes the tides ebb and flow. The sun warms us in the summer and increasingly fades during the cold winter days. All things or events that are perceived or that act upon each other are intelligent energies that are interrelated and connected, even if they appear to be completely different aspects or manifestations in our world. They're essentially considered parts of a whole, and we form part of it too.

'The inundation of energy-intelligence of thought to which we're subjected in this life comes from the cosmos. The inhabitants of Planet Earth are the only participants in this revolution. There are time in which we become vulnerable to negative activities, so we must be cautious with our actions during those particular periods of intense negative cosmic influences.'

'I understand a lot of things now,' said 'white coat'. 'Your beliefs go against Catholic morals and against the principles outlined in the Bible and by the magisterium of the Church. Those are the kinds of superstitions that good Christians are meant to avoid, particularly in a Catholic institution such as San Patricio, directed by the Unholy Father. The fundamental principle of Christian morality is that only God knows the future of man, and that of the whole of mankind. And that leads to a very uncomfortable question. What of the free will given to us by Christ if humans are, in fact, ruled by the stars? We're up against the church! Still, there has to be more to this. Your beliefs may well go against the Vatican, but that doesn't justify you being locked up here. You've spent longer in a mental facility than almost anyone else I've ever met, and yet you're far more lucid than any of them. There's a missing piece to this puzzle somehow.

'I remember seeing in your painful medical history that you gave birth to a healthy baby girl just a few months after arriving here, but I don't understand why they insist on hiding that fact, or making you believe it never happened.'

'During all my time here, I've witnessed the arrival of hundreds of women with "paranoid schizophrenia", which other doctors tend to diagnose as "hysteria". These were single women without children, single mothers and widows. They were suffering from anxiety, were disruptive to family life with their behaviour, had suffered from heartache, an abortion or had been abused. We're their favourite prey – perfect fodder for redemption.

'During my morning walk on a particularly foggy morning, I came across a woman with a grey bun on top of her head who was looking at some birds and smiling. My presence surprised her and she immediately approached me and stroked my growing belly, her eyes filled with sadness. Lola told me as best she could that she was also expecting when she arrived here, but that they'd forced her to abort and then sterilised her. She denounced this practice with words – some more comprehensible than others – and with gestures, such as placing her hands on her temples, making a grimace as though she was biting something hard, and showing true pain all over her face. I hugged my belly instinctively, as if trying to protect my baby, and was overwhelmed by pity for her. I thought that poor woman had lost her mind! Although time made me see that Lola had spoken the truth. I was so scared that something like that could happen to me and, over time, I felt increasingly guilty for not having believed her. The abuse Lola suffered is nothing compared to the way they used drugs to block her emotions, the way they called her by shouting her last name and how they denied her any hint of privacy. When I met her, she was beautiful, sweet and docile. Now, she has a very bad temper. When she gets angry, she raises her voice and waves her arm around, telling everyone to get lost. When she's in a good mood, she sings the hymns that the Unholy Father forced her to learn. All these years of imprisonment have taken a terrible toll on her body – she's very hunched over, she always seems tired and she weighs only thirty-seven kilos. She passes the time in the facility's chapel.'

The Argentinian 'white coat' stared at me as if I was one of the mysteries of the Holy Trinity. I imagine that after hearing my story and what little he'd seen since arriving at San Patricio a month ago, he was wondering how I'd been able to overcome such tragedy and remain so physically youthful. He raised his eyebrows until they touched his messy fringe and continued with his conclusions.

'I know the concept they can have about single mothers such as yourself here, Amelia, but that can't possibly be the reason for such a severe punishment. There's something very dark going on here, it doesn't make sense, and I just can't see it. I noticed that all the folders featuring the patients' names on the spine are divided into medical history and psychiatric history, as if to separate body and soul, and that yours was the only blue one.'

He seemed so passionate about his cause that, for the first time in years, I began to feel hopeful and wanted to share my secret with him.

'There was a time when I really doubted myself. I was convinced that there were ghosts in my head that didn't exist and I wondered if it wasn't all just my own madness. They made me believe that weeds had grown in my head, making me say stupid things. I didn't even know who I was any more. That's when I began to write everything down in a secret diary, so I could save myself one day, if necessary. It was a place for me to find answers when I was struggling, and it could also help others preserve the original version of events should my memory suddenly succumb to scepticism. I made a commitment to my inner reality that would protect me from the cowardice of an uncertain future. It became my time capsule – a safe in which to keep my story, safeguarding it so it wouldn't be forgotten. I needed to shine a light on the truth.'

> For within you is the light of the world – the only light that can be shed upon the Path.
> If you are unable to perceive it within you,
> It is useless to look for it elsewhere.
>
> Mabel Collins

Chapter 13

The Message from Venus

There was no way back now, life was pushing me forwards. As though I'd been tricked by a nymph, having already drunk the potion, not even the magical powder that Belly would add to my buttered toast as a child and whose sweetness would make my troubles disappear could free me from my disastrous life.

'You have no idea how much I envy you, Rafaela,' said Esther, hiding her face behind a mug of hot chocolate as I packed all my broken dreams up into a small suitcase. With it, a passport that would take me to the island of forgotten memories, where I would rise again like a plucked and pathetic phoenix from the ashes. I didn't feel like smiling, but a hysterical burst of laughter escaped me without permission.

'C'mon Esther, don't be ridiculous. Since when are you a masochist?'

'Seriously, you're so free… You can do and experience whatever you want.'

The truth is that, at that precise moment, I was blinded by disappointment, fury and pain, and completely unable to see the other side of my reality. I felt lost, sitting firmly on fear, my feet dangling over the edge.

'Come to Granada with me. Together, we'll start again from scratch,' I encouraged her, impulsively.

Esther was full of excitement for a moment, but she soon let it go, the way we take off expensive dresses we know we'll never be able to wear.

'I wish I could, Rafaela. Nothing in the world would make me happier. I miss you already, but you know that's just not an option for me,' she replied, letting out a deep sigh.

'Esther, who were you before the world told you who to be?'

'I'm where I belong.'

'You only belong when you're doing what you want to be doing,' I stated categorically, observing the invisible chain that tied her to her husband's will.

She went silent, lowered her head and looked at me sadly.

A broken marriage is considered the worst possible thing that can happen to a woman among the Jewish community. The flower of her youth was wilting in a chorus of children and a stern husband, indoctrinated by a religion that was holding Esther's soul hostage. An arranged marriage that was unbreakable in the eyes of a woman whose mind was devout but whose spirit was free.

Esther often visited me in secret. I'd become a best friend to her, and a terrible influence in the eyes of those around her. Her husband rarely allowed her to leave the house unaccompanied. Despite her life surrounded by people, she felt desperately trapped and alone. As a Jewish woman, she couldn't get out of her marriage, even if she wanted to. Jared's brother would never give her the *get*, the document required to carry out the process. A woman is forbidden to date anyone, remarry or have any kind of relationship with another man until a divorce is finalised, otherwise she will be considered an adulteress. It's one of the most extreme forms of emotional abuse because she's confined to solitude, as if locked up in an emptiness as infinite as silence or space.

On one of her clandestine visits, I took her shopping. Esther would choose the clothes she dreamt of wearing and I'd try them on for her. I remember the way she looked at me. She was a child gazing at the moon, thinking that the moon was looking back at her. She observed me completely spellbound, wrapped up in her many layers of clothing. Modest women believe that by dressing this way earns redemption for themselves and for the rest of their community. She'd arrange the pieces on my body perfectly and would combine items and colours beautifully. She had exquisite taste and we wore the same size, so I became her perfect model. That day, we made a pact: the clothes would be hers, I'd keep them in a secret part of my wardrobe, and she'd wear them whenever she came to see me until she had to leave again. The only thing she would keep on was her wig, because she didn't like to see herself with a shaved head. That day, she chose a black leather skirt with fringe on the sides, a loose mint green shirt and some wedge sandals. She stared at her own reflection even on the doorknobs, sucking her cheeks in and blinking, saying to herself, 'looking good, babe'. We took heaps of photos. It's such a shame she never let me keep them. I loved seeing her so gorgeous and happy. We couldn't have been more different. Never have two human beings had more different personalities. It was almost as though we came from distant planets; our stories were so wildly different that only a miracle could have brought us together. But that miracle did take place, and from the moment we met, nothing could tear us apart. She was as modern as I was, which made me realise that there was more than just one type of modernity: there were at least two – hers and mine.

It had been two months since my relationship with Jared had died. I thought I'd die too. Jerusalem wasn't the place for me any more. I felt differently every single day. Either way, I was sure it was time to move on. Although I was angry at life, I couldn't turn my back on reality. There was nothing left. Not even hope. So it was *adiós* to the prototype of my perfect man, the same man who once said he loved all my defects. *Arrivederci* fairy tale. *Auf wiedersehen* to a relationship that I had stretched out like a piece of gum, fooling myself. If only I could've opened my obstinate head, searched in my brain and cut out everything that had to do with him! When I was finally able to make sense of it all, I saw only one open door. Actually, there were two. The first wasn't viable, because I knew exactly what happens when you let life do the work for you: absolute nothingness becomes the title of the next chapter of your life. I couldn't just stand there like an idiot watching as everything around me changed, looking for an excuse good enough to make me take the next step. Change is always uncomfortable, but we must accept that it's the only constant in life.

I had made a very tough decision. Any separation, no matter how necessary, is always a catastrophe. I had a long road of mourning and rebuilding ahead of me. But, why was an abused woman such as myself dedicating so much of my time to thinking about him? I was being held by an invisible string that I refused to break. It turns out I was no less of a slave than Esther was to her master. I was a captive to my memories of him, to his scent, and to the resentment that he, the thief of all my romantic dreams, had left me. It was as though my life had somehow ended up at a pawn shop. I knew it was mine but I couldn't live it.

'I have an idea, something that can help you,' said Esther, excitedly.

'I'm scared of your ideas, *amiga*. I think meeting me hasn't been so good for you, after all. Your ideas get crazier all the time. Honestly, I don't think I can handle any more free-falls.'

'This one's different. I want you to meet someone.'

She never gave up.

'Wait, what? Are you setting me up on a blind date? You're out of your mind, lady!'

'He's a very well-known man, with a life story that's far superior to that of any mere mortal. He works at a place called Venus. He's a professor at Atlantic University, in Virginia, and is the founder of the parapsychology department. Venus is a very prestigious clinic. My contact…'

'OK, are we going to stop talking about this already?' I interrupted, pretending to hold my hands up in defeat.

'It's not what you think. It's about your future,' she replied, circling around me like a hen flapping its wings.

'My future? Esther, really, I'm very grateful, but I just want to switch off and forget this nightmare. I'll be fine, so, don't worry about me.'

'He has very good references. It might help you find some answers.'

'C'mon Esther, a Jewish woman believing in paranormal phenomena? What's he going to tell me that I don't know? I'm a psychologist, remember? I know exactly which stages I'm going through right now.'

'I've been reading. There's a connection between spirituality and psychological experiences, extrasensory events and even the psychology of religions. You told me you've been having strange recurring dreams for some time, remember? This might help you resolve them.'

'I almost would've preferred the blind date,' I sighed in resignation.

'At least tell me you'll think about it. His name is Derek Ríos.'

Suddenly, I imagine this Derek character running through, gloomy castles and haunted houses trying to catch ghosts. My friend seemed to read my mind.

'He isn't a ghostbuster, Rafaela; he's a scientist. Among other things, he studies premonitory dream experiences, dreams that seem to predict future events. Apparently, through his studies, he's discovered that some people tend to remember the dreams that come true, and forget the ones that don't, and also seem to be very good at finding connections between seemingly random events. That's one of your skills, isn't that amazing? Go on, Rafaela. This'll be our last adventure together. Please, do it for me.'

Actually, maybe the only ghosts I was seeing were those of my breakup, and they seemed to have made themselves at home in my head like squatters. Besides, I couldn't refuse my friend's request, no matter how crazy it sounded. My friend, my sister, had shown me such incredible loyalty and love, that her words always managed to make my heart melt.

You never truly know someone until you see them in the best and worst moments of their life. There's no point thinking you know someone if you've never seen them hit rock bottom, or touch the sky. It's only in those two scenarios that you truly discover the vulnerable being that inhabits their body. Esther was one of those few people who knew me almost better than I knew myself. At my lowest points and at my highest ones. It only took a few minutes for me to agree to go along with her suggestion. I figured it may be better to preserve my energy for what lay ahead, than spend it arguing.

It was just an ordinary day. I think it may have been a Thursday. I got off the bus feeling very cold; September was particularly rough that year. I didn't want to admit it but it wasn't the month, it was my clothes. I was wearing shorts and a camisole top with just a light stripy long-sleeved shirt on top for protection. I'd already packed my suitcase and had only left out two changes of clothes, enough to last me a couple of days until I caught my flight back to Granada. I was never good at dressing in-between seasons, maybe because I never liked doing anything by halves. Call it radicalism, if you like. For the first time, I watched as Esther revealed her wig in public, removing her bandana without a word to tie it around my waist like a long skirt. It was a very meaningful gesture for us both.

'Welcome to the first day of the rest of your lives,' said the sign at the reception of the clinic called Venus, which we found at number twelve of a very narrow street. I followed my friend warily down the corridor that led to a cosy waiting room full of people who could have been spirits or apparitions waiting to be freed. I was expecting to find a haze-filled, mysterious place with creepy music, but instead, Raffaela Carrá enlivened the atmosphere to the rhythm of one of her hits 'En el amor todo es empezar'.

'Esther, what a coincidence! We come in and the singer that welcomes us has my name. And the song… I mean, "when it comes to love, everything starts over" feels like it's meant for me, doesn't it?'

'Maybe it's not such a coincidence,' she said with a know-it-all tone.

A chirpy girl suddenly appeared in front of us as though she had been materialised by a magician's wand.

'Does it bother you?' she asked, pointing at the stereo system. 'I love it. Life is so much better with good music, don't you think?'

'Yes, of course,' I smiled, giving her a thumbs up. 'Life is better like this.'

'You must be Rafaela,' she said confidently, as she typed on her computer.

'Maybe they really do have powers of premonition,' I whispered in Esther's ear, somewhat mockingly.

I found it very entertaining just watching the people who were waiting with us, imagining the gruesome stories that had brought them to this place. The door to the parapsychologist's office kept opening and closing, not letting me see his face despite my best efforts. His patients were a motley crew of people; some would leave seemingly happy and others looked horrified, while some would even look straight at us, encouraging us to go in. Finally, a voice emanated from the door calling my name. I went in alone, swallowing hard, feeling a combination of scepticism and curiosity. A large white beard softened his hard features, covering a thick neck. I found myself standing in front of a short, stout man with a very normal appearance, who must have been about to turn seventy. His face, tanned and covered in wrinkles, was pleasant and friendly. His manners couldn't have been more welcoming. I immediately felt at home.

'I don't really know what I'm doing here, to be honest. My friend practically dragged me…'

He stopped me straight away. 'You can leave at any time. We'll just tell her that everything's sorted out now and she won't bother you with this again. It'll work. Seriously. I promise. I do it all the time. I won't blame you for not believing in something you don't understand,' he said, with a knowing smile.

I hesitated for a few moments. The last thing I wanted to do was to give the image of being a coward with a narrow mind and zero personality. What I needed most was to feed my self-esteem and feel like I was in control of my life once again. A silent question invaded me: 'why not?' In an instant, those four walls became a place for me to open up and explore.

'OK, let's do it. But no candles, crystal balls or anything like that.'

'Deal,' he said, holding out his hand to make it official.

I explained that ever since I was a little girl, I'd been experiencing very strange recurring dreams, and that I'd lately been having them more often. Sometimes, when things happened, I felt as though I had already lived them out in my dreams.

'What kind of dreams, Rafaela?

'I see myself in a place I've never been before, with people I don't know.'

'Do those people communicate with you?'

'Yes, but in a very strange language. I can't understand what they're saying.'

'And what happens in those dreams?'

'I feel as though many eyes are looking at me, as if they're expecting something from me.'

'Is it frightening?'

'No, not at all. Actually, I feel at home. It's as if everything looks familiar. After these experiences, what usually happens is that I begin to see signs, coincidences and I begin to connect dots that only I understand. Sometimes it has to do with numbers, or simply a synchronicity of events that all seem to be designed to send me a message.'

'I understand. Could you describe this place?'

'Of course. I went there on so many nights as a child that I could describe it in detail. In fact, I'm sure I drew it for my mother when I was little. Now that I think of it, I remember I didn't finish the drawing that night, so she completed it for me. It was just as I had dreamt it. I got the feeling she also knew that place.'

What you're telling me is very interesting, Rafaela. Did you ever tell your mother about your dreams?'

'No. I've never shared this with anyone other than my best friend, Esther. I didn't want anyone to think I was crazy.'

'I see you've studied psychology.'

'Yes, that's right. I'm fascinated by the mind and I love being able to help others get to know themselves better.'

'And wouldn't you also like to find some answers for yourself, Rafaela? Did you know that we're all energy sponges? This reality is an undeniable truth to many, and something completely incredible to others.'

'Well, I don't doubt that parapsychology is considered a science and that it's divided into extrasensory perception and telekinesis, but, frankly, I've always been rather reticent to go any further than my rational mind could understand. My grandmother may have influenced me in that way. She's never been very religious, but she speaks openly about superstition. Her hair stands on end when people talk about spirits or karma. I grew up always wearing one sock inside-out to protect me from the evil eye. Unfortunately, it didn't protect me from being laughed at by the other kids at school. It's impossible to make her walk under a ladder, and she runs away from black cats just in case they cross her path. She may not have always been wrong, though. Every time she caught me wiping my feet, she would say, "don't do that or you'll never get married," and, as it turns out, cupid has declared war on me.'

'It's too early to give in, Rafaela,' he said with a laugh.

'Would you allow me to work with you as a hypnotherapist?'

I'll admit that this question made me jump out of my chair. Up until that moment, everything had made sense. But hypnotising me and putting me in the hands of a complete stranger was another thing.

'Is it really necessary?' I asked, hoping the answer would agree with my wishes.

'Look, some people have a much more developed sensitivity than others when it comes to perceiving what may happen in the future. They may not always see things clearly with detailed accounts of what will happen, but they do have the intuition that something will happen in relation to something specific. Dreams are a gateway to the astral plane, a realm where there's no time or space. Although it may seem odd, premonitory experiences in dreams are a very common thing.'

'Do you mean to say that I have the ability to see the future?'

'I'd like to explore that possibility with you, if you'll let me.'

Dreams transmit information that doesn't come from known facts. They go beyond normal human comprehension, therefore turning those experiences into a parapsychological perception process.

I admit that I once went to a hypnosis show featuring a mentalist-cum-hypnotist. When he appeared, he explained to the public that we would be journeying through hypnosis to become a part of the great stories of literature, with medieval knights, clandestine lovers… even pirates! But before he could do this, he had to test us to see who among us would be the most open to suggestion and, therefore, easy to hypnotise. He assured us that while everyone could be hypnotised, not everyone was equally open to suggestion at all times. When I heard this, I hoped with all my might that I wouldn't fall into that group as I had no intention of dropping to the floor like a ragdoll in front of hundreds of people, including fellow students from my university, when this 'super man' worked his magic on me. I avoided all eye contact just in case.

In general, I've never been scared of supernatural things. In fact, they've always inspired curiosity in me. But to experience it myself was a completely different matter. Luckily, I wasn't very receptive that night and wasn't chosen to go on stage, which I was grateful for once I saw some of my classmates being turned on and off like robots. Of course, this time it would have much more of a therapeutic approach.

'What? Now? Here?' I asked, hoping he'd give me an appointment for another day so I could use my trip back as an excuse not to go.

'Yes, we can do it now seeing as you're already here,' he replied, inviting me to lie down on the comfortable-looking sofa.

I don't know why, but this Derek person inspired confidence in me, so I put myself in his hands. I considered the situation carefully and thought, 'Rafaela, if you have the opportunity to take an hour out of your day to lie down on a comfortable couch and relax, then that's already a step up. If, on top of that, it can benefit you personally, then make the most of it!'

He explained what was going to happen at all times. I followed his instructions. I closed my eyes and began to count backwards, focusing on slowing down and taking deep breaths. The truth is that I found hypnosis very pleasant. It was almost like sleeping, but being aware of everything happening around you. At no time did I 'disconnect' from my body, nor did my mind switch off and leave me trapped in a dark place while he manipulated my brain at will. I learned that it really wasn't like what you see in the movies. As the session went on, my state of hypnosis became deeper and deeper, although I did actively participate during the entire process. Seeing as I'd decided to jump in, there was no point in resisting; it was better to just cooperate. So, paying special attention to his words, I followed the suggestions given by a pleasant voice that said, 'You are standing at the top of a staircase, with a banister on the side to steady you. You can go down the stairs slowly. Each step takes you closer to a sense of calm and relaxation, going deeper and deeper into your subconscious. You are calmly and effortlessly falling into a deep sleep. Where are you, Rafaela?'

I told him that I saw myself lying in a field of tall yellow grass in the late afternoon. A man came towards me and handed me something. It was cold and hard and had a peculiar shape. I couldn't tell what it was, but I felt that it was very valuable. Suddenly, from my lips emerged the words 'I found it', though I don't recall saying this consciously.

'Is anyone else with you?'

'I see blurred faces in the grass and the outlines of some animals moving around further away. I hear whispers in a foreign language, *"The Layet Mai. The Mai Layet."'*

'What's happening now?'

'The grass is beginning to flatten, forming a path, and the man in my vision is starting to glide over it, moving faster and faster towards a light in the shape of a star. I want to follow him but I'm dazed and confused. He disappears.'

Derek counted down to bring me back to a waking state and told me to hold on to that calm feeling when I came to. I opened my eyes, my limbs feeling very heavy, with a feeling of calm and exhaustion all at once.

Listening to the recorded audio afterwards was amazing. There were so many descriptions that I didn't remember giving, and my voice was much slower than usual. I barely recognised myself. Derek wet his lips. My heart was beating out of my chest when I felt that he was about to solve the mystery.

'Rafaela, we have to figure out what *"The Layet Mai. The Mai Layet"* means; that may be the key.'

His knock-kneed legs began to move around the room, spinning round abruptly from time to time. He seemed to be guided by a well-trained sense of smell. He reminded me of one of those Belgian Shepherds used by the army that are trained to identify smells from under demolished buildings in order to locate survivors buried beneath the rubble. They pick up the scent emitted by humans that are affected by catastrophes of this kind – the smell of a drowning victim, of burnt human bones, of the stress experienced by people in life-or-death situations, and of corpses. The parapsychologist's nose directed him to an enormous book titled *Extinct Tongues*.

For more than twenty minutes, I had the feeling that the pages on that book had swallowed him up. I experienced one of those moments where, if you're not used to dealing with silence, you can start to feel uncomfortably ignored. With everything that was happening to me, my mind had become so active that it was practically impossible to remain still and in silence. Keeping quiet when silence provokes panic and discomfort is such a difficult task that improving our relationship with that nothingness requires expert help. It took me a long time to understand that having a good relationship doesn't necessarily have to involve always knowing what the other person is thinking. I firmly believed that having those moments of silence and boredom truly determined the quality of those relationships.

'Jared, what are you thinking?' That was the recurring questions I'd use to fill the empty spaces that suffocated me.

'Nothing' was also his recurring answer. I just couldn't believe that anybody was able to not think things at all times, which led me to think 'he doesn't want to talk about it', 'he's bored with me', 'we don't have anything in common', 'he doesn't trust me', 'I'm sure he's hiding something' and so on. That gave me a destabilising sensation of losing control and of insecurity. I was horrified at the sight of couples just sitting on a bench, having dinner in a restaurant facing each other, or simply walking down the street without saying a word. That was the antithesis of the perfect relationship that I'd pictured in my head. I saw silence as the ultimate annihilator of couples.

Now I know that silence is a barometer of trust and intimacy. The day I can walk hand in hand with a man along the beach and simply enjoy doing nothing else, without the need to fill the silence with words at all times, is the day I'll know I've found the love of my life. Communicating and talking about feelings is a way of keeping love fresh and, of course, dedicating some time every day to building 'us' is essential. Words are the doorway to reality, but it has to be based on silence so we can really savour them and make them our own.

The heart is a lone hunter and the only true listener. We have to see beyond words.

There was a loud thud. Derek had closed the heavy book, freeing a cloud of old dust.

'Rafaela, I can definitely tell you that your dreams are full of meaning. They're giving you information about the future. I was able to decipher the words in your vision and this is the literal meaning of a secret and forgotten Native American language: *'Your destiny is laid out for you, you just have to follow it.'*

Chapter 14

The Deflowering Ceremony

They were running barefoot and laughing in the gardens, picking colourful flowers along the way, all of which seemed to bow at their feet, begging for a space on their laps. We took in the scent enveloping those beautiful creatures whose elegantly sculptured shapes were clad in petals. They looked like nymphs, spirits of nature, and appeared before us like beautiful young, virgin brides. There was great merriment in that fertile land filled with lush and blooming trees high the mountains. Its creatures praised nature infinitely and paid attention to every detail with extreme care. They were sisters, daughters of the earth, with long hair wrapped around them like buds. A white flower resembling a water lily bloomed on their chests. This strange species had both stamens and carpels, as if it were a bisexual flower with both male and female floral organs all at once.

Our presence didn't appear to disturb their celebration. On the contrary, seeing us look shy and distant, one of them opened her arms with a welcoming gesture, inviting us to join their dance. Elsu put his arms behind his head, lowering his elbows to his heart. She responded by making another similar gesture. They communicated through a type of sign language. I was surprised to hear that the only sound that emanated from her plump lips was laughter, and some whistling sounds when the wind raised her clothing.

'Amelia, the daughters of Virgo do not talk very much, because they know the true weight of words and how much value they hold. They will not speak unless absolutely necessary.'

Those words entered my consciousness like a thought and, for a moment, I forgot we were communicating telepathically.

'Come!' he said, taking my hand and copying the soft movements of the other goddesses.

I followed shyly, but I was enjoying myself. Our adventure around the Purple Lagoon had been by far the most human experience I had ever had. I desperately wanted to dance with Elsu, despite the strange circumstances. We mixed in with the beauty in motion. Our bare feet tapped rhythmically on the stellar soil of Virgo in time to her beat.

Elsu explained to me that they were heading to the temple to join the sacred circle where they would deposit the large bunches of flowers they were carrying. That was where the deflowering would take place, in the presence of all their sisters. Along the floral path, they played with the clear water of the rivers and springs they came across.

'The temple?' I asked excitedly, 'Do you think they mean the Temple of Light we're looking for?'

'We will find out when we get there,' he said as he continued dancing.

'What is a deflowering?'

'You will understand each thing in due course, Amelia. Now enjoy this moment that will never come again.'

My Earthling mind made me feel envy. I feared that Elsu would fall in love with one of them. They were perfect, and no matter how hard I tried to find their defects, all I saw was beauty and virtue. The white that surrounded them reflected purity – the very essence of those virgins, whose inner calm and peace mirrored nature's harmony and benevolence nature that pervaded everything.

I was embarrassed for having felt that way and remembered Leonardo da Vinci's words *'sooner will there exist a body without a shadow than virtue unaccompanied by envy'*. It also occurred to me that nobody could take away what was never yours to begin with, a thought that gave me some semblance of peace, although it didn't make me feel better. I covered up my feelings by playing with Vodka who was also dancing around on two legs, not sure which rhythm to go with. We took a break on an open field overflowing with flowers tinted sky blue and apricot. I tried to stay close to Elsu, as it was only by remaining at a certain distance that I could telepathically understand everything in that enchanted fairy tale world.

'No, not like that. You have to place each flower at the same level as the others, you see? And you have to alternate the colours. It has to be perfect,' said one to another using signs, as she rearranged one of the bunches hanging from her basket made from dried stems.

I found this perfection a bit much, to be honest. Is there anything more utopian than perfection? They seemed to centre on the here and now, and on planning and preparing. And what were they preparing? Their perfect plan, of course.

As we advanced, everything was kind of... similar to... just like... I couldn't identify any familiar smells nor identify any of the colours in the forest, the sky or the water. The air was dominated by a diffused white, as if there a creamy translucent glass curtain hung before my eyes, blurring the outlines of all the living things around us. I sensed we were arriving somewhere magical and that we would witness a special event. It was as though we had come out of the womb of one fantastic world and entered another. The wandering moon, accompanied by one or two stars, and my body's tiredness let me know that we had been dancing a long time. I didn't know whether it was the intoxication from all the dancing or the excitement from feeling Elsu's hands around my waist that made me feel hungover. It was a hangover that only affected my body, freeing my soul. Vodka followed his natural instinct and lay down near a riverbend, waiting for me to do the same.

'Are you hungry?' asked one of them, looking at us.

'They're fresh shells,' she explained, offering us a kind of oyster that she had just taken out of the water.

'The white ones are sweet and the black ones are saltier,' she said.

Elsu thanked her for the gift by making a subtle movement with his fingers. I did so by bowing my head slightly as I gazed impatiently at that delicacy. It looked amazing! She left some near Vodka and sat with us, doubling over with laughter when she saw how much he struggled to open them.

'The fresher they are, the harder they are to open. It is the same with virgin souls,' she added.

I waited for another explanation that would give more meaning to her message, but she would only say the bare minimum. As per usual, Elsu answered my questions.

'Amelia, these creatures' actions speak much louder than their words. The daughters of the constellation of Virgo are able to express a great deal and to feel a great deal, but all within reason, so as to not release everything they hold within them at once, which would make it lose its value.'

'Do you mean to tell me that things have value not because of their worth, but because of what they mean? Is that why they remain virgins?'

'Valuable things must be conquered,' he answered.

That truth really impacted me, bearing in mind that I came from a world where we knew the price of everything and the value of nothing. A world of masked beings where being able to see someone's soul is a true privilege. A consumer society that was consuming us. Earthlings such as myself, were resigned to the materialism that forces us to shop, pay and own, always on the lookout for the right price, the best bargain, the final offer. Up until that moment, I hadn't stopped to think clearly on just how absurd we were. We lived surrounded by prices, and this had become second nature to us.

'Amelia, that is one of the tragedies of the generations that inhabit your planet nowadays. You know the price of giving birth in a private clinic versus a public hospital, but you do not understand the value and the dignity of each and every human life. You know the price of an apartment and the furniture inside of it, but you ignore the value of the love inside it. You are experts on the prices of mobile phones, but very few of you appreciate the value of being able to talk, listen and share experiences with loved ones. It would be great for the future of your planet if its inhabitants showed an interest in economy of the heart and soul; you would experience infinite abundance.'

I could maybe agree up to that point, but what was virginity? I could only see it as a social construct, even as a tool through which to control women and their bodies. For a feminist such as myself, it was very difficult to accept that a woman's value depended on her purity, and purity was nothing more than virginity. No way, I wasn't going to put up with that!

'You're not going to tell me that you agree with that, are you?

'It is not about agreeing or not, I mean valuing the value of our values.'

The answer sounded like a tongue twister. The term 'losing one's virginity' always felt somewhat old-fashioned, as if it were something you drop behind the couch along with the crumbs from your lunch. Historically, virginity had been venerated, but the script was finally changing. After a ten-minute monologue about sex and how liberal I was, I was inevitably asked the question that only a loudmouth like me could answer.

'How did you feel your first time?'

By now, I'd already learned that I couldn't fool Elsu. My emotions would give me away on his emotional radar, but I tried my luck anyway. What would he think once he knew my big secret? Yes, I was a virgin just like them but at least I could have avoided giving my expert speech. I still wasn't used to the fact that he wasn't from my world. I couldn't stop seeing him as someone I was attracted to and whom I was madly falling in love with, like when you leave a car on a hill and forget to put the emergency brakes on. Despite how modern my mother was in a lot of ways, we never ever spoke of sex at home. The only thing she told me at one time or another was that her parents, despite being engaged since the age of fourteen and burning with desire for one another, belonged to a category that became extinct a long time ago, meaning that they didn't get in each other's pants until their wedding night. I always thought my parents were asexual angels, above right and wrong. It's not that it was a taboo subject or that I had been brought up with religious beliefs, I think it was mostly cultural. Both had grown up in patriarchal families that constantly deny everything that makes women stronger. In my case, I'd say there was a glitch in the communication: they didn't explain and I didn't ask either, so I eventually had to figure it out on my own. At school, we had four sex education classes that dealt with the vulva, the vagina and the penis, and yet somehow left out the clitoris, considering it a secret sexual organ waiting to be discovered somewhere in limbo.

Up until that point, my virginity had never bothered me. After all, I was young and still had so much life ahead of me. That one fact didn't define me. I had been very busy studying and travelling so I could have a profession and not depend on anyone in the future, as my mother had taught me by example. My love life had never been my priority. I trusted in the fact that one day I'd meet someone who would truly love me, with whom I could experience my own deflowering ritual. I also remembered how, little by little, I freed myself of taboos and shame, and was comfortable getting to know my own body, experiencing incredible orgasms by myself. That was the story of my entire adolescence and part of my youth. Why, then, was the word 'virgin' echoing around in my head, in many different voices, as if everyone I'd ever met was saying it to me?

It was probably just that I didn't want Elsu to see me as someone desperate and unsure of herself who promotes something she's never even experienced. I had to come up with something convincing, and quick, that would get me out of this mess.

That moment is usually a very important one in most women's lives, so my story had to be brilliant; no way would mine involve losing my virginity in the backseat of a Ford or something along those lines. I'd watched hundreds of idyllic and romantic movie scenes, and my friends had told me of their sexual exploits loads of times, so improvising shouldn't be that difficult.

'It was an unforgettable experience,' I declared, starting with my improvised account. 'It was with a gorgeous and very attentive Swedish guy that I met one summer. He invited me over to his house. The bed was covered in rose petals. I had just turned eighteen and it was the first time for us both. I remember that I was shaking like a leaf, while also intrigued by the unknown. We laughed a lot and enjoyed ourselves despite our total lack of experience. He whispered words of love in my ear in Swedish, running his fingers all over me for hours. Our relationship ended just as the summer did.' I finished by saying that it had been a beautiful memory, sure that he had fallen for it.

Elsu looked at me in an entirely new way and said, 'My soul is glad to be the only one to have seen you naked.'

I then understood that your eyes always belong to the person who makes them shine. I loved the way he saw the world and the way he looked at me. I was dying to ask him the same question and learn how a man from the Elove Galaxy gives in to love and sex, but I didn't for fear that I'd be disappointed by his answer. What if some cosmic dust or DNA extracted from these light beings was in charge of reproducing and continuing the species with no type of eroticism or physical contact at all?

Discreet, without the need to draw attention to themselves, each of the maidens sought out a refuge in which to rest in solitude, just as the flowers on their chests also closed, entering a deep meditation state. They were protected in havens of peace that seemed to have been created in communion with nature, designed to connect with a spiritual power. There was complete calm, a mystic atmosphere, interrupted only by the timid movements of some strange beings that blended perfectly into the forest resembling miniature metallic trees covered in moss. Apparently, we couldn't make direct eye contact with them as they had the power to absorb our energy and turn our blood into fertile soil. We continued our journey to the temple as the sun began to set, guided by the well-rested virgins. Night had fallen by the time we finally arrived, and we had no idea what we were going to find. I expected a building made or marble with sacred altars, but instead I saw four huge flat rocks high up on a mountaintop. It was then that I understood that the magical circle was a defined, yet non-physical, temple – a space closed off by invisible walls that protected energy, delimited by a type of mark along the four cardinal points. It was a pentacle consisting of a bowl of purple salt in the North representing the Earth, burning incense in the East representing Air, a lava rock in the South representing Fire, and a bowl of rainwater in the West. In the centre were the bunches of flowers as offerings. The maidens took floral garlands out of their baskets and placed them on their heads, raising a torch in the form of a long, clear cup attached to a short bark handle. The tiny metallic trees all jumped into the cups one by one, filling them with yellow light like a well-synchronised army. The petals that covered the maidens' bodies fell off as they performed a circular dance around the sacred rocks, illuminating the place in the midst of a magical chant that hypnotised us. I felt privileged to be able to witness such a powerful ancient ritual. Suddenly, a druid priestess emerged from one of the rocks that formed the circle. She was a mature but very attractive woman with green eyes, and her brown hair was interspersed with white in a messy plait. Her tanned skin and perky separated breasts drew attention She was slender with a narrow waist, and she wore a light red and gold cape with a large hood that trailed behind her.

The naked virgins invoked fertility with rotating belly and hip movements. The dancers' exposed abdomens picked up the energy and the power of the sacred rocks as a symbol of fertility, which would make life possible. The priestess, in representation of something supernatural, spread oil and green clay on the virgins' bodies, which would heal their skin after childbirth. She then recited the spell that would seal the circle.

> *We invoke the air for speed,*
> *the fire for purification,*
> *the water for blessing,*
> *the earth for manifesting,*
> *and the spirit for sealing.*

We kept our distance, hidden behind the vegetation, out of respect for this worship of Mother Earth. It was the virgins' favourite time, the deflowering ritual in the temple where each bride happily awaited the ceremony.

Our eyes met, in absolute silence.

'It is the dance of life, Amelia. They celebrate it at the summer and winter solstices,' he said, watching me observe that female celebration with my mouth open.

'It reminds me of belly dancing on Planet Earth. It's a sensual show for men, where women hang hundreds of metal coins around their hips and make them jingle together as they move their hips.' I said.

'They practice to exercise their uterus and to obtain self-pleasure. The dance and their pelvic movements contribute towards uterine ductility and improving the childbirths of these givers of life.'

I felt like a voyeur spying on those naked longing bodies in erotic and exciting situations. It bothered me that Elsu was looking at them. I also wanted to bare my body and stand right in front of him so he could see what he was missing. I didn't notice that my libido had shot through the roof in a matter of a second. I breathed in deeply trying to calm myself down. The caress of the fringe of his jacket on my naked shoulder and the warmth of his breath just inches away from me weren't helping at all. Hundreds of questions and fears were popping up from the turbulent waters of my thoughts, and none of them were positive. The sparkle in his eyes suggested he was clearly enjoying this.

'It is incredible. What do you think, Amelia?'

'Ah... Well... Um...'

Not even Woody Allen himself could have bettered the collection of silly mumblings and the stammering that came out of my mouth.

Feeling exposed, as well as the ease and absolute candour with which he posed the question made me feel small, ridiculous and shrinking. He then brought his face right up to mine, and I was convinced he was going to kiss me. Instead, he just said, 'Do not worry, I also feel like we are desecrating a sacred place, occupying a space that does not belong to us, but we are not bothering anyone here.'

The priestess became aware of our presence and raised her eyes, inviting me to cross the circle. I immediately prepared myself to join in, as I thought that they wanted to make me a part of that ceremony because I'm a woman. I felt honoured and privileged to be able to form part of something so magical and special, but Elsu stopped me.

'No, Amelia. The spirit and time circle is about to open.'

'What do you mean?' I asked, confused.

'In the spirit and time circle, one minute is equivalent to one year on Earth, so whoever enters it ages very quickly.'

'But what about the fertility ceremony?'

'The virgins will become pregnant and give birth this very night. Then, they will offer the blood from childbirth to the goddess of fertility. If you enter the sacred temple, you will never be able to leave this place.'

I took a few steps back as the powerful woman looked on, disappointed, but continued the ritual without insisting any further. But we couldn't stop Vodka. Before we knew what was going on, he'd jumped into the circle.

'Vodka, come back!' I shouted when he already had two feet inside.

'We have to get him back, Elsu. We can't leave him here. I won't leave without him!'

'There is nothing we can do now. We have to wait until the end of the ceremony.'

I bawled my eyes out as impotence took over me, but I trusted Elsu. We witnessed everything from our privileged viewpoint and saw how the flowers that bloomed from the virgins' chests began to spread and multiply their tiny roots, like veins full of sap, leading to their abdomens. Their fertile bellies grew at a vertiginous speed. Before we knew it, the seeds had grown. Then, began the collective, pain-free birthing process, as they all sunk into the ground. From their uteruses emerged creatures as beautiful as their mothers, all of them female. And they also bore light: under the mantle of a copper sky, everything began to glow as an enormous blood-red sun, as large as the moon, rose powerfully before our incredulous eyes.

I can't describe the emotion I felt at that moment; it isn't often that I'm so deeply and wonderfully surprised. Since that explosion of life that ran through me, I've always wondered: is the night the bringer of life and the day the bringer of death, or is it the other way around? Either way, the sun will always be at the centre either by its arrival or its departure.

Mother Earth had had her fill of the virgins' blood, and they had given her new life in return. The offering had upheld the perfect balance between feminine and masculine. In this way, they gave back what they had taken through the principle of cosmic reciprocity. The pact was sealed between the beings from the constellation of Virgo who carried the knowledge of the earth and nature in their souls. By now we understood that this wasn't the Temple of Light we were looking for, but we still had to save Vodka. Elsu gave me a look confirming that the place was now safe. We approached carefully. There was my furry, dying friend, covered in white hair, lethargic, emaciated and too exhausted to even breathe. I caressed the calluses that had appeared on his elbows and knees. His expression was that of an old dog in its dying moment. I'm not even sure he recognised me. My heart broke and I began to cry inconsolably. I couldn't accept that, amidst so much life, Vodka could go in such a senseless way.

'Where's the magic for Vodka?' I shouted. 'Give him back to me, please!'

Elsu lifted his head up lovingly and said something to him, but this time he didn't respond. My desperate screams startled the newborns curled up on their proud mothers' laps.

'Only the priestess can help you,' said one of the new mothers, pointing to the figure of the powerful woman, heading towards the rock from which she had emerged, soon to disappear again.

I ran after her and stood in front of the enormous granite rock with outstretched arms, wanting to block her way back.

'You can't leave. It's not fair,' I begged. 'I'm a mother too, you know?'

This last affirmation seemed to have an effect as it provoked a reaction in her.

'I know you are a virgin. Maybe in the future you will experience what it means to be a parent and create life,' she said with the solemnity of a priestess.

'But I already am,' I answered. 'Vodka is like my only child. I've loved him with all my heart ever since he was a puppy, and even before he came into my life, I wanted him and dreamt about him. I've spent sleepless nights taking care of him when he was sick; isn't that what a real mother does? I pamper him, I educate him and I love him unconditionally. I'm his leader, his guide, like a mother is to her children. True, he didn't come from my belly, but I adore him and I'd give my life for him if I had to. Unlike a biological child, he will never mature mentally, he won't leave home and he won't become independent. I will also never see myself reflected in him, be it physically or psychologically, but every day I'll see the legacy of my love in his eyes. I'm not only the person who looks after him, I'm also the one who'll see him leave the world forever, just like this, naturally. It's our destiny, but I'm ready to make the sacrifice and to experience that pain, in return for having him with me for many more years to come. I'm not his master or his owner. To Vodka, I'm just his family. I don't know whether a child can inspire the feeling I get when I look in his eyes, those eyes that tell me absolutely everything. When I think about making plans, he's in all of them, and I'll tell you something else. Sometimes I wonder who really rescued who. My life simply wouldn't be the same without him, even if he does leave hair everywhere. I have no doubt, and neither does he, that we're a real family. Blood often isn't enough to create families. Aren't connections based on reciprocity and significant relationships; and aren't our real day-to-day lives what truly bind us to one another? Vodka is my silent confidant, but also the one I share my moments of laughter and sadness with, and I know that I'm the centre of his particular microcosm. You must understand that the love between a dog and a human is an incomprehensible for those who've never experienced it, as it is wonderful for those who are lucky enough to have it.'

The priestess bent towards me and spoke, expressing her infinite wisdom.

'Young lady from the other side, your heart has spoken with the passion of one who gives birth. One who loves with a whole heart speaks with nothing else. My condition sets me apart from what is impure, but I would be breaking our mysteries and their justice if I did not recognise the truth behind your words.'

She put her hand on my belly and, as if speaking of a prophecy, she declared, 'You will give birth to an only child, a daughter, in honour of our land. In exchange and as justice, the life that has been taken will return to the animal's body.'

Just as she finished the sentence, Vodka began to jump around full of vitality, wagging his tail energetically from left to right. I gave him such a strong hug I almost killed him myself with an overdose of love.

Elsu thanked the priestess for her justice and then added, 'May I ask you a question?'

'If I know the answer, I will be happy to answer it for you.'

'Could you please tell us how to find the Temple of Light, where the thousand-step staircase is located?'

'The answer is on the other side, traveller,' she said, minding her words.

'On the opposite site of the constellation of Virgo you mean?'

'To get there, you will have to travel through one of the sacred rocks, where the three sources of life and divine energy of the earth's fertility converge.'

'Are you referring to one of the four elements: air, earth, fire and water?'

'Each one of the four sacred rocks opens a path connecting to one of those elements. The Temple of Light is in one of them.'

'How do I know which one is the right one, wise priestess?' I interrupted, bursting in on the conversation.

'Only one element inhabits both above and below. When the sun reaches its highest point, the rocks' sacred doors will close. There is little time.'

Elsu looked up at the sky and then at me. The burning star was about to reach its culmination. I approached the rocks, inspecting them quickly, and realised that each one had a triangle with a symbol engraved onto it.

'Look, Elsu, this is the fire symbol.' The triangle is pointing upwards. This other one must be air because its vertex is pointing up, with a dividing line in the middle of the triangle.'

Elsu immediately began to examine the other two.

'Yes, this one is clearly the earth symbol. The triangle is pointing downwards, with a horizontal line through the middle of the triangle,' he said, excitedly. 'Therefore, the last one left must represent water. The triangle should be pointing downwards.'

I rushed over to confirm Elsu's theory.

'That's right. But which one should we cross?'

I turned around to look for the priestess but she'd already disappeared. We only had a couple of minutes to make a decision that would affect all of humanity.

'Let's go through the one the priestess used,' I suggested nervously.

'No, wait. She said that only one element inhabits above and below. That is not earth.'

'Which one, then?'

He looked to the sky for a moment and then dropped his eyes to the floor, feeling the connection.

'The rivers, springs, lakes and oceans are where the water lives below, but it also lives above us, in the clouds. That must be the one!'

I didn't have the chance to react, he took me by the hand and I dragged Vodka with me, melting into the sacred rock that would transport us to our next challenge.

That adventure, experienced not by choice but by destiny, served to adjust my imagination to reality. I learnt that coincidences do not exist. Every day, we walk towards places, situations and people that have always been waiting for us. I understood that destiny always plays a part, and that it doesn't stop until it has what it is owed.

Chapter 15

Lessons from the Sea

L ife is different at sea. It doesn't consist of hours, but of moments. Its voice speaks directly to the souls of those who are awake enough to recognise its language, proving that not everything is written and not everything has been invented, which is why we discover a new person within us every day.

It was sunrise and a new sun was painting the calm waves gold. A fishing boat was bobbing in the water about a kilometre off the coast. A few seabirds were competing to see which one could make the most outlandish sound as they plunged into the endless expanse of deep blue water.

'I'd forgotten what it was like to have the smell of sea and seaweed in my lungs,' said Conan, sighing deeply as if remembering old times.

'I guess being on dry land for the past five years must be tough for a marine like you,' I remarked, leaning my body on the helm of the blue and white sloop that Conan had hired for the weekend. He'd convinced me, telling me I needed fresh air and to get some sun. I was mad about the sun and the sea, so getting lost on the open sea and discovering a pristine beach sounded like the perfect plan to me.

'Yes, it's been a long time, Rafaela,' he said, with a calm but nostalgic tone.

'Tell me, were you one of those sailors with a girl in every port?'

Conan's honesty had no filter so, if you didn't want to know the truth, it was best not to ask.

'Muslim women conquer you with their eyes, and Angolan women do the same with their breasts. The former are covered from head to toe and only show their pupils and the mystery of their provocative eyes, which convey all their feelings. The latter, on the other hand, are almost naked, and it's their body and the way they move that entice you. And then there are Asian women, who have a unique charm and a combination of sensuality and tenderness that overwhelm your senses. Even though they come from what are considered to be cold cultures that don't openly show their feelings, they know how to win you over very sweetly. And because they're so delicate and slim, it's almost impossible to know their true age. Their silence drives you crazy, so you never know what's going to happen with them.'

'That's why you never settled down and got married then, I imagine.'

'You have a lot to live up to, *chiquilla!*' he replied petulantly and with a teasing smile.

'God, you're so conceited!' I said, throwing a lifebuoy at him, as it was the first thing I could lay my hands on.

The sudden movement made the sheer sarong that was covering my body fall, exposing my minuscule silver bikini. The halter top that tied behind my neck pushed up my breasts. The G-string bottom barely covered the essentials. That morning I had put my long curly hair into ponytails, making me look almost childlike. I looked like a Lolita, despite being closer to forty than thirty.

'Only a jealous woman acts that way,' he said, grabbing the flying object as he laughed at my terrible aim.

'Look here, Popeye, you and I might love each other, but you're not really my type,' I spat out, trying to save face.

Ever since I'd returned from hospital, I noticed the flirting going on between us. Well, he mainly flirted with me and I pretended not to notice. I was starting to remember more and more, but I didn't tell Conan, because I loved that he was trying to win me over as though I were a different woman, and that I had the opportunity to discover him all over again.

The monohull sailboat, which had curiously been christened *The Wandering Falcon*, sailed along Granada's Costa Tropical with the help of only one mast, two sails and a pair of hearts together with one destiny, which was about to take a decisive step. Actually, I was also enjoying the ride.

'Rafaela, wouldn't you like to become a sea nomad and travel the world on a sailboat? But before that, you're going to have to learn a lot of things, including sailing terms. The sea is a world in itself. Did you know that everything has a different name on a boat?'

'The idea of spending a weekend on board is super creative and romantic, but I don't see the appeal in spending an eternity in a minute cabin. What about my claustrophobia? No way!'

'Are you sure it's not just fear of being that close to me for so long, thousands of miles away from civilisation?'

'Rubbish!' I said, faking a smile. 'Living together is a relationship graveyard, but I'd die of seasickness first, and of the horror of sleeping in a tiny cabin.'

'Only someone who hasn't slept on the deck, looking up at the stars while the waves rock you to sleep while a group of dolphins plays with the ship's hull as the candles flicker in the wind, speaks like that. As far as living together goes, it actually makes relationships stronger as teamwork is crucial for a good voyage, and sometimes even for survival. There's nowhere to go or to escape; you have to face reality – something that never happens with many couples in crisis nowadays.'

'Well, you can always jump overboard,' I jokingly replied.

'Why swim when you've got a boat? You're better off just relaxing and enjoying yourself. The sea teaches you that freedom lives within you.'

'I guess people like you who've spent so much time at sea have a different view on things.'

'*Chiquilla*, there are so many lessons that only the sea can teach you. The first one I learnt was that boats are much safer inside a harbour, but they weren't built for that. You have to be willing to take risks and leave the shore behind if you want to discover new unimaginable places, people and experiences.'

I was silent for a few seconds, thinking, trying to make sense of those words and taking into account everything I was going through. Maybe my anchor was too heavy and I didn't have the strength to pick it up, or maybe all my past events had left me stranded on a desert island. I wanted to move on but I didn't know which way to go.

'What else did you learn, Popeye?'

'That you can't always see where you're going,' he answered, as if reading my mind. 'When you're sailing out there on the open sea, just as in life, your senses aren't always able to tell you where you are or where you're headed. The horizon extends outwards in all directions. You have to put your trust on other means to know if you're on the right route. A compass or the position of the stars can guide you on the ocean, but you have to keep a lookout for the signs and trust in them. The beacon of a lighthouse in the distance, the direction of the whales during their migration, or the flight of the seagulls. And, when you lose your sense of direction completely, there's always intuition.'

I glanced over at the wicker beach basket. There was a half-full bottle of tanning lotion, a pair of sunglasses, a pair of strappy sandals and a stripy towel, along with Belly's letters, which I had brought with me for some reason. Would the letters be one of those signs Conan was referring to?'

'Are you going to keep reading them?' he asked me, looking at the pile of letters.

'I'm scared to discover things I won't like.'

'Sometimes the conditions are favourable, and other times they're not.'

'Is that another one of your lessons?'

'At sea, you can get winds of up to fifty knots with strong currents; we call that inclement weather. A good sailor has to be able to manage it, not fight it. He knows that nature is the boss. To the ocean, even a boat made using all the best materials is nothing more than a solitary albatross, a whale or even an insect. It doesn't treat us with dignity or respect just because we're human. Life is precious and delicate. We can disappear in an instant anywhere, but this reality is intensified at sea. During inclement weather, sometimes the best thing to do is just go with the flow. You have to accept that sometimes conditions are in your favour and other times they aren't, and know that they will always change. If you stay the course and are ready to face the onslaught you encounter every now and then, you'll eventually reach your destination.'

'Thanks, Conan. You trained me to be a champion and I'd forgotten that. I don't know what I would've done without you.'

'Here's my final lesson for the day, *chiquilla*. You can't be a lone wolf at sea. It's fine to sail against the wind, but you depend on your crew for everything when you're at sea. You have to work with them, eat with them, live with them and socialise with them. You can't keep to yourself and then try to survive on your own. No army consists of a single soldier. You always have to trust someone, otherwise you may wake up to find that you're a solitary buoy floating in the middle of the ocean, with no chance of ever reaching land again. No matter what you do, you won't kick me out of your life.'

'You know, you just reminded me of Belly and her words of wisdom. *"In sea as in love, you'll enter when you want and leave when you can,"* she'd often say.'

Conan smiled mischievously, adjusting his sailor hat, and said, 'She was a wise woman, your grandmother. Here's another one to add to your collection: *with women, as with the sea, you have to know how to find your way.'*

We laughed together at the thought, and the scent of desire began to float around us again. Next to the railing, with the wind blowing against us, and dominating the world and the bow, we kissed as though we were Kate and Leo, or Jack and Rose, in the emblematic Titanic scene – a kiss that stops you in your tracks, where you can't really tell who's kissing you, that makes you feel like your clothes are bothering you, even if it's only a tiny piece of fabric. All that was missing was for me to stretch out my arms in line with the horizon and say 'I'm flying, Conan, I'm flying!'

Few people have the ability to search for you where you really are. Conan had found me and was showing me that not everyone who wanders is lost. I was wild about the way he refused to let go of my hand, just as the sea refuses to stop kissing the shore, regardless of how many times it gets turned away. We decided to sail wherever the wind took us. To me, sailing was like returning to the romantic ideal of epic voyages, at a time when flying is all too easy and destinations are overcrowded. To him it was a way of life. You could tell he had seawater coursing through his veins. We anchored in a secluded cove where we swam and snorkelled until sundown. It was a truly incredible experience. The sea really is a world in itself. An endless stroll, holding hands, enveloped in the deepest silence soothed my soul. This raised the question: was Conan the partner I had always fantasised about? We shared a night filled with guitar music and fresh grilled fish with a group of young fishermen celebrating a stag party around a bonfire. The men were brimming with stories and jokes. We were caught up in their enthusiasm, their eyes full of dreams. We were like two teenagers, seeking adventure and new emotions, celebrating life at sunset on a secret beach that was accessible only by sea. I was sitting on the soft sand with the best possible company I could think of at that precise moment. It was a perfect night.

We set sail again the following day. The weekend was going incredibly well. Conan explained the workings of the dashboard that contained the steering wheel, where I could see the course and speed at which we were travelling, as well as the water depth and wind direction. This last aspect was essential because, depending on the wind, the sails could be set one way or another to better optimise their use.

He put his enormous muscly arms around my waist to drive the helm. I felt every movement as he steered *The Wandering Falcon*. He took my hands and placed them on the wheel, saying, 'We're going to sail the seven seas, discovering new places all over the world. *Chiquilla*, set sail to your dreams.'

With all the nerves of an apprentice sailor, I got my ports and starboards mixed up a few times. The thought of crossing this immense desert of a sea, depending only on the wind and sea currents, made my heart stop. But it didn't compare to the experience of feeling Conan's heartbeat bringing my own body back to life. I laughed like a child every time we galloped over the waves and the sailboat keeled. I literally felt as though we were flying to the sound of a 'yeehaw!' Looking at the different shades of blue was so relaxing. It was a glorious spectacle, and yet it paled in comparison to the looks that amazing man gave me.

The sun had already risen when I heard Conan running on the deck. It was raining like crazy. I could barely see, but the boat was being tossed like a walnut shell, pushed around by the fury of the gigantic waves. A storm had caught us by surprise, despite all our careful planning. The constant rocking made me throw up. The world of calm, still, silence had turned into a scene of chaos that was completely out of our control.

'Go back inside, Rafaela!' he shouted from the top of the mast, as he tried to lower the sails as fast as he could. Crawling over the teak floor, I took my soaking wet body back into the cabin, leaving my head out to make sure that Conan was also safe. I didn't know that I could do to help. Finally, a lightbulb moment! I grabbed my mobile phone to call for help.

'Put your phone down and don't go near anything metallic; it looks like an electrical storm is coming,' he shouted as soon as he saw me with the electronic device in my hand.

'What do we do?' I asked, trembling from the cold, once I had him close enough.

'First, make sure your life jacket is on right. Striking the sails is the most sensible thing to do right now. We'll have to ride it out. I'm going to set the steering slightly windward so that the vessel can balance itself on the waves, just until the weather settles down and we can safely get back on course again.'

'We're a team, remember? How can I help?'

He looked at me realising I wasn't going to stop insisting. Now was the time to put all those lessons from the sea he'd taught me into practice.

'OK,' he said, his white linen shirt stuck to his body, confirming he hadn't left any part of his six-pack at home.

'We're going to stop the boat. Drop the floating anchor and secure whatever you can onto the deck,' he ordered, and I obeyed like a slow-witted cabin boy.

As clichéd and superfluous as it sounds, the calm really does always come after the storm, and that's exactly what happened. The rough waters didn't take long to calm down beneath our feet and the rain stopped slapping us. The sun came out as though it had simply been on a coffee break.

'You were great, *chiquilla!* Not bad at all,' he congratulated me, giving me a high-five. 'Next time remember to put something on when you come out to greet a storm in the middle of the night or I'm going to think you want something from me,' he said, looking me over with a malicious smile.

'Oh God!' I exclaimed, jumping into the foamy water, when I realised that in the heat of the moment, amongst all that chaos, I had left the cabin in my birthday suit, wearing only an ankle tattoo I didn't even remember getting. It was too late now to feel any embarrassment, so I stayed in and enjoyed the water until a very cheeky Conan casually left a towel hanging on the rail to encourage me to come out.

Once we'd recovered and tidied up the boat again, Conan prepared a spectacular breakfast that we savoured while enjoying breathtaking views. He really made an effort, I must admit. There was toasted rye bread with avocado, tomatoes, mushrooms and eggs, fresh watermelon and carrot juice, some cottage cheese and nuts, and a small bunch of wildflowers. No detail had been spared. The menu had even been printed out on golden cards, ingredients and calorie count included, which he had titled 'Breakfast for Mermaids'. I wondered to myself how I had let a jewel such as this go unnoticed in my previous life. Could this be my fairy tale? I didn't need anything else. No carriage, no diamonds, not even the promise of a happy ending that neither one of us could guarantee.

After the feast, I opened another one of Belly's letters as I got in a dose of natural vitamin D on the deck. Conan was busy trying to fish, throwing furtive glances at me every now and then. I struggled to decide on which one should be next. I shuffled them in my hands very gently, worried that their original scent would get mixed up with the smell of the sea and I'd never be able to remember it afterwards. I closed my eyes. The song of a noisy gannet gave me a signal and I chose at random. It turned out to be one of the oldest and most yellowed. It had a bare envelope, with no sender or recipient.

I was curious to know why she never sealed the envelopes. I figured that a woman as free as her probably wanted to give that same freedom to her thoughts. I took a deep breath, felt the breeze on my cheeks, and got lost in my reading.

Dearest Rafaela, my sweet girl,

I'm happy to think that, by now, you've probably already learnt what it takes to live a brave life with an open heart and have decided that it's worthwhile. I never told anyone my sad story. In everyone's eyes, I've always been a happy woman, and that's true to some extent. At first glance, I don't think sadness has changed me very much. There are times when I think that happiness, just like manners, is an acquired habit. You can train yourself to smile. It isn't necessarily easy, but if you try hard enough, you can manage.

The sunrise in Granada still makes me happy. I like tall men with large hands and a young spirit. I like feeling desired. There were times when I almost told my story because I was eager to share it with someone. But whenever I made the decision and was waiting for a break in the conversation, I was silenced by the fear that my story would run away from me and someday turn against me or, even worse, turn against the man I was so desperately in love with. Besides, I gave up asking people for directions to places they've never been to a long time ago. I've always envied the honesty with which some people talk about their personal issues and wondered if maybe my discretion stemmed from arrogance. The very last thing I wanted was to see your grandfather suffer or to have his name on everyone's lips, reduced to a label that had absolutely nothing to do with his true greatness. Others might have thought that it was nothing more than a tall tale from a woman with an active imagination who, rather than accept her reality, made up a destiny that set her apart from other mere mortals.

It took some time for me to accept that whenever you're feeling defeated, deeply pained, confused, disappointed or angry, you don't have a problem, what you have is a life. You are a human being. I've always tried to avoid being easy prey to society's beliefs that are so closely-tied with stereotypes regarding what you should or shouldn't be. Many people give up their happiness in order to fit in with the imposed models. Your grandfather Esteban fell into that trap and, in a way, dragged me down with him. Your mother was just an innocent four-year-old girl the day he let it all out and told me that he couldn't live a life of denial and deceit any longer.

'I'm sorry, I'm so sorry… you're the love of my life and the person I'll always love above all others, but I'm not who you think I am,' he said, bursting into tears. For a few seconds, he said nothing else.

I guess my female intuition pushed me to ask, 'Are you gay?'

'I don't want to be,' he said, following his initial shock. He told me that he'd tried to be the best husband and a wonderful father. And he absolutely was. He continued to be just as affectionate and sweet, and just as distant and uninterested in sex, until the very last day. At least it was a relief, in a way, to know that it wasn't my fault for being plain or unpractised. I simply couldn't satisfy him. We turned an unlucky marriage into the most beautiful and eternal love story in the world. I hated him at first, but then I couldn't punish him for being honest about his feelings. We still adored each other. Love survived, even without sex. We came to an agreement that we could each have our own lives as long as it didn't sully our family image.

Today, I know that our own liberation also frees those around us.

Remember me,
Belly

'Belly, I don't have to remember you because I never forget you,' I whispered, my lips wet from the tears I had shed all over her emotion-filled letter.

'Are you OK? What's made you so sad?' asked Conan, seeing me so distraught.

My voice caught in my throat again, but not because I was hiding from my own voice. I just wanted to swallow each syllable carefully to properly digest it first.

'I'm just very sensitive lately, that's all,' I replied, not wanting to give him any explanations.

Suddenly, I saw something shining in the sunlight, rolling around and bumping against my bare feet. The strength of the waves during the storm had thrown a glass bottle onto the deck of *The Wandering Falcon*. I thought it was empty at first but when I picked it up, I noticed a type of animal skin, carefully rolled up and inserted into it and tied up with a green, mouldy string. The brown bottle was two-thirds filled with water but still had its cork on. After uncorking the bottle with his teeth, Conan used an intricate tool to remove what was inside without breaking and unrolled it. The uneven piece of skin had adopted the bottle's curved shape and seemed to have been engraved with a sharp object. It was very well preserved, considering how long it must have been out at sea. We wiped off the wet sand covering the text and let it dry for a few minutes. On the top right-hand corner was written 'Montana, United States, August 12, 1822', and it showed a set of coordinates inside a sphere divided into twelve equal parts with symbols inside them.

'What a coincidence! It's dated the twelfth of August, my birthday,' I said.

The message was written in a style of English that Conan had to help me decipher and read:

> You can trust in my words just as you trust in the changing seasons. They are as unchangeable as the stars in the sky.
>
> The day that your feet touch this Earth, you will be standing on the ashes of your ancestors.
>
> My call will reach your ears at the perfect moment and at the exact location, travelling through the water's voice. This same clear water flows through the streams and rivers of our land, which is also the blood of our bloodline, and keeps a love alive between two worlds.
>
> Man has not woven the net that is life; he is simply one of its threads in the weave. What he does to the weave, he does to himself. Follow your own thread.

'To think that this bottle hasn't been touched by anyone in almost two hundred years, and has travelled thousands of kilometres just so we could be the ones to find it. My mind is blown,' I said excitedly, unable to stop touching it.

'The narrow diameter of the bottle's opening and the thick glass have probably helped it soften the blows and preserve its contents,' concluded my favourite sailor, who was just as surprised at our find as I was. 'It's almost as if it found you and not the other way around, *chiquilla.*'

I admit I was overwhelmed with the incredible range of emotions I had experienced in just a few hours. A door had opened through which all kinds of crazy ideas and feelings were bursting, the same ones that made me realise challenges are what prepare normal people for extraordinary destinies, and that, without a shadow of a doubt, there was a thread I needed to follow. Hopefully, I'd be accompanied by good wind and a calm sea.

Chapter 16

Taking Flight

My name is Amelia. I wasn't born on the tenth of July. My mother's name was not Amelia. Neither was my grandmother's. There are no family reasons behind choosing the Germanic name meaning 'work'. Could it have been a premonitory name? Work… I wonder how I can fulfil the 'Great Work' that will give meaning to my existence. I know that, just like myself, there are many others also seeking to resolve this question right now.

I was named Amelia after Amelia Earhart, the most famous aviatrix of all time, renowned for her flights and for being the first to try to circumnavigate the world along the equator in the 1930s. My mother always admired her. Maybe it was because she was a feminist icon that broke all the rules and never gave up her independence, or for her messy hair and brilliant smile, or because no one had ever worn a leather jacket quite like her. I remember that my mother once created a line of gloves, cloche hats and caps inspired by her muse, made using parachute silk and Grenfell cotton, some with feathers and rhinestones, for day, for night and special occasions. In her atelier, she kept a photo of herself looking brash and chic in her breeches, black leather boots and an aviator hat that she wore like no one else. She would tell me that hats were a sign of identity for both men and women at the time, and that nobody left home without gloves on. I loved listening to her stories with the sound of the sewing machine in the background, while

I played with the mannequins, the newly-completed hats and leftover pieces of material.

'My love, did you know that Amelia Earhart was one of the first celebrities to have her own clothing line? A style that was both masculine and feminine at the same time.'

'Like you, *mamá*!' I replied in my childish singsong voice.

She smiled, looking at me tenderly and caressing my nose with the tips of her fingers.

'Yes, Amelia. Her outfits were an obvious nod to aviation and were inspired by plane propellers. It was practical, affordable clothing, yet very elegant and feminine. See? She was a fantastic designer.'

She showed me a book with pearly covers where she kept a collection of cut-outs of famous women in the fields of cinema, law, advertising and mechanic engineering, among which was the daring pilot with her line Amelia Earhart Fashions.

'Can we show her your hat and glove collection? I'm sure she'll love it!' I suggested, excitedly.

'Unfortunately, she disappeared in 1937 during her final exploit,' she said, sadly caressing one of the photos.

'Isn't that the year you were born, *mamá*?

'It's the story of my life. I wish I could've met such a stylish adventurer.'

'Did she have daughters like me?

'No, but I'll tell you something. She had very clear-cut ideas. She thought marriage was a prison and kept her own maiden name. In fact, when she eventually married George Palmer, a renowned editor and explorer whom she had previously rejected five times, she presented him with a letter saying that she would demand an end to the marriage if it didn't prove satisfactory in the first year. She was something, alright!' she chuckled between basting stitches, patterns and needles. My mother always had a needle or pin stuck to her home clothes. She would always end her conversation with one of her sayings. '*You know what they say… he who marries, carries the weight of the world on his shoulders.*'

She identified with Amelia Earhart and unconventional nature. Both were pioneering women with a spirit of adventure. There were only a few small differences between them. The intrepid American was born into aristocracy; my grandmother was a farmer's daughter. For my mother, fashion was her life, while the adventurer's plan was never to be surrounded by sewing machines but to use the money she earned from it to finance her expeditions. Behind the portrait of the 'bird woman' was one of her legendary phrases, handwritten with tight writing, using up every available space, which was so characteristic of my mother. Today, I want to write it in the first page of my diary, so that my bravery never knows fear.

'Everyone has oceans to fly, if they have the heart to do it. Is it reckless? Maybe. But what do dreams know of boundaries?'

I would immediately recognise my parents' handwriting anywhere. Their styles were as different as their personalities. My mother's clear, round letters were unlike my father's minuscule and elongated ones. One thing is for sure, though. They would both reject the wonders of the Internet and the idea of communicating by email. 'All the letters are the same? How can you tell who wrote them?' My father always said that those identical black typewriter letters crushed the writer's personality and annihilated the sense of closeness that you get from a handwritten letter. They preferred to take comfort in writing, in the soft scent of paper, rather than succumb to cold, impersonal emails that could never be smudged by your tears. Because, just like fingerprints, nothing is more personal than handwriting. I always considered them writing fetishists, entrenched in pen and paper, with enough sensitivity to expose feelings through their hands. I couldn't believe it when my father assured me that he could sense the urgency of the words judging by how quickly the writer was hurrying to get to the end of the sentence or, on the contrary, when something was holding them back. The arrival of Sanzio, the postman, who appeared each morning with sleepy eyelids on his yellow delivery bicycle, made their hearts jump with joy, and they welcomed him regardless of whether he was bringing good or bad news. Either way, he was delivering voices expressed in ink. He wore a blue uniform with golden buttons, a hat, a heavy brown messenger bag over his shoulder and black shoes that had become very worn out over time. I remember what a close relationship he had with all the neighbours. He could never finish his shift at two o'clock from all the chatting. Because of her work, my mother received many letters from abroad, and my father collected stamps.

As the words of a popular zarzuela say, *'Nowadays, science advances in leaps and bounds. However, perhaps we should consider rescuing the art of handwriting, which brings us closer as humans and offers us positive effects for our physical and mental health, just as other millenary traditions did, such as Chinese calligraphy or being a scribe for medieval monks.'*

'Amelia, thank you for trusting me with your diary. I'd like to take it with me and give it the time it deserves,' said the 'white coat' once he'd finished reading the first page, realising it would take him several days to finish the rest.

'Of course,' I answered, letting out a sigh of resignation.

The decision had already been made. I would do it however I could, with or without his help. My escape plan was already in motion. I had to get back everything that had been taken away from me at one time or another. Something had come undone inside me. Each passing day was torture and I couldn't stand it any longer. To see Rafaela again, to feel the gentle breeze, to breathe in air that wasn't this air, to look at the moon and the stars from a new perspective had become my new priority. I just wanted to be free. I would stop fighting the world and, instead, flow along with it.

Restoring my relationship with my daughter filled my every thought. Would she accept me after all this time? How would I even begin to explain my absence? Would I have the strength to face her resentment and coldness should that be the case? We'd have to rebuild our bond. Mutually recognise each other. Seek to somehow accommodate what was out of place in our lives and fill the void in both of us. I hoped my daughter would be armed with an endless supply of forgiveness. It killed me just to think how deep her pain might have been. What could I do to fix that? Would she see herself in me at all? Or would I be a complete stranger to her?

Between us, I had the advantage as I'd never forgotten her face. My adult memory had held on to all the moments we shared together and, later on, I had found a way to keep tabs on her, but what about Rafaela? Would her childish mind still preserve my kisses, my cuddles and my immense love for her? Or perhaps her heart had given rise to a feeling of guilt, thinking that she'd done something wrong for me not to love her. It was time to get some answers, heal wounds and recover my own identity and my own story.

An emotional whirlwind took over me as I visualised myself standing in front of her, while she demanded explanations to make her understand what had made me decide to disappear from her life.

I didn't want to tell the 'white coat' that one of the male nurses always tried to sleep with me and that I had to fake attacks of rage for him to run scared. Among the many ideas I had, I thought about seducing him to earn his trust so he could open my bedroom door, which was always locked at night. He would often come in to inject me with sedative. Once I had him under my body, I could take the syringe and make him sleep as they do with me. They hurt me for fun, I would do it for survival. I only had two weeks to concoct a plan and put it into action. They were going to transfer all the patients from the old facility to the building adjoining the new hospital. I was on one of the floors with thirty-two beds. In total, thirty-two souls that shared a television where the world was exploding, that said how terrible everything was on the outside, and that it was better to stay here. Where else would we be safer? Well, apparently they had found a much safer place for all of us. There were endless rumours regarding when this transfer day would be. And, a few days back, I accidentally ended up in a room where the Unholy Father was projecting a video about the new project, where the philanthropists were writhing in pride and satisfaction on their leather chairs, licking their lips as the priest blessed them and washed their souls clean with his leftover charity. Nothing interesting every happened there, so I couldn't pass up the opportunity to listen in. I instinctively hid behind the pillar where the coats were hanging and observed. It was a maximum security building surrounded by extremely high iron walls. An enormous arch made up part of the street frontage, featuring the portraits and names of the founders and wealthy community members who contributed their generous donations to the construction of that monument to their arrogance. A security barrier was located a few kilometres later, controlled by a security guard in a hut. From there, you could see the psychiatric hospital far off in the distance, accessible via a winding road. They'd given it the original name of San Patricio II. They certainly hadn't wracked their brains thinking of it! It was a closed, sombre place with large barred windows.

The newly opened hospital facility with its sloping roof would have twice the number of personnel to cover absences owing to holidays or sick leave. They mentioned reviewing security staffing in order to ensure the security of the inmates. For that reason, we would all now wear a microchip in our clothing that would beep if we tried to exit through a door or the lift without prior authorisation. This advanced technology was connected to a central alarm that would make any attempts to escape impossible. Personnel would have state-of-the-art equipment to protect them from physical aggressions from hostile residents.

'With God's help and your generosity, all these poor unlucky souls will soon have a safer and more comfortable home,' said the Unholy Father, rubbing his hands together.

Poor naive fools. While they boasted that they lived in a rational world, they were unaware that they would never be able to escape the asylum they took with them wherever they went.

In a sudden attack of honesty, I dropped the bomb. 'I'm going to escape from this facility.'

His reaction could not have been more witty or appropriate given the context.

'Are you mad? Whoever put that idea into your head?' he whispered in his Argentinian accent, taken aback and looking around to make sure no one had overheard.

'Crazy or not, it's the most coherent decision I've ever made. I'm saying goodbye forever to this scrapyard where people, like vehicles, come to die.'

'You'll never manage, Amelia. The security cameras are watching all day long, how many guards do you think there are at San Patricio? And what about locks? The only way out of one mental institution is by being committed to another one.'

'No loony bin, solitary confinement room or chains in the world can stop me. I'm leaving orders and reprimands behind. I refuse to believe that anything is impossible. I'm leaving behind the endless years of identical days, where others decide everything for me, what to eat, what to do, how to dress, when to sleep. If there's one wonderful thing we humans have it's freedom and the right to choose.'

'I don't see why you have to do something like this right now.'

'Maybe when you finish reading my diary you'll understand why I can't stay.'

'Do you realise that you're putting me in a very delicate situation?'

I nodded. I was aware of it, but I didn't want to leave without saying goodbye.

'I won't be your accomplice. I don't want to know any more.'

'So, will you turn me in?'

He thought about it for a moment. 'No, I won't. But you're all alone in this.' He took his glasses off to massage his nose and gently touched my shoulder. 'Good luck, Amelia.'

'Luck? I don't need it. I'm being led by the inexorable hand of destiny,' I answered with the inner peace you acquire when you know you are on the right path.

'Of course, I'd forgotten about the origins of life, human beings already have their destinies set out for them.'

'Some people's destinies are straight and very clear. Others, such as mine, are twisted and abrupt. And what we refer to as coincidence is, in fact, already predetermined.'

'In that case, I hope destiny allows everything to turn out the way you planned.'

He said goodbye with a sad smile and a distant wave. I said goodbye to my diary, sure that I was leaving it in the best possible hands.

I knew San Patricio like the back of my hand. I had walked along those hallways, rooms and outdoor spaces millions of times. There was no hidden corner that wasn't noted on my mental map. I knew the rules and protocols as if I had written them myself. Most of the auxiliary staff, registered nurses and other clinical employees arrived between six forty-five and seven in the morning. The rest began their workday at eight o'clock. The nuns that lived on the premises attended the first mass like clockwork, just as the chapel bells would ring at eight fifteen. For those of us who had 'lost our marbles', we began our daily routine at eight thirty. The entrance was guarded by two security guards who we called Tweedledee and Tweedledum because they were two mischievous and shameless twins who always ended up in some sort of mess, and because their original Moroccan names were unpronounceable. I ruled out Sundays because we were usually full up with visitors. I knew it had to happen at night. When they eventually found out the following morning, it would be too late. Who was going to care about one less crazy person? Surely they'd find a new young person to take my place and cover the financial aspect, and they'd forget about me. I wasn't as profitable at my age.

I had kept a small map with some notes on it inside a novel I'd been reading on and off for some time, right on the page where the main character's phone rings at a decisive moment, changing her life forever. The day would be Wednesday after dinner. Finally, I'd ruled out plan A, seduction, and had opted for plan B. I needed a good alibi to leave my room before they were all locked at ten o'clock at night. Sisters Jacinta and Manuela would sacrifice their hours of sleep to tend the terminally ill on Wednesday nights. They provided comfort to them and guided them to their 'Father's house', as if they'd already been there before. They stayed all morning, praying and giving communion. Every week, one of the inmates could volunteer to help with pastoral care. Throughout my entire stay at San Patricio, I had never ever wanted to take part in that activity, though I acknowledge that the nuns performed their mission with great conviction, even if it didn't relieve pain or psychological suffering. I needed an excuse and thought that volunteering seemed like the best option. I just hoped they'd select me for that particular week. I filled in the application form and told the sisters that, as I got older, I had begun feeling the spiritual call and wanted to serve the community. It seemed odd to them but they replied with a 'Praise God!' All that was left for me to do was to present my authorisation and meet them at ten in the chapel located just a few metres from our building. I had fifteen minutes before that time to jump the gate during the change of guards that happened at nine forty-five. There was no margin for error. I knew I'd never get another chance.

The big day finally arrived. I felt like I was falling upwards. I was a bundle of nerves but tried hard to conceal it in the dining room. A steel ball was pressing hard on my throat, my wrists were tingling and my lips were trembling like rippling water.

'Why aren't you eating today?' asked one of the patients sitting opposite me.

'I'm not very hungry.'

'Can I have your potatoes?' he said, grabbing them with his hands before I could say anything.

I left the table at the set time. When I opened the dining room door I suddenly ran into one of the male nurses from behind. He looked straight at me but didn't see me.

'Where are you going?'

I showed him the authorisation and told him I was going to help the sisters that night.

'Stay there!'

I stopped suddenly, leaving my humanity at the threshold, pacing on the spot while he smoked and discussed last night's hockey game with another nurse, as if no one else existed or was worth speaking to. He tapped his temple with his finger to signal that I had a screw loose.

I was used to handling retaliation. The padded cell or more medication, or both, could be in my immediate future if my emotions took control, so I waited the five endless minutes until the nurse authorised me to be whatever he wanted me to be. I had learnt what the rules were, and the consequences for anybody who broke them, or so much as tried to break them. An Oscar-worthy smile covered my face. They liked it when I smiled.

The frantic ticking of the clock made my pulse beat faster and faster. That unexpected encounter had delayed my plan by a few minutes.

'I have to run,' I said to myself. 'It's almost half past nine.'

I'd already crossed the red line and, as if they were two narrow train tracks for a magical train, I slid down the wooden banisters to the first floor, avoiding the lifts. With an acrobatic effort and rugged breathing I was able to reach the Unholy Father's office, where my report and the few personal belongings I had arrived with were kept. That was all I was going to take with me into my new life. That, and a heart to be recycled. There were still two more doors to go before reaching the building's exterior. My heart in my chest, I softy whispered 'Elsu, stay with me.' A few more hurried steps forward and I reached what to others was the main exit door, but to me was my entrance into the universe. Everything seemed to go to plan. I hid in the courtyard until the new guards arrived, then hurried until I could touch the wall with my hands.

'Amelia, stop!' yelled Sister Jacinta hysterically, just a few metres away from me.

The guards didn't take long to subdue me while the nun kept doing the sign of the cross and repeating, 'May God forgive you, my child'. Her black habit had camouflaged her in the darkness and I hadn't noticed her following me. My world fell apart. I was in shock; my body was following my feet but I didn't know where I was any more. Desperation slowly took hold of my mind. They were taking me back to the labyrinth like a wild cat caught against its will. I looked up at the stars, holding out hope that the cosmic threads would anticipate my destiny. As I looked down, I thought I saw a dirty shadow moving a curtain in 'white coat's' office on the second floor, watching as my dignity refused to return, like a wounded wolf that howls more for his wounded pride than for the blood that has been shed.

Sister Jacinta, whom I imagine was as disappointed as I was, went back to her routine after informing the Unholy Father. His reaction was completely disproportionate: he couldn't contain his rage. His screams came over the telephone as though it had come to life.

'We can't allow something like this to happen at San Patricio! It's late. Take her to her room and I'll decide what to do with her tomorrow morning. Who's on night duty today?' he asked, firmly.

'It should be Dr Enrique tonight, but it appears he swapped his shift with Dr Fred just last night,' the nun reported.

The pair of nurses who had become my punishers appeared with their malicious laughter and obscene comments, ready to take me to my cell.

'You've come back very soon, Amelia. Didn't you have fun out partying?' the leader said mockingly. 'It seems you're one of those non-conformist women.'

'If it isn't the psycho pussy. She screams when you put it in and then cries when you take it out,' said his sidekick, laughing at his own joke and raising his hands as though scratching the air.

'That's enough! Leave her alone! You should be ashamed of your-selves!' reprimanded a young nursing assistant who was also often subjected to bullying.

'There's more where that came from, if you're interested,' replied the emboldened leader.

'Idiots!' she sneered at them with contempt, disappearing with the sound of her rubber clogs to patrol other hallways.

Along the way, seconds fell slowly like pollen falling from a tree. I had no idea what they'd do to me. The lock sounded like a death sen-tence. A night butterfly that appeared to be made of glass was sleeping in between the blankets on the bed. It had amazing translucent wings, and you could literally see through it. How did it get there? Suddenly, there was another, and another, and another. The room was filled with living butterflies in an infinite array of colours. The room had become a conservatory that smelled like plants, flowers and mud. I closed my eyes to hear the wings that surrounded me flapping around. I didn't need to see them. I remained as still as a scarecrow. They were all over my body, I felt them on my hair, on my shoulders, on my chest and in my hands. The spectacle taking place before me caught my attention to the point that I almost forgot what had just happened to me.

Life sometimes felt like a party that no one had bothered to invite me to. Elsu taught me not to settle for substitutes, which is why I dreamt of myself as a cosmonaut, travelling light-years to reach his clouds and his galaxy. Could this be another one of those space journeys? Many believe that reality should be kept separate from fantasy, but that's totally impossible as fantasy is nothing more than a reality that's waiting to be switched on. It was never, as they believed, a way to escape from reality but a more pleasant way to approach it. Perhaps this is why crazy people find reality so repulsive.

I trembled when I heard footsteps approaching. The sound of the lock made shivers run up and down my spine. His presence made me happy, maybe more so that I'd like to admit. I couldn't tell whether he was more sorry or happy to be there, but there he was nonetheless.

'Destiny has dealt its cards, Amelia. It looks as though you've been dealt an ace in this hand,' he said, giving me a magnetic key card, like the ones used by the workers and professionals at San Patricio. 'I discovered who the two men that appeared in the guest register were.'

'Who are they?'

'There's not time to explain right now. You must leave at once. Our world can't wait. Go find your daughter.'

'But...'

'Quick, Amelia. I'll find you.'

I thanked him and we said goodbye with a side hug.

It sometimes happens that, not quite knowing how or when, something gives you goosebumps and saves you from the shipwreck of your lost future. We're never alone. There will always be someone there to push us and give us strength when we're ready to give up.

It took me no time at all to exit the building. Taking large strides and with my adrenaline still fresh beneath my skin, I abandoned that nightmare. My heels were on fire. I felt like an Olympic runner whose only goal was to see the outline of San Patricio disappear forever behind me. The darkness of night covered the puddles left by the storm the night before. I discovered them as I ran, as the water splashed on my shaky legs, and my feet sunk deep into a carpet of mud and rotten leaves. The depth of one of them made me trip and fall flat on my face. The mud got in my nose and ears. Squashed against the floor, I felt it seeping into my soaking wet clothes. 'Mud doesn't hurt, Amelia, keep running,' I told myself, leaving behind a slipper like a darker and more sinister Cinderella. I felt the strength of a pair of enormous grey wings carrying me up into the air, its flapping coming to a stop shortly afterwards.

I looked back. There was the facility filled with old stories, some full of suffering, of life and death, of achievements and failures. I would no doubt miss some of the people I'd established a real connection with and, of course, the image I'd keep of them wouldn't be of someone who looked abnormal, with frizzy hair, a disturbed face or lost eyes. The concept of a place that was completely padded, with objects flying from one side of the room to the other, people drooling or crawling with rhythmic body movements that you see in movies has an element of truth to it, but a lot of it is fantasy too. Not everything is aggressiveness or delirium. I can confirm that there's a lot of camouflaged love and encrypted intelligence there, waiting for a genie's magic to free them from the bottle of the diagnosis. Perhaps one of the questions we need to ask ourselves as human beings and citizens of this planet should be 'What do we need to open in order to close the loony bins?' With a humble and brave yell, I loudly wished for a better future for all of those who would be remaining there.

Some time went by, I couldn't tell exactly how long it had been. The moon, now a few hours older, began receiving the impatient rays of sunshine. Like a sleepwalker wearing an outdated ochre coloured dress with white polka dots on it, I looked up at the tall buildings while I chewed on a piece of brown bread that I had hurriedly grabbed from dinner's leftovers. I caught the first tram I saw with no direction in mind, just for the simple pleasure of watching those grey buildings disappear, becoming smaller and smaller, until all I could see were trees, ploughed fields and a blue sky full of tiny clouds. The city of Granada slipped further away, shrinking into the horizon, making me want to jump off the tram in motion, but I waited until the brakes made their screeching sound and the few passengers left marked the end of the line. I got off at the very last stop in front of a lake where couples in love rowed around in little boats, envied by the anglers who seemed far more interested in catching some of that rare and desired feeling that in catching an actual fish. A beggar played a sad song on a violin in the shade of an olive tree, his only audience being two mutts whose pheromones were going crazy for a female in heat. His abundant and messy beard, his socked filled with holes and his unkempt appearance reminded me of Camilo, one of the inmates who wore thick glasses and who would joke around pretending to play classical music on a violin, adopting the Baroque position and using a long stick of stale bread as the bow. They said he had lost his mind, but he was actually just near-sighted. Two old ladies were spitting out sunflower seed shells as the sun rose on their boredom.

I sat on an empty bench, my legs crossed, like a straggling passenger at the end of the world. A large woman wearing fake eyelashes and with a scar on her forehead dropped a few coins into the musician's dish. Then she looked over at me with pity, with her enormous eyes like large seashells, and repeated the same gesture, this time leaving some coins on my skirt. She then continued walking her champagne-coloured toy poodle as if nothing had happened. Until that moment, I hadn't even considered my appearance. I'm not surprised she mistook me for a homeless person. It looked as though I'd been mudwrestling, which didn't bother me one bit ever since I had got on that tram to happiness. By the same process of metamorphosis, I'd gone from an egg to a caterpillar, to a cocoon, and was finally flying like a glass butterfly.

I stopped to think about the terrible consequences that 'white coat' would face for giving me his key card so that I could escape. His code had been registered on the system and that would incriminate him. The Unholy Father wouldn't forgive such sacrilege. The full weight of his fury would fall upon him. He'd lose his job and possibly even his reputation. Those thoughts made my smile fade. I played with the key, taking it out of my pocket. With the stress of my escape, I hadn't noticed the name that appeared on it. It didn't belong to Dr Fred but to one of the nurse bullies. It had been a sublime 'checkmate'. I had underestimated the Argentinian. He'd really done his homework and, taking note of what was really happening at the psychiatric facility, had executed a fair and perfect ambush.

Despite not sleeping a wink, I'd never been more awake, more alert and more aware, because life is pure experience. I felt like a bird that always returns to the place where dreams are born. Life was still the best gift, and even in the darkest times, we can find a star to keep us company.

Chapter 17

A New Beginning

I f you've lived enough, you'll have learnt that in the most desperate crisis, when everything seems lost, a well-deserved rest may be around the corner. On the contrary, when everything seems to be under control, that's when you should worry and anticipate problems.

There he was, just sitting on the stairs waiting for me to come home. His smile never failed to raise my pulse.

'What are you doing here?' I asked after my heart had done a triple somersault.

'I came to get my brown corduroy jacket, unless you want to keep it.'

'Me? Why would I want to keep the jacket of an immature dick, unless it's to wipe my arse with it?' I spat out like an angry child.

'What can I say? I'm a man who fights against what he feels and what he needs. I'm somewhere between what I am and what you want me to be. I know I'm not always coherent. I think I'm going crazy.'

'Rubbish! I don't want to hear the same old story again. I'm leaving tomorrow.'

'Where will you go?'

'I'm taking the path to good luck,' I answered ironically.

'I'm not quite sure what to do with the memories of us and our relationship,' he confessed, crestfallen.

'Put them in the trunk where you keep your failures, along with your clown shoes.' I snapped.

The landing was dark but the light in our eyes still had enough electricity to power the whole block. Sparks were flying like fireworks.

'Can I come in?'

I sighed, knowing that I'd lost this battle. I surprised myself opening the door and feeling his gaze on my back, scanning every inch of my body. Jared looked at my few pieces of luggage piled up in the entry. His jacket was still exactly where he'd left it several months ago, as if time had stood still. I couldn't help but smile discreetly when I read the message on his white t-shirt with red sleeves: 'Without you, today's emotions would be nothing more than the dead skin of past emotions.'

'I bought it thinking of you,' he told me, placing his hand on his chest.

'Of course, you did; but was that before or after you stirred up so much trouble and forced me to quit the job I loved so much? Honestly, I don't understand a thing.'

'Life isn't meant to be understood; it's meant to be lived. You were working too much and the vulture, as you called him, was exploiting you.'

'I never said such a thing. Do you have any idea how hard it was for me make it this far?'

'Less curriculum and more vitae, Rafaela. Life is short.'

'Yes, short, but you still have to pay bills and eat, in case you haven't yet figured that out in your philosophical world. Besides, it was about my professional and personal development. It was a unique opportunity and it's gone down the drain now thanks to your insecurities and your obsession with controlling absolutely everything I do.'

Jared wrapped his arms around me from behind. His scent immobilised me. He twisted my hair up near my nape and brushed his lips against my earlobe. I felt the temperature rising. It was one of those romantic Hollywood scenes that make you feel like you have the best partner in the world. I felt as though, following a long break, the impossible love story was being rewritten with a fresh new chapter, full of promise.

I turned my head to face him. His lips crashed against mine and I surrendered to the ambush. I took a deep breath to work up the courage to turn him down. But I couldn't avoid temptation, it was far too strong. Judging by how fucked up I was, I could only conclude that I was a budding love kamikaze, ready to die for love. My body, my mind and my soul were completely disconnected from each other. Basically, I was making every mistake I criticised in others.

As we devoured each other with kisses, I heard my little guardian angel yelling into my ear from my shoulder, 'Rafaela, people don't change. They just take little breaks. What are you doing? Didn't you say you wanted a stable element in your life? I'm telling you, this is going to shake up your stable foundations all over again!' But by then I was a dog tied to the leash of passion. No matter how hard the little angel tried to persuade me, I chose to succumb to the whispers of the little red devil, surrendering to the dark side. The evil brother worked hard planting contradictions and stabbing my heart with his sharp trident, saying, 'What harm is a little roll in the hay going to do? Take it as a nice farewell. It's only sex, woman.'

'Of course,' I told myself, 'only sex. Don't let your oxytocin-filled head confuse an orgasm with love. Someone who makes your life impossible can't love you, end of story.'

I'll never forget my first official patient after graduating. Her name was America, like the continent. She looked angelic and had an intense gaze the colour of a monarch butterfly. She arrived all wrapped up in a black A-line coat that only revealed her long legs covered in black tights with a long visible seam running down the back. It was clear she had no idea where to start.

'I'm so glad my psychotherapist is a woman. A man could never understand me,' she said, finally. 'We have really great sex, you know? But I don't know if he loves me, and that's what I want the most. It makes me so unhappy. At the beginning, I let myself just go with the flow, not thinking about it too much. But after about a year, I began to ask myself, "What is this? Love or just sex?"'

'Has he clearly expressed his feelings to you?' I asked.

'He says he loves me but he won't stop sending me WhatsApp messages asking me to sleep with him. I feel like his hook-up hotline. He does always want to see me, but never for anything outside the bedroom.'

'And what do you want from him?'

'The normal stuff. To go to a concert, or the movies, a spur-of-the-moment weekend away. He never shows any interest in getting to know me in any situation that isn't the bedroom. He says I'm always in his thoughts.'

'You mean when he's thinking about his sheets?'

'If you're as good a psychologist as you are a translator, you'll go far.'

'I see.'

'He never gets tired of telling me how hot I am. In the middle of a sexual marathon, he'll say, "your body should be illegal, what an arse..." I hope you don't mind me telling you the details.'

'Not at all, feel free.'

'Do you think he admires me?'

'He's talking about your body and about how much he desires you, not about you. Intelligent guys know that if they make you feel good, it makes your self-esteem shoot through the roof. Do you think that may be a red flag?'

'Now that you mention it, he never talks about any of my personality traits, just about my body. Last week I won an award for one of the paintings I presented at the modern art exhibit and he didn't even congratulate me. He did tell me I looked amazing all made up in the catalogue photo, though.'

'How is he with you in private?'

'Well... the kisses during sex are amazing.'

'What about when you're not having sex?'

She went quiet for a few moments as if the answer didn't want to come out.

'Actually, he only does it when he knows things are getting exciting and we're going to end up in bed.'

'So, he doesn't kiss you in the middle of the street, in public, or even when he knows it won't lead to sex?'

'He fills me with orgasms and makes me see the stars, but I'm not happy outside the bedroom. He never talks of feelings or of his personal life.'

America began to understand that some bodies connect sexually like two magnets, but it's what happens outside the bedroom that makes or breaks a relationship. Love involves pleasure but that doesn't just mean sexual satisfaction. Someone who truly loves you wants to see you happy everywhere. A man with sincere feelings would love to spoon you after sex and wouldn't let you sleep alone just because he has 'very important' things to do. It's essential that in every sexual experience, outside of emotional commitment, no matter how daring and fleeting it may be, there should be abandon, authenticity and tenderness that only grows over time.

Jared came from a Jewish home, with grandparents who were Holocaust survivors, parents who went to the synagogue every Friday, and circumcised men. Although the idea of mixing sex and religion had never appealed to me, I admit that his way of understanding sex really got me going. While Catholic morality would punish our lust, I discovered that his doctrine had been holding the best-kept secrets regarding sexuality for thousands of years. The way in which we should consummate love, according to him, was an incredible turn on for me. The same devil that encouraged me to let go then entered my body, dominating my sexual impulses. He knew the pleasure it produced in me and the fastest way for me to reach a climax. Judaism dictates that the man must provide sustenance, cover all needs and provide sexual satisfaction to his wife. As a liberated woman, all I was interested in was that last part. The rest was my business.

I remember that after our first intimate encounter, the nutty philosopher told me it would be only fair to have at least another couple of dates. I didn't really understand why I had some sort of debt to him, so he told me the ancient tale of Tiresias. Son of the nymph Chariclo, he was considered the most important and powerful seer by the ancient Greeks. According to the myth, Zeus gave him the power of foresight after his wife, Hera, made him blind. That was how problems were solved back then.

'Why did Hera punish him in that way?' I asked.

He replied with another question, 'Who enjoys sex more? Men or women?' The god argued that women enjoyed sex more than men, therefore she had to compensate him with many more encounters. Hera did not at all agree with Zeus. That was an argument that Tiresias was called on to settle as he was the only one who had been both a man and a woman in the same lifetime. His answer, firmly in favour of women, was not to the liking of Zeus' wife, so she struck him blind. That's why Zeus gave him the power to see the future, which allowed him to become the most powerful fortune teller in all of Greek mythology.

Yes, Tiresias had been both a man and a woman. According to the myth, he became a woman after killing a female snake as it was mating. Years later, in an identical event, he killed a male snake and was returned to his original male condition. Because of his androgyny, he lived as a mediator between men and women. Tiresias read the future in the flights of birds. As he was blind, a guide would describe it to him. There's something pathetic and very wise in this: it is only when you lose your sight that you can see the future. Tiresias is said to have always regretted his long life, and he died after he abandoned the city of Thebes, having drunk the cold water from the Tilphussa spring.

My plane was leaving in less than twenty-four hours. This would be our last encounter, so I though I'd take the bull by the horns and forget about sentimentality and give it my all. Why couldn't I be like America's boyfriend? We clumsily made our way to the bedroom, tripped over the door, knocked over the clothes stand, bounced off the wardrobe and fell onto the bed, stuck together like suction cups. He very slowly removed my sleeveless lace dress. He always said my neck and collarbones were my sexiest part. He tore my tights without a second thought, my ankles closed around his waist, as he slid his knee between my open legs. His intense gaze clouded all my senses. It was all very promising.

Clothes were strictly forbidden during sexual relations. The main action had to focus on giving and receiving, nothing could stand in the way of that. Like me, Jared enjoyed foreplay, although he was very faithful to his Orthodox sexual principles that stated that it could never become the most important part. The path was not the goal.

'I'm going to do it very slowly this time. I want you to feel how special you are to me without having to tell you,' he whispered, having already become an expert explorer of my burning body.

My heart beat faster at his promise. I didn't even answer. I didn't want to run the risk of having a sudden, last-minute attack of sentimentality. There was no way I wanted to get involved in feelings or anything like it. All I wanted was to enjoy myself as I prepared to slam the door shut on an important part of my life. I closed my eyes so I wouldn't remember his excited face the next day, but that didn't stop me from imagining his seductive smile. I bit down hard on my lower lip, feeling that sensation that took my nails to his back, as we completely let go and gave into each other, without any limits.

As far as ejaculation goes, there's something Jews cannot do: waste sperm. A man must direct the sperm to the uterus, even if there's no chance of the woman becoming pregnant. Judaism consecrates the legitimacy of a couple's sex life. People who don't produce offspring

THINGS I KNOW ARE TRUE

are committing a sin akin the worst sort of criminal offence. In that respect, although it was tough for me to convince him, we always used precautions. Well... not always. This unexpected encounter caught me completely by surprise. After our break-up, I stopped taking the pill to give my body a break and, obviously, the last thing on my mind was to buy a box of condoms in case he ever came back to pick up his brown corduroy jacket just before I was due to fly out.

My internal battle with my angel continued. 'Rafaela, don't do it. It's dangerous. Not without protection.' Meanwhile, the little devil was pulling me in the opposite direction. 'C'mon, just this once. What could possibly happen? Don't kill this special moment. Enjoy it.'

I let it happen. Our pleasure gradually and calmly intensified, until we lost our desire-filled heads. Afterwards, he lay his head on my exhausted chest, and I cuddled up to him tightly. We dozed off like two boa constrictors after just swallowing an entire moose.

I have no idea how long we spent talking after that, naked, recognising each other through the maps of our skin. We were in a good mood. I'd almost forgotten all the times Jared had been violent with me or had humiliated me, only to win me back afterwards. He gave me goosebumps with his sugary, persuasive voice, and we'd inevitably start all over again. I used to tell him he had the gift of the gab and would have been very successful as a radio announcer. He was the best at convincing you and taking you over to his side. Light entered the room, which was as lazy and grey as the new day. I opened one eye and looked at the time on my mobile phone.

'Fuck, fuck, fuck! I've missed the plane!' I yelled, jumping out of the bed like a terrified grasshopper.

Jared was looking at me, disoriented, surrounded by sheets that were as messed up as my heartbeat.

'Are you sure you want to leave? Did this mean nothing to you?'

Sleeping with him again had been very special. Feeling the strength with which his arms held me made me feel weak. Even so, my mouth had a mind of its own and tore away from my heart.

'We have no future,' I answered, buttoning up a blouse as quickly as I could.

'I'll never leave you again, Rafaela. I can't live without you. I'm just asking you for one more chance. I won't hold it against you if it doesn't work out. From now on, what's difficult will become fun, and what's fun will be pure happiness. You'll never regret not having tried enough. We can tell our kids we didn't give up when faced with the first obstacle.'

The first part was ideal, but the second screeched inside my head like nails on a blackboard. Kids? That was the last thing I was thinking about. Surely, it was barbaric to make a decision of that kind thinking about someone who didn't even exist. I felt powerful, thinking I was the only battery capable of bringing that toy to life. I sensually caressed his messy hair. There was no wizard or antidote that could undo what Jared had managed to stir in me through his kisses. All my efforts to detox over the past few weeks had come to an end with me succumbing to my emotional addiction once again. Why are we addicted to ones who hurt us?

My well-being and my dignity had taken a step back, closing ranks around a naive hope that I still had everything under control and things would be different from now on. Actually, the surest way of being wrong is to think we're in control of something. I now know that if naivety was a mortgage, I'd be paying instalments until the end of my days, and so would my descendants. I thought I'd conquered the rainbow, but what happens when you set foot on it? You slip and fall into the void, just like I did.

Esther went crazy when I told her I was staying in Jerusalem.

'So... does this mean you're back together?' she assumed, excitedly.

'Yes, I guess so.'

'Oh, that's amazing Rafaela! You're starting over, just like in that song I like, "Volver a Empezar". What's that Spanish singer's name again?'

'You mean the CD I gave you for Christmas?'

'Yes, the really good-looking one.'

'Pablo Alborán.'

'We have to learn to settle for what life has dealt us,' she said, mumbling the song with a strange accent.

Those words produced seismic shift inside me. Settle for what I've been dealt? I saw myself reflected in Esther and that frightened me. That's not how Belly had raised me, and I wasn't the type of woman who settled for anything less than she deserved. It was up to me to keep my life alive, and I wasn't going to let anyone come along and ruin it.

'I didn't decide to stay because I was settling for anything. I did it for love,' I replied, making things crystal clear.

'Of course. Well, whatever. The Hippolyta and Penthesilea duo is back in business.'

Deep inside I knew this wasn't true, but a strange force out of my control made me unable to leave that place.

The one who was extremely disappointed was Belly, when I told her I was staying in the Holy City, even though I hadn't told her why I was going back or why I had chosen to stay. But she knew something wasn't right. I knew it by the way she said goodbye: 'Take good care of yourself, my sweet girl, and you know that they say, "*what starts badly, ends badly.*"' Jared's family wasn't exactly jumping for joy either, but they took it well enough.

I was worried that this second chance would become a third, a fourth, a fifth, until only the ruins of an unconscious love remained.

Reconciliations never start from zero, basically because we can't just reset and delete all the data we've been saving from the past, just as we can't rewrite history. The experiences, adventures, suffering and happy times are still there, dormant, disguised, anesthetised, forgotten or ignored, swept under the carpet of time. Even so, I chose him again. I had to live my story. Who would I be without my story?

All this time had given me a lot to think about and, when the time came, I was going to truly live. *The Layet Mai. The Mai Layet.* Your destiny is laid out for you, you just have to follow it. That phrase kept whirling around my head like a washing machine during the spin cycle. Was it my destiny to stay in Jerusalem with Jared? Or wasn't I reading the signs properly? Suddenly, I had an idea. I'd been wanting to get a tattoo of something meaningful for some time now. I made an appointment and, two weeks later, the words that kept spinning around my head were now tattooed around my left ankle. *The Layet Mai. The Mai Layet* would become an eternal reminder to guide my steps. The person I wanted to be existed somewhere; I just had to find her.

In life, there's a moment when you become an adult. You reach the age when you can vote and drive. Suddenly, you're expected to be responsible. We grow. We get older. But who says we're adults? We continue to have the same problems we had at fifteen. We trip over the same things, we keep doubting our decisions, and we seem to be predestined to always end up at a crossroads, confused, scared, without a road map to guide us. The decisions we make then will determine the rest of our lives.

It happened on the first autumn afternoon, just after a weakened sun had faded from the sky, signalling it was five o'clock. We were coming out of the book and record shop we would often go to. The skies had opened and we were running, desperately trying to get away from the rain. Our bodies searched for each other beneath the fine rain that fell incessantly. After a short distance, we took shelter under a tree filled with birds who, like us, were also seeking refuge.

'You look like a wet chicken,' he said, laughing, as he placed the book he had just bought over my head.

'Oh yeah? You're no Gene Kelly singing in the rain!' I replied, pretending to be offended.

'One of these days I'm going to scare you and ask you to marry me, officially,' he said, fixing his eyes on mine.

My entire life had come down to just one moment, as if my soul had just been saved.

'Oh, my nutty philosopher, one of these days I'm going to scare you, because if you ask me, I just might say yes.'

'Are you serious?' he said incredulously.

We forgot to breathe as we kissed under the rain.

'I'm a lucky frog, the princess said yes!' he began to shout at all the passers-by splashing around the avenue.

A pair of teenagers waiting for the bus came closer to see who was shouting and making exaggerated gestures from the other side of the street.

'Rafaela, I promise to fill our life with adventures, paint our mornings with watercolours, and to love you for all eternity.'

We hugged, submerged in that deluge of happiness, sharing wet kisses.

'Our love will be legendary and it'll begin with our wedding. The best is yet to come,' he said sounding like a greeting card teddy bear.

Maybe we were mad after everything we'd been through... But I felt that this madness was precisely what we felt for one another. I convinced myself that we were like tequila and lemon, born to be together. I told myself over and over that every relationship goes through phases: some are happy and others aren't. We'd only had a passing crisis in that love story. I needed to believe in fairy tales and live out this fantasy. I was dying to find this new and improved Jared, ready to write a new script for our story and, why not, make it better than the original. After all, I wasn't going to throw away the book because of one bad page!

Over time, I've become increasingly fascinated with the neuro-biology of love. Apparently, humans began to fall in love with each other about four million years ago. No matter how long the topic has been around, there are no statistics to prove that we have made any improvements in the field. Who knows if we were unknowingly making the numbers worse? If romantic love is more of a physiolog-ical impulse rather than a rational idea, does that mean our mental state is actually altered? Was jumping in head-first really the best option? I don't know why I was asking myself all those rhetorical questions when the decision to jump back into the ring had already been taken.

There is no more exciting moment in a couple's history than when they decide to get engaged. My first impulse was to call my mother to tell her. How ridiculous, right? What number would I dial? I didn't even know if she was alive, though I still held on to that dream. This would be a secret wedding. I didn't even tell Belly about it. I knew I wouldn't have her blessing, but she wouldn't oppose it either. She had the wisdom of someone who'd lived hard and fast. They say that wisdom is one of humanity's most prized assets. However, only the ignorant get to sleep well at night.

'Before you get married make sure you know what you're doing, you can't undo that knot that easily,' Belly would say to all the brides who were about to get married and who had come to her atelier to try on their bridal headpieces, their pristine white silk gloves and lace garters. These unique pieces were created with each of their person-alities in mind so that they'd shine during their triumphal entrance. No one could deny that she was the best. She had a gift for capturing the essence of every bride. Her creations were put together lovingly and in exquisite taste, so they didn't mind that Belly would warn them to really consider what they were getting themselves into. Anyway, they all seemed to have left their ears in the little box their engage-ment ring came in. They would be deaf to any words of warning. Her legion of die-hard fans only cared about her delicate craftsmanship and her magical hands that gave form to veritable masterpieces designed especially for the big day. Why not continue believing the Earth was flat and that chickens could fly?

We eloped the following Thursday, and gave a resounding 'I do'. Jared wore his lucky jeans and a smoky grey turtleneck jumper. I wore a soft pink cashmere jumper and a simple long skirt in satin of the same colour. We felt no pressure from having to deal with all the preparations, the family dramas, the high cost and all the posing a wedding would entail. It was just the two of us, with love as our only witness and with mystery as an added hint of spice, which gave us an adrenaline rush. What happened later was a whole other story.

Chapter 18

Winter Soldiers

When we arrived, I had the impression I was entering a whole other life, as if I were a character that had just been pushed onto a stage, into a scene where I clearly didn't belong. Where were we? The place, filled in gloomy islets, seemed to have been relegated to the background, only to be observed from afar. A vague unrest and a feeling of oppressive threat had taken over me and my mood, without me noticing.

Elsu seemed to be completely calm and at ease as he followed the course of the stars from the moment the sun set and they appeared high up in the clear night sky. To a layman's eye such as mine, that mantle of sparkly gems always looked the same, unchangeable in its immensity, but Elsu didn't have the eyes of a novice like me. He knew their secrets, their stories. He could read routes, parables, declinations and orbits, all of which suggested infinite possibilities. All that to ignorant beings such as myself was confusing, coincidental and chaotic was full of meaning to this being from the Elove Galaxy. According to his convictions, every infinitesimal event and even the smallest details were all part of the ineffable mind of the cosmos.

'Pisces?' I asked, trying to guess the constellation we had ended up in.

'No. This can only be Scorpio,' he confirmed resolutely, still focusing his gaze on the immense night sky.

A strong burnt smell guided us to the sandbanks licked by the turbulent waters of a reef. Something that looked like a burnt corpse lay in the centre of a circle. Vodka sniffed expertly around it, still smoky and surrounded by ash, trying to reach a conclusion.

'My God, what is that?' I asked, covering my face with my hands, only to remove them again straight after.

Elsu drew closer to the large charred body and crouched down to observe the details close up.

'The body seems to consist of segments. The pincer-shaped arms… and the body's posterior is suggestive of a sting, like that of a scorpion.'

'Suicide? The sting has been turned on itself, as if it wanted to be poisoned. I read somewhere that if a scorpion is surrounded by fire, it will sting itself in order to preserve its own dignity.'

'The beings of the constellation of Scorpio can be very destructive, even among themselves, but they do not have the suicidal instinct. Amelia, this is yet another legend from your world. The truth is something else altogether. Scorpions are unable to regulate their body heat; they become dehydrated near the fire so they begin to arch themselves, provoking frantic spasms and tail contractions until they die. This can make it look as though they sting themselves, turning their suicide into an urban legend, but their sting cannot actually pierce their own skeletons; and even if it did, they would be immune to its own venom. Scorpios will never commit suicide, not even when they are surrounded by fire, or in any other stressful situation. However, they would not hesitate to kill if necessary.'

'Well, I guess we can rule out that option then. What could've happened?'

'One possibility is that the fire produced a rising hot air column that suffocated it. But I would bet that it was, in fact, a trap.'

'A trap? You mean that another Scorpio killed it?' I assumed, feeling rather ill at the thought.

'No. If they are renowned for anything, it is for their loyalty. They protect their own above everything. Betrayal is something they could never forgive.'

'Basically, don't mess up, because if you do and you lose their trust, you'll have to fend for yourself. Is that what you mean?'

'As a child, my father would tell me stories as we strolled through the valleys of the Rocky Mountains surrounding our village. One of them described it perfectly.

'One day, fire, water and trust entered the deep forest together. The fire passionately told its companions, "If I get lost, follow the smoke, for where there is smoke there is fire." Water followed suit and said, "If I get lost, follow the humidity, for where there is humidity there is water." Trust was the last one to speak. With a penetrating look he said, "If I get lost, do not bother looking for me because you will never find me." He ended by revealing to me that trust had the form of a scorpion and had been born in November.'

I loved it every time Elsu would tell me about his world and share pieces of his story with me. It made me feel much closer to him. I wanted to know everything that had to do with this fascinating man, and where he came from, which I imagined to be like an orchard in a paradise full of vast plains, long silences and a powerful presence of the stars.

'What do we do? This is full of keys, islets and reefs. The Temple of Light could be anywhere. We're trapped. We can't even sail to explore other islets. It doesn't really look like the safest place in the world, either,' I pointed out, as jitters spread quickly and surely through all my neurons.

'I agree with you, Amelia. It is not a very safe place. This land is not currently at peace.'

Fear began to take over all of my suspicions. I would have appreciated a white lie at that moment, but I couldn't expect that from someone like Elsu. The night began to get very cold. Vodka was shivering with his tail between his legs, obviously also scared of the unknown. Thunder clapped, giving way to a storm. That night, the rain fell like silver daggers. The gloomy sky was covered in turbulent black clouds, and our bodies were mercilessly beaten by the gusts of wind. Everything was dark. We wandered around the area for several hours without any food or appropriate clothing to help us ward off the freezing cold. No one could have predicted what destiny, chance or – for Elsu – the stars were about to show us.

Furtive sounds were approaching from every direction. I don't know what terrified me more: the fact that we might be the only beings in that desolate, inhospitable place, or the fact that we might not be, and that we'd run into hostile creatures. Everything happened so quickly that I couldn't actually say how the scene began. I remember Elsu covering my body and Vodka attaching himself to our legs. We formed a solid block in the midst of a pitched battle. Everything was happening in our field of vision as we silently crouched like involuntary witnesses to a science fiction movie.

It was a fight to the death. A legion of hundreds of Scorpios emerged from the water, from behind the rocks and from many secret hiding places, poisoning their enemies with endless and seemingly inevitable cruelty, carried away in a spiral of ever-increasing violence.

We found ourselves in the middle of a brutal and ruthless conflict, led by winter soldiers, as they liked to call themselves. Due to their ability to camouflage with their surroundings, they could disappear as quickly as they appeared, moving silently at dusk and at dawn. When they descended on their enemies, there was no escape. They had to shore up the precarious security of the unstable area in which the beings of the constellation of Scorpio were acting in defence of what they considered to be their territory.

Wearing ebony-coloured hauberks covered in scales, the beings with black hardened skin shook their thick black shoulder-length manes. They let out war cries, ferociously shooting lethal venom from their stings – a weapon that was activated psychologically. Their heads were long and strange, like those of some sort of aquatic animal, and they seemed to be floating on tails that were bent to the right, forming a perfect arch. The light was weak, but the continuous flashes of light allowed us to distinguish the silver shields mounted on their chests. Those tides of black shadows moved slowly and in waves, advancing with snake-like winding movements. The nocturnal beings that blended into the darkness looked threateningly at us from behind their awful, shiny black spots. I tried desperately to resign myself to my fate. I had, once again, fallen prisoner to a nameless, shapeless and hopeless terror.

The land above, as I named the place where the stars live, had not lied to Elsu. It was not a land in peace.

Between the raging battle and the darkness, I struggled to identify who the enemies were. They were more defensive than attacking, which clearly put them at a disadvantage.

'They are fighting against the beings from the constellation of Libra,' explained Elsu telepathically, as he always did whenever he perceived my anxiety.

We witnessed as one of them was knocked down like a felled tree at our feet, after one of the winter soldiers buried its pincers in its clear white flesh. Following the assault, it crawled cautiously forwards, its belly hugging the sand, swimming in its own blue blood. It didn't take long for it to succumb, as if it had simply run out of energy. I observed astonished for a few seconds. The creature was a handsome young man with an athletic build and beautifully sculptured features, like those of a Roman. They were falling on both sides, though more on one side than the other. I'm sure the entire sequence didn't last very long, but it felt like an eternity to me.

'I'll never forget this horror,' I repeated to myself, over and over, on a loop.

'You will forget, Amelia,' declared Elsu, 'if you do not insist on remembering it.'

Apparently, Librans are made of antimatter. Yes, I also struggled to understand the concept. Elsu had to explain it to me many times until I was finally able to understand it. They had the energy gene and needed to recharge with the heat of the sun every day. They did so through a belt that acted as a battery, absorbing the energy they needed and turning it into antimatter.

'Can you explain what antimatter is again?'

'It is pure physics. Antimatter, as its name suggests, is the opposite of matter. In other words, it is a type of matter comprising particles with an electrical charge that is opposite to what is normal. When matter and antimatter come into contact, both are destroyed as the matter is converted into energy.'

'But, how can someone be made up of something like that?'

'The universe contains equal amounts of matter and antimatter locked away in areas that are distant to each other. When matter and antimatter collide, they are neutralised and disappear.'

'That would give sense to Lavoisier's theory, wouldn't it? That nothing disappears, it is simply transformed.'

'It is as you say, Amelia. The matter that disappears is converted into gamma radiation.'

'OK, I follow you so far, but...'

'Antimatter can be used as fuel,' he continued patiently. 'On Earth, you humans have discovered the power of this energy. In the medical field, antimatter is mainly used in tomography. Gamma rays resulting from the annihilation of matter and antimatter are used to locate tumours in the body. You also use it in therapies to treat cancer.'

That science masterclass enabled me to analyse their military strategies, and to understand why when a Libran touched a Scorpio for more than four seconds, both would be destroyed in a burst of energy. The children of Pluto would have to inject enough venom into their adversaries before that time if they wanted to survive. On the other hand, if the children of Venus hoped to win, they would have to activate their energy belts at the same time and have a high enough charge in order to withstand the attack.

A young woman came towards us enveloped in shadows like a blue flame flickering in the wind. The rain washed her blood-stained features. Her face was heart-shaped with full cheeks. Her tall and harmonious body bore a huge resemblance to the young man I had likened to a Roman. On her head was a chromed helmet holding back her long, fine and silky hair that fell in soft auburn waves. She was covered in shiny blue skin and wore a luminescent belt around her waist that appeared to be keeping her alive.

'Enough. Please. You have to stop!' she shouted in the thick of the battle, spinning around and addressing the army that pitched Pluto and Venus against each other.

Surprised by this unexpected behaviour, one of the large black beasts lowered its head and stopped, with a defiant pose.

'We do not want to fight you, and we do not want to hurt you. You have to stop harbouring hatred and contempt and allow love to triumph,' said the beautiful young woman.

'You broke the rules and betrayed our pact,' he replied, with an impassive and immobile face.

'I represent peace and concord. I am sure we can find a way to end this dispute that has gone on for many moons now and left many dead along the way,' she declared, in the spirit of conciliation.

'You have invaded our land and broken our pact,' insisted the winter soldier, showing his cold composure.

I learnt that the balanced superficial calm of the Plutonian character is a strategy to hide their ebullient inner nature.

'We must remain calm. Death is not the answer to this conflict,' said the Libran with great diplomacy as she attempted to pacify the situation.

'The damage is done. Millions of words will never bring our brothers back to life or erase your betrayal,' he rebuffed, completely insensitive to her calls to reason.

'Deliver our daughter to us and we will leave your land forever. The pact will be reinstated.'

There was an outburst of screams and raucous voices, with loose and hurtful tongues, that considered the petition an attack on their honour.

'You know us well,' she insisted. 'We have always played fair. It is a fair deal. We have both lost already.'

The fact is that a son of Scorpio had fallen in love with a daughter of Libra, which contravened the pact that Plutonians and Venusians had kept since the beginning of time.

'Why is that?' I wanted to know.

'Physically, they cannot be together because they would be destroyed. Matter cannot coexist with antimatter,' explained Elsu. 'Libra's romantic and idealistic love seems to have erased their memories. The young, sweet Venusian's seductive repertoire managed to change the young Scorpio's personality, breaking the peace and provoking rage in the Plutonian kingdom of night and darkness. To prevent the fatal outcome, they have kidnapped the young woman, aware of her sentimental nature and of the love between them.'

That story touched my heart in a very particular way, maybe because I saw myself reflected in it. I was also living a love story between two worlds – a bipolarity that separated us with the same force with which I loved him. Who had the power to modify the rules of the universe? It felt very unfair and tremendously sad that two young lovers from opposite worlds had to fight their feelings to avoid falling into their own trap. A romantic story in an extraordinary universe, where the stars of two worlds joined by inverted planes couldn't be together because of physical impediments.

As if unsure which tactic to adopt, the dispute was invariably prolonged. The sensitivity of the Venusians was clearly suffering as they needed calm in order for their energy to remain balanced. Any tension around them was destabilising. On the contrary, thanks to the legendary passion of the Scorpios and to the control they exerted over nature, they handled themselves well in conflict and used the dark of night to their advantage.

Upon observing the scene and understanding what had happened, Elsu made his way towards them. I followed a few steps behind. I was literally scared stiff, despite my attempts to lift my spirits by repeating to myself, as if it were a mantra, 'Amelia, don't let yourself be intimidated, face up to them so they know you're not scared and you can hold your own.'

The cold and the stress I'd suffered by keeping completely still and in the cold for such a long time had caused me to develop a very high fever. At one point, I even began to doubt whether all of the things I was seeing weren't actually febrile delusions caused by my brain's inadequate activity.

The man from the stars stood in front of the Scorpios. When he managed to get their attention, their attitude changed suddenly. Their penetrating, hypnotic looks made me feel nervous and uncomfortable. I had to be the one to break the staring contest first by looking away, freeing my eyes from theirs, which were aimed at me as though they were piercing my very soul.

'We are not as ruthless and dangerous as you think,' said the largest one among them.

'I know the ego of the winter soldiers. You know what you are and what you are not. I also know your warm and sensitive nature, even if it does lay hidden beneath your black armour. It is not my intention to expose the morass of deep feelings and emotions that water brings out in you. I understand that you are only trying to preserve yourselves in the most positive way possible, and that sometimes pushes you to appear to be something you are not.'

Elsu's words seemed to soften the intimidating look in their eyes, calming their rage, giving way to a tense calm.

'You know our secret and therefore deserve our respect. We welcome you to our world, but remember that when there is a storm in these isles, the wind blows in one direction and then suddenly blows in the opposite direction.'

He knew they'd observe him from behind their mysterious, masked eyes, and would be able to feel him, allowing his feelings to respond to his observations. The guardians of Elove were emotional experts and both were exposed now. The flow of emotions between them allowed them to reverberate with a feeling of true understanding.

The pair of lovers appeared on the scene when they saw how Elsu had managed to sooth everybody's nerves in an effort to bring peace to that place. The young Plutonian got down on his knees before us, the rain pouring down on him. His heart was on fire despite the wintry temperatures.

'We love each other,' began the brave young man.

'And we are going to be married,' said the young woman.

'We would like you to help us by casting a spell, an incantation or anything you bring with you from your unknown world that can ensure we will always be together,' they said, in unison.

'There is one thing I can do for you, but it is a very difficult task that requires sacrifice,' replied Elsu after a long pause, to the surprise of everyone, including myself.

'We will do anything,' they said.

'In that case,' said Elsu, addressing the young man, 'armed with nothing but a net and your own hands, you must climb the tallest islet and catch the most vigorous ayty, a bird whose speed is like that of the falcon; and you,' he continued, looking at the elegant Venusian, 'from the tallest islet, you must bring me the bravest pirudis, a three-winged orange bird that is like an eagle. Bring them to me alive and without a single scratch on them.'

Both nodded in silence and, after tenderly looking at each other, left with the permission of Scorpios and Librans alike. For some reason, they trusted him in the hope that this would finally solve the conflict once and for all.

The nocturnal truce gave us the opportunity to share our story with those creatures. Both were very interested in helping us.

A female Scorpio slowly approached me from behind. Suddenly, she stabbed me in the shoulder with her half-moon sting, resembling a rose thorn, which was located at the end of her tail.

I felt a deep hot fluid flowing through my body. It gave me intense pain and caused my heart unexpectedly to race. My reaction to the sting was one of terror as I didn't understand why I was attacked.

'Do not be alarmed, Amelia,' said Elsu, calming me down, 'She detected a high fever and injected a small dose of venom into you that will act as an analgesic and anti-inflammatory. You will recover.'

'Fuck!' I exclaimed, 'Could she warn me next time before attacking me from behind?'

'They are scorpions, remember?' he pointed out, laughing nervously. 'You cannot expect them to be other than what they are.'

It didn't take long for me to feel the effects of the venom, for which I was very grateful. Still, I wasn't taking my eyes off any of them.

In the midst of all those experiences and ideas bumping into each other inside my head like sheep that have just been released from their enclosure, I reminded Elsu that when we arrived at the Purple Lagoon, the Geminian who brought the news had mentioned an encounter with a female from the constellation of Scorpio who sang a song inspired by the thousand-step staircase, and that maybe she could lead us to the Temple of Light we were looking for.

'Well done, Amelia. Are there any musical Scorpio women here who could relate to this story?' asked a hopeful Elsu.

'Yes, Afra,' answered one immediately. 'A strong sea current dragged her out to the constellation of Pisces, and as she was drawn to its crystal-clear waters, she never returned.'

'That would make a lot of sense. We are convinced that the Temple of Light is in a constellation that is governed by water.'

'There is no direct access to Pisces by land,' warned the Plutonian, 'You will have to travel a long way, crossing other constellations, in order to reach your final destination.'

We looked at each other in the way that only we understood. His eloquent eyes resisted looking away from mine in a long stare that told me everything he needed to say. We had invented a private language just for the two of us. We were joined by a mission and bound together by the red ribbon of emotions.

The young lovers arrived from opposite directions at the established times with two large nets containing the birds Elsu had requested. He asked them to very carefully free them from their nets. They were undeniably the most beautiful birds of their kind. He tore one of the fringes from his jacket.

'Now,' he continued, 'Without your bodies touching, you must tie the birds to each other by the legs with this leather strip.'

The ayty and the pirudis tried to take flight, but only managed to roll around on the ground. Enraged by their helplessness, the birds resorted to pecking at each other.

'This is the lesson. Never forget what you have seen today and what is your essence. You are like the pirudis and the ayty. If you tie yourselves to one another, albeit for love, sooner or later you will end up destroying who you are and hurting each other. If you really want your love to last, fly together in spirit, but never tied to each other.'

The space became a temple of silence for an indefinite amount of time. There was silence within the silence, responding to the questions of the mind, like matryoshkas, Russian nesting dolls that represented inner growth. No one felt the need to fill that silence, so full it was of truth, reflection and knowledge, because silence holds its own answers.

That experience taught me that when the ego is offended, the soul learns a lesson. Only those beings who were on another level of consciousness could transcend, and this formed part of their treaty of concentrated wisdom.

Elsu admitted to me that he'd only reminded them of who they were and what their true essence was, and that it's essential to connect with it in order to find ourselves, to return home and to allow our spirit to soar the skies. The spirit is an intimate part in constant communion with the universe that we must protect in order not to create a dependency on other entities that are foreign to the genuine and illuminated version of ourselves. The only way to maintain ourselves on at a higher level of consciousness is to connect with our essence because when we connect with it, we connect with the universe itself and become aligned with it, as if we were one and the same. When you let go of your essence, you become weaker, and everything becomes a constant battle where nothing flows, where you feel like you're swimming against the current. You wear yourself out. You feel lost, and finally end up far from peace and balance.

Knowing our essence teaches us that everything we love is free, and therefore fleeting and variable. Not resisting what we must inevitably let go of is the greatest proof of love we can give to ourselves and those we love.

However, our situation was obviously different. Elsu and I could touch, kiss and feel each other. I was convinced that what we had was the result of twin souls colliding. Two essences that had found themselves in different ages that had decided to transit together, as if they were two perfectly-interlocking puzzle pieces, and that when we looked at each other, we in some way felt as though we were returning home.

Something happened when we looked at each other at the airport that day. By some coincidence our eyes met for the first time in our lives or, at least, in this life. From that moment, the magic of the universe started everything up. I don't quite know how, but it started up as impeccably as one of those tiny smart machines that switch on so that the world can continue to be an even more extraordinary place. Who knows? Maybe after millions of years and reincarnations, Elsu and I, two twin souls, were meeting again. And the fact is that I felt a feeling of transcendence that went far beyond the initial crush. Something between us surpassed all expectations and previous experiences. I was able to recognise him by his look and the touch of his hands. It was almost as if by looking at the other person, we were looking at ourselves. He observed me as long as he dared to. In an indefinable way, he was also attracted to me, as if he already knew me, as if we'd already been close friends elsewhere, in a previous lifetime. His mere presence was able to calm down all my thoughts, making him a kindred spirit.

According to Plato, the first beings created by the universe were hermaphrodites that possessed a truly astonishing strength. According to legend, the gods divided them up in order to weaken their huge potential. That's why platonic love is nothing more than attraction that pushes these souls to find each other, to be joined together as one being, in the memory of those two halves that were originally a whole. In the same way, although the experience is portrayed as something magical and wonderful, this phenomenon is also full of very painful obstacles. Precisely because we're dealing with something that transforms, finding your soul mate is destiny's gift, which is why the universe makes sure that the connection happens with millions of coincidences but, ultimately, it will be our free will that accepts the gift. When two soul mates find each other, the universe conspires to make sure they cannot be separated again. Whether they stay with us or disappear, the soul mate will make sure we hold onto our naked truth in order to complete the journey to ourselves.

The energy signals that Elsu emitted aroused my soul and were above any hint of a doubt. I only had to wait and, in any case, trust in the wonderful magic of destiny and in the stars.

Chapter 19

The Shoebox

I was in the middle of my life, I guess. Luckily, I still had the second half of the game to go. I could have started by just saying my age, but I've always enjoyed complicating things to make myself more interesting.

According to quantum physics, the past can be erased. You can even rewind time like you can a film and change what happens. In truth, I wasn't interested in erasing anything and much less in changing my past. What I needed was a time machine so I could relive it all over again, so I turned my memories into the most sophisticated model. Because of this, I could relive the happy times, and the unhappy ones, too. Although, unfortunately, I could only relive them in one dimension – as a memory.

Negotiating with memories wasn't easy for me to do because I had an entire world full of them. Which one should I start with? Some were in the maturing process, some would die as a result of being shared, others would inevitably wither away, and some were destined to be pulverised. There were days where I simply didn't want to continue ageing only to realise that I had wasted my adult life on an unhappy marriage, and there were others when I couldn't possibly imagine a better life partner than Esteban.

'No matter what happens, don't ever try to control time,' he said, 'as it'll always end up controlling you. Just enjoy each moment to the fullest, without worrying about how long it'll last. Don't allow your life to pass you by counting how many hours you have left. Don't make that mistake. Don't try to measure time; time can't be measured. Time isn't the one that is born, ages and dies. Time doesn't pass, we do. Life is made up of hours, and those hours must be filled with life.'

My time machine took me back to a clear spring day. I loved that field because it was always filled with poppies that time of year. The brightest of red, they grew by the thousands all over the place and without permission. Esteban assured me that they were actually weeds as they competed with the crops, aggressively stealing nutrients from cereals such as wheat, barley and oats.

'A field overrun with poppies can cause huge losses for farmers as their germination cycle coincides with that of their cereal crops. Even so, I love them because they remind me of you,' he explained, hugging me from behind as we sat on a blanket in the middle of that beautiful setting.

'Me? What do I have to do with poppies?'

'They're resilient and eye-catching, like you. They represent the simplicity of the countryside as well as spontaneity. Did you know that their seeds can survive for ten years until they germinate? Also, they can withstand pretty much anything. Poppies love movement, they dance just like you do.'

We would watch for a long time as the green and golden wheat in the fields waved in the wind, splashed with a multitude of vermillion dots, until the sun would sink into the horizon as if it were weighing itself on a pair of scales, sitting on one tray and making the orange moon rise on the other side. I knew he was gay, but seeing Amelia in front of us and sharing these moments that filled my life with joy enabled me to forget that my happiness was nothing but a façade. Who said that people are more authentic when they're naked? Esteban was truth, even when hiding from the entire world. I had formed a family with someone special, full of tiny details, whom I could not avoid loving. I felt as though I'd been cheated when my cards were dealt, but I accepted them and decided to play my hand. I preferred having him in my life like this than imagining what it would be like to wake up without him.

We were living our truth, although we didn't share it with the rest of the world. Esteban had trusted me with his secret. I couldn't ask anyone for help and I didn't want to disappoint his family; I also lacked the mental fortitude to accept insults and rejection from his people. He asked me to never tell our daughter. That was the toughest part for me, but I kept my promise.

When we returned home, he came into the workshop that same afternoon holding something in his hands.

'Today's your lucky day, designer,' he purred in a low voice, placing a box with an enormous green bow on my cutting table.

'What is it?' I asked, surprised. 'It isn't my birthday or any other special occasion that I know of.'

'Today's the day of courage and of courageous women. Aren't you going to open it?' he asked anxiously.

'You're insane,' I half screamed when I saw that little ball of love shaking its tail like a helicopter.

'He wants you to pick him up. I told him all about you on the way home.'

'I can't. He'll bite me,' I said, not realising that the puppy was more frightened than I was.

He kissed me softly, nothing scandalous or out of this world. He never forgot how I liked soft kisses. It left me wanting more.

'He just wants to copy my kisses. C'mon, Belly, come closer. I found him abandoned by the side of the road.'

I stared at him. 'You're a pain, did you know that?'

He shrugged his shoulders, then placed his hands over mine, interlocking our fingers and forced me to move my hand towards that new life.

'You see? It's not that hard.'

Esteban had brought me a dog because I was terrified of them and he wanted to cure me, as if fear were like hiccups and you could just scare them away. But the dog fulfilled his mission. Amelia called him Vodka until she realised he was pregnant and that she'd clearly made a mistake as to its gender. By then, she'd fallen so deeply in love with the animal that she refused to change its name. Vodka always had an amazing connection with Amelia and they became inseparable from the very first day.

I saw this event as a magic flying carpet that could transport Amelia to wherever her father was. It was an open door that Vodka would help us cross, hand in hand.

'Amelia, are you upset that Vodka is female?' asked her father, cautiously.

'Well… I'm surprised. Aren't you? For a year, we though Vodka was male and suddenly it turns out he's something else. It's not very normal for a female to be called Vodka, it's going to sound a little strange. I'd got used to the idea of having a male dog and not a female dog.'

'And how do you feel now that you know?'

'A bit disappointed, perhaps. I guess it's to be expected when our hopes for a wish or a person don't come true, especially when you realise that something or someone may actually be different to what to you originally thought. I know it's ridiculous, but it's a type of disappointment mixed with a feeling of loss.'

'But you haven't lost Vodka. He's still with you,' he continued, sympathetically.

'I know, but now it's as thought I have to get to know a whole new dog. I know it's immature but I can't help but feel angry. What hasn't changed at all is how he makes me feel. When I'm with him, I'm happy.'

'So, why be normal when you can be happy?'

'You're totally right, papá. Nothing's changed. No name or gender will change my love for Vodka or everything we've lived together.'

'That's what's important, Amelia. That clash between expectation and reality is important. We have a capacity for expressing our needs while others have the right to not fulfil our expectations or our fantasies.'

'Vodka never listens to me, so I'm pretty sure the most rebellious thing she can do is be herself,' she said, jokingly.

'Amelia, have you thought about this? When a baby is born, its identity has already been predetermined by its gender. That gender, which makes it male or female, has to adapt to a social model. If you're a man, you will wear trousers and must seduce women. If you're a woman, you must seduce men. You will wear makeup and look after your appearance; you will have children and be a good mother. Don't you think it's perhaps time to think differently?'

'Papá, you've become very deep since discovering Vodka's new gender,' she replied, wide-eyed.

'Do you love me?'

'Papá, what kind of question is that? I love you like you only love once in a lifetime,' she replied, jumping into his arms like she did when she was a little girl.

I was so happy that Amelia had dealt with Vodka's new gender so well, in such a positive and mature way, particularly because I knew in the bottom of my heart that it had comforted and freed Esteban's soul. In a way, they'd had the conversation he always wanted to have with his daughter, which he never dared to have due to the fear of breaking his silence and confessing that he liked men more than women.

I recognised some of her reactions and I couldn't blame her for them. I remember how I myself felt when Esteban threw open the closet doors and stood before me as a complete stranger. My disappointment stemmed from my frustration regarding my expectations and my need to control and predict everything, none of which came true. I cried and cried for a very long time. It seemed impossible to me that a 'truth' that was such an integral part of my world, that was unquestionable, could shake my life in such a way. I felt lost and insecure and angry for having discovered that the love of my life wasn't who I thought he was. It hurt me deeply that the 'truth' I thought I possessed was in fact another. Physically, I felt as though something had been torn out of my insides, something that belonged only to me. Over time, I realised that disenchantment and disappointment are two different things, and that the structures upon which disappointment is based are deeply rooted.

What Amelia felt was disenchantment, whereas I felt enormous disappointment. The impact and the shock I felt turned my world up-side down. I experienced fear, rage, frustration and impotence, even feeling unprotected and abandoned. I didn't have enough room in my body to hold all that pain. I didn't know where to hide or how I fit into that new reality. I felt betrayed and convinced myself I could no longer trust Esteban, life or even myself for having made the wrong decision instead of living the life of a free, successful woman as I had always dreamt of. I had to redesign my 'truth' and regulate all my painful emotions in order to refocus my life differently.

When someone disappoints us, we change our image of that person. Maybe we had put them on a pedestal and suddenly they've fallen off. To give without expecting nothing in return sets us free. On the other hand, when we expect something from others, it makes us dependent, because we suffer if it doesn't come true. We often have the feeling that our friends, family or partner have failed us by not saying what we wanted or needed to hear. If I organise a surprise party for him, why won't he do the same for me? If I'm always there for my friend when she needs me, how come I can never find her when I need her? That's when frustration appears, and you feel, in the bottom of your heart, that you're being selfish and you blame yourself for expecting anything in the first place, yet still you get angry that they didn't give it to you.

A disloyal friendship, a love that lets us down, a project that is cut short too soon... it's easy for things not to turn out the way we want them to. We simply don't have control over everything that happens in our lives.

People are always creating expectations, interpreting situations or judging our surroundings, and that makes us go through life with preconceived ideas. When these don't happen, it gives way to disappointment and frustration, starting a vicious cycle.

Why do we believe that others should do what we think is right? If only the school of life could turn us into good pupils so we could realise that life is about accepting the fact we don't own the truth, that we can only control what we control and that we mustn't depend on others in order to be happy. At school, lessons are taught to us first, and then we're put to the test. In life, you're tested first and learn the lesson afterwards. There can be no disappointment possible in a well that is overflowing with freedom. In these circumstances, living with a degree of understanding for ourselves and for others can be a gesture of kindness and compassion when faced with different situations that won't always be in our favour.

I made the most of my disappointment and my low points and made them into an opportunity for learning and growth, aware that disillusionment often walks behind enthusiasm with a big smile on its face. The disappointment I felt when I realised the truth made me see just how important that man was to me.

Our love was always a free verse – a connection that was difficult to understand by those outside of our tiny emotional ecosystem. I'd go as far as to say that even I got lost in it on more than one occasion. The first time I was unfaithful, I felt like the worst kind of rat. I took a deep breath and took off my blouse. I took off my pearly grey bra with the same ease as with which I threw myself into that fleeting adventure. I only kept my grey hat with its birdcage veil on because my lover said he thought it very erotic to see me completely naked with just that on my head. I'd wrestled with the idea so much that I finally decided to just do it. I looked great for my age, without any of the workouts or massages that women have nowadays. I armed myself with courage and didn't stop to think of the consequences that could come from my rebellious act. When I got over my nerves, with my lips painted poppy red the way Esteban liked them, I opened the door I had refused to walk through for years. I felt a stab of panic that triggered my imagination. Scandal was served. The world would be outraged, calling me indecent, a sinner, a snake, because I'd gone against the conservative ideology and the deep-rooted religious and chauvinistic values of the time. We have been taught that infidelity is very bad, which in turn governs how we behave in the world.

On the one hand, I was anxious and afraid that my courage that took so long to build up would ultimately fail me. But on the other hand, I was determined not to look back.

Every couple has codes, and ours were very clear. We were both free to have relations with other people. However, I couldn't help but feel like I was being unfaithful, though not disloyal. I wasn't acting out of spite, or even vengeance; it was about being faithful to myself. My will to cling to life invaded me like the high tide invades the dry rocks. I felt powerful, like a woman who truly knew the power of her own body. I needed to feel sexually desired. All of my weight rested on my own two feet. I stood my ground as far as life was concerned, sure of my decisions. Of course, my shoulders also carried the weight of the puritanism I had absorbed from my family and through my education, and this occasionally caused me an internal suffering that I couldn't ignore. I had previously tried to tell myself that sex wasn't everything, and it isn't, but it does form part of our lives. You can tell your body thousands of times that it's okay if nobody wants it, but it won't believe you, because in that animal part of its being is the need to be desired, to prove that it can still be sexually attractive to someone. It's a primary, animal instinct that always rears its head and has its own reason for its existence because it seeks to be part of the exuberance and the flourishing of life.

I don't know if there are 'cheats anonymous' meetings, but it might be good for us to be able to discuss these issues freely, without feeling judged.

One of my travels around the world took me to a show in northern Senegal, where hundreds of men from the nomadic Muslim tribe of the Wodaabe that inhabit the Shahel region were preparing a festival aimed at impressing women in order to be chosen as their husbands.

This is considered the most impressive beauty contest in the world, where male beauty is put on show every September at the start of the celebration. The rainy season had ended and it was time for the Gerewol festival to commence. For seven days and seven nights, the men tried hard to convince the women to become their wives. The preparation that went into it was like that of any other beauty contest. The men would apply makeup to their faces and bodies in a process that lasted over seven hours. The judges were the tribe's most gorgeous women, and each of them would choose her winner. The candidates had to perform a special dance. If the judges liked any of them, they could decide to be stolen by them, leaving behind their current husbands. They just had to wait for their favourites to touch their shoulders. The fact that the women were already married was no inconvenience. They could have the husbands they wanted and single women could have sex with whomever they wanted, whenever they wanted. The female power in that tribe gave me a lot to think about, particularly about the strict beliefs that had been instilled in me as a child. I'd been educated that way, and questioning all those beliefs all of a sudden felt like being reborn. When you're unfaithful, it's normal to feel like you're worth less than dirt. Then I had to add the label of 'bad mother' to the mix as I was allowing myself to have sex with another man who wasn't my daughter's father. But I was determined to write the story of a woman who learned that a responsible mother isn't one who slowly dies for the sake of her children, but one who shows them how to live life to the fullest, trusting in herself, making peace with her body, taking pride in her fury and her anguish, and giving herself permission to give in to her most authentic and wild-est instincts. The same woman who embarked on the adventure of learning to listen to her own voice that decades of cultural and social conditioning had silenced.

I had freed the deepest war cry I could from the very centre of my being. I was ready to believe in myself enough to overcome barriers and connect with my untameable spirit. To be a woman didn't mean giving up your personal happiness so you could fit in with the predetermined models. If I had accepted that idea in the first place, it had been for Esteban. Wasn't it, therefore, fair to also do it for myself?

I became someone else that afternoon. I had come back to life. I began to buy sexy lingerie again, something I hadn't done for years. I went to see my lover looking beautiful and amazing. It was all about having fun. I ran as far away as I could from the idea of the woman I never wanted to be – a woman living in a small town, with white hair, short nails and tough, calloused hands, without makeup, all wrinkled up with a sun-damaged face, buying bread in the morning wearing slippers and a polka-dot apron, who asked how much a baguette costs with her hands on her hips. A woman who was completely uninterested in the pleasures of sex. I had the image of my own mother in mind. She never enjoyed her body; it was there mainly for my father's enjoyment. When we came back home after mass on Sundays she'd let her stomach out of her girdle, her facial expression would relax and she'd remove her bra, letting her breasts hang down to her bellybutton after all her children had dried up her milk factory. She would then flop on the couch and let all her cellulite hang out. When she took off her stockings, any leg hair that wasn't long enough to be removed could be seen. She never removed the hair on her upper lip or around her crotch. She was always running around after the chickens that in the early morning would try to break into the house to live like people, eating the freshly-made bread from the iron pot. She believed that her job as a woman was done once she'd had a family and that her body served no other purpose than to satisfy others. She was always tired, sequestered by domestic logistics, what we were having for dinner and the constant stress that a child would wake up at any time. She never questioned her daily misery. She left this world feeling like she had fulfilled her role as a woman and within society.

At first, after the first few encounters, I'd go home feeling guilty, torturing myself. I'd be mortified for days and had the feeling that everybody knew. I'd also always end up throwing out my lingerie after each encounter, because it always looked dirty to me, no matter how often I washed it. At first, I went out looking for these encounters. After a while, I simply went with the flow. After fourteen years of marriage, the first man that saw me naked was five years younger than me. He told me I was his skin's obsession and that he found my body extremely attractive. That flattered me. A few minutes later, we became one, wrapped up in passion. I was intoxicated by the moment, the feelings, the lust – a little of what everyone needs to feel alive. When we finished, he insisted on accompanying me to the bus as he showed me his neighbourhood and even tried to hold my hand, but

I let go of it with a polite smile. I made sure there were never any feelings towards any of them. All emotional connections were strictly forbidden. I could only ever love Esteban. In that sense, I was still the same woman who had vowed to love him forever, only in a more modern and practical way.

I began to experience emotions that had been banished and repressed for far too long. I rediscovered myself with this sexual liberation. Following years of drought, this new enthusiasm for truly living was like kerosene to fire. I remained faithful for a long period of time, until I began to wonder what my life could have been like. And then I decided to do something about it. I'd always been an adventurous woman and this undoubtedly spurred me on. I wasn't searching for anyone else, I was actually searching for myself, or at least for certain aspects of the woman that lived within me that had been lost or ignored. I searched for part of my lost identity in every adventure, something that had been a part of my past. My infidelity wasn't motivated by my need to fall in love with anyone else. What I loved was the new, fresh image of myself, this personal rediscovery that came from having others admire my beauty, notice my perfume or my new haircut. I was swimming in dopamine, and that made me stronger.

From the start, it was clear that any 'slip up', for lack of a better word, would not be discussed. Neither one of us wanted to know about the other's relations. It was too painful. Esteban also had his dalliances. He would come home at two in the morning and, without even taking a shower, would put his pyjamas on, get into bed, kiss me and sleep cuddled up to me. Did it hurt me? Of course it did. It hurt my ego deeply. I was trained to be hurt by infidelity. My soul was at peace being with another free, frank and clean soul, capable of showing themselves completely with me in order to build a relationship where both parties could decide what they wanted. No, it wasn't my soul that was in pain, it was my ego that had been fatally wounded. I had his company but I longed to have him as a lover.

Together, we built a solid base for cohabitation. He never tried to be my master and never bossed me around. We travelled together, at a pace that was comfortable for us both, all the way to the end. Even his death was a serene disappearance.

Ten years after his passing, I still missed his laughter, the sound of his voice, his company, and a million other tiny things. I still felt him lingering around in my soul. Our story was that of two free spirits who lived with each other, with love and respect. Parallel lives in perfect symmetry and balance – something that only really happens once in a lifetime. I didn't expect to find it with anyone else. Esteban was one of a kind.

You'll never hear on the news that a chef has tragically lost his legs in an accident, and for good reason. For the universe to teach us terrible lessons we can apply to our own lives, the chef would have to lose his tongue, the musician his ears, the painter his eyes, the philosopher his mind and the athlete his legs. What did I learn? My lesson was that being faithful to oneself has to come before being faithful to anyone else. Now that Esteban was no longer here, I could assume my own story with total liberty, without feeling ashamed of it.

'Listen, Belly,' said Esteban as we sat on a bench. 'Today's lesson is about us.'

He had taken me to the vegetable garden where he had planted potatoes. He opened a green shoebox with a broken cardboard lid. It was full of photographs of relatives I'd never met.

'I want you to see something,' he added, taking out a pile of loose black and white photos. 'This old box is full of lives unlived. Their faces don't reflect the accumulation of resentment and failures, but I can guarantee you that very few of them were true to themselves. I'd hate it if our faces were to be added to this shoebox one day. Even if the world doesn't know about it, you and I must continue to be true to our own feelings. You and I, do you follow? Love is a mystery that matters only to two people. Sometimes, the world isn't ready to receive special people, and they have to invent a new world for themselves in order to survive, just like we did. To me, we'll always be great. We were two, you in your body, me in mine, but with only one heart. Don't think that it's cowardice, I'm speaking precisely of intelligent courage. If we don't make it into the shoebox, we fall away from the memories, and memories feed the future because man is nothing without his memories. If at some point in your life, you realise that you can't go on, don't feel obligated to keep unkeepable promises. First, you have to earn trust in yourself and be faithful to your own values. Then, and only then, will you be able to fulfil your promises, no matter what they are and who you made them to. This means, in particular, keeping the promises you make to yourself and satisfying your own needs above all others, so that you can then be available to others when you make a commitment to them. Never betray yourself knowingly.'

Esteban told me that betrayal doesn't mean infidelity. Being untrue to oneself is the worst of all betrayals, and although it's never the start, it can be the result. The most dangerous betrayals are those that stem from everyday events and accumulate over time, and they answer the question 'Can I trust myself? How faithful am I to myself?' There's no situation more difficult than to live an internal struggle with ourselves, which is why coherence requires determination in order to overcome the fear of being different. It took so much blood, sweat and tears for me to learn that loyalty to others is false if you aren't loyal to yourself first. Maintaining an attitude based on what I really wanted and acting genuinely at all times, without fear, respecting myself, listening to and understanding myself, without going against my own ideas and principles was a very bumpy road, but was also deeply rewarding as it allowed me to take control of my own life without being conditioned by what others might think. Ultimately, the most important thing is to be faithful to our own truth. I only wish I had learned this at the beginning of my journey and not at the end, so I could have lived wild and free.

Chapter 20

Someone Like Me

What we know pales in comparison to what we don't know, much like comparing a drop of water to an ocean.

My mother wasn't like other mothers. That, I knew. I imagined what her childhood had been like in Granada in the 1960s, when the streets were wide and the buildings were low, with very few cars and trams in control of the streets, along with some donkeys that were used as means of transport and carried loads for locals from one part of the locality to another.

It was an image filled with contrasts, between the modernity that was emerging all over the place and had come to stay, and a rural world that, although still present, was slowly fading from the picture. She was probably one of those girls with plaits who played hopscotch, elastics or with a skipping rope outdoors to the tune of a traditional children's song, surrounded by rosemary sellers, weavers, bootblacks and young men who paraded their pigs around the Plaza Nueva. Her childhood would have coincided with the transition between the post-war period and Franco's dictatorship.

I vaguely remember Belly telling me how my mother would sneak away to watch the show put on by the magician Fumanchi, where she would sit in the first row surrounded by other children. The children would shout, 'Peneque, Peneque, where are you?' Apparently he was a hero made of cardboard and felt, measuring around fifty centimetres, who would appear on a tiny travelling stage seeking justice and beating the villains. This brave Andalusian puppet continues to live adventures thanks to the hands of his creator's children, who keep the traditional children's theatre company alive today.

'Your mother always returned with a head full of fantasies and incredible stories after watching Peneque. She always had an amazing imagination,' said Belly, shaking her head as though that virtue had, somehow, been more of a problem.

I was only beginning to get my life in order and putting together my story once again. I'd recovered around eighty percent of my memory, the remaining twenty percent were long-term memories and would eventually come back, although gradually. I went back to work and Conan and I were getting closer and closer as time went on. However, his question made my past blow up in my face.

'Would you like to be a mother, Rafaela?'

My silence said it all.

'Am I asking too soon or too late?' insisted Conan.

'I don't know. Perhaps you're asking the wrong person.'

He hugged me protectively me and made a joke, trying to make light of the issue. We were so close I could feel the vein on his neck throbbing.

'I just wanted to make sure you didn't mind that my sailor sperm is too salty to impregnate you.' Only he could laugh at even the most serious topics.

'Very funny,' I replied, still in his arms.

I did end up laughing, though. At first, just a little. Later, when he saw me he joined in and, by then, no one could stop us. Conan had one of those contagious laughs that begins in his stomach and then expands throughout his entire body, throwing tentacles all over the place that grab you and wrap you up in it. I couldn't help but have a few thoughts: What truly defines a mother? What defines a child? Family creates bonds that cohabitation cannot sustain and, sometimes, these come undone. Did I want children? My biological clock wasn't ticking for maternity; there was no impulse that awoke my maternal instinct. I suppose this was connected to the way I viewed life and to the unresolved trauma caused by my parents' absence.

It just so happened I was working with Alicia for a few weeks around that time. She was a thirty-seven-year-old marketing consultant who was trapped by her own feelings. She began her very first therapy session by telling me, no holds barred, 'I don't want to be a mother. At twenty I thought I'd have kids by thirty, when I turned thirty I thought I'd have them at thirty-five, and now I've come to the conclusion that I just don't want to have them at all. It will never be the right time. I've decided I want a hysterectomy as a permanent contraceptive solution.'

'You seem very sure of your decision,' I said, bluntly.

'I went to the doctor to get an appointment and they were so patronising: they treated me like a child and even sent me to have a psychological assessment. My friends tell me that having children is like coming full circle, that it's part of the natural process. And my partner says that my decision not to have children is a selfish one. All of this is making me feel awful and I don't know what to do about it.'

'You've told me what the others think and want. What do you really want, Alicia?'

'I don't want to take on any more responsibility. I know I'd be a great mother but, even so, I've got other commitments and obligations, and I don't want to add yet another one. That would mean putting the brakes on my projects and professional development for several years.'

'Does this mean that you think you'd be giving up more than what you'd be getting by becoming a mother?'

'Well, obviously I'd have to stop everything, go through the pregnancy, the birth and then maternity leave. As a freelancer, I'd lose clients and opportunities. Besides, I want to do other things with my life.'

'Which metaphor would you use to describe maternity?'

She lowered her head and though for a few moments, then answered firmly, 'Having kids is like signing a contract for things you'll be giving up for life.'

'Right. So it seems like becoming a mother would have a huge impact on your life.'

'That's how I see it. I think everyone has to manage their time as they see fit. My lifestyle simply isn't compatible with the type of dedication a child requires. It makes my skin crawl every time I see pregnant bellies on the street that have become magnets for brothers-in-law, know-it-alls, paediatricians, neighbours and visionaries who use it like some sort of crystal ball that predicts the future, and they speak of their own experiences as if they were dogma or, even worse, not their own experiences but popular theories they've heard about maternity and advice regarding how to be a mother and shave both legs at the same time.'

'I understand.'

'I feel huge pressure all around me. It feels like I constantly have to keep explaining my decision to everyone.'

'As you said yourself, motherhood is a choice, not an imposition.'

'Last weekend, just because I said I didn't like children at my in-laws' place, they looked at me like I was a monster. My mother-in-law resented my comment, later adding that my time would come, "Everyone has children, you know. You're just not mature enough yet." Can you believe that?'

'So, you don't like children and you also don't want to have to give up everything. Is that it?'

'There's more. Now I that I think about all this, I just don't think it makes sense. The planet and our values are going down the drain and I don't want to be a part of this circus. It's not misanthropy; it's just that it doesn't fit in with my values to bring a child into a materialistic, aggressive, competitive, authoritarian, anti-social and voracious world.'

'How would you like to feel about your decision?'

'I don't want to feel guilty, or that my decision isn't normal. I've even been asked what I hope to get out of life if I don't want children, as if I alone am not enough, as if I could never be complete as a woman or as a person if I didn't have them.'

'Alicia, you've told me how you don't want to feel, but you haven't told me how you would like to feel about your decision.'

'Light, brave, and sure that my decision and my way of life is just as valid as motherhood is. It's time to take the batteries out of the pro-verbial biological clock and its insufferable ticking and rid myself of the historically established model mother role everyone keeps insisting on pushing onto me.'

That afternoon, I tried to hide my clumsiness as I attempted to light a stick of incense for the fourth time in a row. I felt uneasy, unknowingly sensing things that I still didn't quite understand, truths that had not been revealed. It was all lights and shadows. I couldn't imagine that I really did have a reason for feeling that way, reasons I didn't yet know about.

I walked along the garden path of gravel and white cement that had quickly become on of my favourite spots. The rosebushes, the orange tree filled with blossoms and the fragrant honeysuckle and jasmine vines at the entrance of the house permeated the air with their delicious aromas. The enigmatic bottle with the hidden message that we rescued on the boat was sitting on the little white iron table surrounded by green vines, and I felt serene and completely enamoured of the secrets that bottle contained. I sat in the shade, on one of the soft cushy chairs around the table, and caressed a velvety rose I just had cut. I thought about how privileged I was to be sitting among so much greenery in that garden I so loved while looking through the misted glass of an icy-cold bottle of lemonade that was my sole companion.

The imagination and the eye of the beholder can make anything more or less beautiful. To me, the garden was like paradise, but I was actually looking at was a poor beggar looking in through the wrought iron front gates. Despite her tattered clothes, her light glowed in the darkness of dusk, shining among everything my eyes could see. She looked like one of those Roman marble statues, except she was wearing far more clothes and her messy hair looked sticky. When she saw me looking and smiling at her, she responded with a smile of her own, clean and free of all malice, and a vague memory stirred within me. I knew then that she wasn't a statue or an angel; she was a woman. She was very still, her arms hanging loosely at her sides. I first noticed her face, a true beauty, then her hands. And as I looked at her, a chill ran through my entire being that I couldn't understand. She was waiting in front of the gate patiently, with the stillness of someone who controls their body and their emotions.

'I know,' she said, thinking that I was judging her dirty, dishevelled appearance, while she smoothed down the front part of her dusty dress with her delicate hands. 'Can you believe it? I've been walking for three days.' She gestured behind her at the distant olive trees.

For a moment, I was speechless as my brain tried desperately to find the appropriate memory. I just couldn't remember.

'Is there something I can do for you? Are you lost?' I asked, raising my voice but without moving.

Her large eyes that had known a life of suffering were moist. 'I'm looking for Rafaela,' she declared, with a timid voice, full of emotion.

Waiting a little for the clamouring in my chest to stop, I stood up as if powered by a spring and walked towards the voice, pulled by some inexplicable force. I stood just a few metres in front of the gate, one hand on the rose, the other in my pocket.

'I am Rafaela. And you are...?'

'I'm your mother,' she answered, as if she were equally expecting a kiss or a slap.

And then it happened. My hands couldn't hold on to a flower or remain in my pockets any longer. I ran and my arms finally wrapped around all that lost time. I thought I heard a sigh of relief.

We rocked each other as if we'd grown roots in the centre of that same garden. We were together again, destiny with destiny. We looked at each other, making sure we were in fact us. I caressed her hair covered in dirt, but to me it felt like the softest thing my fingertips had ever touched. She caressed my cheeks, incredulous. Time had finally been on our side and I burst into tears. We were completely overcome with love.

'We still have so much time and our hearts are still beating,' she said, not letting me go, hugging me tightly. 'We can still set the timer on a new stage of our story, my beautiful girl.'

My soul was shaking, ready to leap into hers, like a bird that learns to flap its wings before taking off into the void for the first time.

'Come,' I said. 'There's no lost time. I've filled every single empty minute with you, *mamá*.'

We were separated, but when two souls are destined to find each other, destiny steps in to bring two worlds together, eliminating distances, bringing paths together and overcoming the impossible. The air whistled, having held its breath to hear the musical sound of our impatient kisses. I thought then of something I can't remember, and even if I did remember it, I wouldn't be able to put into words, because my spirit had left me to surround the both of us. We were living a sweet dream, one that no one could wake us up from.

'Have you formed a family, Rafaela?' she asked, looking at Conan as he observed us perplexed from where he stood, by the stained-glass kitchen window.

'That's Conan, *mamá*. He's the closest thing to a family I've had since Belly died.'

I signalled for him to come closer and he quickly joined us. He tried to hide it, but he was overwhelmed with feelings upon witnessing the high emotional voltage of our encounter. He knew exactly what that moment meant to me. My mother greeted him politely and he pulled her to his wide strapping chest, hugging her tightly. He then wiped the last tear that had slid down my cheek and stopped at my chin.

'Look at that, I finally have a mother-in-law to argue with!' he joked, trying to redirect all that emotional energy. 'Had I known, I would've baked a cake and hung decorations up to celebrate your return.'

I was on cloud nine. She was swinging on the moon. I'd always dreamt about this moment and what it would be like, but never in a million years could I imagine being this happy. I was scared to let go of her hand in case she disappeared all over again, like when I was a child and all I had left of her was an image burnt into my retinas of her hair in a French twist and her old brown leather suitcase.

'Chiquilla, let your mother have a shower and change her clothes. I'll make us some dinner. You have a lot to catch up on, but give her a break,' suggested Conan wisely, realising we had both lost completely ourselves in each other.

She nodded, grateful for the initiative, and entered the house where she'd been raised, her home. The door was already open to let in the air. She walked slowly, recognising every detail. I had kept most of my grandmother's furniture but, obviously, I'd made some improvements and had changed some of the décor. It was a combination of old and new things because, although I wanted to leave my own mark on the place, I could never completely get rid of all the things that went into the character of this family home.

She headed to the kitchen, turned her head towards me and said, 'There used to be a high wooden table here with tall stools where my mother would make her jams, and where I learnt to make canapés for Christmas, which was also my father's birthday. And in this corner was the shelf with all the medicines,' she continued, pointing at where the modern microwave now sat, reflecting off the shiny blue tiles with Moorish motifs that matched the mosaic floor.

She closed her eyes and breathed in deeply, as if wanting to inhale all the aromas of her history. Then she looked for another room.

'I remember the day I got locked in the bathroom and my father slipped one of my favourite books under the door so I wouldn't get bored. This is the same place where I got a gash on my head because I insisted on sliding over the bottom of the bath on a sponge. I would've been no more than eight then.'

I followed her around the entire house, like a dog with two tails, as she shared her anecdotes and childhood memories with me. It was like travelling through a time I never knew; it was a priceless gift that I was clinging to.

'I'll never forget the epic tantrum I had when I was sixteen. I'd asked for a suitcase for my birthday, but I was given a typewriter instead. I threw a fit right here in this hallway. It was painted beige back then. From this window, I'd hear my father talking to the vegetables and the trees out in the garden. I laughed whenever he said they had to grow healthy and juicy because they were going to be prepared by the best cook in the world and tasted by the most discerning palates. That Sunday, when we returned home after his death, coming into this house without him and feeling like part of him still lived on in here, was very strange. The outside and the surroundings have changed quite a lot. The garden is even more beautiful now and the shutters are painted a different colour, but the house still has the same essence. It's wonderful to be able to return home and relive so many special moments,' she said nostalgically. 'Thank you for keeping it this way, Rafaela.'

'Tell me more, *mamá*. What other memories do you have here?'

'The most important place for me was the tree in the front garden. When I was little, I gave him a name, Berto, plus our family surname. We took photos under it on the first day of school every year.'

Upstairs, she showed me her old room.

'When I came to visit you, we'd sleep together in this bed. Do you remember, Rafaela?'

I nodded. That memory lived in some remote part of my conscience. Childhood is like being drunk, everyone remembers what you did except you, but in this particular occasion I must've been particularly sober.

'For far too long, I've been remembering every single scratch on these walls, every creak of the stairs, the smell of my parents, the sounds of my mother's atelier always full of clients, and the image of the fireflies in the vegetable garden looking for the last bit of light. There are so many memories in this house, Rafaela... so many dreams and plans for the future. To be honest, remembering is coming back to life.'

Her words made me realise that a home is the sanctuary where you're expected, and where your heart lives. Like birds, we can rest in an infinite number of places, but we only have one nest. Even when it's empty, it still retains the echoes of our lives. There's a special kind of magic that lives inside the tiny universe of a home that allows tears to dry at their own pace and laughter to burst out of our mouths without shame. It's the place where one rests from battle and takes refuge from the flaming arrows. Home is a living being that invites us to dream inside its warm embrace.

There I was, standing before the person who gave me life, trembling with emotion, trying to discover, I guess, the reasons for her disappearance. And there she was, thin but strong, small but by no means insignificant, attentive to my reactions and incapable of hiding her satisfaction.

Conan carefully observed us from a distance, with the same level of interest with which you study two beings from a different planet who are rediscovering each other. His body language became somewhat more daring. Maybe it was something that the senses notice but can't put a name to – the smell and glow that emanates from people in love. The clock confirmed that the eternity I felt had passed since I had sat down to wait for her to finish showering and dressing in clean clothes was nothing more than a reflection of my impatience to have her back and to make sure she was still here.

We had something to eat. Conan had prepared a cold crab salad and an asparagus omelette. He behaved with such familiarity that he appeared to be the host. Seeing my mother occupy this house again with me in it felt like a mirage. We spent several hours sitting in the dark garden. At first, we spoke about abstract things, life, the future… My mind was boiling over with questions, I was full of doubts, and yet I lacked the courage to ask the one and only question that mattered. Doesn't everyone have a right to be indecisive? She seemed to sense my uneasiness.

'Rafaela, there are questions that you have a right to ask and answers that must be given. We're not going to be strangers any more,' she said, taking my hand in hers.

'Why did you leave me?' I blurted out, finally, like an old car motor that had remained still for too long.

I was sad to have to ask that question, but I think that a cruel question can sometimes do us a favour in the long run. Conan looked for an excuse and left, leaving us alone. Perhaps he thought we needed to spiral into a deep and meaningful conversation, one where you go over and over the same things, and he felt that we needed privacy. It was as though the traffic lights had turned green and the retaining wall had collapsed.

'Shall we walk, Rafaela?' she asked, standing up.

I followed her. We walked slowly along the main avenue, eager to drink up our feelings, oblivious to everything and everyone. We even stopped a few times, without wandering apart so that we could continue to share our deepest thoughts. Had anyone seen us, they would surely have thought we were out strolling on a fresh spring night, thoroughly enjoying one another's company. Perhaps it was me who would draw nearer to her to brush her skin, or maybe she was the one keeping up with my steps in order to perceive my pulse. I felt the urge to hug her many times, the urge that weak animals have towards those who can protect them, but I held back. The sounds of the few cars that were around and the smell of the plants pervading the night air brought back the memory of our walks to the shop of long-lost books.

Certain silences, along with the night breeze, helped me dispel the mental mess that my mother's incredible story provoked in me. It was as if I were rowing upstream trying to make sense of my thoughts. A short sharp phrase hurt me deeply like a dagger when she spoke of Elsu, an otherworldly man whom she presented as my father.

After thirty years, I expected to hear pretty much any narrative except for that tale of science fiction. I would have settled for the story of a young mother who falls pregnant and is unable to care for her daughter. An addict father who abandons his family. An unwanted pregnancy and a grandmother who steps in to raise the child. I would even have settled for the story of a pair of immature parents who break up dramatically, leaving behind a child in no man's land, or that of a cowardly parent who decides to leave their daughter's life in order to start over with a new partner and form a new family. I don't know... I had prepared myself for any one of those sad and dramatic stories that I heard in my office daily. But, how was I supposed to deal with something like this?

I felt trapped, beguiled and enveloped by that unbelievable tale that began over three decades ago. I was so captivated by that enigmatic man that I couldn't stop until I knew everything I possibly could about him. How else would I get to know this stranger? I wasn't sure I was even awake. My head was split in two. One part rebelled and denied everything, saying it just wasn't possible. The other part desperately just wanted to know more.

'Rafaela, remember when you were a little girl and I'd tell you stories?'

'Yes, that was one of my favourite things,' I nodded, nostalgically.

'Well, this could be a chapter from the story *The Atelier of Miracles*, but it's not. It's one of the few things I know are true.'

She told me how she managed to escape from San Patricio, like someone who escapes after committing the worst possible crime, like escaping a tyrannical prison guard by night so no one can see. She came to me as a fugitive. It's beyond my imagination to think how many kilometres she walked with those swollen, tired and hurt feet. I won't deny that when she added the words psychiatric facility to all of that, the first thing I thought was that maybe she was an impostor who had lost her mind and had managed to reach me to tell me what I most wanted to hear in the entire world. Her story sounded like that of someone who'd been kidnapped by a cult and forced to eat magic mushrooms, swearing she had flown to incredible places. Even so, I decided to change my perspective and set aside my logical instincts, even when she began to speak to a caramel-coloured Great Dane, assuring me it had winked at her, because in order to know someone's inner truth we must listen with our hearts.

Upon discovering that the neurosurgery hospital where I had stayed was shared the same premises as San Patricio, making my mother's nightly visits possible, I also came to understand how destiny had played a part.

A flurry of moments suddenly landed on the runway of my memories. I must have been six years old. A child doesn't understand figurative language and I thought that maybe my mother really was insane, as some people had said.

One morning, she was sad when she got up and said to me, 'My love, I'm dressed in gloom today, can you see?' When she was in a good mood, she would show me her dress covered in musical notes and twirl like a ballet dancer in a music box. She'd ask me to turn up the volume for the theme from *Swan Lake*, and I'd pretend I would; and as soon as Tchaikovsky's music began to play, she'd straighten herself and move her arms like one of those wonderful first row ballerinas, and then bend gracefully like a reed in the wind. Her green khaki trousers and simple orange T-shirt still allowed me to see her small waist moving ethereally on long legs that were as flexible as rubber. She would balance from side to side effortlessly to the rhythm of a light, catchy melody. Her floaty imaginary dress with its tulle and white feathers would wrap around my tiny body as I danced with her, placing my bare feet on top of hers. I felt the warm touch of her fingers in every spin. We were two happy souls covered in the pink fairy dust of life.

'Rafaela, I've noticed how upset you get if your friends call you crazy, and that's not right,' she said, still dancing, 'It's natural for a crazy woman's daughter to be crazy too.'

Then, for the first time, I answered her back. I raised my face with a smile reflecting both innocence and bravery, I faced the light in her eyes and vividly replied, 'Mamá, you're wrong. The daughter of a crazy woman doesn't always have to be crazy. Sometimes she can help crazy people.'

'You're right, my love. Keep on listening and dancing. This is music to wake up to.'

Those long, intense hours with my mother helped me so much to clear up the ideas I had about the kind of mother I'd like to be, if it were to ever happen. Firstly, as a daughter, I learned that a mother doesn't have to be a slave to our own idealisation of her. Sure, my mother was different, but that didn't mean she loved me less or that she was, somehow, inferior to other mothers. I would be more like a buffet. Just there. Nearby. Available. So that whenever they needed me they could approach me easily, just as I'd receive them. Bleeding yourself dry and giving every bit of yourself doesn't make you a better parent. As women, we must take care of ourselves, pamper ourselves, carve out a moment to sleep, replenish, delegate, ask for help so that we can have moments in silence and alone, to fly, to care for ourselves so we can better care for others. No two mothers are the same, just like no two children are the same. It's easy to fall into the comparison trap and think 'I wish my mother was more like my friend's mother' or 'why can't my mother be normal?' I'm convinced that every mother comes from a different planet, all of them with super healing powers that can control time in order to get everything done. Over time, they become knowers of everything, first as apprentices and later as experts in many new professional fields, such as nursing, teaching, cooking, entertaining, psychology, among others. Our falling in love with our mothers – regardless of their planet, without judging her, without criticising what perhaps we cannot understand, simply and acceptingly – is the only thing that makes us worthy of them.

As a mother, I'd be the tree that allows each emerging trunk to decide who they want to be, simply observing them and giving them the space to go as far as they want. I'd accept that some of their roots go deeper than others, that some would grow faster and others would need more watering. It wouldn't matter if one extended its branches really high wanting to go far and others had shorter ones because they didn't feel the need to go any further. The important thing would be to make sure they each had the freedom to grow as far as they wanted, and in the direction they chose for themselves. I'd be there to pay attention to how much water they each need and I'd let each extension of myself be as it wants to be, with its own particularities. I would love the ones that are most like me as well as the ones that are completely different. All of my extensions would show me a new and different world, and my roots would remain firm in order to help them one day sow their own seeds, if they so wish. I would grow in the sun and be an example to them, free, unique, true to my purpose, with my wings open wide so I can fly where my heart takes me, wings made with the feathers from each of my babies, who will clear the sky of obstacles to make it possible.

My mother is the way she is, and I love her because she doesn't pressure me and she shows me that I can do anything. Now I know that she's a wild spirit and that she'd die behind the bars of monotony and routine, that she needs to fly free towards unspeakable places, peculiar characters, stellar universes, far away from all that is predetermined, in order to return to me forever with an open mind, full of wisdom.

That same day, I lost my fear that she would leave me, that she didn't love me. The only thing I feared was she wouldn't feel free, that she wouldn't be happy and she wouldn't find a place to call home wherever it was that she decided to be. I didn't want us to love each other any other way. I didn't want to chain her to my fears, my needs or my conditions, imposing my motives and obligations on her. I wanted my mother to be whole, free of my emotional dependence, free from having to explain herself. Mothers and their children don't have to fly in the same direction, dream the same dream or live the same life. There is something much more divine that all that. It is an infinite thread that holds our souls. And even if it gets twisted or tangled, or time passes, spells are cast or wars are fought, this thread never lets go of love. It erases borders, crosses oceans and brings hearts together. It remains strong, without crushing, hurting or drowning love. It doesn't demand presence or gestures; these simply happen.

That night I wrote in my book one of my favourite phrases: 'A perfect mother is a happy one.'

When we got back, there were still some pieces of lemon stuck to the rim of the lemonade jug sitting on the table.

Conan distractedly asked me, 'Where have you been? How did it go?'

I smiled and told him it had gone well. He made one of his gestures, as if to indicate that he didn't need to know more, because he didn't want to delve into private conversations and lives. When it came to emotional issues, he was more tightly sealed than a zip-lock bag, though time had gradually peeled away his tough external layers, revealing his soft centre.

My body seized up in shock when I saw my mother holding the bottle that contained the mysterious message in her hands, running towards me, frightened and asking me, 'How did this get here? Where did you find it?'

Chapter 21

The Frog's Leap

There I was, with a hot coffee on the table, my restless fingers playing on my mobile phone. My name is Rafaela, but it could easily have been Sofia, Paula or Julia; the name isn't important. I could be anyone because my story is that of many other women.

If you drop a frog into a pot of boiling water, it will immediately jump out. However, if the pot is filled with cold water over the heat, the frog will continue to swim around, gradually adjusting its body temperature to that of that surrounding water, keeping itself comfortable. This, unfortunately, means that it doesn't notice the water temperature increasing and that it will die if it doesn't leap out. When the water comes to the boil, the temperature becomes unbearable and the frog will try to jump out. However, having spent all its energy adapting constantly to the changing water temperature, the sleepy and exhausted frog no longer has the strength. Paralysed, its muscles don't allow it to take that leap. It has lost its ability to react and no longer has the impetus to save itself. What began as a refreshing swim ultimately turns into its death.

This parable by the writer and philosopher Oliver Clerc unfortunately became a true law of physics. It was proven that if the water temperature is increased by 1.2 degrees Celsius every hour, the frog will stay inside the pot and die. It shows the danger of adapting, conforming and losing touch with ourselves. It perfectly describes how our lack of awareness of progressive decline makes us unable to make timely decisions that will resolve a situation. So I ask myself, what really killed the frog? Was it the boiling water? Or was it its own inability to adequately decide when to jump out? If it had been put into the pot when it was at fifty degrees, it most likely would have leapt out and saved itself. However, as long as it could tolerate the increasing temperature, it didn't consider the fact that it could and should get out of there. That was me, a woman with 'boiling frog syndrome', who'd become an expert at adapting to what was hurtful and went against my mental, emotional and physical wellbeing. Esther praised my virtuous conduct, but in reality, I was nothing more than a boiled frog, as a result of my own neglect.

Nobody stands for an insult or an aggressive action from someone they've just met, or gives up all their rights or loses their identity from one day to the next. Jumping out in any of those circumstances would be a reflex. Had I known the first day I met Jared that I would go through what I experienced that afternoon, I would have leapt right out of that pot. But if the rot sets in very slowly, it goes unnoticed and doesn't provoke a reaction, opposition or rebellion most of the time. I was paralysed like a frog in boiling water. My emotional muscles were no longer responsive. I felt like I was in a safe space and didn't notice the tiny changes taking place around me that were, in fact, undermining affection, respect and trust. This gradual emotional wear ended up trapping me until I saw no way out. I was a textbook example of an abused woman. At first, I denied the issue's true importance, saying 'we have our ups and downs'. Later, I would justify his conduct by saying 'we're a highly passionate couple'. In order to minimise the situation, I'd focus on the positives: 'he's all I have in this life'. Then I pinned my hopes on change: 'it will all be different when we go to live in Granada'. I went through the guilty phase: 'it's my fault for marrying him'. I felt cheated by my own stupidity. Finally, I tried to justify my presence in that relationship by any means possible: 'well, I'm sure this is a lesson I'm meant to learn'.

Three weeks after our idyllic wedding, life no longer smiled at me; instead, it was pulling faces and giggling nervously. The periods of simple and ordinary happiness were few and far between, so few in fact that I could no longer even see their shadow. I stopped drawing hearts on fogged up windows, instead going back to our painful and heart-wrenching 'love story'. Jared once again saw me as that small green amphibian being with shiny bulging eyes, and I was burnt all over again in his pot.

I began to feel dizzy and deadly tired. It was a demonstration of Murphy's law. Yes, the law stating that toast will always fall on the buttered side, and that if anything can go wrong, it will. In fact, we attribute anything that goes against what we want to this man's law. I've always had ups and downs, so there was no reason for me to suspect anything was wrong. But, suddenly, everything seemed to pick up speed, galloping as quickly as the heartbeat of the tiny foetus during its first ultrasound. Although I'd always dreamt of starting a happy family in which I would be Barbie, he would be my Ken and we'd live in a pink caravan with a dog and a beautiful blond son, the surprise news and just the idea that I'd have to share my maternity with someone as emotionally immature as Jared, with such drastically different traditions to mine, filled me with utter terror. I'd always dreamt of building a home for three people, not for a multitude of people including rabbis, parents and an entourage of many ready to govern your entire life. Neither Jared nor I were prepared for what was coming.

That day of unbridled passion, when we made up just as I was about to head off into my new life, had resulted in an unwanted pregnancy. If we take into account that there's about a twenty-five per cent chance of falling pregnant with each sexual episode, and the fact that we always used contraceptives, except obviously that one time, Murphy had clearly struck again. I stared at the pregnancy test. There were the two unmistakeable blue lines. An ultrasound was done. I couldn't believe it; I was seven weeks pregnant.

Even though there was a clear chemistry between us as a couple, I didn't see a very hopeful future for us. There can be nothing worse for a child than coming into a situation such as ours. I also didn't want my child to grow up without a father like I did. What could I do?

Sometimes, when someone brings you to the edge of the abyss, you discover that you can fly. Opening your eyes just in time can be a type of victory, and this situation made me see what I hadn't been able to see before. I was terrified and felt completely alone. I hesitated a lot before telling Esther. I couldn't cause Belly this kind of pain. Jared was out of the question as I'd already decided to leave him for good. I alternated between desperate panic, fear and the uncertainty of not knowing where to turn in a foreign land where abortion is illegal and where I felt completely unprotected.

'*Hapala?*' shouted Esther, covering her mouth with her hands not wanting to release the taboo Hebrew word meaning abortion.

'I need your help,' I begged her as I drew nearer.

'Rafaela, Judaism doesn't allow abortion, unless there's a direct threat to the life of the mother or the foetus if the pregnancy were to continue. In Israel, abortion is only permitted under certain circumstances by a special committee: if the woman is single, if she's underage, if she's been raped, if it's the result of an incestuous relationship, if it poses a risk to the mother's health or it's a non-viable pregnancy. None of them applies to you. You'd be committing a crime.'

'It's my only option.'

'Don't you watch the news? Right now the country's in uproar with all those pro-life protests; the streets are covered in pamphlets, and the media's being pressured by religious leaders who are trying to sway public opinion so that the government and the health system keep life in the belly.'

'There's no way I'm the first to have an illegal abortion in this country.'

Esther's furrowed brow signalled her negative response before giving me a definite verbal 'no'. Before continuing, she gave me an icy cold look – the one she saved for her children so that she wouldn't have to yell at them, a look that was both a shout and a slap all at once, a paralysing lightning bolt, a super power that made me feel small and insignificant.

'Israel is number one in the world when it comes to prenatal testing, and abortion is often recommended if they suspect the baby has a problem or deformity. My sister had a legal abortion because they found that her baby had clubbed feet and was missing three fingers on one hand.'

'I would've had my baby in that case,' I declared with a spontaneity that bothered Esther.

'I really don't understand your way of seeing things, Rafaela. According to the Torah, living is a responsibility to God, but also to society, as we're all here as part of a plan in which love for one's neighbours is expressed by placing oneself at the service of others. According the law of Moses, doctors are here to treat human illness, but are not allowed to use their knowledge to shorten or end a life, as none of us are. *Hapala* is a serious transgression that goes against one of our holiest commandments, which is procreation.'

'Yes, yes, I know... life is a God-given gift that must be valued and appreciated regardless of its temporal condition, and man does not hold domain over the sanctity of life to do with it as he pleases... blah, blah, blah. But what about human dignity? What about people's right to a happy life? Do we have the right to bring ill-fated people into this world? Does the life of a wise man not have the same value as that of a man who is mentally or physically disabled? Why, then, is it legal to abort when the baby has a deformity?'

'This baby can save your marriage, Rafaela.'

'Save, you say? A child isn't a lifeboat that turns up at the perfect moment to save your life. On the contrary, it would become an anchor. If we cling to it, we'll sink and drown.'

'For Jews, driving without a seatbelt, crossing the street outside a pedestrian crossing or disobeying any of the traffic or health rules is considered a sin because it's an attitude that obviously puts other people at risk. *Hapala* is bordering on murder.'

'I've made a pro-life decision, Esther, even if you think the contrary. I understand that some people may think that they'd behave differently in my situation, because this is something very personal, but I don't understand people who dictate to others going through this type of thing.'

'I just worry about you.'

'I know, but we can never allow others to rob us of our free will. If that were to happen, we wouldn't have the strength to overcome any situation other than our own personal failure. If ever my freedom to face my destiny were taken away from me, I wouldn't like to be around to see it.'

I sold everything I owned for the procedure. It wasn't much, to be honest. I never liked wearing jewellery, so I didn't even have a watch I could pawn. Letting go of my laptop hurt the most. I'd bought it with the first money I earned here and used it for absolutely everything. It was an extension of my own body. I managed to sell my hair at a flourishing business for *sheitels*, as wigs were called in Yiddish. It was a prestigious object for Jewish women, and I was paid the equivalent of five hundred euros in the Israeli new shekel currency. What I later discovered upon receiving a Christmas card containing a photo of Esther and her children moved me to my very soul. My great friend, my sister, had bought the medium-length wig with a fringe that had been made out of my own hair.

'Now we're really going to look like twin sisters,' I told her when I found out.

In the waiting room, I felt as though I'd pinned a scarlet letter on myself because I was having an abortion. In my case, I knew that becoming a mother just wasn't an option at that time. I was trapped in an abusive relationship. I wanted to go on with my career and become a much better mother someday. I also wasn't in a position to support a child. The more I thought about my decision, the more convinced I was. My future with Jared was hopeless, and we would've made a terrible team as parents. But, above all, I felt justified in wanting to give my child the best life possible as a willing mother, with financial stability and a responsible, mature father. I wanted to raise my child in a safe and loving atmosphere.

It was one of the toughest decisions I ever made, but it was the right one at that particular time of my life. It was an act of responsibility. For many women, abortion carries an irreparable pain, particularly when it goes hand-in-hand with other traumatic events such as an abusive partner, as was my case.

It's interesting how so many people worry about life, wanting to play God, and yet how many children roam the streets, neglected and with nobody showing concern for them. Let's worry about them first. We're not incubators or reproductive machines. Many of those God wannabes have no idea of the emotions involved when they talk about health; they don't understand the danger of a broken heart, or bother to determine how much damage a crushed soul can create. I don't think I have to obey what people outside my life path dictate, particularly when they're nowhere near as qualified as I am to know what I really need. The conscience of someone who acts by listening to their heart will never be sullied, no matter how much others condemn them.

I cried for an hour sitting on a chair next to Esther, who was wriggling uncomfortably on her seat. Despite her beliefs, she didn't judge me at all, which I appreciated enormously. How could she possibly pick a side when there was no other side to pick? It was hard for me to tick the box at the bottom of the page asking if I was sure. My whole body was trembling. I was terrified. Finally, I signed the form, gave my consent and waited my turn. Waiting was torture, the time on my phone didn't seem to move at all, or did so extremely slowly. The uncertainty was killing me.

At first, I considered buying the super expensive pills on the Internet, but many women said they were fake and that they ended up with sugar pills instead, or worse… this made me give up all notions of buying abortion pills on the black market. With Esther's help, we found a midwife who worked outside the official health system in precarious conditions, but offering more safety. She saw patients outside normal business hours. The room was full of women of all ages. We crossed our fingers, trusting that there'd be no complications during the procedure. This would surely be better than parsley stalks or clothes hangers inserted into the vagina. To all appearances, there's nothing to associate a rock, an umbrella wire, a hot bath or a staircase, yet all of these things have been used or are used in certain parts of the world by women who abort at home, putting their lives at risk because they have no access to legal, safe and free abortion.

The year before I arrived in Jerusalem, I had been to a photography exhibition accompanied by explanatory texts describing methods used in ancient times to prevent pregnancy or to abort. It felt surreal to see the fish bladder or sheep intestine condoms that were used back then, and knitting needles. Yes, those implements have been and are still used in countries with very conservative policies to provoke premature labour by introducing the pointy end through the cervix until it reaches the amniotic sac containing the foetus. I thought about the kind of desperation a woman must feel in order to resort to such physically tough measures and I understood them. We were no longer in the eighteenth century when women would place half a squeezed lemon in their vaginas in order to block the sperm during intercourse. It wasn't very safe or effective, and often ended up inside the uterus. Still, many women continue to be judged today when they decide not to be mothers, when their motives are really nobody's business.

I was even more affected by the mind-boggling conversation about 'obstetric violence' that I overheard between the two women seated to our right.

'My friend was sued by her own doctor when she told him she wanted an abortion. Another was cruelly operated on without anaesthetic as a form of "moral punishment",' said the older one, wearing Muslim attire. I couldn't really tell her age by her covered face, but her voice gave her away.

'Many don't survive having abortions in those conditions,' said the other woman, also covered with a black burka that completely covered her round body.

'I prefer to take this risk as opposed to doing what one of my friends did,' said the first woman. 'She was only twenty years old and her mother found her dead next to a note saying that she'd drunk bleach in the hope that it would cause her to lose the baby. Apparently, she tried with a bicycle spoke first. Her uterus began to rot. The septic shock spread to her kidneys and the pain was unbearable.'

I felt sympathy for the poor terrified nurses who had to tell women who begged for help that it wasn't possible, that it was wrong, that the Church would condemn them, that the police would arrest them and put them in jail, that it was illegal when, in reality, it was a right. It was the coldest place in the world and the people were the greyest, most unreceptive people I'd ever seen in a clinic. There was tension in the air no matter where you went, a kind of pins and needles that sent a shiver down my spine. Sadly, I saw many girls alone or accompanied by a friend. All pregnant women in this situation deserve to be treated with respect because we are going through hell before, during, and sometimes even after. No one happily goes to have an abortion.

My turn came and all I could think of was just putting an end to all of this. An unabashedly overweight nurse came to collect me, her red hair matching her round cheeks and large mouth that opened to full capacity whenever she spoke. She wore enormous black-rimmed glasses with tinted lenses that covered her eyebrows and her acne-covered cheeks. I still can't believe that my sense of humour made an appearance at a time like that but I asked her if she could go snorkelling with them. She looked at me, jaded and emotionless. There was a stretcher in the middle of a pile of books, all of them dirty. A knot in my stomach barely let me swallow my own saliva. The questions they asked me before the anaesthetic took effect were outrageous, they scared me more than the abortion itself. 'Who knows you're here? Did anyone see you come in? Erase this address from your mind and don't ever tell anyone you were here. Who is here with you?'

I underwent a surgical abortion. When I woke up I strangely found myself hurting right in my very soul, in a kind of morgue. I was in a row of old stretchers containing other women. The feeling running through my body was as though I had just swallowed half of the North Pole. I felt as if a cold Arctic snap was surrounding my naked body and I couldn't find anything to cover myself with. Everything was bleak, dark and with a feeling of secrecy and covertness in the air. I wasn't sure whether someone would come to find me or if I had to get up. I didn't know what to do. I remained on my stretcher, afraid and confused, observing that giant space. Somebody finally saw fit to take me back to the waiting room where Esther was waiting for me. Her face said it all. I was given some mysterious brown pills.

'They're to prevent possible infections,' said Esther, putting them in my mouth.

I swallowed them, despite still being very groggy. The bitter red-headed woman was yelling at me, 'God is going to punish you'; 'you're going to become infertile'; 'your future children will have birth defects', plus a whole other series of lovely things that were meant to kick you while you're down and make you feel guilty. I tried to get up, but I fainted and collapsed on the floor. Esther was overcome by fear and began to yell for one of the assistants who came calmly, unhurriedly, and helped her put me on a chair.

When I was able to regain my strength, I looked at her and said, 'I'm not some little girl who didn't know how to keep my legs shut; I'm a good mother who made a decision not to give her child a shitty life.'

The red-headed inquisitor closed her mouth and left us in the room, among ten other women who all looked at me as though I was some sort of heroine.

On the way home I considered what could happen next. If something went wrong, what would I tell Jared? That I had just had an abortion? Something was pressing against my crown, crushing my chest against my back. I imagined it to be what a pumpkin might feel like inside a pressure cooker.

It would have been around four in the morning when I woke up feeling sick, thinking that maybe it had all been a terrible, blurry nightmare, but it hadn't been. The bed sheets were incapable of absorbing the river of blood that sprung from between my legs. Between bouts of vomiting and strong convulsions, I made it to the bathroom, where I took a wad of gauze and inserted it into me, like plugging a champagne bottle to stop it from going flat. My eyes went cloudy and I rubbed them with my arm. I managed to control my panic attack, I imagine because I specialised in anxiety and trauma.

'Rafaela! What's wrong?' asked Jared, stupefied when he woke up to see me writhing on the floor against the side of the bath.

'That life is a series of unfortunate events,' I answered.

'Leave Plato out of this. We have to go to the hospital immediately. You're bleeding out.'

'No. I know what I have to do.'

'My love, please don't do this to me,' he insisted, taking me in his arms and carrying me to the bed.

'I had an abortion.'

Jared denied it over and over, not wanting to give any credibility to my words.

'How could you do something like that?' he asked bitterly.

I confessed as calmly as I could that I had aborted my child in an act of responsibility. I went straight to the point, leaving out the details I didn't feel like sharing. He lost it completely. The fury that flowed through him was obvious in his facial expression. Jared was one of those people who hated losing his power.

'If someone invented problems, it was because they knew that another would be able to solve them, otherwise they never would have been created in the first place. We could have solved this together.'

'I'm sorry but I've finally realised that I can't be anything without myself. You make me go far, but you take me away from myself. What we had ends here and now,' I said, unable to make a single gesture, the last of my strength gone.

'You killed our child,' he said, his voice sharp and cutting, like a pair of sharp scissors.

'No, I saved my future. I need a few days to recover and to be able to travel, that's all I ask. I've also asked for a divorce. I don't want to see you ever again, please don't try to get in touch with me. I don't love you any more,' I said in the cruellest way possible.

Those were the words that hurt me the most to say as they weren't true. Tears fell from my eyes, treacherous and abundant like those summer storms that come out of nowhere, catching you by surprise.

I pressed my teeth together, trying to contain my despair and all the love that I still had for him, despite all my best efforts to end it.

Jared lowered his head, still nervous and a little stunned, dropping his belligerent attitude. And, although he could be more annoying than a newsreader at bedtime, on this particular occasion he knew there was nothing he could do to change my mind.

Now that I have a little more life experience behind me, I can psychoanalyse myself objectively and I realise just how strong the legs were on that young frog that was making a historic leap into my life, cutting all ties with a man who couldn't truly make me happy, and who managed to turn me into a switch that only he controlled, turning me on and off at will. And it's not as if life had learned to say 'no' to me whenever I kindly asked for something, or that the sixes didn't exist on the dice I was rolling, it's just that you simply can't go through a door you haven't opened first. I didn't know that I had to jump out of the pot in order to enjoy everything that was waiting for me outside.

Chapter 22

The Afar Brotherhood

'*What keeps me going is what I don't know.*' This well-known phrase undoubtedly expressed what was keeping me going. Elsu, however, went in search of what he did know. That was his purpose.

The land that was open to the world. The epicentre of the Purple Lagoon. A place where everyone greets each other according to their rank and all creatures know their category. A place where the future is lived out in the present, where everything is explored and discovered. The house of the masters, where the most valuable substance in the universe grows – the coveted essence, famous for its capacity to expand minds. That is how Elsu described to me what my eyes didn't believe. I still don't know exactly when we ended up at that floating city, with its three clearly defined levels that were connected by ancient rock tunnels through which transparent, golden orbs resembling giant soap bubbles circulated, transporting beings from one level to another. The levels were known as the incubator level, the laboratory level and the launching level, each one with its own rhythm, activity and rules. However, through the veins of those separate beings flowed the same blood. They were a society with a common goal who chose to call themselves the Afar Brotherhood.

I felt as if I were in a theme park that was filled with attractions I had no idea how to use, a three-for-one in fantasy beings I was anxious to discover. Like a child, I was caught up in the magic of imagination that had so captivated my eyes, my ears and the rest of my five senses, to the point where I had forgotten why we were there and what our mission was. We didn't have to make an effort to search for life, everything was bustling with creatures that intermingled in what seemed like perfectly organised chaos.

It seemed impossible to me that all of that had been there all along and that its inhabitants had remained silent like actors waiting behind the curtain, while we Earthlings spent millions of euros planning manned and unmanned missions to the moon. Apparently NASA had now decided to include a transit area on the moon for all routes heading to Mars and beyond. Could it be that we were possibly looking in the wrong place? How could we be so lost?

Now, everything was beating right in front of me. I still didn't know it, but we were entering the heart of this immensity, the incubator level. Jungle loomed over the mass of roads that travelled in every direction, with a large variety of plants that were not to be found even in the depths of the African rainforest. Blue predominated over every other colour.

A lightning glance caught my eye. I perceived it as rather cold, although I later discovered it to be the result of a profound natural shyness, disguised as snobbism, and a distant attitude. He was hurriedly attending to hundreds of hungry pedestrians in a travelling market, where the food awaited purchase separated into colourful piles. There was a type of skewer threaded with colourful balls wrapped in edible plastic that he would poke into his customers' fingers, which featured holes designed for this purpose. Despite the commotion, and what I identified as stress, I kept my emotions under control at all times. There was a degree of latent serenity in him. His sales strategy was very practical, just as his own personality appeared to be. He was clearly focused on the material gain to be made from his activity. His serious and worried face was focused solely on profits, and he didn't seem to enjoy the pleasure of the laughter, conversations and the spectacle buzzing around him. His lavender blue eyes on the sides of his head showed cross-shaped pupils, allowing him to extend his field of vision and to scan both the floor and the horizon at the same time without having to move his head. Around his horns was closely cropped white hair, with the removed length seemingly added to the plaited goatee that grew from his elongated face. Hanging from his mouth was a small bundle of half-chewed blue herbs that evaporated before being digested.

The clop of baby goats' hooves could be heard climbing and descending the mountains surrounding the market. They played to see who could reach the highest cliff edge. Goats never think there's anything higher up than where they are.

Throughout my travels, I learned that the best way to get to know a city was to learn how the inhabitants work, love and die there. The first thing we learnt was how they worked. A marketplace is always a good reflection of a new place because by carefully observing the products sold there, we can imagine in detail what their homes might be filled with; it means becoming completely immersed in so many different lives all at once that you barely know what to do with them all.

'This is the constellation of Capricorn.'

'How do you know? I can distinguish at least three different types of creatures here.'

'That is correct, Amelia, but most of the ones carrying out the arduous daily work and controlling the actual trading are Capricornians. This is their home and this is where it all begins. The others are visitors who probably come from the upper levels in search of supplies.'

He was right. The number of Capricornians quadrupled that of the others. They also made up the guards and provided security for that floating city. The members of the brotherhood were held in great admiration and respect, and the goats were seen to represent the solid competence that was required. On the incubator level, there was an accumulation not only of provisions but also of experience. There was always a sense of 'I do what I need to do.' They were precise, exact and responsible for cultivating and preserving the greatest treasure, giving sense to the brotherhood.

The old-looking merchant signalled to us with his filthy grey hand, offering us one of the strange products. I tensed up immediately, as Elsu told him we had nothing to pay him with. He scrunched up his face in anger as though we had just refused heaven itself. I was, therefore, extremely surprised when he offered some pieces of food to Vodka, which he ate without thinking twice.

'He does not have to pay, but you do,' he grumbled. 'I have to take this box to the laboratory level but I have to stay here until I sell everything,' he continued, looking over all the merchandise covering the stall. 'If you do that for me, you can eat whatever you want,' he concluded.

Something told me that this encounter, in this market with this particular grotesque merchant, was neither ordinary nor fortuitous. You also didn't have to be much of a negotiator to know that we'd accept. Elsu knew that Vodka and I needed food to live. He had read the old goat's emotions and his offer wasn't malicious. This would be our free pass to the next level.

We had to leave our fingerprints on the Capricornian's horns in order to gain access to one of the golden orbs. Apparently, it was an advanced control system that the disciplined protectors of the flying city had established to restrict traffic. Excessive precaution and the need to ensure the community's existence and preserve its secret were its core principles. Their minds didn't work fast, but they were organised and structured. They were practical thinkers who worked with precision when performing mental efforts for useful purposes. I can imagine that same merchant as a child, playing in the water and reflecting on how dams were built instead of playing with paper boats, or thinking about something poetic related to the sound of the water.

I closed my eyes, exploring the sensation I felt upon touching those horns, which radiated a heat so intense that the burning sensation ran up my arms. As we let go, I noticed that our fingertips now had marks bearing the symbol of the Afar Brotherhood on them – a Celtic knot representing protection and the cycle of life, the universe and eternity.

The merchant raised a finger to announce that he was going to say something important.

'You have two estias in which to carry out your task and return. After that time, the symbols will disappear and you will be on your own, with no protection.'

'Two estias?' I repeated looking at Elsu.

'Here, time is measured in estias, one of which is about three hours and twenty minutes in your Earth time.'

I felt like time had never been on our side since our travels through the Purple Lagoon began. We left that vast landscape of rugged slopes on which there were ordered lines of immense workshops filled with merchandise ready for distribution and managed by an army of Capricornians that controlled the inventory and production. We rode in those orbs that travelled at high speed inside the tunnel, breaking the limits of the unknown. The beings that had created that form of aerospace travel, which reminded me of a supersonic train I had seen in a futuristic movie once, could only have been geniuses. As we floated, I was tempted to open the secret white lacquered wooden box, but Elsu, who seemed to only practise absolute honesty, wouldn't allow me to give in to my mad urge. He distracted me by showing me a colony of large insects with yellow and green exoskeletons. They were split down the middle and flew around feverishly looking for their other halves.

The journey was short but fascinating. I was no longer sure if whether I was asleep or awake. One of the things that impressed me the most was the cloud station they used as a source of humidity in order to keep a constant temperature in that place right out of science fiction. The orb began to deflate, and it released a jelly-like slide that I guessed we were meant to exit down. It wasn't that I was a genius or anything, we just copied the other creatures moving around naturally and comfortably through the tunnels. We also followed another of my mother's sayings: 'When in Rome, do as the Romans do'. Vodka weighed so little he was spinning out of control, trying desperately to grip onto the winding surface, over which he was sliding upwards. Yes, upwards. I had never seen a slide suck you up like a vacuum toward the surface instead of letting you free-fall towards the ground. I couldn't help laughing when I saw his face, looking like that of a child that had been unexpectedly pushed down a water slide. He finally arrived, shaken and with a broken nail, as he had worn them down in a failed attempt at stopping the ascension. Everyone seemed to enjoy themselves; even Elsu seemed like more of an Earthling and was allowing himself to go with the flow.

The laboratory level was impressive. It was clearly the scientific and mathematical headquarters. How can I describe that place and those creatures? It was never night there; there was always light. Elsu felt lost without his stars. The level was governed by the beings from the constellation of Aquarius. To start with, they didn't have feet: they moved around quickly on a pair of tiny wheels connected to a pair of mixed and augmented reality glasses. To say they used a combination of sensors, cameras and artificial intelligence would be a grave insult to their intelligence. Enveloped by a green wind, we bumped into one of them riding quickly and absentmindedly, just like the rest of them. He was completely absorbed in reading his minuscule book the size of a thimble that spun around incessantly and seemed to contain enough entertainment to last a lifetime. He travelled along the tracks as if there weren't enough distance for him in his world, because a path means a beginning and an end, and his mind was infinite. His lost self breathed in something new, unknown, perhaps something to be invented. Suddenly, he was stopped by a force stronger than curiosity – the discovery of our presence and of the unknown, something different. His pupils dilated. The leopard yellow colour of his iris extended along the oval, making the white part of his eye disappear altogether. His pinkish face gave him a peculiar childlike appearance, as if the last traces of his distance youth refused to disappear completely.

'I want to know, I want to see, I want to understand,' he said as a means of introduction.

His short body was as covered in layers of clothing, as was his idea-filled head. Their cerebral energy consumption was so high that they were constantly cold. He looked as though he collected the strangest and most unimaginable bugs.

'We are looking for section seven. We have to deliver this box,' said Elsu, signalling to the tiny box in my hands. 'We do not have much time.'

The being from the constellation of Aquarius opened up a map in the air as if he were casting a fishing net. Its interpretation was truly complex but we both recognised the Pisces symbol, our desired final destination. I jumped in and asked him, pointing at the place in question.

'How can we get there? I'm sure you have a supersonic spaceship that can take us there immediately,' I suggested desperately.

'Wait, this makes no sense. You are looking for section seven, correct?'

'Yes, yes, but we have to get to the Temple of Light,' I answered, confusing the friendly Aquarian even more.

'Where is the logic in that? You should accompany me to my lab so I can examine you. There may be a new type of algorithm in your way of thinking, and who knows? Maybe it will lead me to discover a more ecological way to save humanity from mental illness. We have learned that a mental pandemic is threatening your species.'

'This is all normal,' I said, stunned.

'Normal? That is a forbidden concept in the laboratory level,' he said quickly, shocked, as though he had been terribly insulted. 'All our children are vaccinated against the germ of normality as soon as they are born. You would not happen to be infected, would you? The vaccine allows them to have an early, intuitive conscience so they can accept all that is new and incredibly unique. We are lovers of all that is original here. We understand that it is necessary to steer away from traditional routes in order to arrive at unusual and innovative ideas.'

We'd arrived at the kingdom of abstraction where everything from concepts to conclusions were preserved. The obstinate, rebellious Aquarians with their innovative and brilliant minds had turned that level into a place where extravagant ideas blossomed, fed by pure logic.

'The best way to communicate with them is by using a rational method. If it is not logical, do not consider it! Their mind will refuse any emotional interference within the thinking process. You must be careful with your displays of emotion, Amelia, they can be disturbing for the strange mental atmosphere of these creatures. Be direct and stay away from anything even remotely emotional,' warned Elsu.

'I see,' I said, snorting in resignation.

'They are ruled by a completely impersonal objectivity that allows them to accept ideas that would otherwise be incomprehensible and even reprehensible to others. They have no trouble believing what, to others, seems utterly deranged.'

'I can't believe they've been able to create all this!' I exclaimed. 'I would love to have a child born under the influence of Aquarius. If he or she's capable of believing in UFOs and extraterrestrials, it'll be pretty easy to explain this outrageous adventure to them.'

As it turned out, section seven is where he worked. He promised to help us after the mental exploration. He was only interested in my human brain, which, apparently, was worth studying.'

'Wait outside,' he ordered Vodka and Elsu, separating us. He then encouraged me to follow him.

Independent Aquarians need their space and, predictably, one stranger was an object of curiosity, but two was an invasion. The peculiar creature leaned over the box. He scrutinised its interior with an arched back, as if deciphering an enigma, oblivious to everything else around him.

'Interesting. Now I understand why you grow in hundreds from the same genetic strains, just like clones with sleepy mentalities that are easy to manipulate as workers in a working class. They educate you incorrectly, in such a way that prevents you from being curious about universal laws and complex spiritual sciences. That is what keeps you in a state of voluntary deficiency, imposed on you during gestation, with a limited mental state and a weak and fragile body. I see, there is no doubt about it,' he said to himself. 'Finally, here are the waves of rhythm and lights that affect humans when they cross the threshold of several unknown dimensions. There is no positive reaction to the fantastic arts. You are clearly an emotionally unstable species because you live under the alienating principle of "me". It is, therefore, logical to assume that the narrow-mindedness of your introverted brains can only lead to a slow decadence and the eventual end of your planet's species. Your world is not yet sane enough to allow insanity in. You cannot lose touch with a reality you do not yet understand. I can see a clear psychological mutilation.'

I looked up, confused by all those notions that bore no connection in my brain, apparently affected by a severe lack of fantasy, and observed it from the couch of my own scepticism.

'And what's the solution?'

I felt ridiculous asking that question, like someone who goes to the doctor and is diagnosed with an unknown virus.

'You have to make love to magic on a daily basis, and recover the lost key to your childhood. Well… I have seen everything I needed to. I am going to try to break the chains invading the vigilant part of your mind. Do not worry, it is a return trip,' he predicted, brushing back his noisy metallic hair with his hand.

Everything was spinning around me when he made me inhale that shiny white mandarin-scented powder that was inside the box. For an indeterminate amount of time, I couldn't find anything to hold onto or any place to belong. Little by little, I began to see light again, as an intense headache came over me at the same instant. I then became aware that I was awake, in a mental coma, but awake. What happened after, I don't exactly remember.

Just four days ago, I thought that the world I knew had gone crazy. Now, I knew it was dying. Four days isn't very long in a human life, but at the Purple Lagoon it felt like an eternity. In a sense, I'd acquired a lot of knowledge, and yet I felt like someone who suddenly knew the name of the illness that was killing them, but was unable to do anything about it.

If I had my own travel magazine, something I'd always been interested in, I would undoubtedly rank the launching level number one as I'm sure it wouldn't disappoint any of my readers in search of meaningful adventures. I would describe it as if an unhinged professor had thrown their box of colours into the sky in order to blind the world's inner eye, letting the ochre colour of the Earth and the opal colour of fire drip down, liquefying them with the rays of the silver moon that illuminated the arrows of the archers, the proud and hospitable residents of that space. To capture such a location with just one, spectacular photograph to accompany the magazine text, one that truly reflected its immeasurable beauty, I would use the image of the archers with the moonlight caressing their long and wild ash-coloured manes, reaching unparalleled distances with their silver arrows.

Journeys, like artists, are born not made. And this was of the sort that inspired an irrepressible urge to pack your bags, sure that you'd have a truly spectacular experience. It doesn't matter what type of traveller you are, and there are many.

Photographers: you'll never see them without a camera, and despite having evolved with the digital age, they continue to stand out because of the seven kilos of equipment they carry around their necks, plus a bag full of accessories. The spark of the flash is always around them. They know they've been to India because, when they get home and downloads the photos, they get to see the Taj Mahal for the first time. We know they've been there because they tell us, but they never appear in any of their photos.

Collectors: they're preoccupied with creating an endless list of 'things to see' and tick them off throughout the journey. Whether they've enjoyed it or not is irrelevant, the important thing is to put a tick next to it. They consult blogs in search of other people's comments telling them what's worth seeing and what isn't. They've memorised Wikipedia and act as tour guides for friends and anyone else they come across. They're true 'bucket listers' who won't stop to admire anything unless they've seen it in a guide book first, but they're capable of taking a million photos of a monument they don't even like just because someone somewhere said it was important. Once they arrive at their destination, they're easily bored because they know more about the history of the place than its own inhabitants do. They keep a multitude of tickets used to enter places they can no longer remember because they didn't spend long enough there to even make their presence known. But at least they have a photo in front of every illustrious building they've visited. They know how many countries they've been to by heart and view the Earth as if it were the board on which you play the game of Risk.

Consumers: the typical people who always gets stopped at airports because of their overweight luggage. Their bags weigh five kilos when they depart and forty kilos when they return. Their need to acquire souvenirs knows no limits. They go in search of special deals and love to buy knick-knacks at bargain prices. They visit all the souvenir shops and their credit card burns a hole in their pocket every time they travel. All their family and friends have the same Sydney Opera House figurine and only bring it out when they come to visit.

Chameleons: one of my favourites, they have an incredible ability to completely immerse themselves in the customs and culture of a place, even changing their clothes, language and the colour of their skin if necessary. A week later you can't tell them apart from the locals. They're particularly sensitive to details that go unnoticed by the rest, such as a listless expression on an old man's face, or the smile on a waiter at a beach bar.

Intrepid travellers: people find it hard to believe the stories they tell about their travels, but end up being convinced some blurry photo proving that the shark was real. They know no fear. They feel completely at ease in dangerous neighbourhoods and clear a path for themselves in the Amazon jungle without so much as a stick to help them, and they eat the bugs that others can't even bring themselves to look at.

Alternative travellers: they're the ones who go on and on about visiting Barcelona without seeing the Sagrada Familia, or touring through China and avoiding the Great Wall completely. Their goal, above everything else, is to avoid tourists and any other focus of public interest. The truly beautiful street is the one at the back; the most amazing views are seen from places nobody else can get to; and the best places to eat are never the ones recommended by guide books.

Sheep: the typical travellers who can go anywhere in the world, provided they have a good guide to lead them and a flock of their own kind. Naturally, they've never crossed paths with an alternative traveller. They need someone to guide them at all times, even to go to the toilet. They're totally blown away to hear that somebody went to a nearby island without going through a travel agency.

Shepherds: they're the complete opposite of the previous type. They're always in control of the situation and make all the decisions, even when they have no idea what they're doing. They'll talk to anyone and in any language, interpret indecipherable maps and trust their instincts to find their destination. Purebred shepherds prefer to forego all of that, though. If you ask them why they're going around in circles, they'll tell you with great conviction that it's to familiarise themselves with the area.

While what impacted me most about the laboratory level and its refreshing beings was their capacity for dreaming, imagining, inventing, seeing the invisible and sensing the infinity of the universe, what amazed me so much about the hospitable inhabitants of the launching level was the magical aspect of their spirit of adventure. They were constantly moving from one place to another, pushed by the need to explore and discover. For me, someone truly in love with travelling, this level made me feel at home, and the beings that inhabited it felt like kindred spirits. Now it made sense that I had been born on the twelfth of December. I carried this in my cosmic DNA. The beings of the constellation of Sagittarius live out their existence as if on a travel adventure. If there were any kind of prize for the 'happy traveller' who you should always take with you, it would go to them. All types of travellers fit in on this level.

All the men bore the arrows, which varied in number according to the archer's rank. The tip was shaped like a backwards heart. It was a small transparent capsule that contained the famous white powder. When it disintegrated, it spread its contents over the infinite space at the end of its stellar journey. The arrows are held in a quiver adorned with precious gems. The women bore the bows, which were fitted with extremely light and hard-wearing silk strings. When the moon rose and the sun no longer blinded them, a hail of arrows would constantly be shot towards the universe. They were incredible equestrians who handled the bow a with unique mastery to shoot the arrows so far that the eye could no longer see them. The arrow's flight meant the spirit's liberation, and also the penetration of knowledge, the gnosis. The arsenal of arrows had little to do with war or death, and more to do with life and hope. They were peaceful warriors. They had expert aim and their target was to complete the circle of brotherhood, expand the coveted essence that had been turned into white powder – cultivated and sourced from the highest and hardest mountains in the incubator level by the persistent Capricornians, then purified and improved in the laboratory level by the Aquarians – in order to achieve the best version of all the inhabitants of the cosmos.

Through a west-facing window lit up by the last of the sun's rays, a group of six archers expertly arranged their bows and arrows. Clearly enjoying themselves, they hummed a song as they tensed the strings, checking their endurance, elasticity and strength. The fire in the centre never went out. They were lively beings with passionate, happy hearts.

Nobody was better suited than they were for this extremely important mission. They were perpetually optimistic and observant, and their senses were as clear as they were acute. They alone could shoot their arrows with the speed of a meteorite to the furthermost part of the outer abyss. The equestrian archers understood the complex routes into and out of that world, making them a natural and unwavering force.

I asked Elsu what *sebel* meant in their language, as the word seemed to be stuck to their tongues.

'It means free spirit, Amelia.'

Then I asked him to tell me about the song.

'It is a song about wishing for a better world, where everyone is brave and noble, encouraging us to love what is pure and true.'

'It's very idealistic, don't you think?'

'Being idealistic is part of their nature. It would be impossible to shoot arrows to the end of the world if they did not think that they would reach their final destination. Seeing people as they should be helps us to treat them as they are. Remember? They operate in search of truth, like you, even if you have never realised this before. Amelia, fulfil your obligations, never stop wondering and never stop chasing your ideal, with determination and joy, in the certainty that even when you do not know the way, you are on the right path. This is the gift given to us by the Afar Brotherhood.'

Outside, a group of children was having a conversation that caught my attention. They had found a container full of manure, probably waste from the steeds the horsemen used to get around – a much faster, more sophisticated version of a horse with six legs. I could clearly distinguish two Capricornians, two Aquarians and a tiny Sagittarian.

'Ugh, it stinks! Why would they leave all these droppings here? We should tell someone,' the first one complained.

'Who said they were droppings? Let us take a closer look,' said another.

'There has to be a baby here somewhere for me!' said the last one, smiling excitedly, as if floating on cloud nine.

Even with my eyes closed, I could've easily distinguished who said what.

I was fascinated watching the spectacle unfold from the launching level, at the highest part of that floating city. Bursts of arrows, much like fireworks, disappeared into the horizon at lightning speed, headed who knows where. I wondered how many of them would end up on my own wounded planet.

Chapter 23

Uniting Promises

H e was twenty-four years old and he'd just celebrated his birthday on the twenty-third of May, the day on which the Church
celebrated the Solemnity of Pentecost – when Christ's promise to his
apostles came true, and his Father sent the Holy Spirit to guide them
on their evangelical mission – which also coincided with his feast day,
that of Saint Giovanni Battista de' Rossi.

Jambi, as he was called by all who knew him, was tall and stocky,
with a face like an archangel, and like an archangel, he had great power
and strength with which to fight the enemies of the soul.

The first mass by a new priest is always a big event, particularly in
the small town that saw him grow up, supported by the community
in which he had found his calling. He'd just left the seminary, and to
celebrate his very first mass as a newly ordained priest with his family
and inside the homely church on the town square where the devoted
parishioners awaited him, far exceeded anything any human could hope
for. It was the dream of anyone who is ordained into the priesthood,
the charge and the dignity of the ecclesiastic rank given to those who
become priests, to be made responsible for a sanctuary or parish church.

On the eve of the big day, the act was announced by ringing all the
bells, and a flag was placed on the tower as was the local custom. The
new priest's childhood home was the place chosen for the guests and
authorities to congregate. From there, they'd accompany him solemnly

to the sacred place where the liturgical mass would be held. People had always believed in the bishop's special gift, a miraculous ability to see in each young person whether they had received, or not, the call from God. He was considered almost a type of saint. 'You'll be a priest forever', he repeated every time Jambi would attend the spiritual exercises with his mother, who would wear her black lace shawl and carrying a rosary in her hands. In fact, Jambi had been tricked into believing that he was the chosen one. He wasn't very devoted, to tell the truth. He would sit with his cousins in the rows located right in front of the altar, and the priest was constantly made to stop the service in order to scold them and tell them to be quiet. His interest was more geared towards complimenting and chasing the girls who attended unwillingly, as if they were lambs to the slaughter. Seeing as he couldn't be a rock star, which is what he truly wanted, he became a choirboy, and he never looked back.

Over time, Jambi became a servant of God, kind, very polite with impeccable manners and equally impeccable dress sense. Though he refused the rich robes, he never forgot to wear his sparkly pastoral ring, which he wore on his hand, which was as white as the hand of a duchess. He became used to a priest's life. He got a certain amount of pleasure from the feasts he was often invited to after each service. Weddings were his favourites as they never economised on food, and only he only considered his part to be complete once his stomach was fully satisfied. He'd say that it was just as ethical to eat a good chorizo in the house of a poor man as it was to feast on pheasant in that of a rich man. As evidence, he revealed that it wasn't just their taste for good food that made so many priests overweight; he was convinced that the hand of God was behind every delicacy, and, therefore, it was mortal sin to refuse it. They nicknamed him 'Father tablecloth' as there were no tablecloths that hadn't been graced by his presence at one time or another. For Father Jambi, everything was ambrosia. It was rare not to see him scooping up the crumbs that fell on his white chasuble. In fact, on the very few occasions when he was truly honest with himself, he admitted that what actually fed his soul at weddings was not the food so much as his secret wish that he were the groom. His cassock wrestled with his need for caresses and passionate kisses, all the gestures he witnessed among the newlyweds, and he desperately wanted to make them his own. Not even holy water could quench the desire that sometimes consumed him. The black he wore was more expressive of his feelings of loss and the memory of an unfulfilled dream, rather than of the protocols of priesthood. Still, what kept him in line was his vocation to help those in need.

'I was an atheist, Father Jambi, but now I believe,' said one of the young grooms he was about to join in holy matrimony. 'Without a doubt, he has performed a miracle by bringing this woman down from heaven. You must have a direct connection with God, please ask him to forgive me for the things I do with her in bed. I see religion in her hair, in her mouth and in her face at all times. You couldn't possibly understand me, Father, but once a man has tasted the venom of love, he's capable of burning in hell if necessary.'

But he understood all too well. His vow of celibacy didn't stop him from having intense feelings or desires.

As it says in the New Testament, *'The ways of the Lord are inscrutable'*, which supports the belief that, even when something bad happens, it actually has a positive connotation, or at the very least a reason. So, even if Father Jambi didn't understand, he had to put his trust in the divine decision. Or, perhaps in the stars? His life transpired with expected normality. After spending five years as a teacher and missionary in Africa, he was sent to one of Granada's oldest churches, which he found in a ruinous state. The crumbling church, like all the oldest churches in the Granada diocese, had been founded over six hundred years earlier following the city's conquest by the King Ferdinand and Queen Isabella, the Catholic Monarchs. Now barely standing, it had been built over a forgotten mosque located in what was now one of the poorest areas on the city's outskirts, only occasionally visited by a few 'alternative' tourists. The bishop wanted to send him to Rome to train him to teach at the seminary, but Father Jambi didn't have much faith in the rigid training that took place at the Catholic Church's neurological centre, so he decided to create a community of parishioners and help revive the inhospitable enclave. At that time, his eyes were as closed to what was to be found in that place as they were during prayer.

He settled into one of the cold stone rooms, turning it into a combination of office, prayer room, alcove and dressing room. The only thing to bring any life to that three square-metre space was the camp bed that he had covered with a colourful blanket in an ethnic floral design, a farewell gift from one of his African parishioners. A cold and spartan iron clothes rack contained all his clothes. The simple earthenware bowl propped up on a pile of old books served as his washstand. In order to acknowledge his presence, he left a piece of broken mirror, void of any life, hanging by a rusty nail just above the yellowing candles that lit the alcove, just enough so as not to encourage vanity. The first few months were the most austere. Then, with the help of some locals, he fixed up some rooms to the best of his ability, turning the place into his home and into the house of God, welcoming any souls brave enough to go to such a remote place. Using a piece of wood and a sharp rock, he designed the motto for the reborn church, 'Our faith is our strength'. He made sure to read it several times a day, in order to remind himself that his faith, unlike his body, had not weakened.

He hadn't been able to sleep through the night for several days and had given up trying. There was no space or clear distinction between a new day beginning and an old one ending. He awoke abruptly when the rays of sun began to shine upon his town's fragile little houses. He blinked, turned over on the mattress and closed his eyes again. Nothing. It only worked momentarily. He decided to get up and peak sleepily through the window. He liked it when his cheeks froze in winter, so he could sit in front of the chimney afterwards and come back to life in an instant. He browsed through some books, flipping them from cover to cover, without reading a single line. To distract himself, he decided to think about whether lightning fell from the sky or shot up from the ground. 'Who cares, anyway?' he said.

The sound of the storm had abated, albeit briefly, enough for him to hear loud knocking coming from the main door. Father Jambi went over quickly to open it.

'You're soaking wet! Come in, my son,' he said, opening the door wide.

'Thank you, in the name of Allah. I wasn't sure if anyone lived here,' said the visitor hoarsely, with no strength and wheezing lungs.

A young imam walked in from the dark. His skin was the colour of burnt sand and he was wearing a brownish-purple djellaba. His long, wrinkle-free face was a reflection of his youth. A mane of black curly hair could be seen underneath the grey scarf that covered his head. Further accentuating his mystique was a long beard. He looked like a kind man, with no inkling of fanaticism whatsoever in his large, dark eyes.

Father Jambi knew it wasn't right to find defects in others, but the stranger's quick steps made with his turned-out feet seemed more like those of a comedian than a clergyman. He envied the man's round belly that pushed his djellaba outwards, resembling a store of food and drink, a characteristic of a gluttonous and lustful man. It reminded him of himself before melting away in Africa. When his visitor sat down, his bare feet, full of calloused and deformed around the toes, became visible.

'I've come on a pilgrimage from Morocco to visit the mosques of Granada,' he declared, massaging his calves and his scarred ankles. 'And yes, I know that everyone thinks we only go on pilgrimages to Mecca,' he added before Father Jambi could say anything.

'For us, Granada is also a very important place. We consider it the home of Islam. History tells us that before the Catholic Monarchs completed their Reconquista in 1492, the Nasrid Kingdom of Granada was the last Muslim stronghold remaining of a presence that had lasted almost eight centuries in the Iberian Peninsula. The presence of Islam has remained in the city's culture, architecture, music and customs, and we also consider it our own, despite what any maps or politicians say. There is a good basis here for our people to return. We Muslims are looking to continue the history that the Catholic Monarchs interrupted,' explained the imam whose name was, predictably, Ahmed.

'I've always been very curious about Mecca. What does it mean to you Muslims?'

'The pilgrimage to the Great Mosque of Mecca is a visit that every Muslim must complete at least once in their lives, it is one of the five pillars of Islam along with fasting during Ramadan, almsgiving, praying five times a day and the testimony of faith.'

'The Great Mosque of Mecca? Is that the holy city found in Saudi Arabia?'

'That's right. Our pilgrimage is called *Hajj*. It takes place once a year during the Muslim lunar month of *Dhu al-Hijjah*.

'I'm curious; why do Muslims have to complete a pilgrimage?'

'We go to Mecca to complete a unique series of rituals. During *Hajj*, waves of worshippers wearing white tunics, to symbolise purity, seek forgiveness, walking seven times around the *Kaaba* anticlockwise. When we pray, we kneel facing the direction of Mecca.'

'Of course, Mecca is your spiritual centre. And those pilgrimages guarantee you a place in heaven, is that right?'

'Exactly. The culminating moment of the pilgrimage is when we climb Mount Arafat, which we call the Mountain of Mercy, in the Mina Valley.'

'And what is the symbolism of that place?'

'It was on that mountain that the prophet Mohammed bid farewell to the Muslims who had accompanied him on his pilgrimage towards the end of his life.'

'Many non-Muslims feel that your women are oppressed. What do you think about that?'

'A woman is like a crystal,' answered Ahmed. 'There is a place reserved for them inside the mosque in order not to mix energies and to respect their privacy. People think it is discrimination. No. We are different. The custom of marrying more than one woman allows us, for example, to protect our brother's wife if she becomes a widow. It's a shame that this is forbidden by Spanish law.'

'But it's bigamy!' he protested, upon hearing such blasphemy.

'But why can a man not marry more than one woman, particularly if it is for noble reasons?'

'The best thing about the city is its food culture, don't you think?' asked Father Jambi, taking the conversation off on a tangent to tone things down; it was getting a little tense owing to the enormous differences between their religious ideologies.

'Without a doubt. It is truly unique, especially the tapas,' he agreed, touching his stomach and licking his lips.

'Tapas, flamenco, Iberian ham and Holy Week,' added Father Jambi, winking as he mentioned the religious holiday, one of the most authentic expressions of what it means to be an Andalusian Christian.

Ahmed wasn't in the least offended by the joke. In fact, he let out a loud laugh, giving him a golden pass.

'Oh, Iberian ham! The only thing that would make me turn my back on the Koran.'

'Whoever wrote your sacred book and forbade the eating of pork clearly never enjoyed this succulent delicacy.'

'You must know that this restriction is not a lifestyle choice but a divine mandate. It is not just about maintaining a healthy soul, but also a healthy body. Pigs are filthy creatures that eat anything they find, even their own waste. They do not filter toxins or parasites, which then remain in the animal's fatty tissue.'

'So, you wouldn't share a glass of wine with me, I suppose?'

'No alcohol. But I would greatly appreciate a piece of bread with olive oil, and some of those honey figs I see on your table.'

They spoke for hours, until sunrise, learning from each other through an inter-religious dialogue that Father Jambi would normally never have been exposed to within his Christian bubble. Opening the door of tolerance towards different sets of beliefs that we essentially do not understand is the bridge to peace and respect. He noticed that, far from being a threat to his own beliefs as he'd been indoctrinated to think, it actually led to a spiritual and intellectual enrichment. If religions dominate the world and these are inextricably linked to society, shouldn't we at least show an interest in other people's beliefs? Surely, an act of good expands in every direction and, like in springtime, its roots bloom, producing new trees and so on. That night, Father Jambi realised that all religions, while bringing us closer to God, pushed people further apart.

Father Jambi invited Ahmed to be his guest during his stay in Granada. The Imam accepted. Obviously, permission was not requested from the bishop as it would've been denied. They each became accustomed to each other's rituals – Father Jambi to Ahmed's continuous prayers that began with the washing of certain parts of his body with running water, and Ahmed to the aroma of Father Jambi's altar wine, with which he drowned life's sorrows.

The priest had wanted to repair the small chapel for some time. After the midday mass, which was attended by only two elderly souls and a nun from the Convent of San Jerónimo, he asked Ahmed to help him move some of the rugs, a few of the pews where the parishioners sat and the image of the patron saint, for whose intercession the space had been built, which weighed a ton. His intention was to reposition the altar, enabling the problems of rising damp that had appeared on both sides of it to be solved.

'Father Jambi, have you seen this mark below the altarpiece?'

'It looks like some kind of underground access. Perhaps it leads to a tomb of an important person, or even an earlier, hidden church.'

'It's strange how the light that comes in through the dome hits the tiny marble pillars and points directly at that spot.'

'You're right, Ahmed. There has to be some way to lift this slab.'

With a mammoth effort and techniques of improvisation seemingly learnt from MacGyver, a secret agent whose deadliest weapon was his intelligence, rather than from religions with conflicting gods, they managed to reveal a hollow space under the floor containing a marble staircase. Once three more adjoining slabs were removed, the access to an underground crypt was completely revealed. The crypt appeared to be thirteen metres below ground level and was at risk of collapse. But curiosity was more powerful than fear. Both men went down the tiny marble stairs with just as much astonishment as precaution. Ahmed followed behind Father Jambi, holding one of the candles that lit the narrow, vaulted passageway through which they had to duck to avoid hitting their heads on the low ceiling. At the end of the passageway was a small hidden circular door leading to an impressive chamber paved in turquoise blue tiles with veins like marble. There, they found scrolls of old Hebrew manuscripts, prayer books, notes, religious laws, correspondence between Christian and Muslim orders, magical and mystical texts as well as some ancient bibles. It was a type of secret library full of worn wooden bookshelves. A small part of its contents had been amazingly spared from Father Jambi's terrible enemy, damp.

'Why do you think this chamber was sealed?' asked Ahmed, unable to hide his astonishment.

'I have no idea, but it must be a sacred place that conceals much more than just mysterious objects.'

'Look at this, Father Jambi,' he said, gesturing with his hand towards a heavy brown book. 'This book looks different to the rest,' he said as he wiped the dust from the cover using the sleeve of his djellaba. 'There is a fragment with handwriting hidden inside the binding. The paper and ink are truly ancient. I have never seen anything like it.'

Father Jambi examined the writing and the paper very carefully.

'Yes, it seems to be written in an ancient dead language. Look at the symbol drawn in the centre. A purple-coloured sphere divided into twelve equal parts with symbols in each of them.'

'It suggests an incomplete map with some coordinates. Look at these tiny dots that join together. Try to find the one that's missing,' asked Father Jambi, as he himself did the same.

The priest absent-mindedly knocked over a long-necked glass jar standing near to where they found a book; it was some type of still made in the shape of the philosophical egg. It took them a while to understand that it contained samples of the eight metals, corresponding to the eight planets.

'What do you think is behind all this, Ahmed?'

The imam spoke, 'I beg you, in the name of Allah, that you do not speak or write of these findings and that you never reveal the location of this place.' He grabbed him by the clothes, which is the Arab and Muslim way of imposing a mandatory oath on anyone. 'By common agreement and in the spirit of fraternity, we must come together to sign a pact of silence,' he insisted with steadfast obstinacy.

'Ahmed, we can't hide this discovery that has more to do with God's designs than with providence. This goes far beyond our own beliefs,' reasoned Father Jambi, with the weight of his conscience, unable to stop exploring that fascinating space, with its bare walls that were free of any paintings, prayers, or even any stains to distract from knowledge. His impressions were building up so quickly inside his mind, what with so many writings and drawings of the processes of alchemy, that everything became blurred.

The following day, when the sun was high up in the sky and they were sure that they had not imagined any of it, they began to hatch their plan. Due to some unknown adverse force, it eventually descended into a mess of pretexts and evasiveness, at the hands of the mundane problems of daily life, until it became nothing but an illusion. For the next three days, deaf monologues and engrossed looks were the only dialogue they shared. Silent and withdrawn, Father Jambi sometimes pushed his imagination to incredible limits in order to attempt to understand the mystery that lay beneath their feet.

It turned out that Ahmed was such an intelligent and peaceful man that his own entertainment was to sit and think, his eyes completely immobile, hearing the distant rattling of the visiting fortune tellers reading what the future held for the expectant and gullible few who would go to them.

Father Jambi closed the church so that he could finish rearranging the chapel, making the most of the fact that the townspeople were lost in their own streets, distracted by a fair and the presence of street acrobats. Unfortunately, as destiny would have it, the bishop turned up unannounced that same afternoon. He entered the chapel silently, like a fox in a chicken coop, revealing his presence only by the noise of the door scratching against the uneven floor. He was wearing his everyday outfit of black robes with red trimmings, adorned with knotted buttons, a purple sash and a skull cap of the same colour. His pectoral cross was the insignia of his strong faith. He said he was making the most of his few weeks off to drop by and visit one of his favourite sons who, deep down, he imagined as his eventual successor.

'What's this?' he asked, seeing the slab that led to the crypt, noticing that it had clearly been moved. Meanwhile, a stray Siamese cat that Father Jambi often fed was rubbing against the new visitor's legs, leaving white hair all over his dark robes.

'You're Excellency, how wonderful! You've come at the best time. There's no better route you could have taken. The last few days have been very entertaining.'

The prince of the church didn't seem disturbed.

'Christianity is a discipline, Father Jambi, not entertainment.'

But the bishop smiled as he said it because he understood Jambi's nature. He'd known him since the day he was born. Perhaps that's why sometimes he looked the other way when he invited a long-haired pop singer wearing a kaftan to sing one of those hippy hymns during his sermons.

Overwhelmed by the evidence, the bishop reacted by placing his hand on Father Jambi's shoulder, as his heart swelled with both fear and jubilation, knowing that Jambi had come into contact with the great mystery.

'So, you found it at last?'

'Your Excellency already knew about the crypt?' he asked, completely taken aback.

'Who else knows about this?' asked the bishop, eyeing Ahmed suspiciously.

Father Jambi finally worked up the courage to introduce the man who had become more than a confidant and good company, as they were now united forever by a link much stronger than friendship: the awakening to the truth, and the legacy of the mystery of life.

'I always knew you were the chosen one, the one to preserve what has been my mission for so long. I was not mistaken. Now it's your turn. Only one of us can do this.'

I looked over at Ahmed, gesturing to indicate that he also knew of the existence of the crypt.

'Don't worry, the secret has been in hands of Muslims and Christians for several centuries. Ahmed and you will take over the responsibility for your generation. You are both deserving heirs of this honour, and that begins here and now,' he said with the kind of authority and determination that wipes out any risk of argument. 'There would be no greater danger to the church than to let this secret out. It would be our end, as it would compromise the principles of the Holy Scriptures. In the case of the Muslims, those of the Koran and its teachings. That's what has united us in this mission. What this parchment declares contradicts everything that religion has created over thousands of years.'

His words seemed to have riveted their clothes to the floor, because they were completely incapable of moving. They trembled in surprise, unable to believe the evidence.

The imam put all prudence aside and asked the big question that Father Jambi didn't dare say out loud. 'Is it true that the place on that map really exists? And that the cosmos is the force that rules life and not God, the creator, for whom we stand?'

'We can't be certain of this, but that doubt must never be sown. That would be the end of us. The science mentioned in those manuscripts is our worst enemy, the silent army waiting to come out of the shadows to defeat us and take our power away, spreading slander. If the theory of that place and the stars wins, the divinity of our creator will be impossible to defend.'

It was only then, calmly and without the excitement surrounding the new discovery, that Father Jambi was finally able to understand the profound meaning behind it all. The bishop was telling them what their real mission would be. They'd have to dedicate their bodies and souls to protecting that mystery. They allowed themselves to be beaten by their own devotion, convinced that the event that had been so awaited by their ancestors was now imminent. No more had been revealed to them, so as not to surpass the limits of human knowledge, leaving them to torture themselves with fantasies of the unknown.

'Somebody is coming,' he announced to them both, looking at them in a way that created huge uncertainty. Every time the bishop made a prediction, Father Jambi was sure it would come true.

'The fourth is on his way,' he insisted, hurrying towards the door, as if he were skating on ice.

The awaited visitor didn't take long to arrive. A Shiite ayatollah, a rank used only for the maximum authorities who were among the twelve imams of Shia Islam, apparently an expert in Islamic sciences, laws, morals and philosophy, who had earned the privilege of interpreting the law, holding legitimate religious trials and teaching at Islamic seminaries. Ahmed addressed him as the 'Great Ayatollah', a very respected leader in his religious community that had come out of retirement to join them. He held him to be a legend, an untouchable figure, much more than just a man. He seemed no younger than seventy, and he was tall, upright and bearded. His stark and very black eyebrows took all the attention away from his small liquid eyes. Covered with a large black scarf wrapped around his head like a turban, he smiled maliciously behind an astonished expression.

Right then and there, the witnesses materialised the oath. A Christian and a Muslim vowed to maintain and protect the foundations of heaven by keeping the secret that had stayed buried since time immemorial. A piece of knowledge that they would never reveal to the world, whether it was true or not.

If there was a God, he couldn't damn someone eternally for the sin of living with confusion, following his mandates. It was better to die with their beliefs than to accept that the world was completely different to what they had conceived. They had to be everything they had promised themselves to be. But the truth always comes out anyway, doesn't it?

'Is a lamp brought in to be put under a basket, or under a bed, and not on a stand? For nothing is hidden except to be made manifest, nor is anything secret except to come to light.' (Mark 4:21-25)

Chapter 24

Tango Steps

The first excuse was to investigate the psychological part, and the roles of men and women during the dance itself. The second was that I needed something to help me forget the adrenaline rush I got from boxing. The official version was that now, with my life was more or less returning to normal, signing up to a dance class would help me de-stress and keep my mind active. The truth was wildly different. The luminous Argentinian tango academy, located in the magnificent historic building housing the cultural centre, had become our secret meeting place. That afternoon, as we did every Tuesday and Thursday at the magical time of seven o'clock for the past two weeks, I put on my high-heeled shoes and the short black swishy dress that showed off my dance moves, and even a garter on one of my thighs that made me feel ultra-sexy, following my motto of *'if you're going to do it, do it right'*. My best smile, as I was often told by the instructor, Liberto – an Argentinian from Río de la Plata – was detachable, so it was no problem for me to put it on whenever the occasion called for it. In the middle of all those tango classes, I took mental notes about how some couples argued, accusing each other of taking the wrong step or invading their personal space.

'You're stepping on me!'

'No, it's you, you're not stepping back.'

'How the hell can you want me to step back when my foot's in the air?'

'Well, the other women are doing it.'

'The other women are doing it because the other men are setting the pace properly.'

The teacher approached them. 'Do you want to dance tango or sumo wrestle? Don't forget that dancing is a dialogue, not imposing your will on someone else,' repeated Liberto in an exaggerated tone.

But it was to no avail; the dialogue went on to become a monologue instead of a dance between two people, and each would improvise according to the other's movements. They were the same couples that fought constantly when the lesson was over, reproaching each other everything or being silent for an infinite amount of time. For those numbers people among you, I'll say this: tango ignores mathematics in any way, shape or form, because here the sum of one plus one is never two, but one.

Tango had captivated me from the very beginning; I'd never imagined the volume of emotions, sensations and feelings that this hypnotic dance could involve. I'll always hold it responsible for our new start. A tempting adventure that we had sealed with fire, not ice, and a flame that the sensual movements of the tango had managed to revive. We made everyone believe we'd met there by chance. In my case, I didn't need to warm up; as soon as I walked down that immaculate pavement and past the blue wrought-ironwork that hid the brick building from view, the desert heat was already burning my skin. Afterwards, during the playful sequences that characterise the particular way of dancing tango, we smiled at each other cheekily and provocatively – a game of give and take that hid a strong sexual attraction between two souls driven by passions as urgent as life itself.

The sound bounced off the stone walls of the room. Soft lighting was provided by a light hanging from the ceiling with fluorescent white strips designed to resemble a chandelier. Underneath it, we swayed in unison over the wooden floorboards.

'It would love to have a man take me through life like he does, Rafaela. How wonderful it must be to dance with someone who truly understands you,' commented a woman from one of the other dance couples, referring to Jared and to the harmony of our bodies. She had shiny black hair in a side plait and spoke without separating her cheek from that of her partner.

The teacher insisted, 'You have to follow him, it's only three minutes of obedience, honey, no more. Relax, he'll guide you,' said Liberto with exaggerated gestures to one of the couples. They were about thirty years old and were finding it impossible to keep up with the alternating upbeat and downbeat in four-four time.

I did the obedience part well – after all, I'd given in to Jared for a long time – and perhaps that's why I felt comfortable letting myself go, following his lead.

'Let's dance a tango that hasn't been written yet, my love. I could almost hear you this entire time, just from thinking about you,' whispered Jared, head up, light easy steps, as he slid his hands down my naked back, stopping right above my buttocks.

'Take me to new places again,' asked someone with my body, my mouth and my eyes, a nomadic soul. For the duration of that dance, the world fell asleep, only to be woken up again by my senses, one at a time.

'Bodies get to know each other through movement. Tango is like that moment just before orgasm,' said the Argentinian teacher, but our bodies already knew each other well without the need for a GPS or a tango. We danced with a daring closeness and an intimidating intimacy, urged on by those lyrics of disenchantment and heartbreak that we both knew so well.

My feet appeared to vibrate on an ocean liner that plied the seas by night. Tango allowed me to enter Jared's world, and him to enter mine. For others, allowing themselves to be held close, being touched intimately and making skin contact with the other person was the toughest barrier to get over; but for me, it was necessary to allow myself to be carried away by that type of chemistry, the metaphysical connection, trusting in my body and in its capacity for reaction, despite being so hurt by Jared.

Some couples fail at first and then get it right the second time. Others invent new rules that enable them to make it to shore after the shipwreck. Had that hospital visit been a casual encounter or the continuation of an eternal love story? One step forward, one step back, one step to the side... what we had was 'Volver', Gardel's passionate, violent, captivating, romantic and tragic song about returning. The echo of his shoes told me what his mouth did not, picking up what should never have been swept under the carpet of time.

I discovered that life is a tango, and that sometimes we get stepped on while we dance. We hide our need to cry beneath our smiles and, like tango lyrics, life is full of sad farewells. If you slip during one of its impossible moves, you just keep on dancing. I once said that to Liberto, and he pointed out that there were many different types of tangos and that everyone could decide which one they wanted to dance.

'I've been going to therapy. I'm not the same man you left back in Jerusalem, Rafaela,' he said, as if swearing upon a sacred text.

It was during that magical dinner after the dance class that we celebrated how far we had come since we'd been apart. Though, in all honesty, I felt disadvantaged in getting to know someone new because I wasn't aware how he had matured and changed for the better over time, as an ex. I only had a snapshot of the before and the after that motivated me to reconnect, opening up again to his love and to mind-blowing sex, like there was no tomorrow. We knew each other, but certain parts of us were no longer the same. In many ways, we were 'new' to each other.

'That night, you were very cruel when you said goodbye to me,' he said, accusingly.

'I don't want to relive that last night,' I replied.

As impossible as it seemed, talking about it caused me even more pain. I remembered small flashes of the conversation. In what world do two people who want each other so badly say goodbye forever?

'I propose that you set your heart to zero again, and rid yourself of all the kilometres of love that hurt you. I'm ready, and if I were to live a thousand lives, I'd choose you every time,' he declared, before we kissed passionately and impatiently.

I wasn't ready to hear other people's opinions. 'What? You're getting back together after everything? Are you kidding? Why?' But I worried most about Conan, a wonderful man who'd always been by my side. He loved me, and I was betraying him in such an unfair way. The sailor who had healed me, inside and out, sailing in his warm arms, whose dream I was ending in front of an ash-grey, foamy and dirty sea because it wasn't worth the risk or the sacrifices required to continue with the adventure.

But how did we end up reviving this unbridled love, whispering to each other secretly, not wanting to control the lava that sprung from our hearts? It all started when my mother discovered the mysterious bottle and explained to me the symbolism that could be behind it. We needed more information. I remembered I still had the card Jared had given me in hospital when he came to see me in my bag. He told me he was in Granada working on an archaeological research project.

'I know someone who can shed some light on the origin of the bottle and its contents,' I suggested, spontaneously, obviously not mentioning anything about our mutual past, which I was still trying to rebuild.

He seemed equally surprised and happy to hear my voice over the phone.

'Of course,' he said resolutely after hearing my invitation.

I decided to meet him at one of the Jewish cafés in the centre of town, right beneath my office. A light breeze climbed up the wall and straight into my office, bringing with it a combination of smells. The smell of tea became mixed with the smell of roasted coffee with cardamom – a black, dense coffee that had been served there and in other cafés around the city for some time now. The steam that twirled upwards from the cups reminded me of an arabesque motif, and of my time in Jerusalem. Jared was sitting down, sucking on the mouthpiece of a hookah water pipe standing at the foot of the table, surrounded by a column of aromatic smoke. Serene and impressive, he stood up on the enormous Turkish rug to welcome me, gesturing with his hand. I walked towards him as I had done so many times in a previous life. For a moment, I felt like a frightened animal with the uncontrollable urge to run away, not understanding why. His eyes made me feel like prey. I walked quickly to reduce the distance between us and found refuge in the blue leather couch directly in front of his. Despite everything, for the first time since getting my memory back, I felt strong and invincible. Something in my head told me I wasn't the same anymore, and although that I had the ability to rebel against that particular moment, I didn't want to. I had been inside that place dozens of times. However, this time, it was as though I'd entered into another dimension. I didn't expect his effusive hug, which petrified me. I waited desperately for him to sit back down. Everything seemed so familiar, yet so very far away, and I had to make an effort to focus on the present.

'Thanks for coming, Jared,' I said to break the ice.

My hands were digging down so deeply inside my pockets I was worried I might make holes in them.

'Nothing makes me happier than your presence, Rafaela. You look amazing. I thought you'd never call me and that I'd go back to Israel without ever seeing you again,' he replied, with eyes that shone with unrestrained enthusiasm.

'Oh, you're leaving?' I asked, feigning indifference.

'I'm coming back in a month. My work on the archaeological project that brought me to Granada is about to end.'

The button on my orange Manila hemp blouse kept unbuttoning at the level of my breasts, and I kept buttoning it up, so he wouldn't think I was using seduction as a weapon or was trying to trap him in any way. Although the compulsive gesture caught his attention even more than my cleavage would have. I didn't even dare cross my legs, as I remember how that used to turn him on.

'So now you combine philosophy with the work of a modern Indiana Jones?'

'Actually, I spend most of my time working and living in excavation sites, travelling the world, obsessed, willing to melt my skin off under the sun just to reveal ancient discoveries. I'm fascinated by the past. Although I'd be just as happy working in a library full of books as I am surrounded by dirt.'

'And, have you found lots of treasures?'

'Well, a tiny broken piece of ceramic is often worth more than a gold diamond ring to us. We look for information, basically. But I have to admit that the greatest treasure I even found is sitting right in front of me,' he said, ending the phrase with that tone from which there is no escape.

'In that case, and making the most of your insatiable curiosity, perhaps you could give me a hand with something. It's about this bottle and its contents,' I said, taking the item out of my bag and holding it out to him.

'Wow, Rafaela, this is incredible!' he exclaimed with fascination after examining it briefly. 'How did you get it?'

I told him the story of the bottle and everything I considered he might need to know in order to put two and two together. I noticed how his face dropped when I told him of the scene on the boat with Conan, but he didn't mention in.

'What do you think?' I asked impatiently.

'I have to make some inquiries, take the bottle to the lab so it can be tested. I think this might have a lot to do with the project I'm working on.'

'What do you mean? Which project is this, exactly?'

Jared leaned in, making sure no one could hear us, as if he were about to reveal the mystery of the Holy Trinity, and whispered in my ear, 'The archaeological organisation I work for has spent years following the trail of an ancient site whose importance goes far beyond any archaeological remains. It's a secret portal that acts as a kind of astronomical marker, located near a site that's a thousand years old. We're considering several theories, but the most likely is that some religious orders are involved. We still haven't been able to determine its exact location, but there's enough evidence to suggest it's just outside the city. This would be the greatest archaeological discovery of all time, the dream of any archaeologist. You can't tell anyone about this, Rafaela, not until we know more.'

'That place is real, I assure you. My parents have been there. What happened there has never been known, except by the people who experienced the events first-hand. Maybe I'm being irresponsible telling you now, and putting both our lives in danger.'

'I don't understand, Rafaela. I thought you didn't know anything about your parents.'

'I know. A lot has happened since we separated that you don't know about. My mother and I have been reunited, and I finally understand many things that were kept from me.'

'That's wonderful news, Rafaela. I know how much you needed that. Still, I fail to understand the connection between that bottle and your parents.'

I looked around me, thinking. 'We can't keep discussing this here. We have to meet somewhere safer.'

When I first told him about a dance academy, he thought I was joking and threw his head back laughing. When he saw my serious expression, he agreed that it should become our meeting place.

'Who knows? Maybe you'll find one an old lady in there to dig up,' I joked, detecting an amused smile beneath his nose.

The impulsive and dominant Jared that I knew was vanishing into thin air, as I was discovering a different man who still kept what had made me fall in love with him in the first place. It seemed as though the ego that once suffocated him every night had finally gone and retired.

Right there, another coincidence took place that made me believe even more in predestination. A teenager walked past us as we left the café, handing out pamphlets as he yelled, 'The tango academy is celebrating its thirty-seventh anniversary and is offering a month of free classes to celebrate. C'mon, there are only two spots left!'

Jared just had to wink his eye at me and hold up his thumb to know that he was in. I sealed the deal with my lipstick.

Dinner was followed by wine, and the wine by a few glasses of Pommery, my favourite champagne. Before we knew it, it was three in the morning. My phone was full of missed calls and messages from my mother and from Conan. Both were worried about my absence, as this was completely unusual for me. I would always go to bed early and tell Conan about all my plans. But I was having such a wonderful time that I clung to all possible excuses that supported my decision not to break the momentum. My brain resorted to a thousand little tricks to support my theories; it didn't care about the truth. Once again, I ignored the warnings of my little angel, who plucked his own feathers out in desperation. After all, neuroscience has proven time and time again that our neurons have already decided what type of decision we're going to make, even before we're aware of it ourselves. Something similar happens with our motor system, which chooses one muscle from one hand before we even know which one we're going to activate. If I was so consciously disarmed and my own neurons were always going to be late to the party once the decision had already been made, wouldn't it simply be better to respect nature and just go with the flow? To feel better about myself, I kept feeding into the idea that our encounter had not been a coincidence, and that we were destined to come together. Life had led us on different paths, but it had also reunited us, in some way or another. If this theory worked with my mother, why not with Jared? The crazy scriptwriter of my life had given my character an unexpected plot twist, placing me on a stage, wrapped around Jared's body, in a tango circuit with rediscovered tensions.

My motivation was sky-high. I pinched myself to make sure I wasn't dreaming but instead living a reality that no one could tear me away from.

Comparisons are odious, but how can we avoid them? I did it all the time, particularly when I came down from Olympus to go home and find Conan, a simple mortal, after leaving behind a demigod who made me float on air with every step of the tango, only to drop me into my own hell of doubts and uncertainty. Where was this all going? Twice a week at the dance academy was no longer enough, not even three times… it would have to be for all eternity. But what would happen to Conan? What of our rebuilt story and the hero who rescued me and taught me to believe in love again?

In just a few seconds, they'd hear my key in the lock. I had indulged in a very different type of excess; I didn't recognise myself. I would've preferred to feel guilt or remorse, but neither of those had been invited to the party. I knew there'd be problems: we weren't talking about one isolated Saturday night but of feelings, lies and the collateral damage that would result from telling Conan the truth. But I was being driven by passion, and I felt invincible against any obstacle that stood in my way. The belief that moved me was most definitely a triumphant one – 'Love knows no limits'. What was I to do then? Is it possible to love without making mistakes? Could suffering perhaps be an exception and not the rule? I wasn't the kind of woman who could have a parallel life. Under the effects of alcohol and as I walked to the place where the perfect man was waiting for me, I imagined magically replacing Conan with Jared, my ex-husband and now secret lover, and that everything would stay the same as if nothing had happened. But this 'affect displacement' wasn't so straightforward. I faced an huge dilemma that just wouldn't let me live in peace.

'Chiquilla, where have you been? I was about to call the police. Are you OK?' Conan grabbed my face in his hands and came closer, kissing me as he'd never done before. I felt my strength fail me and confusion set in, because that one kiss had suddenly erased from my skin all the ones that Jared had given me that same night. It all happened very quickly; in a matter of seconds, my own emotional rollercoaster looped the loop several times. I guess the impact of this made me say stupid things.

'The class went on for a bit longer. What are you both doing up?' I answered as naturally as possibly, with the long cries of the violins still floating around in my head.

His eyebrows relaxed and he released the tension in his shoulders. Naively, I thought my answer had been convincing enough that he couldn't tell that I tasted differently than when I slept with him and he opened the doors to his paradise to me.

'Rafaela, I knew you weren't in any danger, at least not physical danger, but please don't disappear like that again. We've been so worried,' said my mother, for the first time giving me one of those motherly scoldings that I had so desperately longed for all these years. I was taken aback by the comment that 'I knew you weren't in any danger, at least not physical danger'. I underestimated the fact that mothers know everything, particularly mine, and that I was an open book to her. She knew very well what she was talking about. I made a face like a dog who's being berated but doesn't quite understand that it did anything wrong. Before going to sleep, she found a moment to be alone with me and tried to get me to tell her what was torturing me, but I snapped shut like an oyster.

The following morning, at breakfast, I explained to Conan and my mother that my archaeological contact was making enquiries about the bottle and its contents. I also showed them the letter I had received on my thirty-seventh birthday, announcing the death of my father. My mother became very emotional and was unable to hold back her tears. She looked up at the sky and, before our incredulous eyes, a star became visible in the daytime right above our heads, in the middle of a cloud of carefree monarch butterflies whose migration route was completely off course.

'That can't be possible,' said Conan, taking photos of the phenomenon with his mobile phone. 'Monarch butterflies have a very specific solar compass, and their internal clock allows them to fly without becoming disorientated for thousands of kilometres between Canada and Mexico, in a south-western direction in autumn, and in a north-east direction in spring. Once autumn is over, the monarchs take the longest trip of their lives. These insects are genetically programmed to fly more than three thousand five hundred kilometres south-west from North America to Mexico, where they face the winter. In spring, they complete the opposite route. I saw this process many times when I lived in America, and how they invaded the sky with their colours as they passed. How did they get here? It's practically a miracle.'

'It's Elsu,' said my mother excitedly, while hundreds of them fluttered around her, carpeting the tree in our garden, the floor and everything as far as the eye could see. This immense mantle of orange butterflies seemed even to make the flowers that hung in their pots want to join in.

'They're even more beautiful together,' I exclaimed with my mouth open wide, unable to take my eyes off the bright orange colour and the prominent black lines on their wings.

'Yes, they are, Rafaela. They're one of the most popular butterflies in North America. I spent many summers as a child chasing after them in Canada, wondering where they would go in the winter. I was interested in them and I learnt that they go on one of the longest migrations in the entire animal kingdom.

'*Mamá*, these butterflies are incredible travellers, just like you,' I said, hugging her and trying to support her in this emotional moment.

'Adult butterflies live from four to five weeks. However, one of the amazing things about these is the Methuselah generation. It's a special generation that bears little relation to its ancestors. As opposed to their parents, grandparents and great grandparents, who only lived for a few weeks, migratory butterflies live up to nine months, which is why they can perform such a feat.'

'This means that if we were to live an average of seventy-five years, our children would live five hundred and twenty-five, right?' I said, doing the reckoning.

'Yes, *chiquilla*. You're very good with numbers.'

'Elsu is sending them from Montana,' mother continued, fixed on the idea that this strange phenomenon was my father's work. A message in a secret code that only they understood, connecting them in a supernatural way.

I felt curiosity to know the place that my mother spoke to me about, through Elsu's words. Meeting my ancestors and visiting that world to which I also belonged was an idea that bubbled up inside me – a call that I felt getting increasingly stronger and clearer. Thirsty for information about the beginning of my story and aware of the importance of my ancestors in my own existence, I had an insight. That letter signed by Wakanda, he of inner magical power, also provided a clue that now made sense. Conan recognised a stamp from Montana on the envelope.

I began to feel like my roots were making me stronger and explained a lot about who I was and what I did. They were like a life current through which my history flowed. Knowing my lineage meant searching for deep answers to questions I couldn't yet formulate. I later learned that there are grandiose legacies that you have to look for yourself because they don't appear on a will, as well as ancestors from other galaxies, all of them residing in my spirit and waiting for me to give in to my destiny.

From that chapter of my life, I also developed one of the best couple's therapy techniques for couples in crisis, which focuses on communication and which I still use on my patients today, aptly called 'Tango Steps'. The couples are always surprised when I greet them wearing high heels, a red dress with a long slit going all the way up and my lucky black garter hugging my thigh.

'If you want to tell her something, first you have to make contact, get her attention, otherwise you'll be invading her, surprising her, and in that state of uncertainty, she won't be able to understand you. Let's take this to the dance floor. Look! First you search for her foot, you stop her and then you make the movement. If you don't make contact first, it'll be hard for her to guess that you want to communicate. Like when you want to talk to her. First you call her, and only when you know she is listening to you, then you talk. Otherwise, sooner or later, you'll end up shouting. This is just the same. And you (to the other half of the couple), keep in mind that when he calls you, you have to stop and listen to him, otherwise he'll shout for you to hear him. And if you're dancing, he'll bump into you. Look at what I do. I bring my foot closer to hers, she stops to listen, I make the movement and wait for her to respond. Remember, when you dance, you're involved in a constant dialogue; you impose nothing. One speaks first, and once the other has heard what is said, they reply. Because in tango, much like in life, if you don't show interest in listening, you're going to assume you already know what the other person is going to say, and you never reply. If anything, you'll respond to your own assumptions, but never to what the other person is actually saying. This is how true dialogue ceases to exist and becomes nothing more than a monologue, which ends up destroying relationships. The tango is a loving dialogue between two bodies, where you each handle yourselves with determination, and where there are always moments of silence – a silence that's essential to dialogue, enriching it, never cancelling it out. You can both make suggestions in response to the other, whether it's about the speed, space or direction, even though one takes the initiative of the very first movement. It's then up to the other to reply with the next movement, to decide whether or not to fan the flames or let the fire slowly die down.

'Because of its conquering attitude and hints of melancholy, this dance is also synonymous with self-awareness. We know who we are based on the other person. In tango, you can be the protector or the protected, dominant or dominated, a seducer or the seduced, infinitely tender, violent, even a mix of all the above, and your partner is there to show you this. You can dance a different way every day, but always guided by just one spirit, with one being the shadow of the other.

'The tango's graceful and elegant choreography is stitched together with the threads of life, with embraces that are restrained, not overwhelming. Mistakes are opportunities to create something new together. If I don't give my partner space, they'll take it from me; my partner is there to show me who I really am. Encounters are dialogue, not impositions. Dialogue means listening to each other, not making assumptions. Embraces are about giving space, not trapping the other person. Tango is all about dialogue, dialogue, dialogue...'

Chapter 25

The Pendulum

Everyone has at least one once-in-a-lifetime moment, one occasion or instant of personal enlightenment that gives their life meaning. Sometimes, we can spend years without truly living, and then, suddenly, our life boils down to just one moment, as Oscar Wilde used to say. A minute of loving, intellectual or mystic perfection, an eternal moment promised by the swing of the pendulum, a moment we have to use well.

The gigantic and heavy copper sphere, whose centre featured an engraved sunflower, moved with the isochronous majesty of a pendulum, releasing pale and ever-changing reflections to the rhythm of its wide oscillations as the only light that illuminated that place. The sphere, which moved on the end of a long thread hanging from the enormous cosmic dome, acted like an indestructible power, suspended in the infinite nothingness, spinning at an incalculable speed while moving from side to side. The silent symmetrical movement barely alerted us to the fact that we were in the midst of a void where the strength of the universal law governing that place was determined.

Despite the resistance offered by the air or possible friction at its tethering point, the stimulus that enables the existence of this endless movement seemed to have much stronger willpower. This is the same willpower that the spirits of its guardians possessed, and it was central to their ability to overcome any adversity and choose their own destiny.

It's no coincidence that movement allows both small and large personal achievements to happen, because there's no growth without movement.

We had travelled at such high speeds in the convertible vehicle that we didn't even feel it. The Afar Brotherhood had provided me with a t-shirt made of intelligent fabric that was part of the uniform required to drive that contraption. The fabric contained membranes that were able to diagnose your state of health and increase your intellectual and emotional IQ, based on a potential reactivation of your intuition and your subconscious. Obviously, Elsu had no need for it. In the Elove Galaxy, they moved on another level, which was completely inaccessible to us humans. By then, I'd already established an enduring relationship with the impossible: time travel, force fields, parallel universes, fantasy and science fiction all constituted a giant playing field where reality and imagination were rivals in equal parts. I'd learned that 'impossible' is a relative term and that, as Einstein rightly suggested, *'For an idea that does not first seem insane, there is no hope'*.

To fly like motorised birds was something that would've been translated in my world's dictionary as something impossible and forbidden. But the only way to discover the limits of what is possible is to venture a little beyond the impossible. Life becomes much more interesting when you cook a perfect dish that combines entertainment and knowledge.

'Are you OK?' I asked Elsu, perceiving the formation of new and strange sensations, possibly enhanced by the incredible intelligent fabric.

He looked at me and smiled, with a slightly worried look that I'd never detected on him before.

'You're worried we won't make it in time, aren't you? It's difficult to always choose the right path.'

'How wise you have already become, Amelia. Life is full of choices. We cannot take two paths at once. This enormous pendulum embodies this lesson.'

'Time's running out, but we must be very close. We've travelled through almost all of the constellations. Maybe this is finally Pisces and we can complete the mission.'

'I would like to tell you that we have reached the end of our journey, Amelia, but the stars indicate that it is not so,' he said finally, looking upwards.

I was scared to try although I wanted it desperately. Fear told me clearly that I had to do it and, finally, I did.

'Kiss me,' I said. 'I don't want to risk dying or disappearing in one fantasy or another in this place without holding the memory of your lips on mine.'

He didn't kiss me. But he put up no resistance whatsoever to me kissing him. We were so close that we were breathing in each other's air. He gave in, surrounding me with his non-human aura. Then he retreated slightly, just enough to look me in the eyes. He caressed my jaw with his thumbs and turned the second long, slow, soft and deep kiss into the start of a story that nobody would forget. That kiss was everything. It was a shortcut to heaven, where dying would only be the beginning.

'How do you feel?' I asked him, still not quite believing what had happened.

'Succession,' he replied, sighing the world's final sigh.

'What?' I asked, completely lost. I won't deny I expected something more along the lines of a super romantic line like 'Your kisses are so good they should come with a warning,' or 'I want to kiss you over and over again, every way I know how.' What he gave me, however, was one of his encrypted messages.

'Succession means leaving behind what you were in order to be what you will be.'

'Do you mean that something in time has changed?

'You can live in time for a time, or you can live in time for an eternity.'

I understood that the kiss was like the one between Superman and Lois Lane, an 'I can't be with you, although I'd like to be' kind of situation. One of those kisses that make you realise that oxygen is highly overrated. Now I regret not having kept that kiss in a bottle so I could savour it in small doses every hour, every day, and remember any elusive detail that, like a good Samaritan, would save me from my nostalgia. They say that we're all mortals until we have our first true kiss. I would have given up immortality in return for just one lifetime by his side, because the greatest thing we learn in this life is to love and be loved in return.

'If we're not in Pisces, where are we? This can only be the Taurus or Aries constellation,' I said, my heart now full.

'In both, Amelia. We are in both. Aries is on one side of the pendulum and Taurus is on the other,' said Elsu, observing a strange triangular clock with a single hand that moved anticlockwise and in time with the pendulum. It was divided into two equal parts, one red and other green.

'Have you ever stopped to wonder what your life would be like if you became your opposite?'

'You mean becoming a completely different person to who I am?'

'Exactly. If you could be reborn as that bohemian painter that you never became, or the fun and daring person you dreamt of becoming as a little girl.'

'I don't know... I think I'm pretty fun and daring already, don't you?' I said with my usual spark. 'Are we really ready for that kind of second opportunity?'

He took so long to answer that, for the first time since we met, I thought he had no answer. Obviously, I was mistaken.

'That is what they do here. They open the soul's hidden dimensions, allowing us to free ourselves. The guardians of Elove told me about this pendulum and about the beings that look after it.'

'That would really be like giving dreams wings to fly.'

'Dreams do not need wings, Amelia. They simply need a place to land.'

To the west was a completely flat island that was bathed by warm waters. It was made out of stones of red jasper, whose properties protected the beings of the constellation of Aries against curses, spells and negative energies, while also protecting them from themselves when faced with fear and pessimism, bringing positive energy, increasing courage and determination. When they're born, Aries are given a bracelet encrusted with a red jasper gem as a symbol of power and vitality, which they never take off. The natives of that place refer to it as 'the blood of Mother Earth'.

To the east was another island made out of chrysocolla, a crystal whose shiny blue vitreous surface also contained an intense green. Its energy transmitted peace and well-being, which helped to control the emotional outbursts of the beings of the constellation of Taurus, thus promoting tolerance and patience, and reducing belligerence. Dozens of birds whose nature and colours I found endlessly intriguing seemed to bless its coastlines with whistles as synchronised as the music played by an elite symphonic orchestra. Its inhabitants wore one of those gems around their necks in the shape of horns, as a symbol of their ideal.

Both gems absorbed the rays given off by the immense pendulum that created day and night with its precise balance, illuminating one island while the other remained in darkness. I likened this to the Earth, which by spinning on its own axis performs the miracle of letting some countries enjoy sunlight while others sleep like logs, as is the case with Spain and Australia. Of course, our Sun in this case, our 'king star' and one of the hundred billion stars that make up our galaxy, has the honour of raising and lowering the golden curtain, allowing us to witness such magical hours as those pursued by photographers, dreamers and lovers who tell the story of how the Sun loved the Moon so much that he would die every night just to let her breathe. For these two worlds, the pendulum was that sun, embracing them, shyly at first and then with all its splendour, giving the breath of life to the red brick and green fields of both, which were as united as they were divided by the promise of a new dawn, two sides of the same coin.

'Where ought we to start? Which path is most likely to be the right one?' We were standing right at the start and at the end of either one of them.

'Not all the paths you choose will be the right ones, but some will be necessary for you to grow,' said Elsu, taking me by the hand and heading in the direction of the Aries constellation. 'According to the pendulum's movement, we will arrive at dawn. If we choose the other side, darkness will cover us for hours.'

That was his choice, mine was hope. He told me that I would often realise there is no right path, just right reasons for taking a particular path. It sounded logical and wise, like everything that came out of his mouth, now my favourite spot. Merely brushing against it made all my fears vanish like a jellyfish in the sun.

'One of the limitations of human beings, Amelia, is that you often believe you are on the right path and do not realise that it is not the only one.'

'And if we get lost?'

'There are beautiful paths that cannot be discovered unless you are lost. Adventure begins where plans end. When you stop looking behind you, you will know that you are heading in the right direction.'

'How is it that you're always so sure of everything?' I asked, absent-mindedly caressing the blue petals that snowed upon us, like sparks of life without a compass.

'If there is peace in your soul, there is destiny in your journey. Life is like a boat that never stops; you just have to lead it in the right direction. It is impossible to stop it. Either you move, or the sea current, the wind and the tides will drag you with them.'

We crossed the seemingly endless span of the bridge that connected both islands at the same slow speed at which day was breaking, just as the first flashes of light were beaming from the pendulum to fill the furthermost corners of the place with life. The red earth was drinking up the water around it like a thirsty mouth. Vodka walked a few metres ahead of us, like a veteran traveller simply enjoying our company. I matched the pace of the person who was the source of my energy, the perfect pen who wrote my happiness without any smudges, commas or full stops to slow down my dreams. I couldn't stop thinking about the new unknown landscapes, enigmatic characters and indecipherable messages that awaited us.

Once there, the rams of Aries all seemed to be in a tense calm state, as if on alert. There was a flurry of activity around them. They observed us, unwavering and trusting, and seemed to be far too busy preparing some kind of festivities or competitive games to pay too much attention to us. Brand-new woollen mantles covered their bodies, on which was set enormous raised head with twisted horns. Looking into their eyes, I got the feeling that they were always poised to unleash their ferocity and the irrepressible impulsive nature that ruled them.

'Why are there no children on the island?' I asked, scanning our surroundings.

'There are children, Amelia. In fact, they are taking the leading role today. They must be preparing for the contests.'

'Children in contests? What for?'

'They have an ambitious and adventurous nature. They need to be amused and to compete in order to satisfy their essence that tells them they can always be better. Through them, they will find a good opponent who readily match their skill. This is a very special type of competition, Amelia. When they turn twelve, they have to prove their maturity and their ability to choose their own destiny. They call it the sacred games of "I Am", which represent the deepest truths of life.'

'So, it's a sort of sports therapy?' I asked, pretending to be an expert. 'And what does it involve?'

'In one of the contests, the youths have to walk around the entire island three times day and night, while keeping a steady pace over this great distance. Throughout their walk, they will encounter different physical, emotional, spiritual and mental tests that they must pass. Only in the light of the totality of each Aries can the significance of their purpose be truly understood and valued. This way, they express the mastery they have over their inner lives. These are ritual games that push them to the limits and alter their conscience, allowing them to perform new self-introspections. It is in this state that they can achieve such an extraordinary degree of skill and concentration.'

'They seem like very tough and cruel games for children.'

'Not for them, Amelia. Games allow them to perceive things differently. The participants are more aware of their own existence, of their possibilities and their abilities, which drives them to develop of willpower, discipline, responsibility, commitment and respect for their adversary and for themselves. They are prepared for this moment from birth through a series of initiation and training sessions.'

'Why is it so important to succeed at these games?'

'Only those who are prepared will be able to choose their own destinies.'

'And what happens to those who don't?'

'They call it the power of failure. It leads them to seek betterment through greater effort, discipline, willpower, action and reflection. There is no triumph or defeat. They are given the tools to get to know themselves and value who they are. One day, they will be audacious and independent leaders in their community, pioneers who cut new paths, or they will help others prepare for their big day, but they will be unable to choose their own destiny.'

As I continued to fire questions at Elsu, trying to solve this riddle, a new scene had evolved before us. What seemed like a giant, tentless circus with countless rings had been assembled on the red jasper. Just like pheasants nosily breaking out of their shells, the combative spirit of the young warriors came out of its resting state, exploding like a rocket in search of the challenges they were predestined to face. With their shaved heads adorned with colourful paint, they ran like wolves, hunting hungrily for first place.

It was like being immersed in one of those videogames that was completely indistinguishable from reality, where charismatic characters move at the speed of light and face all kinds of twisted tests they need to overcome if they are to survive and acquire new abilities that will take them to the next level, with even more difficulties of the kind that makes you experience such nail-biting yet spectacular moments that you are unable to let go of the hand controls.

The young rams threw themselves bravely into the competition, taking risks with their temperamental impulsiveness, earning the applause and cheers of the audience. This divine breath made them burn stronger and raise their red jasper bracelets in the air, a sign of pride in who they were.

The finalists, the few who managed to complete the games successfully, were invited to the constellation of Taurus, where luxury, pleasure and opulence reigned. For an entire year, they would experience the essence of its inhabitants, living like them, feeling like them, seeing life from their point of view, behaving like true bulls. They would abandon passion for balance, adventure for tradition, warring impetus for tranquillity, hurriedness for calm prudence, innovation for rational judgement and freedom for roots.

At the same time, their Taurean neighbours were celebrating their own special annual event, at which they would select the new generation of chosen ones, youths who would complete the same journey in reverse, thus obtaining the privilege of having less and becoming more.

Although their story was completely different and the comparison quite absurd, I couldn't help but compare the experience of those youths with those of the Amish community who had no cars, no electricity and no phones. The Amish live in their monochromatic religious world, one in which they're taught that they won't go to heaven unless they're Amish. As if still living in the nineteenth century, they shun a culture where technological progress and prosperity are believed to lead to pride, power and status, and to a breakdown of relationships. Before being baptised and deciding whether or not they wish to join the church, they must take a break, known as *rumspringa*. Basically, they're encouraged to explore the outside world and enjoy the modern freedoms that naturally include riding in vehicles that aren't pulled by animals, parties, sex, alcohol, and even smoking and drugs. This is supposed to help them make an informed decision. To this end, when they turn sixteen, they cross over to the other side to experience the modern world, and they stop being inaccessible and unapproachable. The shock is brutal, to the extent that only about ten per cent decide not to return. Their adolescent testosterone changes their existence, and they exchange family-oriented values and dressing alike – with black felt hats, braces, beards and moustaches for the men, and grey dresses with white bonnets for the women – for a completely different way of life. Very few decide to permanently swap their fresh homemade bread with peanut butter for a burger and fries from McDonald's, the feeling of driving a horse-drawn carriage on a cold winter's morning for the unique sound of snow crunching beneath the tires of a beautiful sports car, sad clothes for jeans and leather jackets, silence for the constant stimulus of large flat-screen televisions and videogames, leaving behind the stone age in order to join a community whose citizens voraciously acquire accessories and possessions, and who don't consider it a sin to use a dishwasher or a computer.

In general, those who decide not to return face a dilemma, though they are no longer confused. They don't stop to consider the psychological impact or spiritual consequences of their actions because they don't meditate on the decision between the Amish world and the outside world; they simply ask themselves what any young person would: 'What makes me happier?' The answer to this vague and fragile notion can only satisfy a soul made of stardust.

Nobody slept in that place. Surrounded by hundreds of lit torches that worked hard to cut a path through the cold darkness of night, the ceremony concluded with thirteen youths ready to embark on an adventure to learn all the secrets of what lay on the other side of the pendulum. This was an invitation they couldn't turn down. It was a chance for them to be everything they were not, the only way to discover who they truly wanted to be, following a period of 'experimentation' that began with the announcement of the pendulum clock's forgotten hour. It was the signal. They looked and each other and smiled, knowing that they were the lucky ones. At times, all you could hear was the excited beating of their hearts.

They idealised their polar opposites, and exploring the other side in order to decide between the two options would make them free to choose later. Once they'd experienced both, learning the positives and negatives of each, they would have the yardstick by which compare them and to decide on which side of the pendulum they wanted to live. It was a major decision that carried commitment. One side had to have enough appeal to keep them from being lost in void in between.

'Your appearance will change. You will look like a bull from now on, if you choose to stay,' the Taurean leader said obstinately, looking directly at the Aries youth with strange liquorice-coloured eyes and uneven pupils.

He wanted to know more.

'Does this mean I will not be able to recover my true self, my own body?'

'No, there will be no going back,' he was warned. 'This will put an end to your past, effectively killing it.'

'What is my meaning in the short dictionary of life? How much is my essence worth?'

'It is not worth everything to you? Essence is the final drop in the deep well of our being, the one that prevents you from being just another name in the history of the cosmos.'

'I am not sure, not completely,' the youth answered, driven by a peculiar impulse, as if his desire had shattered into pieces like an egg dropping onto the shiny floor of hard green chrysocolla. He felt as though the person talking to him was a type of CIA agent working for the universe and the law of the pendulum, knowing perfectly the mechanism that made it what it was and how it was wrapped up and built, as if he were in possession of the manual to disassemble it, bolt by bolt and cable by cable, with no intention of ever putting it back together, indifferent to the fact that eventually all the pieces would fall and get lost in the immensity of the pendulum.

'And if I decide to return?' he asked the muscular figure who combined strength and finesse, and who appeared to be sedating him with the movement of a tail resting on his large and wide feet.

'Your people will welcome you back as though you had never left. You will lose all memories of your time spent here, as if your life had never strayed off course. You will return to your essence and any traces of this time will be erased,' replied the Taurean.

The young Aries was no longer immune to the extraordinary things he'd been lucky enough to discover in that world. However, he felt lost because he didn't know whether he was running away from it or whether he was ready to return home naturally, as though he'd never left.

Much like the young Amish, most would return to their own constellations following this period of experimentation. The ones who decided to stay in the other land were adopted by a new family who recognised them as their own, creating such strong family bonds that they'd eventually forget all traces of their previous lives. The only memory that would remain in their minds would be that of a cold yellow light. The constellation that managed to recruit more foreigners and recover more of their own was rewarded by the pendulum with resources that made the island better for those living there: purer water, more sunlight hours and greater nutrients to make their fruit grow faster and with more vitamins. The fight consisted in acquiring the largest number of beings, with the strongest genes, in order to perpetuate the survival of their species.

Who would I be if I could be anyone else? I remember taking advantage of one of my trips to fulfil a personal project that aimed to reflect on our existence, what we were and what we were not. Like an intrepid photojournalist, I left my digital camera behind and bought an instant analogue camera, which I began using on all my trips. I photographed anonymous people on the street, who I'd encourage to complete the phrase, 'I would have liked to have been...' After the initial surprise, they all asked, 'Anything?'

'Yes, of course, anything,' I said, inviting them to admit their dreams. The comments were extremely varied and opened up a world of endless answers. I loved to observe passers-by and would wonder about their stories, their secrets, their desires, what they were like as children and where they were headed in life. People's true and fascinating stories aren't posted on social media. They're on the street and all around us. I loved approaching people without a specific profile in mind. I chose some by the way they walked, whereas others intrigued me by what they were doing at the time – a simple gesture could inspire me to want to know more about them. Most had captivating personalities and answered with a smile, while others drew on nostalgia. I would go first, telling them that as a little girl I had dreamt of becoming a Bollywood actress and had ended up becoming a tour guide instead. This inspired them to open up and we would both go home with a new story to tell.

More than one would have like to be Julius Caesar on his march towards absolute power. A seventy-year-old man who stumbled around on a wheelchair told me he'd been quite the basketball player in his youth, and that he had lost his legs in a plane accident. He confessed that he'd love to become Spider-Man so he could feel free again. Of course, even superheroes have their own problems. Spider-Man was deprived of his parents' love because they died when he was only six. He had to work very hard, and he also experienced heartbreak and felt alone a lot of the time. And then there were all the battles against enemies, his future hanging by a thread, and not the one that is actually one of his Spider powers. No matter who you want to be, that person will also face challenges and feel pain. We have a tendency to think that others have much better and more exciting lives than we do. But is that really true?

The supreme pendulum was a true revelation for me. I then decided I didn't want to be anyone else in this world, not even for a day. I had my own unique personality, that which made me 'me'. To be like anyone else, even in my imagination, would be rejecting that final drop that contains everything I am and was meant to be.

At some point or another, all good gardeners have found an error in their favourite seed book and have corrected it in the margins, as if it were an ancient book in the library of life. I'd like to be myself at every moment. I hope I can be that person every day of my life.

Chapter 26

Journey to My Destiny

Like a trapeze artist walking a tightrope, I felt that every step I took was a decision and carried the risk of freefalling into the void. I'd felt this way for a while, but I trusted in what was to come, intuitively knowing that the new step would free me from that risk. Connecting all the dots meant opening my eyes in order to know which path to take, whether it was a well-known and visible path or an invisible one. I knew, however, that I couldn't connect the dots by looking forward, I could only do it by looking back, trusting that they would connect in the future somehow, as I observed the constant stop and play of the daily soundtrack that cuts, imposes, delineates, draws maps, unties knots and makes time pass us by. Every line drawn along the way, each tear, each fall, success or failure would make sense later on, when you cast your eyes back and realise that it was all tied together, that everything that happened was meant to happen, because deep down we are all lame sculptors whose destinies escape our grasp.

To live with the borrowed heartbeat of existence, having assimilated into every cell in my being the fact that each tiny beat of my heart could be my last, helped me make some important life decisions. There are no neon lights to show you the way, but there are subtle signs, such as the ones you see when studying your past, that gently guide you towards your future. Once you find that sweet spot where they intersect, the light blinds you to the point where you realise you'll never see through your eyes again nor waste the present as though it were expendable.

Everything appeared to indicate that it was just the start of any other morning. It was eight o'clock on a Saturday when the train of life took off for me, headed towards time – he who devours everything. The fragmented light of that autumn morning reflected on Conan's naked sleeping body. My mother slowly and quietly opened my bedroom door a little, as if to tell me she wanted me to follow her. It was a very faint creak, but loud enough for me to hear. I turned around immediately and saw her figure carefully peeking in. There she was, smiling, wild, so very much my mother, eyeing me curiously. I silently peeled myself off the sheets in order to follow the exhausted but passionate traveller who reminded me of the clouds, ever nomadic, high up on the horizon, free and infinite.

She shuddered a little because she knew that he'd been the only one to come to the truth. Although, his presence might bring back memories of her time at San Patricio, where she'd allowed him to dig around in the dark corners of her mind and dust off over thirty years of suffering.

A gust of wind kicked up some of the dirt in the garden behind her. The wind insisted, pushing her to meet that man, whom she'd obviously been expecting. The friendly and trusting way in which my mother spoke to him baffled me.

'Maybe he'll just provide more clarity, but I don't know if I'm ready for this,' I thought to myself.

My eyes scanned their faces quickly, in search of micro-expressions that could help me read their body language.

'I promised you I'd find you. You look good. I'm glad you finally found your daughter,' he said, finally, looking over at me in a very sweet and familiar way, as though he'd known me my entire life.

'You're not going to tell me?' she asked, still smiling.

He went pale. He opened his mouth to say something but his paralysed throat didn't let him get the words out, like a fish trapped in a puddle.

'Everyone has to fight their own demons, Amelia,' he replied after a few seconds' silence, as if each word were of vital importance.

That sounded ominous to me, as if he were a messenger of fear, but I tried hard not to make any assumptions.

'Lucky for you, I know a lot of angels. Don't worry "white coat",' she urged, placing her hand on his shoulder.

Right there, finally in the privacy of the warm living room, without any type of formalities, we gained access to the treasure of his message. I couldn't describe the magic of the conversation that took place, but we immediately understood so much of what had been hidden from us up until that moment.

The 'white coat' told us who Ahmed and Father Jambi were and why their names appeared on the psychiatric facility's guest registry as regular visitors for my mother during her entire stay there.

'A Christian priest and a Muslim?' I exclaimed incredulous, and somewhat disappointed.

'Every apple has its worm, Rafaela,' answered the psychiatrist, whom I also began to call 'white coat', as if it were his real name.

'What for centuries had been a veil of suspicions, misgivings and hatred that separated Christians and Muslims had somehow brought them together since the discovery of a crypt in some remote church Your mother was a threat to them, someone that had to be silenced and kept away from the truth at all costs. San Patricio became the perfect cover.'

'What about the Unholy Father? What was his role in all of this?' asked my mother as though the Argentinian were an oracle.

'He's just a pawn in the game of diabolical minds. He gets his instructions and executes them perfectly, and they make it worth his while. He casually and innocently revealed your case to the bishop and was immediately told what to do with you, in exchange for the promise of becoming the director of San Patricio if he fulfilled his mission. The mission involved keeping you locked up for the rest of your life. But he didn't know the real interests that lay behind such a decision. He's just a hired thug, someone whose mouth and heart are easily silenced in return for power. Your case became his most important obligation in the sacred ministry.'

'I've seen him kneel before divinity and humiliate it so many times, that nothing you say surprises me,' she said, her voice low and fading.

'Let God punish him as he deserves!' I shouted, feeling how my nostrils widened breathing in the air of outrage and fury, imagining everything that she and other victims had unjustly suffered in that place.

'So, do they all know the existence of the Purple Lagoon?'

'It seems they don't have the complete map.'

'How did you get so much information?'

'After reading your diary and noticing all the strange things that were happening at San Patricio, I began to investigate and tie up all the loose ends. You know how much of a scientist I am!' he said, winking and grinning widely. 'I needed a logical, systematic approach to everything that was happening. A couple of weeks before you escaped, I waited at the reception for the arrival of the mysterious visitors, and after putting my spy skills to good use, everything began to make sense.'

'Spy?'

'Well, the whole analysing of minds business came about once I got tired of leading a double life for a few years, unable to share with anyone what I really did as an agent for an external intelligence agency. I always did enjoy the excitement of knowing things most people didn't know. But still, I don't think I've been able to avoid raising suspicion, especially now that I'm being watched.'

'Counterintelligence', I said, alarmed.

'Amelia, you'll be happy to know I'm back with my wife. I won't put my family at risk. This is where my mission ends. We're leaving the country to start a new life this very afternoon. This is all I can tell you in order to keep you both safe as well.'

Their farewell was filled with joy, which is also what hope is made of. Both were sure that the same reason they had been brought them together was why they were now taking separate paths. My mother's love story had inspired 'white coat' to recover his own one, and he'd become her angel of deliverance in return. A fair exchange always makes the stars smile.

I was still trying to digest it all with a bowl of cereal for breakfast when I was startled by the phone ringing. It was Jared. His phone call so early in the morning seemed odd. He said he had to see me. Every time I heard his voice, it made me unsteady all over again. One day, I was the happiest woman in the world, packing my bags to go to Jerusalem with him, and the next I was preparing my speech to tell him I loved Conan and that I'd never go back to him.

'Hello, my love. I have news about the bottle. It's important that we see each other right away.'

In a way, I felt guilty just listening to such an affectionate greeting that wasn't from Conan. I tried to focus on the bottle and its mystery.

'I'll see you at the reception of the dance academy in an hour,' he said, hanging up, not giving me time to confirm the appointment.

I turned the water on in the shower and, without even waiting for it to get hot, had the quickest shower of my life. There was no transition to warm or even hot. The cascade of freezing water suffocated my burning heart and I barely felt the impact of the water temperature. I put on some turquoise blue leggings, a tight long-sleeved top, also blue, and some sneakers, scooping my hair up into a ponytail and one of those cute baseball caps. I said goodbye to my mother with a brief 'I'm going to jog a bit to clear my head.' In case they were watching, I did some stretches as any other runner would do. I then ran off, advancing in circles to throw anyone trying to figure out where I was going off the scent. After seven kilometres, I sprinted as quickly as I could to the door of the dance academy. Jared was already waiting there.

'Rafaela, I wasn't expecting you so soon… I didn't know you were in such good shape!'

'What is it? What did you find out?' I asked, exhausted, trying to catch my breath.

He quickly took me inside and we locked ourselves in a tiny room where they kept all the costumes and accessories for the annual tango competition. He looked alarmed.

'This map has been a sought-after object for a very long time. In the past, many expeditions were sure they'd succeed where others had failed thanks to the possession of an invaluable piece of manuscript featuring the location of the famous Purple Lagoon, a place people have been searching for since the beginning of time. A map that only one person knew and could interpret, as it had been drawn by her father, one of the guardians of a galaxy that's invisible to our eyes and to our knowledge of the universe. It was apparently originally formed by a tribe of Native Americans living in the United States, specifically in Montana. An unsuccessful quest to find it has cost some people their lives and our organisation billions of euros in research – a Jewish archaeological organisation created in secret, with the sole purpose of finding out the truth. As far as I've been able to find out, the piece of parchment is in the custody of Christian and Muslim leaders. What you possess, Rafaela, is probably the greatest human discovery of all time, everything we've ever asked ourselves but have been unable to answer. Something that can't be found in any of the known historical records. That place contains visible evidence of the start of everything, of the cosmos itself.'

'Wait, wait… let's see if I follow you. Are you saying that the beings of the Elove Galaxy are a wondrous indigenous civilisation and that we, humans, are here because of a unique adventure?'

'They're probably the key to the future that awaits us, Rafaela. These beings are so extraordinary and have such divine qualities that they're capable of explaining supernatural laws. Legends, sagas and religions have all spoken about them in many different ways, about the powerful beings who came from the stars. They are the explanation of the first civilisations. Their knowledge has passed from initiates to other initiates through secret societies for tens of thousands of years. Today, we know them as the occult sciences.'

'Then, my father was one of those initiates who knew and could interpret the map of the Purple Lagoon, just as my mother explained to me.'

'It's incredible, Rafaela, that you're the daughter of one of those beings. I can't believe it! Do you know what that means? Our organisation has discovered that there's a hidden internal report they call *Kura* that mentions all this.'

'And what does that report say?'

'You won't believe it, but the recommendation is to deny it, hide it as much as possible and, if necessary, destroy it. Their excuse is that the possible revelation of the existence of intelligent extraterrestrials could cause such levels of social chaos that political and religious institutions, philosophical beliefs, moral systems, and even the economic structure could be enormously affected, plunging humanity into a crisis of unforeseeable consequences.

'Our Jewish organisation has archaeologists, astrologists, mathematicians, philosophers and scientists who fill blackboards with mathematical calculations, geometric theorems, logical numeric structures, and schemes with traced lines that follow intelligent patterns, any of which could explain how the cosmos is made up.'

'Wow, this all sounds amazing, and I'm a part of that.'

'I'm sure that these being exist, Rafaela, and that they've never left. Everything has been predetermined and it indicates a date. That date is now.'

'Now? What does that mean?'

'I don't know, but they seem to think that something's going to happen very soon. An astrological configuration that will randomly open an enormous dimensional revolving door. The worst thing is that there are still those who insist on keeping the human race in the dark. The phenomenon is already happening, but we have to understand it. Amazing things are happening.'

'Such as...?'

'We've discovered that the Earth's vibrational pattern is increasing. Our team of psychologists has discovered that the children who are being born all over the world, when subjected to IQ tests, are statistically, and inexplicably, obtaining much higher results than in previous generations.'

'Well, as a psychologist I can justify that, given the incredible amount of stimulus they receive nowadays from computers, television, videogames...'

'I don't just mean children in Western countries, Rafaela. This also happens in developing and underdeveloped countries. Very strange things are happening all over the place. Something's going on and I think you're the key.'

'Me? I have to speak to my mother and tell her all this.'

'What makes you think she doesn't know? She's the only human being who's been there, who met your father and had a child with a being from another galaxy.'

'Give me back the bottle and the map, Jared. I've just made a decision,' I said, resolutely.

'But... I thought you wanted us to live this adventure together. Do you know what this means for me, for my career and for my people?'

'I don't want you to tell your organisation about this, or anyone. I'll do it my way. I understand now that we're here to cooperate on a plan that's much bigger than all of us. This may be the last opportunity we have to cross a bridge into a life without limitations, outside the immediate desires of selfish people and their ever-increasing needs, where nothing's more important than being number one. If you ever loved me, or if you still do, I ask that you please respect my decision and forget all of this.'

'I'll think about it, if you also think about your answer after reading this letter,' he said, placing a folded paper under my hat and stealing a kiss, one of those illicit ones that are highly valuable on the black market, because despite it being stolen, you know it belongs only to you.

I couldn't hold back. All I could think about was stopping and reading the note. I stopped halfway, leaning my back on one of the old oak trees that lived in the park that had been newly-washed by the cool, fine rain that had been falling indiscriminately on the streets of Granada for days. It was barely perceptible, but constant and intermittent, like a sign that my soul needed a deep clean. I slid slowly downwards, feeling the rugged bark against my back, until I finally dropped onto the humid ground. I unfolded the fragile paper, which seemed to still be alive in my hands, feeling the heat of words recently uttered, trying desperately to walk in line like a music band during a parade. I blamed all the running and not the emotional galloping of my small muscle, which was being shaken like a cocktail, combining thoughts, feelings and memories. The result was something more like a Molotov cocktail than a refreshing caipirinha. It was only a few lines long, but it was clear enough to make me doubt everything.

Rafaela, my love,

My flight is MVRT7, destination Ben Gurion, Israel. I fly back to-morrow at 2.15 in the afternoon. I bought a ticket for you too, which I'll take with me. It's a ticket to happiness, to a whole new world just for us. If you let me, I'll reinvent this universe specifically for you. If you accept, I'll forget all about the bottle and the map, and of anything that isn't your eyes looking into mine. If I don't see you at the airport, I'll have no choice but to continue pursuing the dream that brought me to your city, using this map that hasn't been able to take me to you, so I can guide my people to the truth. I'll be near the window, imagining your body.

I love you,
Jared.

I slid a finger over the words and tried to envisage Jared as he wrote them. Was he crying as I am now? What a blackmailer!' I thought, two seconds after that rhetoric question, feeling like the star of a novel that could easily be called 'blackmail or seduction'.

'This is insane! I can't believe it!' I repeated, unable to stop reading it. Nervous and excited, I told my mother every detail of what I knew. On this particular occasion, I also had to add my love dilemma; despite having survived a traumatic sentimental past, I was now in love with this man again, or I was at the very least sailing on a strong sea of doubts, making me lose my moral compass. She didn't seem surprised.

Her arms were always my best refuge. Maybe that's why they wrapped around me at that instant, making me feel as I did when I was little and she'd tell me that hugs came from the stars.

'I want to go to Montana, *mamá*, to the land of my ancestors. Something tells me that it's the perfect thing to do in order to get my head and my life in order. I'd like you to come with me. This is an adventure we have to go on together.'

Her eyes danced when she looked at me, as if their shine came from the delirious depth of her soul.

'They've been waiting for you for a long time, and you're finally ready. You don't know how much I've wanted this moment, Rafaela,' she replied excitedly.

'But we don't have the map any more,' I confessed guiltily.

'I gave your *abuela* an exact copy of the map that Elsu used during our trip to the Purple Lagoon. I wanted it to be in good hands in case something happened to me. I asked her to protect it with her life.'

'I've combed the house many times and I've never found it. Do you think Belly kept it?'

'I never knew if she believed my story or if she died thinking that her only daughter had lost her mind. I guess the fact she didn't keep it is definite proof that it was the second option,' she deduced, with a sad voice, her eyes half closed.

'We definitely need that map,' I said wrapped up in one of my unbridled emotions that I found hard to control these days.

'Trust that something will happen, Rafaela. Something always does. Your father taught me that everything's possible, even when we don't know how it's going to happen. Once you've done your part, let the universe do the rest, and make sure it finds you with open arms when the time comes. Can you trust a universe where flowers grow?

Then learn to trust in what is happening. If there's a storm, let it roar; it'll calm down,' she said, completely at peace, which settled my initial discouragement – an inspirational truth that I wrote down in my book. *'If you can't, I'll help you.'*

I had my mother back. I had the love of two men who would, apparently, walk to the ends of the Earth for me. My veins carried the blood of the secret of creation. Shouldn't I be jumping for joy? I should, but instead, there I was questioning my past and my future, carefully picking apart my present in search for the piece that just didn't fit in. A part of my past was still nagging at me, although I accepted the undeniable reality that I'd been far too naive in matters of the heart. I thought I'd left behind that part of my life with Jared, and that there were no longer any grey or dark tones around me. Having recovered from that awful time, I could see bright, lively hues again in my relationship with Conan, and I had clung to them with enthusiasm. But now I was seeing flashes of colour that were blinding me once again, while I was jumping around acrobatically and in pure delight. What I thought was frozen fish turned out to be fresher than ever.

That night, Conan invited me to dinner. He said we were going to celebrate our *ikigai*. Besides being the name of the restaurant, it means 'life purpose' or 'reason for living' in Japanese. We were alone when we arrived and remained so until we left. It was a cool fusion place, apt for well-travelled people who were addicted to the very latest in Japanese cuisine and who loved Asian food. It was a small, cosy place that never disappointed, where order and the minimalist zen silence dominated everything. The light of the moon reached every corner, creating that characteristic warmth of the Japanese culture. It was decorated with rice paper lanterns, prints of fish hanging on the walls, a porcelain geisha inside an urn, red vinyl chairs and a bamboo *tatami*, where we were served a delicious sake, accompanied by tuna nigiri with marinated mackerel and shredded truffles. Mmmmm, my weakness!

I remembered Esther because the chef explained to us how it had been decorated in accordance with Feng Shui principles, to create an energy balance that would make visitors feel calm. Just what I needed!

'You look sad. I thought you'd be happy with everything that's happening,' said Conan. His face was calm, as always, but a fleeting look appeared on his face. 'I know, *chiquilla*. Even so, I can't stop loving you. I have the stupid habit of stopping my entire life in case you arrive late,' he declared, without any further explanations, in a resigned and conciliatory tone.

I looked at him, suspiciously, wondering if maybe he knew. He always had a special knack for reading me, even when I didn't say anything at all. He cleared his throat and continued talking.

'Is there still space for me in your *ikigai*?'

I tried to get out of answering that question by looking behind the bonsai centrepiece, concentrating on holding my chopsticks that were dancing around my fingers nervously, like two drunk ballet dancers.

Intrigued, Conan awaited the magic words that every person in love wants to hear, as he took my hands sweetly in his, helping me hold the chopsticks correctly.

'Remember,' he said. 'Chopsticks must never come into contact with your mouth. It's considered bad manners to lick or bite the end of the utensils. You mustn't skewer your food with them, and don't ever let them lie in a cross on the table, the plate or on the chopstick holder. It's a symbol of death. Try to make sure they're always parallel. It looks easy,' he added. 'Hundreds of millions of people do it every day. But when you first face this challenge, you realise there's a trick to it.'

'Yes, well, I never thought you needed a master's degree to eat with chopsticks.'

'I mean some situations that you have to face in life, *chiquilla*.'

It was at that moment that I got the hint. He knew. I didn't imagine it. You had to be lacking all your senses and not know me as well as he did, to not understand this. He had no proof, but he didn't have any doubts either. I felt like his comment gave me permission, so I decided to tell him everything, no matter what happened. If there was one thing I was not, it was a coward. Time stood still; my mind wandered back into one of memories. It was of one of my boxing competitions. I was practically out of combat, when Conan came near me and said, 'Iris, if an egg breaks from the outside, life ends. But if it breaks from the inside, life begins. Important things always begin on the inside. Some boxers earn a living by losing, but you're not one of them.'

He woke me up from my thoughts, snapping his fingers in front of me.

'What are you thinking?'

'That you're right. You've taught me a lot. You've been my best friend, my lover, my life coach, my everything. I can't imagine my life without you.'

'I have? No secrets, remember?'

We had far more things in common that I could've imagined and that made us special. I told him the truth, I expressed how I was feeling. At the end of the day, I always wanted to be with someone I could talk to about anything and share my most intimate feelings with. Again, I ventured down that difficult path where you open your heart, waiting for someone to either hold it and accept it as it is, or reject it, disappointed by the truth.

Belly always said that we have two great loves in our lives: one who'll break our heart into a million pieces, and the other who'll do the impossible to put it back together again. The problem is that I didn't know what I wanted. I felt as though I was being carried away like a leaf in the wind, unable to make a decision. One gave me a home and the other gave me life. One was unbridled passion and the other was my guide. One gave me peace and the other scared me. I was lost between two loves: one normal and the other poison. I slept with one, but I dreamt of the other. I lived with one and died for the other.

As expected, I couldn't sleep a wink that night. In an attempt to escape from myself, I floated around in my dark bedroom. I missed Belly and the nights she would stay up with me, listening to me when I had a problem. She'd prepare one of those old earthenware mugs full of hot chocolate, which she'd replenish every time it got cold because I was so absorbed in my problems that I'd forget to drink it. She wasn't bothered by the fact I'd go over and over my problems, she always listened to me as if it was the very first time. She was my shoulder to cry on. I looked at the clock, it was four minutes to four in the morning. I went to her room and took her letters with me, followed by the white smoke of memories. Reading her words would make me feel closer to her. I closed my eyes and, after caressing the pile of letters, I took one out randomly among the nine I still hadn't read, hoping it contained one of those wise responses that come at the right time. One of those lights that, though far, shines brightly enough to show the way.

Dearest Rafaela, my sweet girl,

Here, you'll learn more about your origins, how you were made with love, and finally became the wonderful and extraordinary being that you are. Since that hot twelfth of August, you've had so many experiences, some sad, but most joyful and happy. None of those best ones could ever beat the first time I saw your mother holding you in her arms. You were her breath and her strength from the very first day. Even when she was exhausted and broken, she never let herself fall. You had such pink, almost purple, skin and golden eyes that really caught our attention. You were a very fussy baby. Ever since you were born, your mother slept less, but smiled more. You're so much more than just another step in the ladder of life. I can't deny that, at first, I was overwhelmed by the circumstances, but then nothing exceptional ever arrives in a traditional way. Being your grandmother is one of the greatest honours life has ever bestowed upon me. Don't doubt for a second that you were the most wanted girl in the world, and that we cared for you as our greatest treasure. You were never a mistake, as you yourself innocently told me one day in anger, you were our greatest achievement. Your parents made a wish and along you came. I merely made sure to enjoy their gift all these years, knowing that I was not only caring for my granddaughter, but also for the future of all humanity.

Behind his letter is something I've kept for you since then. Something that belongs to you and that I promised to protect. I'm sure that when it reaches you, it will be the perfect moment for it to be revealed.

I love you,
Belly

I immediately turned the letter over and there was the map. It was as if my wishes had suddenly become the centre of the universe. Just as my mother predicted, things would happen in due course. No later, and no earlier. They would simply happen at the right time. Even if we insist on shaking the hourglass, each grain of sand will fall when the time's right. I opened my eyes like a pilgrim who's been shown the way by a sudden burst of lightning. A tingling sensation spread all over my skin as I imagined my mother's happy face when she finds out that her secret had been carefully kept by Belly – a secret rooted in a very distant past that was now returning to threshold of our consciousness. I filled my lungs with air in slow, deep breaths. That was probably the smell of magic. My thoughts were all stumbling over each other, almost as if they were pushing each other toward the door that had just been opened.

It took us two days to organise the trip and land in Montana. When we arrived, a strong wind had been blowing for the past three days, carrying snow and ice particles all over the place, painting all those wide-open, half-wild, half-untamed, half-inhospitable spaces white. The men in the snow weren't able to answer us. They didn't know the location of any tribe vaguely resembling our descriptions up there in the mountains.

'Nowadays, Native American communities like that don't live in the big sky country anymore, and neither do the bison,' said one of them, riding a black horse with a blonde mane and tail, who was just as gorgeous as Kevin Kostner in the series Yellowstone, where he plays the owner and master of Montana's largest ranch.

We came from the prairies with our hearts swimming in doubts. We experienced many discouraging days, but never lost our high spirits. We lived with old sorcerers and their fire gods. We decided to let ourselves be swept away by the perfection of the moment, and by the American Wild West, offering us a golden opportunity to see our own reflections in alpine lakes, to enjoy each other's company during long walks, over rolling plains, and to contemplate the wildlife that welcomed us like prodigal daughters.

A new trail surrounded by tall yellow grass, casually opened to reveal the most luminous and unsettling landscape after ten days of walking. There, my body was past, present and future all at once.

'This is the place,' I told my mother, walking ahead of her. 'I've been here so many times in my dreams, wrapped in the slow golden waves of these crops.'

A man with long hair and dark skin appeared behind a bright light, like a glowing multifaceted diamond. His presence embodied the purest nature. His smile seemed so very familiar… He appeared to greet us, holding his right arm up. He then approached us and hugged us with immeasurable love. No words were needed.

I met Elsu, my father, though his people, his land, and through the stories Wakanda would tell me each day that we remained in that place surrounded by mountains. My eyes were constantly in a state of daze, lost in the altitudes of the mountaintops and the flights of the eagles and the falcons. When night fell, I raised my eyes to the stars and wondered how many beings were looking down at us.

I saw children wetting their hands in the light of the snow, encouraged by adults to let their souls escape through their dreams. Those faces I'd never seen felt familiar, opening the temple of knowledge before me. I felt the miracle of returning home, to my true home. I discovered my purpose, and for the first time I heard Elsu's voice telling me *The Layet Mai. The Mai Layet,* wrapping his hand tightly around my tattooed ankle, letting me know that the spirit never dies. I may never be able to prove it but I know it's true and I have to try. It's perfectly clear, now I know the meaning of everything.

I know that awareness, truly great awareness, can be light years ahead of expert knowledge. Wakanda prepared me by wishing me to reach maximum perfection. With the authorisation of the guardians of the Elove Galaxy, I acquired the experience and accepted the legacy of being who I was. My perpetual memory would not allow me to forget that coming together with a man from this moment on would put the future of humanity at risk. As a recently-initiated hybrid, a combination between a human and a being from the Elove Galaxy, I could never again fall in love or have a sexual relationship with any man. Going against this oath could make me vanish into the sky in the form of stardust, as was the case with my father. It was only at that point that I finally understood the love that brought me into existence, the sacrifice and high price my parents would pay for being who they were, and for loving each other as they did. Did I have a choice? Of course, I did. You always have a choice. But choosing to be exactly who you are is always the best option.

Now that I was in space, no Earthly power could prevent me from floating eternally among the stars. All I needed was the infinite fuel of my destiny that made me fall like a dart into that new world – a work of art so majestic and immutable that no thinking being could ever possibly imagine. My voice no longer hesitated or contradicted everything I thought I knew. I closed my eyes, ignoring the cold, and concentrated on the darkness behind my eyelids. It was like coming out of an underground world, full of moles, blind animals that never knew another existence other than that of their own dens. An entire race colonised by moles whose entire life transpired in the blackness, their habitats logical and natural to them. Far from awareness and knowledge, whose light was considered the product of insanity, fantasy and science fiction. A minuscule world that had no space for truth and where their slightest attempt to open their eyes was thwarted to maintain the established limits and borders.

I was undergoing an invisible change within myself, and I saw myself being transformed and readying myself to receive what the universe was about to grant me. The mirror would never again reflect the image I had known up until that moment. I had acquired the ability to feel the emotions of others, just like my father. This limitless empathy made me feel the weight of the fear that paralysed those who were terrified. I experienced the longing and desire of lovers. Sometimes my body became incensed with fury, despite not even being angry. I was overcome with embarrassment and my cheeks blushed, as a result of a stranger's humiliation. At first, I struggled to distinguish which were my own feelings, because I was living immersed in a type of emotional spiral that was incredibly difficult to control. This legacy both burdened me and brought me closer to who I really was. But the legacy was a just one. It's not enough to put on somebody else's boots and start walking. What looks easy ends up revealing your own clumsiness and isn't easy at all. Well-argued pieces of advice from the library of the know-it-alls end in nothing but frustration. The dreams of others are nothing but unattainable pipe dreams. Because we are no one in somebody else's shoes. We look in the mirror and all we see is a person who's drifting, insecure and unstable, whose boots will never fit them properly as long as we're living on a blue planet that makes us red.

My mother decided to stay in Montana, where I visited often. There, she would be safe and protected by our new family. Like the traveller she always was, she bade me farewell by saying, 'Pity the human that has a homeland, for their space in the universe is very tiny.' I liked to imagine her swimming naked in the crystal-clear waters of a mountain stream, or enjoying the splendour of a calm sunset, with Elsu's spirit. With the help of the guardians of Elove and the updated map to the Purple Lagoon, I found the Temple of Light in the Pisces constellation, something my parents never managed to do as the door closed before they were able to reach their final destination. The original map seemed to have an error in its calculations, something that Elsu discovered and led him to redo the map altogether. It eased my mind knowing that Jared and his organisation would never find the Purple Lagoon, and that its secrets would remain safe forever, until humanity was ready. I was the chosen one to lead the 'Great Work'. The dots were all connecting, offering me an image that had remained blurry and unclear for a very long time. I am ready to tell the world about the grandeur of reality and of the things I know are true.

Book soundtrack

They say that music gives meaning to our lives. It makes us feel alive and transports us to that magical world where we're free to be and to feel. These songs have given a soul to the universe depicted on these pages. They may have entered through my ears but there's no doubt that they stayed in the hearts of the protagonists, like the voices of spirits connecting us with the flight of joy, enchantment and imagination.

Esta tarde vi llover (Armando Manzanero)

I Will Survive (Gloria Gaynor)

Todos locos (Los Caligaris)

Cry to Me (Solomon Burke)

En el amor todo es empezar (Raffaella Carrà)

Volver a empezar (Pablo Alboran)

Swan Lake (Tchaikovsky)

Ateo (C. Tangana, Nathy Peluso)

Entre dos amores (Ana Belén)

The Spirit Carries On (Dream Theater)

About the author

Pilar López (Granada, Spain) is an inspiring international author who currently divides her time between Spain and Australia. She is renowned in the world of coaching and personal development for her revolutionary vision and unconventional ideas.

For the past twenty-five years, she has passionately devoted herself to her mission of contributing to the creation of a new and improved human being. She likes to call herself 'the awakener' as this is, in fact, what she does: awaken our consciousness.

She collaborates on a number of radio shows and leads corporate programmes that focus on fostering human talent and internal transformations. She is an expert on personal change and empowerment processes, and travels frequently as a motivational speaker, promoting movement in order to live happier lives.

A true entrepreneur, she has founded several organisations, among them the NGO House to Grow, from which she actively supports society's most vulnerable members.

She is also a wonderful and relatable communicator, who knows how to seduce audiences and hold the public's attention, reaching their minds and conquering their hearts.

Her previous work includes the self-help book *Como crear una vida maravillosa,* also available in English under the title *How to Create and Amazing Life.*

Did you enjoy this book?

Write to us at farfalle7@icloud.com

Share your thoughts
Pilar López Cardenas

Book Pilar
for a conference,
a seminar or a personal
development programme